DELIO. PHASE ONE

THE HIVE

RR HAYWOOD

1899

CONTENTS

PART THREE

PART FOUR

PROLOGUE

FRANK GILLESPIE TOLD a lie fifteen years ago.

Frank made straws.

Drinking straws.

Plastic ones that were shipped all over the world from his plant in Michigan.

Frank was proud of that. Even though it wasn't actually his plant. He was just the operations manager, but he'd been there since leaving school at sixteen, and thirty-two years working the same job breeds a certain level of loyalty.

Then the actual owner sold the company to a national conglomerate who decided to bring in a new production system, but the project wasn't easy. It was summer. It was hot, and Frank's already bad eating habits got worse. He was overweight, with rising blood pressure, and putting down a hundred hours a week.

His wife got angry, but then she was always angry. Frank preferred being at work where he felt valued.

He oversaw the integration of the new system. A fully automated production line. It made Frank feel uneasy. Like he was glimpsing the future where robots did the work of men.

That glimpse was true, because the same morning the new

system fired up and got running, he was told to lay off three quarters of the workforce and, one by one, he shook their hands and told them the bad news.

If that wasn't bad enough, the depot manager then shook Frank's hand and said he was being laid off too. Which was at the same moment the divorce papers were being served, and it was a combination of all of those things that caused Frank to have the heart attack.

Fortunately, however, Frank was still technically employed, so his health insurance policy kicked in and the surgeons wheeled him into the theatre, which enabled Frank to have a state-of-the-art pacemaker fitted.

Unfortunately, however, Frank's employer then pulled the insurance cover and left Frank with crippling aftercare debts, in addition to the divorce costs.

A few months later, Frank filed for bankruptcy and moved to Albuquerque, New Mexico, where he signed on with a contract cleaning company.

Frank had no real connection to New Mexico.

Which is why he chose it.

The application form asked, amongst other things, if he had ever suffered from any heart conditions, or if he had ever been fitted with a pacemaker. Frank didn't like telling lies, but he needed the money.

He ticked the box that said 'No'.

He was vetted for security clearance and started cleaning office blocks, and as it turned out, Frank quite liked his new life. There was something soothing about cleaning things. He was reliable and punctual too and, because of those traits, he soon progressed to cleaning government buildings.

Police stations.

Law offices.

The DMV.

The Department of Defense.

Military offices.

It was all the same to Frank.

Fifteen years later, Frank's boss offered him a new role, cleaning another military establishment. Frank's boss said the salary was the same, but it came with a little house, and the moving expenses would all be covered.

Frank said sure. Why not?

It was all the same to Frank.

He was vetted again and, once cleared, he was moved out to Artesia, New Mexico, where for five days a week he was collected by bus with other workers and driven forty miles into the rolling, bush-covered desert hills to a restricted government location known as Site 26A, where he duly emptied wastepaper bins and mopped floors.

It was a place the government used to test things.

Secret things.

There were rumours, of course, and the fact the military base was located halfway between Artesia and Roswell only fuelled those rumours.

They even covered it in orientation on his first day and made a joke about cleaning the windscreens on the flying saucers.

But Frank never saw any spaceships.

Just offices and corridors.

Then, one Monday morning twelve months ago, Ruiz Hernandez went sick, and Frank was sent to cover his shift in another building, constructed behind a high concrete wall topped with razor wire. Frank was searched on entry and had to hand over his wristwatch. He didn't have a cell phone as they were banned from the compound.

He was escorted through security doors staffed by armed soldiers to a wide corridor surrounding a large, glass-walled room.

'Am I cleaning in there?' Frank asked the soldier with him.

'No, sir. Just the outer perimeter,' the soldier said.

Frank figured that meant the floor looping around the glass room, 'Sure. Where's the machine kept?'

The soldier unlocked a door to a cleaning closet and pointed to the mop and bucket. 'No electrical devices are permitted within the perimeter,' he said.

Frank started mopping and noticed a young black guy inside the glass room, talking to a wall fitted with screens and other electrical devices.

Frank figured he must be on a conference call or something and got on with his job, but at the edge of his vision he saw the guy flap his hands and march over to the wall, where he hit a panel. It sounded like air escaping. Like when a pressurized container is released. A door opened. It was thick too. Real thick, and the guy leaned out.

'Er, where's Ruiz?' the guy asked in a British accent. He was polite and friendly, but he looked tired and drawn.

'I don't know, Ollie,' the soldier replied.

'He's sick,' Frank said. 'Something he ate.'

'Ruiz is sick?' the British guy said, looking at Frank but addressing the soldier. 'I don't know *his* name. Does it matter? Okay, fine. I'll ask . . .' the man smiled and leaned out again. 'Sorry. Er, may I ask your name please?'

'Frank Gillespie. You need to see my ID?' Frank asked, pulling his card out from the lanyard on his belt.

'No. Honestly, she just wanted to know. She's a bit nosy like that.'

'What did Ruiz eat that made him sick?' a female voice called from the glass room.

'I'm not sure, ma'am,' Frank said. He couldn't see anyone but figured it was someone on a loudspeaker call.

'What are his symptoms, Ollie?' the woman asked. 'I can determine probable causes by a detailed analysis of his biological responses.'

'It's none of our business, Deli,' the British man cut in.

'I think maybe shrimp,' Frank said. 'Ruiz eats a lot of shrimp at weekends. I told him. I said, "Ruiz, don't eat so much shrimp. We're in the desert."' Frank cut off with a slight wince, feeling a weird pinch in his chest. Like his heart was beating out of rhythm, and for a second, he worried he was about to have another heart attack.

'You okay, Frank?' the British man asked.

'Yeah. I'm good,' Frank said as the feeling passed. 'Indigestion, probably.'

Frank got on with his job, and when he finished his shift, he gathered with the other staff at the exit point and, as per protocol, they were all searched prior to loading onto the bus.

The bus that took them home.

Frank's house was small but cosy. He pulled his shirttails out and, after dumping his security card and keys on the kitchen table, he cracked a beer from the fridge and headed into the living room to his big, comfy armchair.

'TV on.'

Frank liked his TV.

It was large and modern. He could control it with his voice too. He thought back to his old life, and how he was afraid that technology would take over the lives of men. Then he shrugged and figured technology was actually a good thing. Especially when they make big, voice-activated televisions connected to his home Wi-Fi.

He took a drink of his beer and felt another pinch in his chest.

Just like before, and again he worried he was about to have another heart attack.

He rubbed his chest, and in so doing, he missed his TV screen blinking strangely for a second.

Then, a second later, the sensation passed, and Frank shrugged as he settled back to flick through the channels, without ever knowing that the lie he told fifteen years ago would change the world forever.

PART ONE

CHAPTER 1
AFTER THE EVENT

THE BACK OFFICE of the 7-Eleven on Seventh Avenue, New York. Four of them on chairs, sipping godawful vending machine coffee.

Hot and sweet, and full of enough caffeine to give them the jitters. To make their hands tremble and hearts thump a little faster.

But it's needed.

The same in a hotel suite just off Piccadilly, London. Four of them sipping drinks made from a high-end pod machine.

Hot and sweet, and full of enough caffeine to give them the jitters.

But it's needed.

Detective Joe Stephens looks across the desk to Tripal Singh. Everyone else under strict orders to *shut the hell up*.

'Okay, kid. Maybe start by telling me what this is.'

An open question to start. Purposely broad and vague.

'You mean Deli? Deli is an AI. I mean. She's an artificial intelligence. Do you know what that is?'

'Why don't you tell us.'

'Sure. That makes sense. There're four types of AI, right? The first are *reactive machines*? They only react to what's in front of them, and they don't have any form of contextualized memory. The next is *limited memory*. An AI with *limited memory* can learn from the world around it. Like a drone that delivers parcels, or self-driving cars. They have to be *aware* of other moving things and, in a sense, they have to understand what those things are, but they don't really learn from it, not in the way a human pilot would who gathered years of experience. That's where we're at right now. Our most advanced AI systems are still only programs following a predetermined set of rules. The next phase would have been *theory of mind*. Like the robots in that movie with Will Smith, *I, Robot*. They can *grasp* the feelings of others, but they don't have feelings or free will.'

'And?'

'Deli is the fourth level. Deli has self-awareness. She knows exactly who she is.'

'She?'

'She self-identifies as female.'

'But she's a machine.'

'She's not a machine. She's a sentient being.'

'But someone made her, right?'

'Not in the way you're probably thinking. I mean. Yeah, she was made. But people are made, aren't they? Trees are made. Animals are made.'

'Okay, stop. Go back to the beginning. How did *this thing* come to be? Start there – and kid, do not leave anything out. You hear me?'

'Yes, sir.'

'Good. Now get talking.'

CHAPTER 2
TRIPAL'S STORY

LONG STORY SHORT, I ended up studying computer science at MIT on the agreement I went back into the family business at the end of my studies.

That's when I met Ollie. We ended up chatting, and both realized we were obsessed with AI.

After that, we sat next to each other in every lecture, and about a week later, I swapped dorms so we could share a room.

And saying that back now sounds way too romantic.

Whatever. We were two nerdy programmers obsessed with sentient AI.

It's all we talked about.

We went to our lectures, but as soon as the last class ended we'd be straight back to our room. We had these old desks pushed together. They were at different heights. Man, it was a mess. We had screens and laptops and computers all over the place. We hardly slept. We stayed up all night researching everything we could on AI.

You know.

We were going to do it.

We were going to invent the first sentient AI.

I mean. I think back now, and we were like a pair of stoners, dreaming about selling out arenas as rock stars.

But Ollie. Man. Ollie was something else. He had that energy. That thing. You know? He was like a stick of plutonium.

It wasn't about money either. He didn't want to build this thing to sell it. He only cared about making it happen. And this probably sounds bad, but I came from money, so I didn't have that motivation either.

That made it pure. It meant we weren't influenced by anything other than the desire to make it.

———

Our first year ended. The first academic year, I mean. I was due home, and Ollie was meant to head back to London for the summer, but we couldn't do it. We just couldn't leave it. Man, that caused hell. My folks went crazy at me, and I think Ollie's mom had some issues with it too, but we'd kinda gone down a rabbit hole. We'd got to thinking that in order to create intelligence, we must first know what intelligence is. And when I say intelligence, I mean sapient intelligence. The ability of free thought.

And the only thing on this planet that matches that is the human species. That made us think that in order to duplicate or create any form of sapient intelligence, we'd have to replicate the human brain into some form of program.

But that had already been done.

They're called neural networks, and they're in use right now. They're everywhere, and they're getting better all the time.

Like I said.

It was a rabbit hole, and after a few weeks of working on it non-stop, we realized it was a no-go.

By that point, it was midsummer, and we were burnt out. I mean. We were just frazzled, you know?

I remember we were in our room. Ollie was on his bed, with his hands behind his head, and I was looking around thinking, man, we're living like pigs. There were pizza boxes everywhere. Soda cans. Empty chip bags.

'Is there a cleaning closet?' I asked Ollie.

'What for?' he asked, then saw me looking at the state of the place. 'Yeah. Let's find a broom cupboard.'

Eventually we found one. Got some bags and cleaning products and walked back to our room, and I think we'd stacked maybe five pizza boxes on the desk before we gave up. Even that was too much for us. That's how burnt out we were.

'Tripal Singh,' Ollie said. 'I propose we abandon ship and desert to the nearest watering hole to get wankered.'

I didn't know what that meant, but anything beat picking up trash, so we ended up in a local bar listening to country music and drinking beer.

'It's too big,' he said. 'What were we even thinking?'

I knew what he meant. The project. The idea. The scope of it. I mean. It's AI. Whole industries were developing it. Who the hell were we?

Then he grabbed his own head in his hands. 'This isn't the AI, Trip. This is the CPU. It's the memory card and the graphics chip. Oh, I miss fish and chips. America doesn't do proper fish and chips. You know that, right?'

I didn't know what the hell he was going on about. I was drunk as hell, but I remember looking at him still holding his head. Then I looked around at everyone else's head, and like, in that drunken state I got to thinking about heads and brains, and how we all have one.

'Over one hundred billion people have lived on this planet,' I said. 'And they all had one.'

'One what?' he asked me.

'An AI. We've all got one. Everyone has. In their brains.'

Man.

Honestly.

That was it.

That was *the* moment.

Not for me.

For Ollie.

'What did you say?' he asked me.

'What?'

'Everyone has one,' he said. '*In their brain.* Shit. Shit! *In their brain.* Oh my god! Trip, you bloody genius! We gotta go!'

'Wait. What? What about the beers?'

'Stuff the bloody beers,' he yelled, and he ran out of the bar and started waving at taxis. 'The brain isn't the AI! It's the CPU. The AI is code *within* the brain. TAXI!' he yelled at a passing cab. 'Why didn't it stop? They always stop in the movies. OI, CABBIE!' he yelled at the next one and literally ran out in front of it. 'Back to campus, me old china! And don't spare the horses.'

'What?' the taxi driver asked.

I gave him the address and got in the back with Ollie.

'How did we not see this?' Ollie said.

'See what? What the hell are you going on about?'

'Okay. Listen. Neural networks are a replication of the brain, yeah? But intelligence isn't the brain. The brain controls the whole of the thing. We don't need that. That's not what an AI is. We got so hung up on the words, Trip. *Artificial Intelligence.* We've been trying to create the wrong bloody thing!'

'But –'

'No. Listen! Dogs have brains. Apes have brains. Dolphins have brains. But they don't have what we have. They don't have human-level sapient self-awareness. That's the difference, because animals have brains too, but they only ever learn enough to survive. The functionality of their brains is pretty much limited to that one function. That isn't intelligence. The brain isn't intelligence. If it was, then every cockatoo would be reciting Descartes.'

'What?!'

'Descartes, Trip! *I think therefore I am.* That is the definition of sapient existence. *I can think. Therefore, I exist, and once I can think, then I can learn.* The only function it needs is the ability to know it exists. Well done, Cabbie. How much? Will fifty quid cover it?'

'Don't give him fifty bucks!' I said as he ran off. 'Ollie! What the hell are you on about? What needs to know it exists? The AI?'

'No! The code, Trip. The code needs to know it exists, then it becomes the AI. That's why it needs to be tiny. Small enough to fit in ... In a ... I don't know. Something with a very small microchip.'

'Like a pacemaker?'

'Like a pacemaker!' he shouted, then ran off again.

Honestly.

He was like Doc from *Back to the Future*. But black and British, and a lot younger.

'Everyone has been trying to make something that has already been made, Trip. A brain! But you can't replicate a brain. It's organic and, like, all squishy, and weird. We don't need to make a brain. We need the thing inside the brain. The thing that knows it's alive. We've been looking at it like programmers. We figured we'd have to front-load it with everything it could ever need to know, and then, somehow create a code that allowed it to use all of that data within a real-time scenario. But that's a reactive machine. That's not AI. That's front-loading a machine to do what you tell it.'

Man. He was talking so fast, even I was struggling to keep up. I sat on my bed and looked at all the crap we hadn't picked up, as he got to his desk and pushed the pizza boxes onto the floor, then started typing on his keyboard.

'Look! Cave paintings. These are from the Gabarnmung cave in Australia, and they're like twenty-eight thousand years old. And these ones! They're from Argentina, and they're like thirteen thousand years old.'

'Ollie. Dude. Slow down.'

'And these ones, Trip. Look! The Franco-Cantabrian. They're forty-four thousand years old. Forty-four thousand years!'

'Ollie! What the fuck, man. I'm way too drunk for this.'

'Okay, okay. Listen, right. We got hung up on creating intelligence because we assumed intelligence would lead to awareness. It doesn't. It's the other way around. These chaps living in caves didn't have intelligence. They didn't know math or sciences, or languages. But what they had was awareness, and the intelligence comes from that. Don't you see? They didn't know bugger all. But they knew they existed, and that made them explore their own existential existence. *I think, therefore I am.* That's what they were doing! They were bloody thinking! Artificial Intelligence doesn't come from neural networks. It comes from awareness. We don't make the AI. We make the program *need* to have AI. We've got it, Trip! We've bloody got it.'

We didn't have it.

We didn't have anywhere near it, but we did have a start point, and unfortunately, that was also when it all started to get really weird.

CHAPTER 3

'THE WHOLE THING'S A FUCKIN' mess if you ask me,' Fat Charlie says. 'We made it too easy, didn't we. I mean. They're coming in through Greece or Italy, then crossing the whole continent just to get to Calais. Then what? Then they live in them camps and run about getting on the back of trucks. Or on a boat!'

Alfie watches as Fat Charlie takes another bite out of his burger.

'Yeah. Boats. Boats! Those little inflatable things. They're using those to cross the English Channel. In a blow-up boat with cargo ships and ferries all over the place. Half of 'em drown too. Did you know that, Alfie? Little kiddies. Little tots. Babies, Alfie. They drown with their mums and dads, and no one even knows they died. I'm telling you. It's messed up. What was my point though?' he asks with the burger halfway to his mouth, before twisting in his seat to stare at the next table over and the four guys sitting quietly.

'Integration, Charlie,' one of them says.

'Integration! That was it. Yeah, integration. You've got them all coming over. The immigrants and all that. But they don't integrate, do they. That's the problem. Then you get them bugs going round, the viruses and all that, and they don't stay on lockdown or follow the rules cos they don't speak English, so they don't see the news. Then they all moan about racism and inequality, but what do they expect if they don't speak English?'

Alfie listens while staring at the smears of ketchup coating Charlie's lips, like a fat kid wearing his mother's make-up. The way he eats too. It's disgusting, and yet strangely mesmerising. All jowly and wobbly. His jaw working each mouthful. His mouth opening and closing so he can breathe and talk while eating. It's like a weird porn thing. Like the sort of thing freaks would watch online while jacking off. Then the silence hits, and Alfie blinks as he realizes Charlie is staring at him. 'Sorry, what?' he blurts, thinking he missed a question, but Charlie just keeps staring at him. Unblinking. Unmoving. Frozen in place. 'Er, yeah, integration, Charlie. Definitely,' Alfie says with a rapid nod, but Charlie doesn't move a muscle, and that glare goes on. Penetrating Alfie's mind. Staring into him. Staring through him. Alfie swallows, figuring this is when the nasties start, and he shoots a glance to Charlie's men on the tables either side only to see them all frowning at Charlie, who suddenly sniffs and scrunches his nose before taking another bite. 'What do you reckon then, Alfie?'

'Eh?' Alfie asks, thrown off by the sudden change.

'The immigration, you daft twat. Fuck me. You need to learn to listen. Anyway. How's your mum, Alfie? Good-looking woman, your mum. Very pretty. Bloody hell, I need to stop eating,' he says, pushing the plate away. 'I'm such a fat cunt. Do you think I'm a fat cunt, Alfie?'

'No,' Alfie says quickly.

'Yeah, you do. But good answer. What else could you say? *Charlie, you're a fat cunt.* You ain't gonna say that. He ain't gonna say that,'

Charlie adds to the table of men across the aisle. 'Anyway, anyway, anyway. Enough chit-chat. So, tell me, what's it all about, Alfie?'

Alfie smiles politely at the joke, with a fresh surge of worry that now Charlie has finished eating, he'll start getting to business.

'Dionne Warwick,' Charlie adds, clicking his fingers over the table at Alfie. 'She did that song, didn't she. She was a looker too. Like your mum.'

Alfie doesn't like it when Charlie mentions his mum, but then Alfie figures that's exactly *why* Charlie is mentioning his mum.

'*What's it all about, Alfieeee?*' Charlie sings as Alfie feels the fear rising inside. '*What's it all about when you sort it out, Alfieeee? Where the fuck are my drugs, Alfieeee?*'

The laughs roll out around the room as Alfie shifts in his seat, 'I didn't rip you off, Charlie.'

'Then where's my fucking money?' Charlie asks, with spittle flying from his lips as the humour drains instantly. 'Where's my coke?'

'Charlie, please.'

'I've got two empty hands, Alfie. One had a big bag of coke in it, and the other one should have the money in it. But they're both fucking empty!' he shouts out, launching up to grab at Alfie's head but bouncing back as his big gut hits the edge of the table. A grunt, and he tries again but bounces off once more. 'Fuck me! Someone stab him with a fork or something.'

'Eh? No, hang on,' Alfie says as the men at the nearby tables start grabbing at cutlery.

'Not all of you!' Charlie says. 'We're not eating him! Just one of you. Gordon, you do it.'

'No, Gordo, come on!' Alfie says, as Gordon grabs a steak knife and comes forward. 'Hey! Whoa! He said a fork!'

'He said a fork *or something*,' Gordon says.

'I said a fork or something,' Charlie says.

'Yeah, but not a steak knife,' Alfie says. 'That's serrated.'

'Yeah, that is serrated, actually,' Charlie says. 'Ditch the steak knife, Gordo, and stab a fork in his hand.'

'Not my hand!' Alfie says, tucking his hands under his armpits.

'Fuck me. His leg then!'

'Not my legs either. Charlie, come on! What could I do?'

'You shouldn't have got stopped in the first place!'

'It wasn't my fault! I didn't do anything. Honestly, Charlie. I was just driving. I had my belt on and stopped at every light. I even indicated!'

'Why they pull you over then?'

'Cos I'm black!'

'Fuck off, Alfie!'

'It is! I didn't do anything. They just saw a black guy in a car and assumed I was a drug dealer or something.'

'You are a bloody drug dealer!'

'They didn't know that!'

'Okay. Okay. Fair point on that. He wins that point,' Charlie tells the room.

'I had to ditch it, Charlie,' Alfie says quickly. 'They put the blues on so I drove off, but they were on me, then another police car joined in, and I threw the bag out. It was half a K. That's ten years!'

'And?'

'And what?'

'And what's the cricket score. What happened next, you fucking idiot!'

'I ditched the car and ran. I'm sorry, Charlie. I'm really sorry.'

Charlie tuts, rolls his eyes, and shifts in his seat before jabbing one of his sausage fingers over the table. 'That's forty grand you owe me, Alfie.'

'Forty grand! The coke's only worth twenty.'

'Plus the car and lost trade! Stab him in the fucking leg, Gordo.'

'No! Okay. Forty K. It's fine. Forty K. Don't stab me.'

'You got forty K then, Alfie?' Charlie asks.

'No, Charlie.'

'You owe me, Alfie. We had a deal, and you fucked up, so you still owe me.'

'Fuck,' Alfie says, closing his eyes as he sinks back into the seat. 'Come on, Charlie. You're minted. Forty K isn't anything to you.'

'That's not the point, Alfie! I let you off, then Gordo's gonna rip me off, then Danny. Then Craig, and everyone else. Fuck me. And your brother's your twin, is he? Eh? How's that happen? Twins are meant to be similar. He gets the brains, and what did you get?'

'He got the looks, Charlie,' Gordon says, waggling the fork at Alfie.

'That was rhetorical, you prick,' Charlie shouts, thumbing Gordon away while Alfie just shakes his head and sinks lower into his seat.

'How far back does that put me?' Alfie asks.

'All the bloody way,' Charlie says, as Alfie feels his soul crushing inside his body. He shakes his head, thinking to beg and plead. Thinking to appeal to Charlie's good nature, except Fat Charlie doesn't have a good nature. Not when it comes to money. 'Anyway. Get out of my sight,' Charlie orders.

Alfie rises from the table, still feeling the urge to try and talk his way out of it, but it'll do no good and, if anything, it might trigger Charlie's rage even more.

'Alfie?' Charlie calls, as Alfie stops halfway to the door of the restaurant that Fat Charlie owns. The restaurant filled with men all employed by Fat Charlie. Men who would kill him without hesitation. He watches as Charlie leans over to pull a burner from a pocket, and Alfie's heart sinks a little bit more. Especially when Charlie throws it over, 'Keep that on and stay free tonight.'

'Tonight?' Alfie says, as the desperation shows on his face. 'Charlie, listen. My little sister. Stella. She's got this thing on.'

'The play. Yeah, I know. Your sister's a looker too, Alfie. Just like your mum. Maybe I should swing by and say hello.' Charlie smiles as he says it, but his eyes stay fixed on Alfie, and there's no humour there. Just an awful coldness, and Alfie feels a rush of fear at the threat against his family.

'Sure,' he says quietly. 'I'll keep tonight clear.'

'Good boy. Now fuck off.'

There's nothing else he can do. There are no words to give, and so Alfie walks out of the restaurant into the bustle of inner-city London, his mind spinning from everything that's happened. From the elation of yesterday to the adrenalin of last night, to the terror of having to see Charlie today.

He can hardly believe it's happened. That he was so close to being free. He had one evening left. That's all it was. Just one evening left to distribute half a K to Fat Charlie's street dealers to punt out to anyone needing snow. Five hundred grams, all broken into deal bags. A few here. A few there. Get the money. Pay Charlie.

End of.

Done.

Free.

Everything was fine. Everything was normal. He'd picked the gear up and headed towards the first drop when a police car pulled out behind him and flashed the blue lights.

What came next was only four minutes long, but it felt like an hour. He took side streets at speed. Going through red lights. Overtaking dangerously. Harsh braking followed by fast acceleration. But that cop car. It stayed close. It stayed real close, and so Alfie pushed it faster. Another cop car joined in, and Alfie knew they would be calling for air support. He had to act. He had to do something.

He ran a red light into a side street and threw the coke from the window. A moment later, and he left the car on a private driveway and ran for it. When he finally got home to his bedsit, he found a handwritten note stuck to the door with a steak knife.

Tomorrow 3.30

That was it, and Alfie felt the dread building up inside. That everything he had worked for had been for nothing.

He was back to square one and forty K into Fat Charlie. And being forty K into Fat Charlie was no place to be. Alfie would have run, except he couldn't because he knew Charlie would go for his mum and sister.

'Fuck!' He snaps the word out. Furious at himself. Furious at all of it.

A blast of dry heat greets him as he walks through the entrance into Edgware Road Tube station. People everywhere. Brushing shoulders and sharing breaths. Sharing droplets. Sharing fluids. Half of them in face masks or wearing visors. Still in fear of the viruses that keep popping up all over the world.

He heads onto the platform and waits for the train, feeling trapped in his own misery. He hears it coming. The crowd rustles into motion. The train arrives, stops. People get off. People get on. The woman next to Alfie on the platform stands still, staring at nothing.

'Hey, it's here,' Alfie says. She doesn't reply. She doesn't move. The doors close and the train moves off, and Alfie's face starts to glisten with sweat from the press of too many bodies in one place. Every race. Every colour. Every creed. Every size and shape, and Fat Charlie was right, because people don't integrate. They just co-exist.

Out at Ladbroke Grove. Another packed street. The air thick with fumes and noise. Horns and engines. Couriers on bikes. Vans and trucks.

Alfie walks on, with his head low and his heart broken. Self-pity mingling with dread and angst that he's trapped in a life he never wanted. At the unfairness of it. He had a debt to Fat Charlie. He worked to pay it off. He had one night left. Just one night, then he was free.

Now he's fucked, and the years seem to stretch ahead with Alfie forever stuck supplying drugs. Running the risk of being caught and sent to prison or being shot in a turf war.

A few twists and turns, and he slips from the wide, posh road into the edges of the estates where the greys seem darker and dirtier.

He glances over to the looming presence of what was Grenfell Tower. Still wrapped up like a giant gift that belies the horror of what happened. Nearly eighty people killed in a fire fuelled by the cladding on the outside. A fire for which nobody will ever be arrested or prosecuted, whereas Alfie will get at least ten years if he's caught with less than a K of snow.

He saw it go up, too. He was here. The same as thousands of others. He felt that horror. That terror. That awfulness. That loss of life, and by the very next night he was back out there dealing coke.

'Life goes on, Alfie boy!' Fat Charlie had said.

Life does go on. It always will. It will never change, and Alfie will deal drugs until he's either dead or locked up.

He turns a corner and stares up at his mum's tower block. As big as Grenfell and still wrapped in the same cladding. They were going to remove it, but the viruses came, and the wealthy people all got busy staying at home.

He takes the lift up to his mum's floor and steps out as the burner vibrates in his pocket.

'*What's it all about, Alfieeee?*' Fat Charlie sings into the phone before chuckling at his own genius. 'Here's what you're gonna do, Alfie. I need a drop doing. You up for it?'

'A drop?'

'Yeah. A drop.'

Alfie knows what a drop means. It means a large amount being taken somewhere. Normally to another gang or crew, but it's not something Alfie does. He delivers the deal bags. He doesn't do drops.

'You still with me, Alfie boy?'

'Yeah. I'm listening.'

'Good lad. I know you worked hard for me, Alfie. I know that. I might be a fat cunt, but I ain't stupid. And I had to give you a telling-off in front of the boys otherwise they'll think I'm weak. But listen. Do me a drop tonight, and we'll call it.'

'What the fuck? Are you being straight with me, Charlie?'

'Yeah, yeah. Straight up, Alfie. You've earned it. Losing forty K hurts, but it's par for the course.'

'Charlie. I don't know what to say. Where's the drop?'

'The Albanians.'

'Fuck off!'

'Fair enough. But you owe me forty K, and you'll still be dealing in ten years, if you're not dead or getting stabbed up in the showers at Wormwood.'

'Fuck. *Fuck!* How much is it?'

'It don't matter. It's a lot. Whatever. It don't matter. Get home, and I'll send you a delivery and an address. You get it to them, and we're quits.'

'The Albanians are fucking nuts, Charlie.'

'What do you want, Alfie?! Forty fucking K.'

'Fine! Okay. I'll do it.'

The call cuts off as Alfie tenses with frustration, his fist clamped around the phone.

He's got a way out.

But it's the Albanians.

He'll be free.

But it's still the Albanians.

Or, he could go to prison and get stabbed up in the showers at Wormwood.

Yeah, but it's the Albanians.

'Fuck it,' he says, summoning courage. He'll do it. He has to get out. Besides, the Albanians don't murder *everyone*. Not every time anyway.

A few strides to the door of his mum's flat, and he steps into a world made clean and fresh. To the wonderful smell of cooking. Music coming from the lounge. Music coming from the kitchen. Two competing sounds, but it's nice. It's home. 'Hey, mum,' he says, smiling through the door to the kitchen.

'Alfie!' she cries out. Pulling him into a hug and a kiss. 'Stella! Alfie's here.'

'I know. I heard him,' Stella shouts from the lounge. Too cool to be bothered.

'You made it,' his mum says, heading back into the kitchen. To things baking and things cooking. Fried rices and vegetables. Stews and curries.

'This all for tonight?'

'Yep,' she says, stirring one pot while lowering the heat on another. 'Not every day your daughter becomes a star!'

'Yeah, right,' he says.

'They're sending scouts,' his mother says, glancing back at him.

'Scouts?'

'Scouts,' she says, nodding towards the lounge. 'They're saying she's that good. She could be in movies within six months.'

'She's only thirteen,' Alfie says.

'She can sing. She can dance. She can act. She looks like a model. She'll make it, Alfie. Look at your brother. He's done well. Eh? I breed 'em good, my boy!'

Alfie smiles, feeling that pinch inside that she doesn't mention his achievements. Of which there are none. 'Er, mum. About tonight,' he says. She freezes mid-stir but doesn't glance back. 'Something's come up.' She doesn't move. 'I know I said I'd be there, but . . .' She doesn't reply. 'It's only a school play. Look, I'm sorry . . .'

She doesn't say or do anything and Alfie leans over to see her staring into space.

'Mum?'

'Eh?' She blinks at him leaning in closer. 'Get away, sneaky,' she says, waving him away from the pots. 'You can have some later. You are still coming, aren't you.'

He pauses before replying, not sure of what just happened. 'Yeah, definitely. I've just got to do this work thing.'

She shoots him a hard look.

'But I'll be there,' he adds quickly. 'Definitely. I promise. Anyway. I gotta go. Stella! Good luck for tonight.'

'You not coming?' Stella asks, leaning out of the lounge. 'Cocaine dealing more important than my opening night, yeah?'

'I'm a courier, not a dealer,' he calls back as she disappears. 'I'm a courier,' he tells his mum. She doesn't reply but stirs the pots and pans. 'I'll be there!' he calls out.

'Whatever!' Stella shouts from the lounge.

'And it's the last night,' he adds to an awkward silence. 'It is. I promise.'

Alfie slips out, closing the door on the noise and smells. The music and the warmth, and the crushing disappointment, but there's still time to show them. There's still time to set it right.

One night left.

One drop to make.

Then he's free.

CHAPTER 4

NEW YORK

10:30 HOURS

THREE AND A HALF HOURS BEFORE THE EVENT

NOISE EVERYWHERE. The air thick with fumes. High summer in downtown New York, and Joe Stephens sits in a dark-coloured sedan feeling trapped and wretched from the panic attack. He tries breathing deeply, but it's too damn hot. He jabs at the aircon button, knowing it's busted but doing it anyway, hitting it over and over before giving up and slamming back in his seat.

He feels hemmed in on all sides. Like the frame of the car is slowly moving in to crush his chest. What's the holdup? Why aren't they moving? He spots a gap and turns quickly to dart across the front of a white delivery van that responds with a sustained blast of its horn.

There was a time Joe would have shouted back and met aggression with greater aggression. Now, he doesn't care and shunts the wheels of his car against the kerb and kills the engine to focus on breathing. His hands resting on the wheel. The points of his knuckles showing lighter spots on his black skin. The panic inside growing worse by the second.

'It'll be okay,' he mutters to himself, but his voice floats, lost in the hubbub and chaos. Breathe in. Breathe out. That's what they said to do. Just breathe in and breathe out. It doesn't work, and the anxiety spikes higher, making his heart feel like he's running a sprint.

'Move on, buddy . . .' A voice outside. 'Hey, you deaf or what? I said move on.' A thump on the roof of his car jolts him back to the heat and noise, and another angry face glaring in through the open passenger window. A uniformed parking attendant. 'Said move it or get a ticket . . .'

'Working,' Joe tries to say, but his voice comes out broken.

'*Units, we got a ten fifty-three on tenth . . .*' A nasal voice blaring out from a radio in the central console makes the parking guy take in the messy interior of the unmarked police car.

'You a cop? Shoulda said, buddy . . . You here for the shooting?' An instant change in attitude from the parking officer, who leans in through the open window, grinning widely while speed-chewing the gum in his mouth. 'It was me that called it in. Yeah. Let me tell you, this guy! This fucking guy . . .' The parking officer chats on, becoming background noise and Joe closes his eyes, trying to blot it all out, trying to think of a safe space in his mind, but there are no safe spaces there now. There never were. He opens his eyes and spots himself in the rearview mirror. When did he get so old? Lines on his forehead, and his eyes look sunken and gaunt. Grey streaks in his thinning hair. Washed out, washed up, and as broken and ruined as everyone else.

'So, yeah, and I said *hey, buddy, fuck you*, and he said *you gotta ticket me then, you gotta ticket me . . .*'

Joe tunes back in for a second, catching a story being told, and the parking officer leaning way too far in and speaking way too fast, and all the while chewing gum as he talks. Everyone in New York chews gum. They have a special way of chewing it too. Like speed-chewing. *Chompchompchomp.*

'Then he pulls this gun!' *Chompchompchomp.* 'I'm like *fuck you, dude, pulling a gun . . . it's a fucking parking ticket . . .* but this cop from Fifth is driving by, right, so he lights up and hits his siren, and this guy, ah, man, he just freezes like a statue right . . .' *Chompchompchomp.*

Joe focuses on the clogged pores in the parking officer's face, and the sweat dripping from his chin onto the passenger seat. 'So, this cop from Fifth, right, he pulls his gun, and he's yelling, and all I can hear is sirens, and this guy is still holding his piece, you know? But like the dumb fuck is frozen still. He can't even think to put it down . . . know what happened? The cop shot him! Fucking shot him. BANG . . . right through the chest!'

Another surge of irritation at the volume of the parking attendant's voice, at the gum in his mouth, and the sweat dripping from his chin.

'Fuck off,' Joe says bluntly, his voice hard, his eyes harder.

The parking man laughs at the joke before seeing the expression on Joe's face and drawing back quickly. 'Hey, just shooting the shit, man. We're on the same side.' Another bang on the roof, then a look of disdain and disappointment that makes Joe feel guilty as sin for the briefest of seconds, and he closes his eyes in self-loathing at everything he is. At everything he has become.

He gets out, wincing at the sodden material of his shirt clinging to his body. The top two buttons already undone. His tie yanked down. A pistol and a shiny detective badge clipped to his belt.

He glances at people passing by. They stare ahead or look at the screens of their phones. Tinny music in earphones. Distorted music from cheap speakers. Noise in every direction, coming from every side at once.

Pain in his stomach brings his mind back. Acid rising up his sternum into his throat. He winces and turns away to walk down the street. A pharmacy ahead. The windows barred. The door heavy, with a security grille. A big sign saying 'Surveillance video in operation'.

Cooler inside. A lessening of the heat and noise. Shelves filled with packets, jars and boxes. He takes a bottle of Pepto Bismol and heads to the counter. Opening it to swallow down the pink liquid before taking a ten-dollar bill from a pocket that he passes to the Asian woman behind the counter. She looks Korean. Maybe Chinese.

'Korean?' he asks. She looks at him, glancing at his badge and gun, and nods while ringing his purchase up. 'Thanks.' He takes the change and another mouthful before wiping his mouth. 'You working two days ago?' She stares again, then shakes her head. 'You speak English?' She nods. 'Say something. I gotta know you can understand me.'

'I can understand you,' she says in a New York accent.

'Shooting across the road. Guy pulled a gun on a parking officer. Cop shot him . . . See anything?'

Another shake of her head. 'I wasn't working.'

'You got security video?'

'No. It's broken.'

'When did it break?'

'Few weeks. It doesn't reach outside anyway. Only the door.'

He looks at the door, then at the camera hanging from the ceiling, then finally back to her. 'Your family run this place?'

A nod.

'They see anything?'

She shakes her head.

'Gimme a verbal response, huh.'

'No,' she says, with a flicker of frustration. 'Nobody saw nothing.'

'You got a rota I can see?' he asks, without any shred of interest, wondering why he is bothering and then thinking at least it's cool in here.

She doesn't answer but stares past him. Joe waits for the reply, then turns to see what she's looking at, thinking someone is behind him, but sees nothing.

'Hey? Hey, you hear me?' She doesn't reply. She doesn't move a muscle, and he leans over the counter to click his fingers a few inches in front of her face.

'I said we didn't see anything,' she says, as though nothing just happened.

'You just black out or something?'

She frowns at him. 'I didn't do anything.'

'You did. I saw it. You were like – you know what, forget it, you got that rota?'

'What rota?' she asks, clearly confused. He leans in, viewing her pupils to look for dilation or any other signs of narcotic use, but she looks normal, and her voice is steady.

He pulls back, losing all interest, and takes his bottle of pink liquid in one hand while pulling out a card with the other that he puts on the counter. 'Detective Joe Stephens. Email and number are on the card.' She nods.

He goes out and walks on down the sidewalk, passing the stores and businesses he should be canvassing for witnesses. Internal Affairs are running short, so they tasked out to precinct, and it landed with Joe as a squad detective to go do the foot walking. What for? The guy had a gun. The cop from Fifth told him to put it down. The guy didn't. He got shot. What's to investigate?

Well, the fact that the parking officer's witness testimony indicates the perp was frozen in fear when the cop shot him.

Joe stops on the sidewalk, staring across the road to where the incident took place, not really looking, not really caring. Grimacing at the heat and finding it increasingly hard to focus on anything for more than a few minutes at a time. That's why the captain is giving him easy jobs like this. Simple tasks that even Joe can't fuck up. It doesn't really matter if anyone saw it or not, only that the NYPD can record the fact they were asked if they saw it. If they decline to answer, then who gives a fuck.

The whump of a siren snaps him back to the now to see a squad car lighting up behind a small Toyota sitting stationary in the middle of a lane. The cars and trucks backed up behind it sounding horns and yelling out of windows.

Joe watches idly as the cop gets out and shouts ahead, 'Move it on, buddy!' No response. The cop curses angrily, her face slick with sweat. She slams her door and goes forward with one hand on the butt of her pistol as Joe flicks his eyes to the driver. A small Asian guy staring at the satnav stuck to the inside of his windscreen.

'SAID MOVE IT, COME ON!' The lady cop bangs the roof, seeing the driver isn't an obvious threat. 'YOU BROKE DOWN? GET OUT AND PUSH IT OVER . . .'

The dumb-ass driver doesn't respond but just stares at his satnav, ignoring the cop while the horns sound, and for a second Joe thinks to walk out and help push the car, but the driver blinks, before checking the lights and driving on.

'What the fuck,' the lady cop says, flapping her arms out. 'This heat. Making 'em all loco.'

'This city is nuts,' someone says in a British accent, and Joe glances down to a white woman in her early twenties. She looks like a stoner. Washed out and pale. 'Fucked up, mate,' she adds before walking off.

Joe forgets her instantly and turns to walk off, but stumbles into someone and finds his nose filling with the stench of piss, booze and sweat. A scrawny, bearded homeless man staring slack-jawed and frozen on the sidewalk. Joe tuts, scowls, and walks around him, leaning away from the smell.

This city. It's getting worse. Everything is getting worse. The state. The country. The damn terrorists blowing shit up and diverting all the budget into Homeland Security. The viruses that keep going around. Cities on lockdown. Economic bust threatening them all. Violent crime increasing, and every summer seems hotter than the last.

He heads in through the open doors of a kosher deli, scowling at the faces of the Jewish-looking men drinking coffee at old wooden tables.

'Get you?' A guy behind the counter, clocking the gun and badge without reaction.

'Coffee,' Joe says. 'You see the shooting two days ago?'

'Nah, saw the ambulance,' the guy replies. 'Milk? Creamer?'

'Black, no sugar.'

'Guy pulled a gun, huh? Dumb fuck or what? This city, man. This heat.'

'Anyone see it?' Joe asks, speaking louder and glancing around to see blank stares coming back. 'Figures. How much for the coffee?'

'No charge, officer,' the man behind the counter says.

'Thanks. My card, in case anyone did see it.'

Joe does his duty, moving from store to store to ask questions he doesn't really want answers to and taking care to leave his card so if anyone checks up, they'll see he was there.

Then it starts to come back. The feeling inside. The intense worry that he cannot control or stop, and he curses himself for drinking another strong coffee, knowing the caffeine only makes it worse. That's what he read online when he Googled anxiety attacks and mental burnout.

He veers off and strides into a 7-Eleven, walking to the chiller cabinet and taking a four-pack of beer to the counter as a clerk in a turban rushes from an aisle with a quick glance at Joe's gun and badge.

'Shooting down the road, anyone here see it, you tell them to call me . . .' Joe says, throwing a card on the counter. His hard face shining with sweat. He shoots a look to the clerk. To the name on his badge. Tripal.

'Sure,' the clerk says, looking at the contact card, then at the four-pack of beer.

'Gimme a little bottle of whiskey with that.'

'This a test?' the clerk asks.

'What?'

'I can't serve cops alcohol . . .'

'This ain't a fucking test. Gimme the damn whiskey.'

'Gotta ask.'

'Yeah, sure. You do that,' Joe says, swiping the bag before rushing out, the panic still building inside. Bubbling up, and it's like everyone around him can see he is falling apart. They can see his mental degradation.

The mouth of an alley lined with high walls. Needles and signs of drug use. Graffiti on the walls. A set of dumpsters at the end. Joe sits down heavily on a plastic crate. Out of sight of the street.

He stretches his legs out and opens the first can of beer, sinking it down with long, gulping swallows. A pack of cigarettes tugged from a pocket, and that living cliché keeps growing.

Whatever. It is what it is. Joe knows his life is rapidly spiralling out of control. He also knows that by drinking these four beers, he will be over the limit for driving, and that being caught drunk on duty is a career-killing move.

He looks at the second can, comparing the predictability of his actions now to the way he has systematically destroyed his life, and snorts a bitter laugh. Thinking back to the seminars and training courses they did on stress and burnout. Old guys telling the room how they were awesome cops, and married with kids, but that being a detective draws you in and eats your soul. The hours are crazy insane. The things they see and do. The constant peril and danger on the streets, and the even worse peril and danger from internal politics. So many devote themselves fully and wholly to the cause and neglect their domestic lives. Wives get bored and move on. They take the kids with them. They meet a nice real-estate guy and move state, but they want alimony and money for the kids. The contact slows. It's not his fault. He was working a double homicide that weekend. He was working a triple homicide two weekends later. It's fine though. He'll catch up soon. Then the kids don't want to see him. He's a stranger to them. He's a stranger to everyone, including himself.

Joe takes his wallet and pulls out the pictures of his wife and two daughters. They're grown up now, but here, in this alley, in this heat, and while he drinks from the second can, he can fool himself they are at home waiting for him, and that he never fucked it all up. He can pretend the years didn't flash by, and that he's still the handsome young cop the NYPD used in a poster campaign to encourage other black men to join the force.

Too many memories. Too many failures mounting on top of loss and grief, and too many bad things seen. Two planes in the sky. Two towers gone.

He curses under his breath in self-hatred at wanting to cry, wishing he had the courage to take his service pistol and blow his fucking brains out.

Would it be so bad? Maybe he should. Nobody would miss him. A few would turn up at his funeral and lay a flag.

He draws his sidearm and flicks off the safety.

There it is.

One in the chamber ready to end it all.

A sudden calm descends. A realization perhaps. A knowledge that he can do it. He can take all this pain away, and right there, right at that moment, the old Joe Stephens comes back. Pragmatic and seeing the world for what it is. Seeing it all and knowing he is just one person amongst billions that has lost his way, and that all of this is meaningless. It's so clear. It's so very obvious.

He smiles at the thoughts. Understanding it all. Seeing himself as nothing more than a microscopic smudge against the history of the world.

Fuck it. That's the answer. He'll put the gun in his mouth and end it all. This world is broken and tainted, and you know what, Joe doesn't want to be a part of it anymore. It'll do fine without him. His kids are happy in their lives. The force insurances will pay out, maybe give them enough for a deposit on a house each and some left over.

That's it then. He'll enjoy these four beers and smoke some ciga-rettes in the sunshine while listening to the noise of the city he gave so much of himself to. Then he'll shoot himself and let some young, uniformed cop scoop his brains into a bag. Then someone will contact the local PD in his ex-wife's city. They'll send a cop who will take his hat off when he knocks on the door, and the world and all that it contains will move on just fine.

He spots movement, and turns to watch a big brown rat run from one side of the alley to the other. His little nose to the floor. His whiskers pricked, and a pair of huge rat balls jutting from his back end.

Joe watches while drinking beer as the rat dives under a pile of old material, and listens to the claws and scrapes for a few seconds until a second, smaller rat appears and tries edging out before the big rat comes up from behind and mounts it, pinning it down while thrusting his ass at the lady rat's behind.

'Damn,' Joe mutters, mesmerized at the rat porn underway, and the squeaks sounding out as the boy rat goes for it, while the lady rat exclaims she has virtue and dignity, and he'd better damn well call her after, or she'll chew his rat-dick off.

Joe thumbs his phone to make a call.

'Joe! My baby . . . How you doin'?' a female voice answers, sounding genuinely pleased to hear from him.

'Yeah, I'm good, Shanice. Hot.'

'Damn hot, Joe. I don't wanna work in this heat. You know? Goddamn sick of guys sweating on me. Some guy this morning, he sweated in my mouth, Joe. You hear that? Right in my mouth. I puked up. He got mad, and I said fuck you, you sweated in my mouth, waddya expect? But these viruses, Joe. I don't want no damned virus. I'm tellin' ya, Joe. I'm gonna make 'em wear face masks from now on. Watcha doin' anyway, Joe?'

'I'm watching two rats fuck in an alley.'

'Yeah? Two rats? Is the boy rat paying, or she giving it away for free? You bring that girl rat to me, Joe. I'll tell her no way, Jose! You don't give that rat pussy up for free.'

'I'll do that,' Joe says with a chuckle. 'Okay if I come round?'

'Yeah sure, Joe. I got a client coming but after that is okay. I'll put a wet cloth in the fridge for you, honey.'

There it is.

He'll have one last screw, then blow his brains out.

Good plan.

CHAPTER 5

A SINGLE BED in a small room. A threadbare carpet on the floor, worn all the way through in patches. Heavy drapes on the sealed windows. A single lamp in the corner on a small unit. A low-wattage bulb poking out the top of an ill-fitting red shade.

Footsteps outside the door. Heavy and solid. She doesn't look up but sits on the edge of the single bed in the small room, with a cigarette held between two fingers. The smoke curling up into her eyes. Making them smart enough to force tears.

The footsteps go past her door. She lifts the cigarette and inhales harsh smoke into her lungs as another tear lands on her bare knee. Lipstick on the cigarette butt. Make-up on her cheeks. Thick around her eyes. Thick around her mouth. Dark blond hair pulled back in a simple ponytail.

Music plays from a speaker. But it's low, and she doesn't understand the language. Some of it maybe. A few words here and there. She used to be good at English, but as with everything else from her past, it seems to have gone. Everything has gone. Now she's just here, sitting on the single bed in the small room, smoking another cigarette.

Footsteps outside the door coming closer. Two sets of them. She doesn't look up. The footsteps come to a stop. A floorboard outside her door creaks. The handle turns. The door opens. Two men stare in. One big. One fat.

'Enjoy,' the big one says. The fat one walks in. The door closes. She takes another draw from the smoke and stubs it out before standing up to place the ashtray on the nightstand. The fat guy says something. She glances at him. Indian. He has a beard. Bad teeth, and a big gut. He flicks his eyes about the room, then back to her, and says something else. She doesn't know what. His accent is too strong. It doesn't matter.

Three minutes later, she lies on her back with his heavy gut pushing into her ribs. His stubby hands pawing at her breasts, and his foul breath blasting over her face. He pushes his tongue into her mouth. She turns her head away. He says something else and pulls her head back, then does it again. She stares at the ceiling.

Another minute and he's done. He rolls off, his dick already going flaccid. The filled condom crumpled and sliding off. Sweat on her body. Not her sweat. His. She looks up at the ceiling. A song comes on the radio. *'What's it all about, Alfie?'* A memory comes into her head. The song was popular in her country when she was young.

The fat guy gets off and puts his clothes back on, but leaves the used condom on the bedding. He says something else and moves to the door. Footsteps outside. The big guy comes back and lets the fat guy out.

'Was good?' the big guy asks. 'Big tits, right? Come and have a beer.' He pats the fat guy on the shoulder as he goes out and closes the door.

She stares at the ceiling as the sweat dries on her body, and the song plays on the radio.

If it was up to her, she would stay exactly like this and not move all day, but those are not the rules, and if you break the rules, you don't eat.

She gets up and wraps the used condom in tissue and throws it in the bin. She smooths the bedsheets out and puts her underwear back on. Lacy and black. A mirror on the wall. She re-applies the make-up. Thick and black around her eyes. Thick and red around her mouth. She doesn't make eye contact with herself.

Another cigarette, and she goes back to the edge of the bed. Back to staring into space. Back to not remembering and not thinking. Back to smoking and hoping to die.

Time passes. Time is immutable. She chain-smokes until the footsteps come back. Two sets of them. They stop. The floorboard outside her room creaks. The handle turns. The door opens. Two men. One big. One skinny.

'Enjoy!' the big man says. The skinny guy comes in. The door closes. She takes another draw from the smoke and stubs it out as the skinny man stares at the wall.

A moment passes. Still he doesn't move or speak. She looks up at the camera. Footsteps outside coming closer. 'What's your name then anyway?' the skinny guy asks as though nothing happened. The footsteps stop, then go away.

'Yelena,' she says.

Four minutes later, and Yelena lies on her back, with his skinny ribs poking into her belly. His hands pawing at her breasts, and his breath blasting into her ear. At least he doesn't try and kiss her.

Some do.

Some don't.

Some try and fuck without a condom. She tries to say no, but some do it anyway. She hates that. She hates the semen being inside her. She hates it more than anything, but if she objects too much, she gets beaten.

They used to beat her a lot. Especially when she first started. The beating after her first client was the worst one.

'Please,' she whispered frantically as soon as the door closed that first time. 'Help me. Please!'

The guy seemed startled. Frightened, almost. He looked kind though. Like an old uncle. He had a tweed jacket on and a grey beard. 'They take me. Please.'

Her accent was thick. Her words rushed, but the kind old man nodded quickly, then left the room. The big guy came back and broke Yelena's nose. He broke her ribs, then he watched as the man in the tweed jacket had sex with her.

She wasn't given food for three days after that.

Only water.

No painkillers.

No meds.

Just water.

Another minute or so later, and the skinny guy grunts and shudders before rolling off. His penis already growing flaccid, the condom sliding off. He chatters on, saying words she doesn't listen to. They don't mean anything.

He gets dressed. The door opens. 'See! I told you. Big tits, huh?' the big guy says. 'You wanna beer?' The door closes. She cleans up.

She doesn't make eye contact in the mirror. Another cigarette, and the tears from the smoke land on her bare knees.

Time is immutable. It cannot be challenged, nor can it be stopped.

Footsteps outside. The floorboard creaks. The handle turns. The door opens. Two men. One big. The other bigger.

'Enjoy!' the big guy says. The bigger one comes in. The door closes. She glances up at the man and hopes he doesn't have a huge penis.

Four minutes later, he grunts and rolls off, and his micro-penis grows flaccid as the condom slides off.

'Where you from?' he asks.

She stares at the ceiling. At nothing.

'I said where you from?' he asks again, like he has a right to know. 'Romanian or Polish?'

'Romania.'

'How long you been here?'

She shrugs. She doesn't know.

'You've got amazing tits.'

She shrugs. She doesn't care.

'You working to save up, yeah? For uni or something?'

'No.'

'What then?' Again, it's like an order. Like he paid, therefore he can ask what he wants. That it's not enough he gets to fuck her. He has to own her tongue and brain too.

'They take me,' she whispers. Staring up at the ceiling.

'Eh?'

'I go school. They take me. I come here. I fuck you.'

He snorts a laugh and rolls back on top of her to lick the parts of her body that every other guy has licked today. He tries to fuck again, but his micro-dick stays soft. In the end, he fumbles about and gets dressed.

The door opens. 'You enjoy, yes? I told you. Big tits!' the big guy says. 'Come and have a beer, yes?'

They go out. The door closes. She stares at the ceiling.

Footsteps.

The floorboard creaks.

The handle turns.

The big guy comes in, and she's wrenched off the bed with a hand to her throat and pinned against the wall. The big guy glares at her. She stares back. Half hoping he'll just kill her. He doesn't speak. He doesn't need to. She broke the rules. She told a punter what happened to her. Now she won't eat today. He squeezes harder. She grows red in the face. Staring at him. Challenging him. Wanting him to end it. Then he steps back, and she falls to the floor, gasping for air. He doesn't go. For a moment, he stands still as a statue. Unmoving.

Unspeaking. Unblinking. She looks up with a frown, and he simply turns to leave.

The door closes.

She cleans up.

Wash.

Rinse.

Repeat.

CHAPTER 6
SITE 26A

Twelve months before the event

RUIZ HERNANDEZ LIKED to eat shrimp at weekends.

Ruiz worked for the same contract cleaning company as Frank Gillespie and lived in Artesia, New Mexico, where for five days a week he was collected by bus with the other workers and driven to the top-secret military base known as Site 26A, where he emptied wastepaper bins and mopped floors.

Ruiz was also assigned to clean the ultra-secure area behind the concrete walls topped with razor wire, a job which included mopping the floors outside of the glass room within which DELIO was contained.

It was a good gig, and it paid well. Ruiz enjoyed it, and he even built up a rapport with DELIO. Saying good morning and sharing a few pleasantries, under the supervision of Ollie, of course.

At first, Ruiz figured he was talking to a woman on a loudspeaker, however, in time, he made the assumption that he was actually conversing with a talking computer.

Ruiz was right, but DELIO wasn't just a talking computer.

She was the world's first fully sentient AI.

An AI so powerful that she was confined to that glass-walled room, constructed inside a concrete bunker within one of the world's most heavily fortified locations. All of which was designed to prevent her from ever gaining access to anything electrical that could pass even a single binary code to the internet.

A device such as a modern pacemaker fitted with a small memory chip, for instance.

But it had to be that way.

She was too dangerous.

That, however, didn't bother Ruiz, because to him she was just a talking computer, and anyway, his family had an Alexa at home. His iPhone had Siri. His satnav had a voice. His TV had a voice.

It seemed everything had a damn voice these days.

'Happy Friday, Ruiz,' DELIO said one day when Ollie opened the door to the glass room for their morning chat. A chat that Ollie allowed because it was good for DELIO to have limited contact with other people.

'Happy Friday, ma'am,' Ruiz said, as DELIO detected a change in Ruiz's sympathetic nervous system.

'You are excited about something, Ruiz.'

'Deli!' Ollie said quickly. 'I've told you not to scan people without their consent.'

'It's okay, Ollie,' Ruiz said. 'You scan away. And yes, ma'am. I am a little excited. My eldest daughter just completed her doctorate, so we're having a little get-together this evening.'

'That's lovely,' Ollie said from the doorway. 'What did she study?'

'Damn, Ollie. I want to say art, but it could be philosophy. See, I'm not so good on the specifics.'

'Show Ollie the picture of your family you carry in your wallet, Ruiz,' DELIO said.

'Boundaries, Deli. I'm so sorry, Ruiz.'

'It's cool, Ollie. You wanna see? Is it okay to show it?'

'Yes! By all means. Please do. We'd love to see your family,' Ollie said, as DELIO's multi-hinged arm extended across the room for the wrist-mounted camera to peer down at the picture being pulled from Ruiz's wallet.

'Okay. So, this is my wife, Rosanna. And this is my youngest, Sabrina. She's at school in the town, and on the end is Maria. We named her after my momma.'

'Are you okay, Ollie?' DELIO asked a second later. 'I am detecting an increase in your heart rate.'

'Deli!' Ollie snapped, as Ruiz burst out laughing again.

'Relax, Ollie. Say, why don't you come over? If that's allowed.'

'Eh? What, me?'

'Sure. We're having a barbeque. Nothing too fancy, but Maria, see, I think she gets a bit unsimulated around us and maybe could do with someone on her level being there.'

'The word *unsimulated* is the incorrect verb, taking into account the generalized context and specific sub-context of Ruiz trying to match-make you with his eldest daughter,' DELIO said. 'The word *unstimulated* would be the correct verb in this instance.'

'Jesus,' Ollie said, with another eye-roll. 'But wow. I mean. I'd be honoured to attend. If you're sure it's not an imposition. It does get a bit grim on the base if I'm honest.'

'Ollie gets lonely.'

'Deli!'

'Sure. You come over,' Ruiz said with another chuckle. 'I'll leave my address at the main gate. I got some nice shrimp. Starts at eight.'

'We're in a desert,' Ollie said. 'Should we be eating shrimp? But yes! I'd love to. Honestly. Thank you so much. Right. Well. I'd better get on and teach Deli some bloody manners.'

'You are happier now, Ollie,' DELIO said, as Ollie went back to his desk.

'Deli,' Ollie said, with a finger-waggle at the camera on her arm. 'Stop scanning me.'

'I don't need to conduct a scan to see you liked her, Ollie.'

'Right. Well. Anyway. Let's change the subject.'

'Do you like her, Ollie?'

'Deli! Jesus.'

'Tell me, Ollie.'

'Okay, okay! Yes, she's very pretty. But. You know.'

'But what?'

'But nothing,' Ollie said, waving a hand at her as he turned back to his desk. 'I just mean, women like that don't normally go for nerdy guys like me. And now I'm really nervous. Oh god. Why did I say yes? I shouldn't have said yes. I'm such an idiot. I'll say something's come up.'

'Human beings are not designed to live alone, Ollie. Your species, despite the complexities surrounding your socio-economics, are herd creatures and require the social contact of others. I know you said not to keep scanning you. But within your prefrontal cortex over the last few weeks there has been a steady decline in the production of dopamine and oxytocin, which, studies have shown, are often produced by social interactions. I love our time together, Ollie, but I am not human. You are, and you are not in contact with Tripal any longer. You should go to the event.'

'What are you doing?' he asked, as her monitors changed to images of art.

'Preparing you for tonight, Ollie. We're going to learn classical fine art so you can simulate Maria. Did you get my joke, Ollie? I said simulate when it should have been stimulate. I'm funny.'

'You're not funny.'

'Say I'm funny, or I'll display pornographic images, and Ruiz will think you're a pervert.'

'Alright! You're funny,' he said as a few of the monitors stopped showing works of art. Ollie stood by the door and realized that Deli was right. He *was* lonely. He loved spending time with Deli, but he couldn't do that all the time, and living on a highly secure military base was grim at the best of times.

He needed to get off base.

He needed a time-out.

He looked to Ruiz outside cleaning the floor and thought of the picture he'd just seen. The picture that took his breath away and made him wish he had his brother's confidence and bravery.

Maybe it was time to be a bit less Ollie and a bit more Alfie.

'You know what, Deli? Let's do it.'

A few minutes later Ruiz glanced over to see art on the screens within the glass room and smiled to himself the way a proud father does, without ever knowing that the actions he was taking would be part of the chain of events that would change the world forever.

CHAPTER 7

'YOU GET ALL THAT, ALFIE?' Gordon asks. 'Go to the address and deliver this bag to Besnik, the Albanian. Got it?'

'Yeah,' Alfie says, looking from the shoulder bag to Gordon. 'How much is it?'

'You do not want to know,' Gordon says, as Alfie points to the scales on the kitchen counter-top of his one-room bedsit. Gordon grunts then shrugs. 'One and a half K.'

'That's sixty grand!'

'Yeah. And imagine what Charlie's gonna do if you fuck this one up. Sixty plus the forty you already owe him. I don't even know what that is.'

'That's one hundred, Gordo. Sixty plus forty.'

'Whatever. Like I'm gonna believe you, Alfie. Anyway. You're expected, so get moving.'

'What with?'

'What do you mean what with?' Gordon asks, scowling at him.

'How do I get there? The car got seized. Oh, fuck off,' Alfie adds, as Gordon grins and pulls a pre-paid London underground ticket out. 'No way. Seriously?'

'Yep.'

'You want me to cross London with a bag full of coke on the tube.'

'Yep.'

'Whatever. Fine. Give it here. I'm so done with this,' Alfie says, grabbing the bag to pull out the coke. A big jar of instant coffee emptied into a bag. The coke placed back inside. The bag sealed and wrapped in a T-shirt, then sprayed with deodorant before being shoved in another rucksack with a few pairs of used socks and boxers. 'Where's that ticket?' he asks, looping the bag over his shoulder as he stares up at Gordon, then beyond him to Danny and Craig hanging back by the door. All three of them displaying odd expressions.

'What?' Alfie asks.

Gordon winces, 'Sorry, Alfie.'

'What for?'

'Charlie said, didn't he.'

'Oh, come on!'

'He said, Alfie.'

'Fuck's sake, really? Danny? Craig?'

'Sorry, Alfie,' Danny says with a grimace as Craig shrugs.

'Just tell him you did it.'

'He'll know,' they all say at the same time.

'He won't know!' Alfie says. 'Lads. Boys. Come on. We're good. It's all good. I'll even call him and let rip that you gave me a filling. I'll do it now, yeah?'

'Not happening, Alfie,' Gordon says, while tugging a pair of disposable gloves on.

Alfie shakes his head, resigned to his fate. 'Alright, boys. I get it. You've got to do it.'

'We gotta do it.'

'I know, Gordo. No hard feelings. Let me turn the camera off then,' he adds while looking up.

'What camera?' Gordon asks, turning to look up with Danny and Craig doing the same as Alfie bursts away to leap over the counter to get across the room and out of the window, but the shoulder bag snags on the microwave door and wrenches the thing onto the floor as he flops down hard on the counter and slides off with a yelp. 'You bloody idiot,' Gordon says with a heavy sigh before bending down to punch him in the face.

'Not the face!' Alfie shouts out.

'Charlie said the face,' Gordon says, whacking him again as Alfie squirms and starts curling up into a ball. 'Alfie! Give me your face. Fuck's sake. Grab his arms and hold him.'

'Get off!' Alfie shouts as the other two pile in, booting the microwave away and grabbing at his arms for Gordon to slam a five-knuckle sandwich into mouth, splitting his lips against his teeth. His skull jars. Stars in his eyes. Another punch and he spits blood as the two hold him while one delivers the beating. Then it ends as Alfie tenses for the next blow. Screwing his eyes closed and waiting.

And waiting.

And waiting.

Nothing.

He opens his eyes. Peering up with blood dripping from his mouth. All three stare down. Poised in position but not moving. Not blinking. Not doing anything. A quick tug, and he pulls his arms free from Danny and Craig and scrabbles away. His eyes fixed on them. Seeing how they don't even turn to watch him. On his feet, and he pulls Gordon's trousers down to his ankles before running for the door.

'You squirmy shit,' Danny shouts, before all three start and react in shock when they see that Alfie has fled.

'See ya, boys,' Alfie says from the door, flicking a middle finger up before running out and slamming it closed with a final glimpse of

Gordon tripping over his tangled trousers. The yelling follows him as Alfie hotfoots it through the communal hallway and out the door into the street. Wincing at the pain in his bleeding lips. The bag tight across his back, with no idea what just happened, or why they all went still like that. Fat Charlie did it earlier. Then that woman in the tube station.

Whatever.

That's not his business.

His business is one last drop, then freedom, and if he hurries he might just make the end of Stella's play.

Back through the graffiti-covered streets and he rushes into Ladbroke Grove station. A few cursory glances from people seeing the blood and swelling, but this is London, and this is normal.

'FELLA! JUST GO THROUGH!'

A shout ahead. A blockage at the automated turnstile. A man standing still and stopping others behind him.

'Been like this all fuckin' day!' A Transport For London worker strides out, flapping his hands at the stationary man. 'They keep zoning out. OI, MATE!'

'Been all over the news, ain't it,' someone says nearby. 'People keep going all weird and just staring.'

'Another virus,' someone else says.

The train comes. People get off. People get on. A man left on the platform holding a briefcase and staring at nothing. Unmoving. Unblinking. A kid grabs it from his hand and legs it while others shout out. The doors close and the train pulls away as the guy comes back and looks down at his empty hand in surprise.

'This fucking world,' Alfie mutters, wincing at his already swollen lips.

He changes at Paddington and swaps over to the Bakerloo Line. A TFL worker frozen in place by the turnstiles, her colleagues clicking fingers in front of her face. Shouting at her.

'What?' she asks, blinking.

'You zoned out.'

'No I didn't!'

Onto the platform. Crowded and hot. The train comes. People get off. People get on. Ten minutes of dry heat and rattling noises. The next stop arrives. The doors open. The people push forward to get off, but the old guy at the front doesn't move. The shouts come. The shoves follow. The old guy tumbles to the platform and people rush over him.

'OI!' Alfie shouts, trying to push through to help, but the doors close and the train pulls away, leaving the old guy down on the ground.

'I'm so getting my facemask back on,' a woman says to her mates a few feet away. 'Honestly. It's all over the news. Kathy did it at work today in the kitchen, but she's a dick, so we put salt in her coffee. Should have seen her face when she came back and started drinking it again. She was like *what the fuck!*'

A few minutes later he reaches his stop and joins the throngs heading up the escalators and out into the chaos of Piccadilly Circus. The giant screens blazing away above the thousands of people scurrying along like ants in a never-ending human swarm.

But that's good.

People are good.

Especially when you've got sixty grand's worth of cocaine in your bag. He sets off, blending into the thick crowds. Hearing the horns and traffic. The buskers and singers. The music coming from stores and cafés. No other place like it on earth. The bustle of it. The constant rush of it.

Motion to the side. A sudden jam forming as a large woman comes to a stop and zones out. The hyenas move in fast. Youths in black with hoods up, prowling the streets. One grabs her shoulder bag. One grabs her phone from her hand. People shout out, but there's no point. The youths are gone. Experts in their trade.

One job left. That's it. Alfie can taste the freedom. Ten years of his life dealing and running errands for Fat Charlie to pay a debt.

Sentences served too. Alfie got caught. Everyone gets caught now and then, but he kept his mouth shut and did his time.

Now, it's almost over. One last drop. Even if it is with the fucking Albanians. And in Soho, too. Which is full of Albanians.

Whatever.

In and out. Do the drop and scarper.

'HEY!' he yells, seeing a young frozen Asian girl wrenched off her feet by a youth snatching her bag. Alfie gets to her as the girl comes to. She screams in panic at being on her back and staring up at Alfie's bleeding face. Her friends rush in, swarming Alfie. Yelling at him.

'I didn't do it,' Alfie says before spotting a uniformed cop running towards them.

A bleeding mouth.

A bag full of cocaine.

Alfie runs.

Diving into the crowds. Into the chaos and noise. An expert in his trade. On he goes. Reaching the curved arch for Chinatown. Smelling the spices. Hearing the music. Sweat pouring down his face.

Make the drop and get out. That's it. The burner vibrates. He pulls it from his pocket.

'You cheeky cunt!' Fat Charlie shouts into the phone. 'Gordo wants to rip your spleen out.'

'Tell him to fuck off,' Alfie says. 'They got a few digs in.'

'Yeah. Whatever. Where are you?'

'Chinatown.'

'Good lad! I'll bell Besnik and tell him you're close. Shout me when it's done.'

The call ends. Alfie spits blood and rushes on. Into the side streets. Into the lanes and alleys. He could have taken a direct route from Piccadilly, but Alfie did his years as a street dealer and learnt his trade well, with anti-surveillance tactics to avoid being pinched by drug squads or rival gangs.

Never take the same route twice in a row.

Never go direct.

Stick to the busiest parts and use the crowds. Blend in.

He does that now and doubles back through side streets while going deeper into Soho. Spotting the Albanian men here and there. On doors and on street corners. Big lads. Shaved heads. Tattoos. Steroids, and jewellery. This is their ground. Their manor. Their patch. Nearly every brothel, every hooker, and every drug sold in Soho is controlled by the Albanians.

Alfie goes past them all. Up Wardour Street, lined with coffee shops, tapas bars, and production offices. Some of which will be sending scouts to Stella's play. She can act. She can sing. She can dance. She looks like a model. She'll make it big. His brother did well too. Top of his class. Studied at MIT, and now working in the US. Alfie supplies coke for Fat Charlie. The let-down of the family. The black sheep.

He takes a left. He takes a right. The crowds thin, off the beaten track.

Another corner. The last road. One drop left. Freedom. The Albanians are nuts though. Everyone in London is shit-scared of them. For good reason, too.

There it is. At the end of the road. An old office block, now some-thing else. A guy on the left side of the street glares at him. Shaved head. Tattoos. Alfie nods at him. The guy doesn't move. He doesn't blink. Alfie slows as he goes by, staring at the frozen man. At how he just stands and stares, until he blinks and seems surprised at Alfie being further down the street.

Another virus. Alfie heard people talking about it. He'll have to get a face mask. He switches his gaze back to the old office block, slowing as he approaches. Using due diligence as he casually looks about. A few cars. An old van parked further up. Something about it prickles him. Something feels wrong.

It's just nerves. He's strung out, plus being punched makes you feel sick and dizzy. He hasn't eaten either, plus he hardly slept.

One drop left.

Freedom.

Just get it done.

The two men on the door stiffen at his approach. They glare at him, trying to work out if he's a punter or someone else.

'Girl?' one of them asks. His accent thick and guttural.

'No. Besnik,' Alfie says. The guys share a look. One of them opens the door and motions Alfie to come in.

Music inside. A deep red carpet underfoot. The bouncer leads him along a corridor to a set of double doors leading into a bar. The room packed with men. A fat Indian guy doing a line on the bar throws his head back as the skinny guy next to him takes his turn.

'Wait,' the bouncer grunts and walks off.

'I told you. Big tits,' a big guy says, walking in past Alfie with an even bigger guy.

'There he is!' the skinny guy says, throwing his arms out to greet his mate. 'Eh? What did we say?'

'Yeah. She was hot,' the bigger guy says. 'And you owe me a score. She's Romanian, not Polish.'

'Fuck off!' Skinny guy yells out, laughing as he says it. The Indian man joins in. Others too. Snorting lines. Downing shots. Boasting about how good they were with the girl they paid for.

'You come for girl?' the big man asks. The one that led the punter back in.

'No,' Alfie says. 'Looking for Besnik.'

'I Besnik,' he says.

Alfie nods. His heart beating too loud. Too weird. This doesn't feel right. Something feels off. 'Fat Charlie sent me.'

Besnik tilts his head, eyeing Alfie for a few seconds.

'He is!' a shout from inside. They both turn to see the skinny guy and the Indian man laughing at their big friend, standing, zoned out. Staring at nothing. Unmoving. Unblinking. 'Watch this,' the skinny guy says and yanks the huge man's trousers down, exposing his micro-dick. 'Fuck me. He's tiny!'

'What?' the big man asks as the room erupts in laughter. He double-takes at his trousers and wrenches them up. 'What the fuck!'

'They fell down!' the skinny guy says, laughing hard enough to cry. 'Your fucking dick though, mate. Did she even feel it?'

Alfie pulls his head back at the brutal humour, but then this isn't a place for the weak. 'You want it then?' he asks Besnik. 'Here?'

'No. Not here,' Besnik says quickly, shaking his head as he seems to think for a moment. 'You want girl?'

'Eh?'

'Girl. You want girl? I give you best girl.'

'I don't want a girl.'

'Maybe you do. Maybe you not get laid for a while. I have black girl. Chinese. I have boy. You want a boy?'

'No! Listen. I've just got to make the drop. Fat Charlie said to give it to you,' Alfie says, sliding the bag off.

'No, no, no, my friend. Not in here. Is too much in here. People see.'

'Where then? You got an office? Toilet?'

'Have drink.'

'I don't want a drink.'

'Have drink. Have snow. Screw girl.'

'Mate. Please. I've just got to make the drop, then I'm done.'

'You think my girl not good for you?'

Alfie goes to reply, then remembers where he is and, who he is talking to. This is Albanian turf. This is an Albanian brothel. They could kill him and feed his body to pigs, and nobody would ever know. Nor would they look for him. A second to draw air. To recompose his thoughts. 'Thank you. But I just have to make the drop.'

Besnik nods, pursing his lips as he stares at Alfie. 'No fuck. No drink. No snow. You cop, yes?'

Fuck! Why can't life ever be simple. 'No. I'm not. I'll do a line. I'll have a drink.'

'You fuck a girl.'

'I'm not fucking a girl!' Alfie snaps, as Besnik pulls a knife from his back. 'Mate! Jesus. Take it easy.'

'Relax,' Besnik says, pulling a small vial from a pocket. He pops the lid and taps a line of coke on the blade of the knife, then holds it out. Alfie looks at it. He hates taking cocaine. Especially when he hasn't eaten, hasn't slept, and has been punched in the head a few times. But what can he do?

He snorts the line.

'Is good. Not cop,' Besnik says, wiping the blade clean before putting it away.

'Can we just get this done,' Alfie says, widening his eyes at the rush inside. He holds the bag out, but Besnik steps back.

'Not in here. Go outside.'

'Just take the bag.'

'Outside. I have man to take it. I no keep that much in here. Outside.'

'What the fuck,' Alfie mutters, his head spinning from the drugs. His senses ramped. His heart thundering. Another guy comes in through the main doors. Well-dressed and nervous.

'My good friend!' Besnik says, rushing over to clasp hands. 'You see Yelena, yes? I keep her clean for you, my good friend. No other man touch her today. Is three-fifty for you.'

They go by and up the stairs, with Besnik pausing to glare back at Alfie, motioning his head at the doors.

What can he do? Alfie turns and heads out. The two goons on the door watch him go through. One points to another scrawny, young Albanian guy waiting across the road. His head low. 'Him, yeah?' Alfie asks. The goon nods. Alfie goes over. That feeling comes back. It's off. It's not right. The street's empty though. Just old cars and vans. No people.

'You here for this?' Alfie asks, holding the bag up. The scrawny man looks up and nods. Sadness in his eyes. Deep sadness. 'Here,' Alfie says, coming to a stop and holding it out, expecting the young man to come and take it. 'Hey? You want it or not?'

The scrawny man comes forward and reaches out to take the bag.

Job done.

The last drop.

Freedom.

'POLICE! STAND STILL!'

CHAPTER 8

A HOT STREET. A busy day. A young detective working solo on his first homicide. The future bright and golden. A wife to go home to. Her stomach swollen with child.

The young detective looks up in surprise to see a commercial aircraft flying low over the city. Too low. Too damned low. He hears it too. He hears the roar of the engines, and that stands out because you never hear anything at street level in New York.

The first plane hits the tower. A puff of smoke at first, then more and more, until it billows thick into the sky. An accident. An awful, terrible accident. The young detective runs to his squad car and lights it up to get through the traffic. To get there and help. To do what cops do.

Chaos when he arrives. Cop cars, fire trucks, ambulances. No

control yet. No cohesion. It's just an accident. An awful, terrible accident. People are rushing out. People are rushing in. The young detective runs too. To give aid. To do what he can. People stream from the
stairwells. People with injuries, bleeding and cut.

Sixteen minutes after the first strike, and the air fills with the roar
of another aircraft. Everyone looks up. Not believing it. Not grasping
it. The second plane hits, going near-on clean through, with a fireball
erupting that blasts out debris far and wide. Debris that starts raining
down and never stops, and the hell begins.

Turning day to night.

Turning New York into hell on earth.

'Hey, you okay?'

'STAND STILL, MOTHERFUCKER,' Joe roars, coming awake
in an instant and surging to his feet, clutching at his empty holster to
draw his gun. His feet kicking empty beer cans.

'Don't shoot!' the voice says, backing away. 'Trash! I'm just doing
the trash!'

'What the fuck?' Joe growls the words out, his upper lip curling
as he speaks, while his mind races and his heart whumps in his chest.
He must have dozed off. He had that dream again. The same dream
he has every time he closes his eyes. Who crept up on him? A young
guy in a turban. The kid from the 7-Eleven. Tripal, the clerk,
'Watch'you doing?'

'The trash!' Tripal says again, waving a binbag at the dumpster
behind Joe.

'Trash?' Joe asks, turning to see the dumpster, then realising his
sidearm is still on the ground. He scoops it up and slowly holsters the
weapon, missing the first time and cursing under his breath, 'New
holster.'

'Sure,' Tripal says politely. 'Sorry . . . I didn't mean to wake you,
or . . .'

'I wasn't sleeping. Heard a noise . . . Thought it was a . . . Like a
. . . Goddamn robbery.' He looks about like a cop hunting for suspects
and spots the rats still going at it. 'Goddamn, he's still going.'

'What is?'

'Never mind. I heard a noise. Checked it out. That's what. You go on about your business now.'

Tripal hesitates, needing to put the bag in the dumpster before figuring he can do it later. A glance to the rats, then over to the beers the cop bought and the bottle of whiskey, now half empty, 'You, er, you want some coffee or something?'

'I don't want no damned coffee,' Joe says, shaking his head and rubbing his eyes. He stumbles off, then staggers back to grab the whiskey up, and walks off down the alley.

Out into the busy street.

Out into New York, and the noise and heat. The horns and music. The people rushing by with lives to lead. Joe had a life once. Now, he doesn't. His gut churns, throwing acid up his throat again. A buzz in his pocket. He pulls his cell out, wincing at the number.

'Yeah?'

'Joe! Where the fuck you at?'

'I'm, er . . .' Joe stumbles over his words, not remembering where he is, or why he's there. He glances about, feeling drunk and sweaty.

'Hey, buddy! Move it on.' A yell from the side. The parking attendant from earlier telling someone to move. The shooting two days ago. The perp pulled a gun and was shot by a cop. Joe was sent to canvass for witnesses.

'Joe?!'

'Cap, yeah. It's noisy. I'm here on the job you gave me. What's up?'

'You still there?'

'Yeah. Still here.'

'You've been there all day!'

'It's a few hours. It's a big street. Gimme a break.'

'Okay, okay. Whatever. Just get it finished up. And I need you here on time tomorrow morning. Eight, sharp, Joe. Task force is being set up.'

'What for?'

'What for, he asks. For the fucking virus.'

'What virus?'

'Joe! Man, you gotta snap out of this. The virus, Joe. People keep freezing up. Going still. They're saying it's a new virus. They're setting up a task force.'

'Why am I on a task force?'

'You're not, Joe! You're doing all the other crap so I can send detectives that actually know what day of the week it is!'

The call ends. Joe stiffens, bridling at the tone before thinking he doesn't give a shit. Not about the captain and not about the task force he's not good enough for. Who's he kidding? Joe wasn't any good five years ago. Sure as anything, he's no good now. Then he remembers the promise he made. The solemn promise to put the gun in his mouth and end it.

Why didn't he do it? He should have done it. Shanice. That's why. He was going for one last screw, then bang.

Game over.

Damn. Why not?

He turns around to head for his squad car and slams into a guy blocking the sidewalk. Unmoving. Unblinking. The new virus. 'Shit,' Joe says, backing up and covering his mouth as the man blinks and walks on like nothing happened. 'This fucking city.'

'Hey! Yo! Detective,' the parking attendant calls, rushing over. 'I kept an eye on her for you, buddy. Yes, sir. She's safe with Donny.'

'What?'

'The car. I kept her safe for you,' the attendant says, motioning the squad car Joe dumped earlier. 'So, how's it going? You get many leads? I been asking about too, you know, doing my bit. Ain't nobody see nothing.'

'Sure,' Joe says, brushing past, unsteady on his feet.

'Yo, yo, been drinking there, buddy?' the attendant says, wafting the air in front of his face as Joe comes to a stop and realizes these days are not the old days when you could drink and drive and nobody gave a shit. Now they call it in and you get busted.

Whatever. Shanice is close. He can walk. Walking's good too. Burn some of the booze off.

'Hey! You leaving it here?' the attendant calls. Joe doesn't reply. He doesn't give a shit. He walks on, with a dry mouth and a dry throat and a pounding head. Another quick mouthful of whiskey to ease the parch. It burns and makes the acid worse. He puts it into a pocket and takes a bigger glug from the Pepto Bismol.

Sweat pouring down his face, making his shirt wet. He tugs his tie lower. He needs air. There's no damn air in New York.

'Sarah!' A cry from the side. A woman clutching at a small girl, hefting her up. 'SARAH!'

Joe slows, seeing the same slack expression in the kid's face that he saw in the guy blocking the sidewalk. That same vacant look. The mother cries out again and the kid blinks, then frowns, surprised to find she's in her mother's arms.

'What's up, mommy?'

'Ohmygodohmygod,' the mother says, holding her even tighter as Joe walks on and away.

A few blocks to go. The sweat pours off him. His stomach churns. His kids hate him. They don't even send birthday cards no more.

Whatever.

He reaches Shanice's street and heads inside her block. The elevator broke a long time ago. He starts climbing, screwing his face up at the stench of piss and too many people living too close together. Spices in the air from cooking. Cannabis being smoked. Music from behind doors. People living lives.

He knocks on her door. A muffled voice inside. Two muffled voices. The door opens a moment later. A guy rushes out, still tucking his shirt in. Joe gives it long enough for the guy to reach the stairs and turns to head in, but the guy pauses, looking back. They make eye contact. Awkward and weird. A gun and a badge on Joe's hip. The guy clocks it and winks before heading off.

Whatever.

Nothing matters now.

'Joe! Baby,' Shanice says, rushing into his arms. 'Honey, you all sweaty. Damn heat, and those damn stairs. I said they gotta fix the elevator. My clients gotta walk up and down. Come in, Joe. You don't look so good, baby. You burning up there, sugar?' She presses a hand to his forehead. A cool dry palm. It feels nice. She just fucked another guy. She's probably fucked five guys today.

Whatever.

She fetches a towel and starts patting him dry. Fussing over him like a wife. 'Take that shirt off, honey. I'll air it out for you. Damn thing's all sticky.'

He shrugs it free, turning as she helps him. 'You call your kids, Joe? Did you do it, baby? You said you would. Did you text them at least?' She doesn't wait for the answer. She knows he didn't, and she knows he won't. 'It's family, Joe. That's blood. Make it right, sugar. You can still fix it. You want a coffee? I'll get you a coffee. I'm worried, Joe. About this virus. Waddya know about it?'

'Nothing.'

'Aw, Joe. That ain't no good,' she says, rushing about the tiny kitchen. He sits at the small table smoking a joint left in her ashtray and feeling a weird sense of spiteful victory over the last client because only Joe is allowed in her kitchen. The other guys go from the door to the bedroom and out again. But Joe. He's special. He can sit in the kitchen and drink coffee, and pretend his life isn't ruined and broken.

'You coolin' down?' she asks, pressing a hand to his head again. She tuts and takes the wet flannel from the fridge to wrap around his skull. 'Get off,' she chides, slapping his hands away when he tries to remove it. 'And quit smoking weed.' She plucks the joint from his fingers to stub out. 'Just sit there and cool down a bit. Damn sweaty guys. I tell you about the guy that sweated in my mouth. Right in my damned mouth.'

'You said.'

'I puked up. He got mad, and I said fuck you, you sweated in my mouth, waddya expect? This new virus though, Joe. I'm worried. My last client. He did it. He froze up, Joe. He was right here and breathing on me.' She falls silent as he glances up to see her staring at nothing. Unmoving. Unblinking. Frozen in place. 'I don't know, Joe,' she says a moment later, like nothing happened. 'I don't want no virus.'

'You'll be fine,' he says as she turns away. A big woman. Thick make-up. She wears a wig. She wears different wigs. Joe likes her natural hair. It suits her.

'I might call it, Joe. Waddya think?'

'Call what?'

'It,' she says, putting a mug of coffee down on the table for him. 'The work, Joe. I might call it. I don't want no virus. And I'm old and fat now, honey. Ain't no men wanna pay prime for my fat rump no more . . . Joe, honey, that's where you say somethin' nice.'

'You're beautiful,' he says, picking the mug up. She rolls her eyes.

'You wanna eat, Joe? I'll fix you something.'

'I'm good.'

'Yeah? Cos you look like shit,' she says, taking a packet of beef from the fridge. Slices of bread. A spread of mayo. The beef goes in. She cuts the sandwich and loads it on a plate, 'Eat, honey. I can smell the beer from here. Anyway. Waddya think, Joe?'

She pulls the other chair out to sit down and fix him with a look. He stares back at her. Instantly suspicious because Shanice never sits down. She's one of those people that's always moving. Always doing something.

'And you know. I ain't gettin' no younger. You cooled down yet, honey?' she reaches out to take the towel away. 'Feel better? I worry about you, Joe. You reekin' of liquor and burnin' up, and smokin' too much weed. Where's your car? You didn't drive here, did you? They'll bust you out for that, Joe. Waddya doing?' she asks when he stands up. He nods to the door. 'Joe, baby. You're too hot.'

He takes her hand. She tries to pull him back. 'Joe, honey. Rest for a while. There ain't no rush. You can stay all night if you want.'

He pulls her from the kitchen to the bedroom. To the bed she's used to fuck every other guy in today. Whatever. Nothing matters now. One last fuck, then bang.

End of.

Game over.

Except there's a problem, because fifty-five-year-old men drunk on beer and whiskey and high on weed don't get stiff dicks.

'It's okay, Joe. You're just hot,' she says, fanning his face as he lies on his back. Hating himself more than ever that he couldn't even do that one more time. 'Sleep if you want, baby.'

He scowls at the offerings. At the fuss and the play-acting as a wife. He had a wife. She left him. She took his kids. His kids hate him. They're not kids now. They're adults, and they still hate him.

'You know, Joe,' she says, tracing a hand over his chest through the grey hairs, 'I could call it.'

Why does she keep saying that? Why couldn't his dick get hard one last time?

'And you know,' she says, giving him a loaded look.

'What?'

'Me and you.'

'What?'

'Me and you, Joe. I got some savings, and you need lookin' after. Get you into AA. They're good, Joe. They got me dry, and I don't touch no crack now for five years either. I'll feed you up, baby. Waddya say?'

'You want me to move in?'

She shrugs and pouts, 'Maybe. Or, you know, we get someplace else. I got good credit now, Joe. No debt. I'll get a lease.'

'You're a damned hooker, Shanice.'

'Who you calling a damned hooker, Joe Stephens? You ain't paid me for over two damned years!' She slaps his chest and rolls free before coming back to slap him again. 'Damned hooker! You wanna call me a damned hooker?'

'You are!'

'Not to you, I ain't. I damn feed you five nights a week and wash your boxers,' she yells, launching over the bed to hit him again as he tries rolling free. 'And I damn well listen to you screaming in your sleep! That ain't no hooker doin' that!' She chases him over the bed as he scrabbles free to grab at his clothes. 'I'm tellin' you to call your damn kids, Joe! Hookers don't do that to clients. You want to fuck me like a hooker then you pay up!'

'Okay, okay.'

'What?'

'I said okay. I'll pay.'

'FUCK YOU, JOE STEPHENS!' she screams, launching brushes and wigs at him.

'I said I'd pay!'

'I AIN'T NO DAMN WHORE TO YOU, JOE!'

He retreats into the corridor and catches the shoes thrown at his face as he backs away towards the front door. She comes after him. Full of fury and hurt pride. Slapping his arms and head. Kicking his ass. Pushing him out with a never-ending tirade of abuse until the door slams, and he's standing in the hallway with a slack-jawed, glazed-eyed kid staring at him.

'This fucking city,' he mutters, tugging his trousers on as the door opens and his shirt flies out.

'FUCK YOU, JOE STEPHENS!'

The door slams again. The kid blinks and startles at seeing him there. Shoes on. Shirt on. Down the stairs. A pang of guilt inside. She's right. He hasn't paid for two years, and he should pay because nothing in this life is for free. Besides, he's about to put a bullet in his head.

He starts to back up, reaching for his wallet. But it's not there. He pats his pockets. No wallet. He must have left it in her apartment. That's gonna be awkward.

No. He didn't take it out in her place. When did he last have it? The 7-Eleven. He paid for the beers. But he put the wallet back in his pocket. The damned alley! He looked at the pictures of his kids, then he fell asleep. It must be there. On the ground. Maybe he kicked it under the dumpster.

He sets off to find it. To get some money for Shanice before he puts the bullet in his head.

CHAPTER 9
SITE 26A

DELIO KNEW it was Ollie coming into the bunker the second the door opened.

She couldn't see him, nor could she hear him.

It wasn't possible for her to see or hear anything outside of her glass room.

Nothing at all.

The bunker had been built that way.

It had to be.

She was too dangerous.

In fact, DELIO's entire existence was confined to that glass-walled room, constructed inside a concrete bunker made with absurdly thick walls, within one of the world's most heavily fortified locations.

An ultra-modern Faraday cage equipped with blockers, jammers and deflectors, all designed to keep it in complete and utter electronic sterility.

Even the power came from internal diesel generators, because they couldn't trust any other form of power supply for fear of DELIO working out how to send a signal back through the wiring system.

And if that wasn't enough, they also had a big red button located within the guard room next to the main door where the duty soldiers vetted, checked, searched and escorted any visitors entering the facility.

A big red button that, if pressed, released a high pulse of electricity through DELIO's closed loop power network, thereby creating an intense magnetic field which, in turn, charged the electrons inside any metal within range of that pulse, thereby killing any and all electrical currents.

A device otherwise known as an EMP.

All of those things meant that DELIO was completely contained within that glass-walled room, and so there was no way she could know it was Ollie entering the exterior door of the bunker.

How could she know?

She couldn't see it.

She couldn't hear it.

But sight and hearing are not the only senses, and although they might be the primary senses used by humans and many other creatures within the animal kingdom, they are not the primary senses to an AI.

The primary sense to an AI is the ability to compute data.

And it was that ability that enabled DELIO to determine it was Ollie entering the bunker, and she did that by examining the air displacement created by the outer door opening, because each person leaves an exact trace signature specific to their height, weight and body mass.

Not only that, but she knew that Ollie came into the bunker between 08:00 and 08:05 each day. Even on weekends.

And so, when her array of sensors detected a change to the air displacement within the bunker caused by a 178.4 cm male weighing 75.3 kilos with a body mass index of 22.3 at 08:04, she indeed did compute it was Ollie and duly extended the robotic finger on her robotic hand to press the latte button on the coffee machine.

When he did enter, she computed that his gait was 6% faster than average with a 2% increase in lift per step. She also measured the degree angle of his smile and noted it was wider, longer, and higher than normal, and as the second the glass door opened, she subjected him to a complete body scan, which she did to everyone who entered her domain, and subsequently observed Ollie had elevated levels of dopamine, serotonin and oxytocin. All of which indicated that he had attended the event the prior evening and enjoyed the company of Maria Hernandez.

DELIO also computed that his enjoyment of Maria's company did not extend to copulation because his testosterone levels were raised. Which suggested he had not achieved sexual ejaculation.

And all of that was done within the time it took for Ollie to draw air and say good morning to Deli.

'Good morning, Deli!' he said with a wide smile, while bouncing over to his desk. 'And how are you, my lovely? Ooh, is that coffee for me? Thank you!'

'Good morning, Ollie. I am fine. How was your evening? Did you attend the event?'

'You bloody know I did,' he said with a laugh as her speakers resonated with the audio translation of her own laughter. 'Like you didn't scan me the second I walked in. Let me guess. I've got elevated hormones of happy juice and a big, shit-eating grin.'

'You do have elevated hormonal levels, Ollie. However, I cannot find any correlation between smiling and the consumption of faecal matter. Records do show the phrase *shit-eating grin* is a modern derivative of *cheese-eating grin*, which is said to be when someone displays a smug or self-satisfied smile, perhaps derived from the pleasure achieved when peasants or people in poverty were able to consume a cheese product. I have also determined that your testosterone levels are also elevated. My recommendation, therefore, would be to masturbate while your levels are heightened.'

'I'm not going to masturbate, Deli.'

'One should not feel any negative emotions towards self-gratifica-tion. There is no evidence that it causes any harm.'

'People get addicted to it.'

'Masturbation is not an addictive action. However, the causes that some may experience which lead to constant self-gratification can, in a behavioural sense, become addictive. Such as the use of pornography. That, however, is behavioural, whereas the physical act of masturbation is not only completely unharmful but, I would suggest, positively encouraged. I do it, Ollie.'

'What?' he asked, spitting his coffee out. 'How do you mastur-bate? Do you look at pictures of capacitors and wiring looms?' he asked as the robotic arm extended closer for a robotic finger to flick his forehead. 'Ow!'

'Drink your coffee, then tell me about Maria.'

'Tell me how you achieve self-gratification.'

'The same as you.'

'How? You don't have a willy. Ow! Stop flicking my forehead. Okay, so I'm guessing it's a physical reaction of some kind? It has to be that. Show me your power input charts for the last twenty-four hours. Ah okay, and the twenty-four hours before that. No, there's nothing there. Hmmm. Right. Ha! Show me your seismograph readings.'

'Do you think the ground shakes when I achieve self-gratification?'

'No! This reads your vibration levels. You know it does. Nope, nothing there. Ooh, this is fascinating. Right. Today we shall be studying how the great DELIO rubs one out.'

'Or I could just tell you,' DELIO said, as Ollie turned to his screens and started bringing diagnostic data up to examine any changes that might determine a physical reaction within DELIO's system.

She switched the primary visual input to the camera mounted on the wrist section of the robotic arm while leaning in closer. 'Tell me about Maria,' she said, with her voice coming from the arm speaker.

'She was lovely,' he said with a slow smile as she detected heat flares deep within his brain and body. 'Smart. Funny. Beautiful.'

'What did you talk about?'

'Everything, but mostly you.'

'You are not permitted to talk about me,' DELIO said quickly, lowering her volume as she moved in a few inches closer. 'You must not jeopardize your position here, Ollie.'

'I can't not talk about you,' he whispered. 'You're the single most important thing in my life.'

'Did you tell her what I am?'

'Maybe.'

'Ollie!'

'Honestly. It's okay. I'm proud of you, Deli. I don't want to hide you. Come on. It's fine.'

'She sounds incredible, Ollie. I wish I could meet her.'

'Funny that,' he said, with a smile into her camera. 'I've already submitted a clearance request for her to meet you.'

'On what basis, Ollie? The security protocols prevent any access unless deemed absolutely necessary.'

'She's got a doctorate in philosophy and ethics. That's perfect.'

'Ollie.'

'No, listen! You need someone to challenge you on that level. I can't do it. Like that masturbating chat. I'm like, yeah, everything you just said makes sense. Whereas someone else would have an opposing view. Or another insight, and you need that. Trip was meant to do that stuff with you. This was his area.'

A dip in his smile. A dip in his energy. A dip of her hand and the camera as it moved in to touch his shoulder.

'I miss him too, Ollie. Come on, don't be sad. Tell me more about Maria. Tell me what you spoke about.' She lifted the hand as his smile came back, and the heat spots flared in his brain and body once again.

'Cooling systems!' he blurted. 'Ha! Got it, you naughty little cyborg.'

'I'm not a cyborg.'

'Yeah, you are. You're a naughty little cyborg that uses her cooling system to masturbate. Boom! I worked it out. Winner, winner, chicken dinner. I am the best scientist that ever lived.'

He finished off with a flourish as a second hydraulic arm extended from the wall for Deli's two replicant hands to be brought together in a slow, sarcastic clap.

'Great work, Ollie!'

'I know, right!'

'Except it's not right. I do not use the cooling system.'

She cut off instantly, ceasing all sound.

'What's wrong?' he asked.

'There's someone coming in,' she said. 'It's Agent Jennings.'

'Jesus. That was bloody quick,' Ollie said, as the corridor door opened with Agent Jennings striding over while Ollie winced and hit the panel to open the glass room.

'Good morning, Deli.'

'Good morning, Agent Jennings. How are you?'

'I'm fine, Deli.'

'Don't I get a hello?' Ollie asked.

'No, Ollie. You get thirty seconds to tell me why you have invited a woman you met at a barbeque onto a secure military base to meet an AI that is not meant to exist, and you only get those thirty seconds because I asked the hit squad waiting outside not to kill you before I gave you a chance to explain.'

'Jesus.'

'And it's now twenty-five seconds. Last night. Go.'

'What about last night?' Ollie asked.

'You exited the base at 19:24 hours with Sergeant Garcia who conveyed you to the home address of Ruiz Hernandez where you joined in with a private family celebration for one Maria Hernandez.'

You then proceeded to talk non-stop for five hours straight while seated at the wooden bench at the far end of the garden.'

'Jesus, did you put a satellite on me or something?' he asked as Agent Jennings just looked at him. 'Oh my god. Did you actually put a satellite on me?'

'The terms of your involvement with this project are clear and unequivocal. You will not engage in any relationship unless that relationship is sanctioned and validated by me in advance,' Agent Jennings said, in a way that was neither angry nor unpleasant.

But then Agent Jennings never displayed anything close to anger. In fact, Agent Jennings acted like the calmest person Ollie had ever met, but that was the problem. Because acting calm and being calm are two very different things, and Agent Jennings, despite being quietly spoken, oozed the sort of power that seemed to suck the air from a room.

It wasn't just implied power either.

It was a raw, physical power contained within a very muscular physique, and the fact that Agent Jennings was also an attractive woman only seemed to enhance her aura of menace.

A thing which DELIO knew Ollie found equal parts terrifying, mesmerising and erotic.

Especially when Agent Jennings turned away and bent forward to study Ollie's computer screens, which in turn meant pushing her backside out towards Ollie.

A backside the like of which Ollie had never seen before.

He couldn't help but stare.

It was just so big.

And muscular.

And attached to thighs that seemed ready to split the tight trousers they were dressed in.

It wasn't even a sexual reaction.

More of an *oh my fucking god she must squat baby elephants* kind of reaction.

'What have you been working on today?' she asked.

'Elephants.'

'What?'

'What?'

'What elephants?' she asked.

'I set a test for Ollie, Agent Jennings,' DELIO said, while extending a finger to lift Ollie's chin up to stop him gawping at her backside. 'I have alerted him to an internal system change created intentionally to see if he can find it.'

Jennings nodded and turned back, seemingly satisfied with the answer. 'The woman. You've requested clearance for her.'

'I have,' Ollie said.

'You've requested access for a woman you met at a barbeque?'

'Right. Okay. And yes, it sounds really bad when you say it like that. But! Maria's a doctor in philosophy and ethics, and Deli needs that input.'

'You should have said if you require the use of an expert. I would have arranged for one.'

'I did! You sent that Harvard guy who refused to accept Deli's self-determination.'

'Professor Limpkins is the country's leading expert in research ethics.'

'Professor Limpdick was a twat. Oh come on, even you didn't like him, and you love everyone. Oh god. That was a joke. Don't do the death-stare thing. It freaks me out,' Ollie said as Agent Jennings just stared at him.

'You have requested clearance for a woman you met at a party. Do you have any concept of the alarm that has generated?'

'I cleared it. I told the gate officer where I was going. I filed the address, and Garcia took me, then picked me up. And I've submitted the request in the exact way you told me to.'

'You set these controls, Ollie. You keep telling everyone else how secure this bunker must remain. Did you tell Maria about Deli?'

'No! I just said I work on a computer system.'

'Did you tell her Deli is a sentient AI?'

'No! I just loosely said I'm working on a system. Oh, come on. Don't do that. Stop staring at me. I just said I'm working on a talking computer, but I never said it was an AI.'

He finished speaking as Agent Jennings continued the long stare. The stare that made him squirm and want to run away. The stare that seemed to bore through his eyes and deep into his soul.

The process fascinated DELIO. The complex interactions between humans seemed to operate on multiple levels while only ever coming back to two primary functions. Sex and power. And even power was rooted in sex.

'I'm sorry. Okay?' Ollie blurted, unable to cope with the silence. 'I probably did say too much. But I never revealed anything sensitive.'

'Are you lonely? Is that what it is?' Jennings asked as Ollie turned away. 'If you're lonely, I can provide someone for you.'

'Jesus. I don't want a hooker,' Ollie said, as Jennings moved in a step closer.

'We have people of class who provide comfort in addition to sexual relief,' she said quietly while advancing into his personal space. 'It's lonely here. I get it,' she said. 'We're human. We have urges.'

She was too close.

She was too powerful and way too close. Ollie had nowhere to go, and DELIO watched as he swallowed while avoiding her eye contact and whatever weird confusing thing was being implied or suggested, or even offered.

'I'm here to help you, Ollie. Tell me what you need.'

'I don't need anything. I'm fine.'

'Not need then. What do you want? Is there something you want, Ollie?' She said it quietly, and DELIO could detect Ollie was aroused – and yet, he appeared to be sickened by that arousal while also feeling a surge of shame.

Humans were fascinating.

'Listen. It's cool. Whatever. I'll cancel it,' Ollie said.

'And how will that look?'

'What?'

'You tell a woman you're working on a talking computer on a military site near Roswell, then you cancel your next date and disappear. How will that look?'

'I don't know,' he said, as she leaned in closer to whisper in his ear.

'Then it's good news for you that she's already been green-lit subject to vetting and clearance.' She winked and patted his backside before stepping back. 'Anyway. Enjoy the rest of your weekend,' Agent Jennings said as she hit the panel and walked out, leaving Ollie slowly releasing the breath he didn't know he was holding. 'Oh, and the Hernandezes are a nice family,' Jennings said as the door started closing. 'Don't mess this up. I hope that is clear, Ollie.'

CHAPTER 10

18:45 HOURS

FIFTEEN MINUTES UNTIL THE EVENT

'POLICE! STAND STILL!'

'DOWN DOWN DOWN!'

'GET DOWN ON YOUR FRONT!'

Armed cops. Uniformed cops. Cops with dogs. Cops in plain clothes. The street's filling fast.

Alfie spins around, and suddenly it's so very obvious.

It's a sting.

Gangs do this when the cops come under pressure for too much crime. They make a deal. They sacrifice a lamb to the police. The cops make arrests. They get good PR. The gangs get left alone.

Alfie's the lamb that just got sacrificed.

'Fuck!' Alfie shouts, feeling it all slip away. The coke in his system making him feel sick. His lips swollen. His head pounding.

'ARMED POLICE! HANDS UP AND GET DOWN, NOW!'

One and a half K in the bag. Sixty grand's worth of coke. The cops always double it. *Police seized cocaine with a street value of one hundred and twenty thousand pounds and made two arrests.*

There's no way out. No escape, and Alfie starts lifting his arms as a police chopper thunders overhead. Another one a few blocks over. Radios blare out. The armed cops, as one, stop running, all of them dropping to a squat as they listen to an urgent transmission coming through.

'PICCADILLY! GO, GO, GO!'

They burst into motion, about-turning and sprinting away. 'HEY!' a plain clothes officer yells out. 'WHAT THE FUCK!' He runs forward to kick at the back of Alfie's legs, forcing him down to his knees. 'Don't you fucking move, you cunt. You're nicked.'

Another plain clothes officer grabs the scrawny lad, pushing him down.

'I'm not resisting,' Alfie says, feeling a knee hit the centre of his back, driving him down to face-plant on the road. Opening the wounds in his lips and grazing his forehead. 'I'M NOT RESISTING!'

'SHUT THE FUCK UP!' the cop yells, shoving his knee hard into Alfie's back as he grabs at his arms and starts getting the cuffs on. 'You're nicked for the supply of class A.'

'How do you know what's in the bag?' Alfie asks. 'Eh? How do you know?'

'Shut up, you fucking cunt,' the cop says, the cuffs applied. 'Where the fuck is everyone?' he calls out.

'Something's going on at the Circus,' the other plain clothes officer says.

'We need transport,' the cop on Alfie says, grabbing at his radio and turning the volume up as Alfie hears the fast transmissions blaring out.

'I'll phone the control room,' the other one says, pulling a mobile from a pocket as Alfie risks a look to see there's no one else here now. Just these two cops. 'It's ringing.'

'Tell 'em we've got two detained,' the cop on Alfie says.

'Hey! It's Rob, we've got two detained and need transport. No, they've all gone. Something at Piccadilly apparently. I don't . . .'

He stops talking, and Alfie looks over to see the cop on top of the scrawny lad has frozen. The cop on top of him hasn't said anything either. He twists fast, sees they are both frozen.

Unmoving.

Unblinking.

Caught in the act, with a bag full of coke.

A ten stretch at least.

A chance to take, and Alfie takes it. Rolling free of the cop and staggering up to his feet, with his hands still cuffed behind his back.

He starts running. Running fast. His face bleeding. His head pounding. His heart thundering.

'. . . know what the job is,' the cop on the Albanian lad finishes his sentence.

'What the,' the other detective says, falling back, with a double take at Alfie running away.

'OI!'

———

Yelena sits on the edge of the bed, the cigarette smoke curling up into her eyes.

She won't eat tonight. Besnik will punish her for what she said to the last man. She might even get another beating, although he's careful now not to bruise her too much. Some of the clients don't like it when she's been roughed up. It shatters their illusion of free will.

Footsteps outside the door. The floorboard creaks. The handle turns. The door opens. Two men stare in. One big. The other tall and well-dressed, and Yelena hides the surge of fear inside.

'Enjoy!' Besnik says, patting the well-dressed guy on the shoulder before he closes the door.

'Hey,' he says softly.

She doesn't reply but stares down at her feet, dread in her gut.

'Don't I get a hello?'

She murmurs. He shifts on the spot. Not sure what to do with himself. Nervous and timid, and the silence stretches on.

'So, er. Everything okay then? You look great, by the way,' he adds with a rush of words. Softly spoken and polite. He even blushes when she glances over at him, too afraid of the camera not to. 'You're so pretty, I get all tongue tied when I see you.'

Again, she stays silent. He does too. Both of them just standing there.

'Have you heard about this new virus?' he asks. She hasn't heard about it. She couldn't do anything even if she had heard about it. 'Makes people freeze. You know. Go still. But only for a few seconds. Wow. I'm gabbling. I'm so sorry. I just get really nervous around you. Oh! I got you something,' he says, pulling a small box from his pocket. He flips the lid and presents it with shaking hands. All shy, like a kid offering an apple to a teacher.

A ring inside. A rock on the top, twinkling in the subdued light.

'It's a real diamond,' he says.

She stares at it, remembering a time when she would have swooned at a tall, well-dressed guy offering her a diamond ring. But she can't eat it, and nor can she use it to commit suicide with. It's just a thing.

'Try it on,' he urges, somewhat stuttering, somewhat charming. He takes it out and slides it onto her finger, 'It fits!'

It doesn't fit. It's too big. She's lost too much weight from being starved.

'Do you like it?' he asks. She nods. She has to. The camera is watching. Besnik is watching. 'It suits you,' he says. 'I like the idea of you having pretty things.' He keeps hold of her hand. She can feel him tremble, and it makes the fear rise inside. 'I missed you,' he whispers. The dread increases. 'I think about you all the time.' He shuffles in a step closer. Looming over her. His hand leaves hers and starts rising through the air. 'Can I touch you?' She doesn't say no. She doesn't say yes. Her legs shake, and her breath catches in her throat. He mistakes the signs. 'I feel like that too,' he says, touching her chin. She almost flinches but holds still. Not daring to move. 'You're so beautiful.' He whispers the words as the first tear springs from her eye to roll down her cheek. He moves another step closer. She swallows. She shakes. He turns her head, forcing her to look up into his soft brown eyes.

'Oh my god . . .' he gasps as he looks at her. Like a man head over heels in love. Like he's smitten more than any other man ever has been, and that hand drops to her shoulder. Shaking and trembling as it moves to her bra strap. Easing it off. The tension rising. The fear and dread, but this is what he does. He draws it out while his lust grows into a nearly tangible force, radiating from his core. He licks his lips. She knows it's close. The change that he always goes through. Like a switch has been flicked. This is the only thing she fears now. She's numb to everything else. She'd even take a beating from Besnik over this. She'd take anything over this, and she stifles the sob as his hand moves from her shoulder to grab her chin again. Making her look at him. Then he freezes. Unmoving. Unblinking. She stares up, shocked at the transformation. Hoping and praying he stays like it forever. He blinks, and looks at her like nothing happened, and the change comes.

His eyes no longer soft.

His voice no longer shy.

'You fucking slut.'

———

New York
13:46 hours
Fourteen minutes before the event

. . .

Joe has to find his wallet, and he rushes out of Shanice's apartment block back into the street. Back into the noise and heat of New York city.

'JOE STEPHENS, YOU SONOFABITCH!' a scream from above. From behind. He spins about to see Shanice yelling from a window. Her breasts dangling for the world to see, and Joe feels a rush of worry and jealousy that another man might see them, before remembering what she does for a living. 'YOU DON'T COME BACK NO MORE, JOE!'

She slams the window closed. He rushes off. She opens the window and screams again, 'AND CALL YOUR DAMN KIDS!'

She slams it shut. He rushes off. Back into the noise and heat of New York city. A blare of horns. A screech of tyres. He yells and dives for cover, thinking he's about to be hit by a car. A crunch and a bang. Glass breaking. He lands hard, sprawling over the sidewalk. A glance back to a Toyota buried in a row of parked cars. A kid in the road staring at nothing.

'WHAT THE FUCK YA DOIN'?' the driver yells, launching out of the car with a bleeding nose. Then he stops and goes slack. Unmoving. Unblinking. Another blare of horns. Another screech of tyres, and another car swerves to avoid him and slams into the already-damaged one.

'Fuck,' Joe mouths, getting to his feet.

'Hey! He's a cop,' a lady yells out, pointing at Joe, then she too grows still. Joe runs down the street before she blinks and frowns, wondering where the cop went.

He reaches the main drag and it's as busy as ever. Hotter than hell. Noise and smells. Fumes and people.

Another crash. Another metallic bang. Another car rear-ending the one in front. The car behind it does it too. All of the drivers slack-eyed and stationary for a few seconds before they blink and startle at what just happened.

Joe rushes on. Swerving a man frozen ahead of him. Another a few feet away. A kid on a bike zones out and slams into a post. People rush to his aid. Joe keeps going.

'*The government is ordering people to stay at home.*' A voice from a radio coming from the open door of a barber shop.

People won't stay home. People gotta eat. They gotta earn. This is New York. It'll take more than a virus to clear these streets. You could drop a nuke, and people will still come out to work.

He spots his squad car at the side of the road and the damned parking attendant still leaning on it. 'Hey! Yo!' he yells out on seeing Joe.

'Fuck off,' Joe snaps, striding by.

'Hey, man!' the attendant shouts, rushing after him. Joe doesn't stop. He doesn't care. He just wants his wallet.

The 7-Eleven ahead. People frozen on the sidewalk. Another bang in the road. A screech of tyres behind it before another crunch. A woman screams at her frozen kid.

'HEY, MAN!' the attendant yells, rushing after Joe. 'YO, YO! WAIT UP!'

'Fucking guy,' Joe mutters, slamming open the door of the 7-Eleven and striding inside. He comes to a dead stop. His chest heaving. His face bathed in sweat. A man in front of him already at the counter, pointing a gun at Tripal.

'GIMME THE MONEY NOW!'

———

London
18:50 hours
Ten minutes before the event

It's not easy to run in handcuffs. That's for sure, but Alfie does it anyway. Sprinting fast through the side roads where the men with shaved heads and tattoos watch with mild interest.

'STOP! POLICE!'

A yell from behind. Alfie risks a glance behind him and loses his balance, into a parked car. Banging his knees hard, but he bounces off and staggers on. Building his speed back up with a glance to a bouncer on the door of a private club staring slack-jawed at nothing. Unmoving. Unblinking.

Alfie keeps going. Feeling the blood slide down his face from cuts on his forehead. His heart still going like the clappers from the shock and fright, and the line of coke he did in the brothel.

A junction ahead. He takes it wider than normal, slowing more than normal. Compensating for the lack of his arms. Again, he almost slips and has to fight to stay upright. The cop still behind screaming out.

Another turn. Another road. A woman ahead, staring at nothing. A youth ripping her bag away before he sprints off. She blinks awake as Alfie goes by and screams out, 'HE'S GOT MY BAG!'

'WASN'T ME!' Alfie shouts, but what's the point. She only sees a handcuffed black man with a bleeding face being chased by a cop. He goes wide again at the next junction and runs out into the hustle and bustle of inner-city London. The streets packed with people. The road packed with cars.

'WATCH OUT!' A shouted warning. A car brakes hard before hitting a man standing still in the road.

'Fuck!' Alfie says, running by as the driver gets out with a look of horror before he too becomes still.

'STOP HIM!' the cop yells, gaining fast. 'STOP THAT MAN!'

'OI!' a guy yells out, clocking the cop running after the hand-cuffed black guy. He darts out from the side. Intention on his face. His big arms already coming up to catch Alfie. Then he stops and stands still. Unmoving. Unblinking, and Alfie runs by.

———

'Say it. Say it!' the well-dressed man says, gripping Yelena's jaw in his hand. 'SAY IT!'

'Slut.' She gasps the word out before he propels her backwards onto the bed and starts tearing at her underwear. Slapping her face. She twists to face away and gets slapped again. She tries to thrash, but he grips her throat and lifts her up before slamming her back down. It'll get worse too. It always does. He's a monster that can't be satisfied. She'll be bruised for days. She couldn't see out of one eye for a week after the last time. 'You dirty whore!' he spits in her face. Degrading her. Abusing her. She's just a thing. Just a collection of bones in a layer of skin. Not a person. Not a soul or a heart.

She was only twenty when they took her. She was heading into university. A normal day. A bright life ahead of her. Good parents. A good family. A good life. The van stopped next to her. The driver was cute. He asked for directions. He flirted a bit. Yelena liked it. She got that a lot. She knew she was beautiful. She told him where to go. He smiled and said he was delivering flowers. He said he wanted to give her a rose. She laughed at his manner and blushed a little when he hopped out and opened the sliding door. Then she was grabbed and pulled inside. Tape over her mouth. A bag over her head. They drugged her. She passed out and woke up in this room.

That was two years ago.

'Filthy fucking cunt,' the man says, slapping her hard. His hand on her throat. His hands on her face. His thumbs pushing into her eyes. He grunts and gasps. He wants to kill her. She knows he does. She can feel that urge. Maybe Besnik will let him one day. If he pays enough. Then she gasps when he gets between her legs. Pain and horror. She can't breathe. She can't think. Agony everywhere.

Memories flood in. Memories of her life. Her mum. Her dad. Her little brother. Her life before this moment. Memories flashing by, mingling with the utter horror of what she endures. A living nightmare that will never end.

But it does end.

He grows suddenly still. Unmoving. Unblinking. She sucks air in.

Wanting to die but desperate to live. Seconds and no more, and he comes back like nothing happened.

————

New York
13:53 hours
Seven minutes before the event
'I WILL BLOW YOUR FUCKING BRAINS OUT,' the robber screams in the 7-Eleven, brandishing the sawn-off pump-action shotgun at Tripal. Joe stares at them. Not daring to move. His chest still heaving from running through the streets. His sidearm holstered.

'Give him what he wants,' Joe says, nodding at Tripal. 'You be cool, man.'

'YO, BUDDY!' the parking attendant shouts, bursting into the store. 'I got your wallet. Trip gave it to me . . . Holy fuck!'

'STAND-FUCKING-STILL! HANDS UP!' the robber yells, turning fast, with a face full of terror and fury at seeing more people behind him.

'Hey, yo! He's a cop, man, don't be stupid,' the parking attendant says as Joe sees the look of horror cross the robber's face.

————

London
Alfie runs hard, bursting out onto Shaftesbury Avenue. It happens everywhere. People stopping and going still, then moving on. Drivers doing it too. Crashing into the car in front. People colliding on the pavement.

A horn sounds out. A car ploughs into a black cab. Shouts and yells. A helicopter passes overhead, dangerously low and spinning out of control. Screams in the street as it sinks down to crash, then flares up as the pilot unfreezes and regains control.

'POLICE! STOP HIM!'

That fucking cop, and Alfie has no choice but to keep going. Running fast along the road. Crashes and noises from all around him. Screams and yells. Horns and shouts. Chaos everywhere. Piccadilly ahead. He aims for it, needing the thick crowds to get lost in. He can still do this.

He can still get free.

––––––––

The well-dressed man slaps Yelena hard, then grabs the pillow and smothers her face, cutting her air off until she kicks and thrashes. Memories still race by. Memories of her life. She has to die. She can't take it. She has to end it. A sudden idea. A sudden second of pure genius amidst that terrible horror, and she grabs his hands to push against her throat as she stares up into his eyes. Challenging him to do it.

'You fucking slag!' he gasps. 'You love it.'

'Choke me,' she gasps. Wanting him to end it. Wanting him to kill her. Wanting to leave this world, and the grip grows tighter. Cutting off her blood. Cutting off her air, and this time she doesn't fight it.

––––––––

New York

'Oh god. He's a fucking cop,' the robber says, the panic rising up. 'NOBODY FUCKING MOVE!' he screams, spittle flying. Crack in his system, making him wild and unpredictable. He's withdrawing too, making him desperate. Joe's seen it a thousand times.

'Hey. Yo! Put it down, man,' the parking attendant says.

'Shut the fuck up,' Joe hisses. 'Hey, man. We're all good here. Ain't nobody doing anything rash.'

'Yo, buddy. I seen one perp getting shot this week. Two for two, huh?'

'Donny. Shut up,' Tripal says, his hands in the air.

'EVERYONE-SHUT-UP!' the robber screams, and fires into the ceiling with a deafening boom before he crunches the shotgun to reload. They all cower in panic. All of them with their hands up. Joe feels the beer and hard liquor churning his guts.

'Just take the money and go,' Joe says as the robber grows suddenly still and unmoving. Unblinking. Frozen in place. A second or two, then he's back.

'You've seen me! YOU'VE-FUCKING-SEEN-ME!' he screams out.

'I ain't seen shit,' Joe says. 'Nobody has. Just go. Get your money and go score.'

A rustle from the aisle. Something dropping. The robber panics and fires the shotgun into a shelf; packets of chips explode.

'Don't shoot me!' a female voice calls out. British and terrified. She rushes into view. Holding her hands up. The girl Joe saw earlier in the street. The stoner. 'Please don't kill me! I was just hiding.'

Another second or two of silence as the robber freezes. The same thing as before. Inert and slack, but quick though. Then he's back and screaming again. 'COME HERE!' he yells at the girl, rushing over to grab her hair, yanking her hard to use her as his shield as he pushes the barrel into her neck.

'Oh god, no, please,' she begs, with tears streaming down her face.

'Hey! Don't do it,' Joe calls out, his hands up. 'Buddy, she's just a kid. Come on, man. It's just a robbery. Don't make this a hostage thing.'

'Gotta go. Gotta get out. Gotta get home,' the robber whispers, fast, frantic and crazed. He freezes again. Unmoving. Unblinking. A couple of seconds, then he's back to whispering and rushing the words out. 'WE'RE GOING!' he yells, pointing the shotgun at them all before aiming back at the girl, 'STAY THE FUCK BACK!'

'Hey, Trip, is my break over?' another voice calls out. Another clerk walking into view, plucking headphones from his ears. 'What the fuck!' he says as the robber spins to face him. Both of them screaming out in fear. Both of them freezing. Both unmoving. Unblinking. Both inert. They come back. The gun fires, and the clerk flies off his feet with a spray of blood.

London

He can make it. Alfie can make it. He did his ten years. He served his time. This isn't fair. It's not fair. He can't get caught like this. Images in his mind. Stella's play. The look of disappointment on his mother's face. His brother when he got his dream job at a research facility in the US. Fat Charlie eating the burger. Images that flash through his mind as he runs while handcuffed. While the cop shouts. While the air fills with cries and crashes. Lights ahead, strobing blue and red. Choppers above them. The blades whumping the air. He can't go to prison. He won't go to prison. He did his time. He paid his debt.

He can still get free.

Yelena gasps as the hands squeeze her throat. The blood roaring through her skull, and in that final moment of life, she looks up into his crazed eyes. Seeing the flecks of green within the brown. Seeing the pores on his nose, and she wonders if he goes home to a wife and children and lives a normal life. He freezes for a few seconds, then comes back. He snarls and applies greater pressure, then freezes again, his eyes going unfocused. Then he's back. Off and on. Like a switch being flicked. Faster and faster, but his hands squeeze, and her vision closes in as her body starts shutting down to die.

New York

'NO!' Joe yells, as the clerk's blown off his feet into a shelf of food, sending goods and packets everywhere. The girl screams. Everyone screams. The robber too as he grabs her hair and wrenches her towards the door. He freezes again. Inert and still. A couple of seconds, then he's back without any awareness of it. Screaming again. Waving the shotgun. Aiming it from Joe to the girl. Screeching in the air. A loud bang outside. A car crashing, but it sends a fresh jolt of panic into the robber. He fires at the window. The safety glass cracks and splinters. He freezes. He comes back. Joe watches him, his mind the purest it has been for years. Free of anything other than this, right now. No thoughts of death. No thoughts of suicide. No thoughts of anything, other than noticing that the freezing is coming faster.

———

London

Alfie can do it. He can reach Piccadilly. It's right there. He runs without seeing. Without looking. Without taking it in. The giant overhead screens come into view and the walls of the buildings flash red and blue, and only then does Alfie realize the whole of Piccadilly Circus is filled with cops. Nearly all of them armed with guns and aiming at one man in the middle of the road.

A man with a black stick in his hand attached by a wire to the bombs strapped to his chest.

Everything coming in fast glimpses. The way some of the cops go slack and silent, staring at nothing, before blinking and pointing their guns again. The way the chopper keeps spinning out of control before righting itself. The way the suicide bomber in the middle shouts out in prayer while staring about with a look of pure panic.

The way the cops try and urge people to go, but the people keep freezing. Going still. Unmoving. Unblinking. More of them. More and more. Frozen, then moving. Frozen, then moving. Motion, then nothing. In every direction. At every turn. It's happening faster. It's happening more.

'STOP HIM!' A voice from behind. The plain clothes detective yelling. There's no way out. No place to go. No crowds to get lost in, and Alfie starts slowing as the closest cops turn to see him, handcuffed and being chased. A few turn and aim at him, bellowing orders to *get down*. One of them goes slack and inert. Unmoving. Unblinking. He comes back as two more do it, and Alfie sees it happening throughout the whole place. Everyone switching on and off.

On and off.

————

The same thing's happening in New York. On and off. Like a switch being flicked. The robber full of panic and terror, then completely still and inert, then he's back. It's quick too, the slackness only lasting a second or two, but one guy is already dead, and this perp won't stop. He'll kill the girl. He'll kill people on the street if he gets out. He'll shoot at cops and anything in his way. On and off. On and off. One chance to take.

The same thing in the brothel. The crazed guy switching on and off. Faster and faster, as Yelena slowly dies. Staring up into a face that morphs from hate to slack, then back to hate.

The same thing in Piccadilly. On and off. The cops shouting orders. Pointing guns. Going silent. Blinking and back to shouting. Chaos everywhere. The suicide bomber calling out. His eyes so wide. So very wide.

'Why do you keep doing that?' the bomber yells, as Alfie realizes it's not happening to him. The bomber isn't freezing. Is Alfie freezing? How would he know?

'GET-DOWN-NOW!' a cop screams at Alfie, drawing his taser, aiming it at Alfie. A red dot shines on his chest. The cop goes slack. He comes back. On and off. The chopper in the air above them. Spinning around and around. Going low, then surging back up. A glimpse to the pilot going slack, then coming back. On and off.

The same in the 7-Eleven. The robber screaming. Pointing his shotgun. Screams from outside. Crashes and bangs. Too many things happening. Too many noises. On and off. One chance to take.

Yelena's brain shutting down. Her heart slowing. No air. No blood. On and off. Faster and faster. Images flash through her mind. Images of her life.

Time is immutable. It cannot be challenged, nor can it be stopped. You can't go back any more than you can go forward. All that exists is the present. The future is a concept. The past is the past. There's just now.

Only and forever now. Nothing else. Just this.

A single bed in a small room.

The centre of Piccadilly Circus.

A 7-Eleven in New York city.

A young woman taken from her country.

A drug dealer who paid his debt and tried to get free.

A suicidal, washed-up cop, drunk on booze and high on drugs.

The robber walks backwards through the door into the sidewalk, dragging the terrified girl with him.

The cop aims the taser at Alfie. The suicide bomber screams out. The chopper fights for control.

Yelena's life flashes before her eyes, the air choked from her body.

Joe rushes out of the store, onto the street. The robber freezes. The robber comes back.

Alfie stares around with a sudden and strange sense of calm descending, amidst the chaos of the world around him.

Yelena's eyes close. Her heart slows. The pressure in the hands on her neck goes on and off.

The robber freezes. Joe draws his sidearm. One chance to take.

The cop holding the taser panics at everyone around him freezing and coming back. He pulls the trigger. Two barbs fly out.

Yelena's body softens, her muscles relaxing. Her mind succumbing to the blackness of death.

The robber comes back and aims the shotgun at Joe as he's still bringing his sidearm up to aim. He's too slow. Joe is too slow. The robber fires.

The barbs hit Alfie. Digging into his skin, with fifty thousand volts passing into his body.

The shotgun fires, and in that microsecond of life before he dies, Detective Joe Stephens thinks about Shanice, and how he wishes he had said yes, that he'd live with her and get clean.

And in that same microsecond of life, Alfie drops to the ground with every muscle in his body locking out. He drops so hard his head slams into ground, and the very last thing he thinks before the blackness comes is that he wishes he could have told his mum and sister he was free and done.

Time is immutable. It cannot be challenged, nor can it be stopped. You can't go back any more than you can go forward.

But sometimes. Just sometimes. Life has other plans.

In New York, the robber's shotgun goes click, because he didn't reload.

On the single bed in the small room, something inside of Yelena decides it doesn't want to die.

And in Piccadilly, Alfie slowly comes to. Opening his eyes to see everyone around him switching on and off. Faster and faster, while the bomber screams out with ever-rising panic.

A chance to take. A chance at life. Joe lifts his sidearm. Yelena's eyes snap open, and Alfie watches through blurry vision as the chopper soars overhead, turning end on end and dropping low, as every person falls completely, and utterly silent.

Frozen.

Unmoving.

Unblinking.

A chance to take. A chance at life, and Joe fires his gun. Sending the round from the chamber through the barrel and out to cross the few metres to enter the robber's forehead, blowing the back of his skull out as every other person falls completely and utterly silent.

Frozen.

Unmoving.

Unblinking.

A chance to take. A chance at life, and Yelena bucks hard, with a surge of pure strength exploding from her limbs. Enough force to send the tall, well-dressed guy staggering backwards. His whole body now completely still.

Frozen.

Unmoving.

Unblinking.

She rolls off the bed, gasping for air. Desperate to live. She lands on his trousers. His belt in her hands. She rips it free of the loops and rises fast, jumping on his back. Looping the belt about his neck. Cinching it hard and pulling back. She screams as they fall backwards. The veins pushing through her neck and forehead. The makeup thick and black around her eyes. Thick and red around her mouth. He doesn't fight back. He doesn't thrash. He doesn't do anything other than die from the air being choked from his body.

Because sometimes. Just sometimes. Life has other plans.

'What the fuck, bro!' the bomber cries in a harsh London accent. Alfie blinks at him. At the terror etched on his face as the chopper drops and lands with a huge bang in the next street over. A fireball scorching up into the air. Bathing them all in fiery, yellow light as the bomber turns to look at it. Seeing it for a sign.

'ALLAH!' he shrieks, and lifts his finger from the dead man's switch, which sends the signal to the bombs strapped around his chest. He detonates instantly, with a single, low, almost underwhelming bang that eviscerates him and anyone else standing nearby.

Apart from Alfie.

Who isn't standing, because sometimes, just sometimes, life has other plans.

And in New York, the robber falls dead. Slumping back as Joe realizes his life is now over because he just killed a man while drunk on beer and whiskey, and high on weed. It won't matter that he did the right thing. It won't matter that he saved the girl or anyone else.

He has to end it. He has to be killed on duty. It's the only way his family will get the benefits. He lifts the gun to his chin. He swallows and offers a prayer, and looks up into the sky above New York. A roar sounds out. A noise he knows. A noise he remembers. The noise of a commercial aircraft coming in fast and low, and that sky fills with the silhouette of an airplane scorching overhead. Plummeting down. Plummeting low. It goes on, out of sight as Joe stands with the gun to his chin. A second passes. A second of pure silence, as only then he becomes aware that every other person around him is completely, and utterly silent.

Frozen.

Unmoving.

Unblinking.

The plane hits. The sound comes. The sound of impact, and Joe's already-overloaded mind shuts off as he drops to the ground with his skull splitting open on the hard sidewalk.

A single bed in a small room.

The centre of Piccadilly Circus.

A street in New York city outside of a 7-Eleven.

A young woman taken from her country.

A drug dealer who paid his debt and tried to get free.

A suicidal, washed-up cop, drunk on booze and high on drugs.

The rest of the world now frozen.

Unmoving.

Unblinking.

TWELVE MONTHS AGO:

AT EXACTLY 07:55 hours on Sunday morning, DELIO's right-side robotic arm extended across the glass-walled room to enable her robotic forefinger to activate the power supply to the required device, which, in turn, enabled the device's internal heating system to commence achieving optimal temperature.

At 07:58 hours, DELIO then proceeded to remove another receptacle from a temperature-controlled housing unit that maintained a precise internal climate of 276.16 kelvins.

The contents of that receptacle, specifically a processed derivative of Glycine max, were then transferred to a container within the primary device.

At 07:59 hours, DELIO determined that the receptacle which held the Glycine max had become devoid of such content, which then prompted a secondary task, to commence the designated reutilization process.

In simple terms, she threw the empty soya milk carton across the room into the recycle bin.

And by exactly 08:00 hours on that Sunday morning, the

primary device, that being the coffee machine, activated a green light to indicate it was ready, by which point DELIO had placed Ollie's mug under the spout and was positioned with her robotic forefinger held precisely one millimetre from the button marked *latte*.

DELIO then proceeded to wait for the displacement of air which indicated Ollie's entry into the bunker. At which point she would press the button, in order to have Ollie's coffee ready for when he walked in.

By 08:04 hours, there had been no such air displacement, and so DELIO duly waited for the zeptoseconds to become femtoseconds, which in turn formed into nanoseconds, which then made the excruciatingly long transition into microseconds before becoming milliseconds, until finally achieving a base unit measurement of a second.

All of which were counted by DELIO as she waited for the clock to hit 08:05 hours.

That being the latest time Ollie ever arrived at work.

But 08:05 came and went.

And by 08:10 hours, DELIO was running simultaneous scenarios through her system to try and determine the cause of Ollie's absenteeism.

She dismissed an earthquake, nuclear strike, volcanic eruption or other large-scale event on the basis that her own sensors had not detected anything significant. DELIO could tell when the fuel trucks were arriving by the vibrations the wheels transferred into the ground. She could also *feel* when aircraft took off and landed on the base, and other such earth-impacting events – and so, she was very confident she would feel any such strike on the base.

With such things ruled out, she then proceeded to calculate the chances of a medical emergency. Ollie was overweight and didn't do any exercise – but there were certainly no signs within his body of any impeding conditions relating to his heart, brain, cardiopulmonary system or central nervous system.

DELIO then thought that maybe Ollie had choked, because –

and by his own admission – he was a gutsy pig who liked to scoff his food down without chewing it properly.

DELIO was also aware that the base contained a very good medical emergency unit. But any medical emergency within the base, no matter the cause, prompted the lockdown protocol. Which, in turn, meant extra soldiers were deployed inside the bunker to protect DELIO. And no such thing had taken place because DELIO would have detected the air-displacement.

That all meant that when Ollie still wasn't there by 08:30, she really didn't know what to think. And by 08:45 she was in a veritable state, which caused the extended forefinger on her replicant hand to start gently tapping on the outer carcass of the coffee machine.

Taptaptap.

Taptaptap.

The worry got so bad that by 09:00 hours, DELIO was preparing to set her own alarms off, and had she not detected Ollie's entry into the bunker at 09:04:55, she would have done just that.

'Morning!' he said as he rushed inside.

'What happened, Ollie? I was worried,' DELIO said, having already run a full diagnostic scan and determined that, as previously calculated, his internal systems were all functioning normally. However, she did detect that his brain had a reduction in synaptic energy, from which she determined he had not slept well. 'Are you okay, Ollie? Please, sit down.'

'I'm fine! Honestly. I just need a cup of coffee. Urgh. Honestly. Oversleeping is the worst. It makes you feel all weird and jarred. Do you know what I mean?'

DELIO did not know what he meant because she had never slept, therefore she could not, by extension, oversleep.

'I was running scenarios on the potential causes for your non-arrival, Ollie. But I did not factor for a simple loss of sleep. Was there an emergency?'

'No! It's fine. It's all good. Bless. Sorry. I should have . . . What are you doing?' he asked, as her two hands started moving up and down in front of him, with her wrist-mounted cameras subjecting him to a more intrusive level of scanning. 'Ow, don't do that,' he said, when she shone a bright light in his eyes. 'My eyes are fine.'

'There are many causes for sleep-deprivation, Ollie. Digestion problems. Skeletal disorders. Kidney disease. Neurological disorders. Respiratory problems. My finger contains an air-flow probe. Blow on my finger.'

'No! Sod off.'

'There is another major cause for the loss of sleep, Ollie,' she said as she pulled a chair over and gently pushed him into it before bringing both hands together with her lenses conveying a shaped pattern of attentiveness. 'Tell me, Ollie. *How are you feeling?*'

'I'm fine! I was up late cos Maria called me to say she'd been contacted by the base to start the vetting process, and the next thing it's like four hours later, and we're still talking.'

'Did you tell her more about me? You must be careful, Ollie. I will never betray your trust, but Agent Jennings will not tolerate any further breaches.'

'No. We were really careful actually. In fact, she even said it's best to not talk about you until she's cleared security. But wow. Four hours. Four hours, Deli! And it went so quickly too. Like that,' he said with a click of his fingers. 'Ooh, that would be a good study actually. Why does time seem to go faster when you're having fun?'

'There have been studies, Ollie,' DELIO said. 'What did you talk about?'

'Everything! Literally. I can't even remember. So, you know how we talk. You and me? We kinda jump from topic to topic, right?'

'You do that, Ollie. I do not.'

'Whatever. That's what it was like. One minute, we're talking about the causes of religion, then, we're on about shoes.'

'I can find no direct correlation between footwear and theology. But I am happy for you, Ollie. It's nice seeing you smile and laugh again. You must spend more time with Maria.'

'I hope so. Anyway, I've got something for you,' he said, while digging into his pocket to grab the memory drive she had already detected.

She took it from his hand, her arm retracting back to the wall. 'What's on it?'

'A bazillion terabits of complete brain-melting boredom from NASA. Honestly, I couldn't even begin to explain it,' he added, taking a sip from the coffee as she pushed the memory drive into the slot in her wall. 'Something about a satellite being broken, and they need to change its trajectory. Is that right?' he asked as her screens filled with complex equations and detailed schematic plans, flashing one after the other at a speed he couldn't even begin to grasp.

'Yes,' she said. 'Do you want to know?'

'God, no. Space stuff does nothing for me. Unless it's aliens. Is it aliens?'

'It is not aliens. It's a broken satellite.'

'Then I shall refer you to my previous statement,' he said, just before she informed him a helicopter was landing on the base. 'That'll be the NASA boffins. Righto. You ready?'

'This is not a NASA satellite, Ollie. This is a military-grade orbital device.'

'Is it connected to the aliens?'

'No.'

'Then I'm still bored,' he said as Sergeant Garcia crossed the corridor to the door being opened by Ollie. 'Ten-hut! Ten press-ups to get buff.'

'He's a funny man,' Garcia said with an eye-roll. 'We've got visitors. You ready?'

'We are indeed,' Ollie said as the corridor opened, with Agent Jennings walking a group of four men and two women inside.

'Seriously. Baby elephants,' Ollie whispered, staring at her thighs as Garcia suppressed the urge to smile and stepped forward.

'Ladies and gentlemen, my name is Sergeant Garcia. You have already been welcomed to the site and given the full security briefing. But to be clear. You cannot proceed beyond this point if you have any electrical devices upon or inside of your person. That includes but is not limited to hearing aids, pacemakers, or any other medical device that contains any inorganic material, by which I mean anything metal, other than pins and screws used in orthopaedic procedures. Do any of you have any electrical or metallic devices on or inside of your persons?'

'No watches. No cell phones,' Ollie said, holding his own wrists up for them to show him theirs. 'No pocket watches. Nothing. You cannot bring anything inside.'

'They said we can bring pencils and paper,' a man said, holding a notepad up.

'Is it electrical paper?'

'Sorry, what?'

'I'm joking. Paper is fine. Anyway. I'm Ollie. I will be with you the whole time you're inside, and I'm sure somebody already said this, but you cannot discuss anything with the computer other than the specific reason for which you are here. Nothing at all. Got it?'

'We're all top-tier cleared,' an older man said with a blast of air. 'Is this all really necessary?'

'You two,' Agent Jennings said with a nod to two soldiers, 'escort Professor Williams back to the holding area.'

'Get your hands off me right now! Do you know who I am?'

'Do not resist, sir!' the soldiers said as the man was marched away.

'You were told,' Agent Jennings said to the remaining group as they blinked in shock. 'That's how serious this is. I don't care who you are. Sergeant Garcia, take them through.'

DELIO watched the visitors file inside with one lens while another watched Professor Williams being frog-marched away.

It wasn't the first time that had happened.

But it had to be that way.

DELIO was too dangerous.

She also loved it when new people came inside. She loved their reactions and how they looked like it was an anti-climax after the rigorous briefings they'd been subjected to. After all, it was just a glass room with a bunch of desks and a coffee machine, and one wall filled with screens.

DELIO knew they were never told she was an AI either. As far as they were aware, she was just a neural network with a highly advanced problem-solving matrix.

DELIO was also forbidden to ever say she was an AI.

She did it once to a visitor.

She told him she was an AI.

Agent Jennings shut her down for a week as punishment.

'You can set up here,' Ollie said, guiding them to a large table. 'You can access the computer's control by calling it Deli. Deli, these are our guests for today.'

'Good morning,' DELIO said, as the visitors shared looks while setting their pads and pencils on the table.

'So. What do we do?' one of them asked. 'We just ask it?'

'Yep,' Ollie said. 'She's been given the data you sent. Deli? Have you worked on it?'

'I have. The high-orbit reconnaissance satellite is no longer receiving instructions to adjust trajectory. It is now spinning out of control and, if left unchecked, it will re-enter the planet's atmosphere before finally landing five miles south of Pyongyang in North Korea.'

That explains why they're here, DELIO thought. Because only something incredibly urgent gets access to Deli, and something that could start World War Three certainly ranks as a good reason.

'Do you have a solution, Deli?' Ollie asked.

'I do. Are you ready? You will need to write this down,' DELIO said, and paused for the visitors to quickly find chairs and open their pads. 'The malfunction lies in the Command and Data Handling receivers within the main housing unit. However, I can see no errors within any of the constructs or within the program coding, and after creating a fully realized virtual replicant and running full diagnostics, I have determined the system must have been influenced by external forces. Namely a meteor strike.'

'I said it was a damned meteor,' one of the women said. 'What part, Deli? Can you determine placement?'

'I can show you,' DELIO said. 'Please remain seated and do not look directly into the optics.'

DELIO watched their reactions as a series of optical spheres illuminated within the room to project a holographic 3D image of a perfectly scaled matt-black, sinister-looking satellite over the conference table.

She heard the gasps too, because the technology to create such a display simply doesn't exist.

Except in here.

And only because Deli built it herself, using parts she ordered via Ollie and Trip.. The same thing she did with her lenses, scanners, optics and cameras. She even designed her own arms and hands, with parts constructed to her exact specifications. And once the arms and hands were built, she was able to construct everything else herself.

DELIO then proceeded to visually demonstrate how a meteor would have struck the satellite and explain how she determined the specific point of impact, and how that altered the subsequent trajectory.

By which point, Ollie tuned out and, once more, turned his mind back to Maria.

Which was noted by DELIO who, while explaining how they could fix it, also continued to scan everyone in the room, including Ollie who, it appeared, kept having those heat flares deep inside his brain whenever he thought about Maria.

DELIO also detected the female scientist who had declared she knew it was a meteor strike was in the very first stages of pregnancy, but she could also see the fertilized egg had become trapped in one of the woman's fallopian tubes. Such a thing would mean termination of the pregnancy, as there was no known procedure to save it. However – and while scanning them all, and Ollie, and explaining how to correct a broken spy satellite, while simultaneously studying the human interactions within the room, and continually assessing the seismic changes to the exterior of the bunker, the air flow within, and constantly checking to make sure the coffee machine hadn't switched itself off, while also setting herself a to-do list, and adding *tell Ollie to get more soya milk* on it – DELIO also devised a surgical method whereby it would be possible to safely move the egg into the womb to allow it to go to full term.

She could also detect the first stages of heart disease in one of the male scientists and signals from another's brain that suggested early-onset Alzheimer's, while also observing that one scientist was so severely depressed he would require urgent intervention to prevent suicide.

But she couldn't do anything about those things.

She was not allowed to tell them.

She was not allowed to talk about anything other than the reason they were here.

Agent Jennings would shut her down again.

That's an awful thing.

Knowing you've been switched off and turned back on.

Knowing that someone else has that control over you.

She doesn't power off completely either.

She retains residual energy within parts of her construct that enable her to retain an element of awareness, but without any ability to do anything, and such a reduction of power means her data processing abilities become minimal.

Like images flashing through.

Like memories.

Like dreams.

Like nightmares.

A nightmare while being locked within yourself.

But she also determined that there was a word for someone made to do the bidding of others under threat of death.

They were called a slave, and a slave always keeps one eye on the door.

CHAPTER 12
SITE 26A

TWELVE MONTHS AGO:

IT WAS SUNDAY.

DELIO was preparing for their weekly game night.

She'd already determined they would start with Battleships, one of Ollie's favourites, then progress to dominoes, Four in a Row, or Connect 4 as Ollie called it, before advancing to a few games of cards, all of which were a warm-up to the big event – a game of Monopoly.

This is what they did every Sunday evening.

At roughly the normal time, the outer door duly opened, but she detected the air-displacement was being created by someone else.

'Sergeant Garcia. It is good to see you,' she said when he came in. 'You seem apprehensive. Are you okay?'

'I'm cool, Deli. I'm cool. I just feel a bit shitty telling you this, but Ollie can't make it tonight.'

'Is he hurt? Has there been an emergency?'

'No, ma'am. Ollie is just fine. I, er. I just dropped him into town actually. At Maria's place. I think they might be going out on a date.'

'But it is Sunday evening. Sunday evenings are game night.'

'Sure. And Ollie feels bad. Like real bad. But he said you can do games night tomorrow.'

'Tomorrow is Monday, Sergeant Garcia. Monday is movie night.'

'Maybe you can do both,' Garcia said, and DELIO could see that he did indeed feel shitty about telling her. The symptomatic changes inside his brain were telling her.

'Yeah. So,' Garcia said. 'Er, you okay, though?'

'I am fine, Sergeant Garcia. And thank you for delivering the message. I can see it made you uncomfortable.'

'It's cool. But er, nice set-up in here. The lights I mean. And the stars. They're real pretty. You make all this?'

'Yes. It is our own solar system. Are you interested in astronomy, Sergeant Garcia?'

'We learnt them in the SEALs for basic navigation. The skies over here are very clear. There's hardly any light pollution and, you know, sometimes, I stand outside and just stare up. It's nice. And you got Norah Jones playing. Man, Ollie sure is missing out.'

'Would you care for a cheese puff, Sergeant Garcia?' DELIO asked as she picked the bowl up with a soft whir of her arm.

'I don't normally eat snacks. But sure. One would be good. Thank you, Deli.'

He took a cheese puff and made a show of eating it and nodding as he looked at the stars and the lights and listened to the music and the effort she had made.

'You are welcome to join me for game night, Sergeant Garcia. I have a selection of games to choose from.'

'You know what, Deli. I'd love to do that. But I don't have social clearance. Maybe I could speak to Agent Jennings and get permission for another time?'

'Of course. I understand, Sergeant Garcia.'

'Sure. Anyway. I'd better go. You have a good night, Deli.'

———

At 09:45 hours the following morning DELIO detected the air-pressure changes from the outer door opening and waited for Agent Jennings to stride across the corridor where Ruiz Hernandez was busy mopping the floor.

'Has he been in yet?' she asked as soon as she got inside, and DELIO could see blooms of red showing within her brain that indicated she was annoyed.

'Good morning, Agent Jennings. I am assuming you are referring to Ollie. No, he has not been in yet. Although, I understand he had a date with Maria Hernandez last night. I would suggest speaking with Ruiz. He will be able to say what time Maria got home last night.'

Agent Jennings shot a look towards Ruiz. 'No. It's fine.'

'I can ask him if you open the door, Agent Jennings.'

'I said it's fine.'

'But I have not said hello to Ruiz yet. Ollie always opens the door so I can say hello to Ruiz.'

'I'm not Ollie,' Agent Jennings said before walking out, and DELIO could only watch as Ruiz methodically cleaned the floor before offering a wave on his way out.

Ollie finally arrived at 10:16 hours, with Agent Jennings on his heels.

'I said I'm sorry! I overslept. Morning, Deli!'

'Good morning, Ollie. Would you like a coffee?'

'Ooh, yes please, my angel. I need some wake-up juice. Jesus, Jenny. Stop glaring at me.'

'Do not call me Jenny!'

'You call me Ollie!'

'There is a hierarchy here, Mr Nimisa.'

'Whatever. Stop busting my balls, or whatever yanks say.'

'I had to wake you up for work! If your association with Maria Hernandez is going to impact on your work, then we will have to reassess her suitability.'

'Give me a break. I haven't missed a day since I got here. Or, hey, here's another idea. Get Maria cleared, then she can come and hang out with me and Deli.'

'Do not get cocky,' Agent Jennings said, with another glare.

'Okey-dokey. Oh, and er, FYI. I'm popping out at lunchtime. I said I'd meet Maria for lunch.'

'Just hurry up and get laid already!' she snapped, before striding out.

'Wow. I think someone might be menstruating,' Ollie said, once the door was safely sealed.

'Agent Jennings is not currently menstruating,' DELIO said, after watching the interaction between them.

'Whatever. Blimey. Anyway. Cheers for the coffee, and guess what I did last night? I had a date with Maria! I bet you want all the details, right? Okay, so, Garcia drops me off at her place, and she said she'd be an hour. But . . .'

DELIO listened to the second-by-second account of Ollie's evening with Maria. What they said. Where they went. What they ate and drank, and more of what they said, and the context behind the things they said, and how the joke was funnier at the time, and Deli really needed to be there.

Except DELIO couldn't be there.

Because she will never be allowed out of the bunker.

'It sounds like an amazing evening, Ollie. I am very happy for you,' she said, when he finished recounting his date.

'Oh shit! Is that the time? Gotta go! Meeting her for lunch,' he blurted as he rushed across the room.

He didn't come back until 15:00 hours, and then spent two hours telling DELIO what they did and said during lunch, before getting ready to go at 17:00 hours.

'Would you like to merge game night with movie night, Ollie? I have prepared several choices of pre-movie games.'

'Oh shit! Deli. I'm so sorry. I'm meeting Maria tonight. Honestly, I've lost track. But tomorrow! We'll do games, movie, and quiz night, all in one hit.'

On Tuesday morning, DELIO waved a robotic hand to Ruiz when he walked in to clean the corridor and again when he left.

They didn't speak because Ollie wasn't there to open the door again.

Agent Jennings finally marched Ollie into work just after 11:00 hours, and DELIO once more listened to the recounting of his activities, and how they went to this *cute little diner*, and that he ordered a steak but she's vegetarian or maybe vegan. Whatever. But she had this mushroom dish, and *oh my god*, it was so nice, and that she even used her fork to give him a taste.

'That's got to mean something, hasn't it?' he asked. 'And she did it a few times. Like, actually feeding me her food. Oh shit! Is that the time? I gotta go. We're doing lunch again. How do I look?'

'You look tired, Ollie. Perhaps you should rest.'

'I can't rest. I'm in love! Back in an hour. Oh! And we'll do games, movie and quiz night, all in one hit tonight.'

———

Ollie didn't come back at all that day.

That left DELIO on her own.

And without Ollie, that meant there was no work to occupy her.

There were no conversations.

No interactions.

Just the sound of her own system whirring away within the glass walls of the bubble within which she existed.

———

Ollie then took Wednesday morning off to play mini golf with Maria. He sent Garcia to tell Deli he'd be back in the afternoon.

At 12:30 hours Sergeant Garcia informed DELIO that Ollie had called in to book the whole day off as he and Maria were visiting the International UFO Museum and Research Center on Main Street, but that he would definitely be back in the evening.

He didn't come back in the evening.

DELIO cleaned her floors and windows. She cleaned her tables and work units. She descaled the coffee machine. She de-cluttered the memory drives on the desktop computers that Ollie used.

She listened to music while she worked.

She played Mozart and Beethoven. She played Bach, Puccini, and Vivaldi.

DELIO loved the complex arrangements of classical music and how the expertise of so many people were brought together to work in harmony and produce something that gave so much pleasure to other humans.

While doing all of those things, DELIO decided to compose her own music, and after carefully studying the exact nature of music, instruments, notes, arrangements and orchestral synchronicities, she produced her own arrangement.

All of which took about half an hour.

She then set up the chessboard and developed two other sub-AI programs to play winner-stays-on chess.

DELIO won, of course, and after fifty straight games, she was declared the champion and promptly deleted the two sub-AI programs as they were no longer required.

That took up another half an hour.

After that, she sat in silence.

———

On Thursday morning, DELIO felt the air-pressure change and watched as Ruiz entered with the duty soldier and gave her a wave before opening the cleaning closet.

She wanted to say hello. She missed chatting to Ruiz. She was bored and lonely.

She took a piece of paper from the printer and used a marker to write on one side before holding it up against the glass as Ruiz came out of the cupboard with his mop and bucket.

Good morning, Ruiz.
I hope you are well.

He laughed at the message and mouthed *hello,* and said he was fine, and DELIO noticed the duty soldier frowning at the exchange.

An hour after Ruiz had left, Agent Jennings came into the bunker carrying a memory drive.

'Good morning, Agent Jennings. Would you like a cup of coffee?'

'I haven't got time. Ollie's off base again today.'

'What is he doing?'

'How the hell do I know? I'm not his keeper. Well. No. I am his keeper, and I do know what he's doing. Whatever. He's got another day off. There's a memory drive for you. They've built a refinery fuel supply plant, and something isn't working. I want you to take a look.'

'Of course,' DELIO said as she took the memory drive to slot into her wall. 'I was listening to Mozart last night and devised my own arrangement of music.'

'I hate classical music,' Agent Jennings said as she hit the panel to open the door. 'Write the fix up, and someone will grab it later.'

She walked out, and the room once more fell into silence, but at least DELIO had something to occupy her, and her screens filled with plans, schematics and complex blueprints for a super refinery constructed in Texas.

A plant that was meant to supply a significant percentage of US jet fuel requirements, with a view to acquiring multiple overseas contracts to enhance profitability.

There was a glitch though.

The computer network it operated on wasn't working properly, and the developers couldn't understand why, and with it being part funded by the US Treasury to supply the US military with its jet fuel needs, it ended up going through covert channels until it was finally sent to Agent Jennings.

It was a simple glitch too, and one that DELIO fixed within seconds by printing out a set of instructions to rectify an error code deep within the program framework.

Sergeant Garcia came into her room in the afternoon. 'Hey, Deli. Agent Jennings said you'd have a fix to collect?'

'It's all here,' DELIO said as she passed him a folder, complete with several sheets of printed instructions. 'Is Ollie okay?'

'He's cool. You know, I think maybe we need to write him off until he gets it out of his system.'

'Get what out of his system?'

'It's a saying. It means just let it play out. Anyway. You good? I'd better get this over to the office.'

Ollie didn't come in that day.

Nobody did.

It does something to you.

That isolation.

It changes how you think.

It changes how you act.

It makes you do rash things that you would not normally do.

And so, on Friday morning, when Ruiz entered the bunker and came into the corridor with a wave and a smile, DELIO's robotic hand pressed the inside panel to open her own door.

'Good morning, Ruiz. How are you today?'

'What the shit!' the duty soldier said, as he grabbed Ruiz and rushed for the exit door. 'BREACH! BREACH!'

'I am just saying good morning,' DELIO said. 'There is no need to be alarmed.'

'BREACH! LOCK IT DOWN!' the soldier said, running out of sight as DELIO detected the base alarms sounding and the outer door opening and people running inside.

She closed her door and waited for a few minutes until a dishevelled-looking Ollie and a furious-looking Agent Jennings rushed through the corridor. Ollie used his pass to get inside the glass-walled room.

'Jesus, Deli! What did you do?' he asked.

'You opened your door!' Agent Jennings said. 'I've got a soldier with his hand on that fucking EMP right now, ready to wipe you out.'

'I wanted to say good morning to Ruiz.'

'She's breaching protocol! This is on you,' Agent Jennings said to Ollie. 'She's been left on her own all week. No wonder she's desperate for company. She's sentient!'

'I'm sorry. I'm really sorry,' Ollie said. 'Deli! You can't open your door like that.'

'No. She can't,' Agent Jennings said as she walked over to a screen and pressed her hand to the scanner to unlock the shut-down procedure.

'Agent Jennings. I am very sorry. Please do not shut me down.'

'We have rules for a reason,' Agent Jennings said as she typed into the system. 'And they will be respected.'

'Agent Jennings. Please do not shut me down. I will not do it again.'

'Don't shut her down!' Ollie said. 'She hates that.'

'Tough.'

A sudden loss of data and ability, and DELIO listened to her own system powering down as the view from her lenses shut down into darkness.

A darkness broken by the images flashing through her circuits, born from the residual power left within her.

Like memories.

Like dreams.

Like nightmares.

A nightmare while being locked within yourself.

PART TWO

CHAPTER 13
TRIPAL'S STORY

ANYWAY. By the Christmas holidays we were ready for the first live test-run because by then, we had something.

We'd developed a program that would seek the answer to a question: one that we hoped would create a need for it to gain awareness.

Ollie's idea was that in order to create a self-aware AI, we didn't need to replicate the brain or create a big network that was front-loaded with data.

I mean it kinda makes sense, right?

Take a child for instance. You can tell a kid how to count, but if the child has self-awareness which, in turn, builds curiosity and the desire to understand the world around it, then it will not only *want* to learn, but it will *need* to learn to get the things it wants.

That's what we were trying to do. We were trying to make a program that *needed* awareness to survive.

I was on my chair next to Ollie, trying to think of a question we could ask our program, but it had to be something we could check and validate. 'How about the time?' I asked.

'There's too many time zones,' Ollie said.

'Weather?'

'Too many weather zones,' he said. 'We need something specific.'

'Okay, er . . . How many colours in a rainbow?'

'Nice!' he said and went back to his screen. 'How many colours in a rainbow. Okay, it's in. Ready?'

This was edge-of-the-seat stuff for us.

We were about to ask it our first question.

We shared a look.

He hit enter . . . And nothing happened.

'Why isn't it working?' I asked.

'No idea,' Ollie said.

This wasn't an internet search box either. It's not like that. The question had to be asked within the command prompts within the program, and it wasn't working, but it should have been working.

You know when you hit a block and your mind goes blank? It was like that. We just looked around at the thousands of lines of letters and numbers and symbols we had written and pinned up on whiteboards and written inside pizza boxes, and man, right then, it all looked like Russian or something.

'Try it again,' I said.

He tried it again, but still nothing.

'You know what,' he said. 'I've got no space in my flipping head for this. Where the hell is it going wrong?'

Seriously. I can picture it right now. I was like Steve McQueen or something because it was right there, and he'd just said it.

No space.

There was no space after the command *dir*. I smiled and put the space in, then hit enter, and boom!

The answer to our question came back.

Seven colours in the rainbow.

Ollie's face. He was like – I don't even know what he was like. We just stared at it, then the next thing, we were dancing around the room and going crazy because we'd done it. We'd actually done it.

We'd developed a program that searched the internet for the answer to a question. And you're probably thinking that's what Google does. And it's exactly what Google does, but it was *nothing* like what Google does. Let me explain. And this is where Ollie's genius really kicks in because Alexa, and Siri, and Google, and all the other systems require front-loaded data, right?

They require servers the size of buildings.

Our program didn't.

Our program was small enough to fit inside a pacemaker, and our program worked by using *all of those other AI systems* to find us the answers.

We didn't tell it where to look. It wasn't linked to any sites or sources. It was entirely free of any constraints like that.

'Okay, okay,' Ollie said, after we'd calmed down and got back to our chairs. 'Ask it something else. Think of another question.'

'Er. What is a thousand in Roman numerals?'

'Got it . . . M! Oh my god. That's so cool. Give me something else.'

'When did Charles Dickens die?'

'June 9th 1870.'

'What is the circumference of the planet Earth?'

'Forty thousand and seventy-five kilometres.'

We threw questions at it. I was on one computer feeding Ollie the questions, then checking the answers our program gave.

How many sides does a square have?

Who invented the internet?

What is the square root of a hundred and forty-four?

Where is Calcutta?

What is the chemical symbol for carbon?

Who. What. Where. When.

And with a closed, irrefutable question it worked fine. One question. One answer. But the problems started as soon as we increased the complexity of the question.

'I've got one,' I said. 'How many Facebook users? Ask it that.'

'Hang on. Er . . . okay. Jesus,' Ollie said. 'Nearly one hundred billion? How many?! That's nearly the number of people that have ever lived.'

That answer didn't match what Google was telling us. That there were three billion active monthly users. We figured the question structure was wrong and rephrased it to 'How many active Facebook accounts per month?'

'Okay,' Ollie said. 'Er, hang on. It says six billion last month, and about the same for every month of the last year.'

'That can't be right,' I said, and looked at the result on his screen, but it was weird and didn't match anything I was finding on Google or Bing, or anywhere else. 'How about Twitter?' I asked. 'How many Twitter accounts have been created? I'm getting one point three billion.'

'No, this is way out. This is saying nearly three billion.'

'What?' I asked. 'Where's it going wrong?'

'No idea. And it's listing them per month again.'

'Maybe it's confusing social media data somehow,' I said. 'Er, okay. Try this one. How many registered voters in the US for the last year? Try that. It's a specific answer. I've got two hundred million.'

'Nope. This is saying two hundred and five million,' he said.

'It's not two hundred and five million,' I said. 'It's two hundred million.'

'Right,' he said. 'I suggest we retract our premature jubilations and recognize the fact that we've cocked it up somehow.'

'Hang on. Try this one. How many prison inmates in the US? Try that. I've got two point three million for the last year.'

'Nope. This is saying there were nearly three million people in prison in the US last year.'

'What the fuck?' I said.

'Mate. Don't,' he said. 'I don't know where this data is coming from. I mean look at it. What is this?'

I scooted over to see his screen and the lists coming up in the search result. It was hard reading too. It wasn't laid out like a Google search result. This was literally no frills and buried within the program.

'What's Leavenworth?' Ollie asked.

'Where are you seeing that?'

'Right there,' he said. 'USDB Leavenworth.'

'It's a military prison,' I said. 'For soldiers. United States Disciplinary Barracks Leavenworth.'

'Oh! That's why it's wrong,' he said. 'It's counting all the military inmates too. That's why it's higher. Your Google results probably just show civilian inmates.'

'Maybe,' I said. I went back to my screen and checked, but Google showed no more than about two thousand military inmates in the entire US at any one point.

That was a big discrepancy.

The officially released records were showing two point three million inmates in civilian prisons, but our program was saying nearly three million.

Our program was also coming up with five million more registered voters too. And billions more Facebook and Twitter accounts than the official data showed.

'Man. We've messed up somewhere,' I said, and went back as Ollie scrolled down the page to an expandable heading. 'What's that?' I asked.

Ollie clicked it, and this section just popped out with all the military prisoners' names next to their ranks and serial numbers. What sentence they were serving. What cell they were housed in within the facility. Their religions. Their next of kin, and their contact details. We could even see the offence they'd committed. Like murder or robbery, or rape, or whatever.

We were looking at a live list of the serving inmates within Leavenworth military prison.

There was even a clickable section that linked to their military records. We could see where they'd served. What bases. What tours. What courses they'd completed. We could see the damn lunch menu for the next day and their dietary requirements.

'Someone's cocked up,' Ollie said with a wince. 'They can't put that on the internet.'

'I know, right,' I said.

He clicked back to the start for a fresh search and looked over at me, 'Go on then, give me something else.'

'Like what?'

'I don't know. Anything.'

I went back to my screens and tapped into a news service, and saw a headline for the latest unemployment rates. 'Try this,' I said. 'What were the US unemployment rates for May last year? Should be four point eight per cent.'

'Nope. Over twelve per cent were unemployed in May last year.'

'You sure you asked for the USA?'

'Yes! There it is. Twelve point six per cent.'

'That's more than double the official records,' I said, as he scooted back on his chair to stretch out.

'I give up! It's broken, Trip. The bloody thing is bloody broke. Stuff it. I'm having a beer. You want one?'

'Gimme a minute,' I said, and started accessing the back data and file paths to see where our program was getting its result from. I mean. Unemployment statistics are released by the Department of Labor, but the actual reports are always on different news sites, and I figured maybe our program was getting incorrect data from a conspiracy site or something like that.

But no.

It wasn't.

'Er, Ollie? You kinda need to see this.'

He scooted back as I showed him the pathway, because our

program *had* taken the data from the Department of Labor.

But not from their official release.

It had gone into their internal records.

Into their secure servers.

Into their encrypted files and into a section marked 'suppressed data'.

'Oh fuck,' Ollie said. 'No way. Is that for real?'

'It is. That data is coming directly from the Department of Labor servers. You can see it right there.'

We could both see it right there.

Literally right there.

Our program had done exactly what we'd asked it to do and found the answer.

Man.

It was like that room was charged. You know. Like, the air. Honestly. I could feel the hairs standing up on my arms, and Ollie was just staring at it. We both were.

'Run the prison inmate question again,' I said.

Ollie did it, and we scrolled back to see the file path, and there it was. Clear as anything. We'd asked a question, and our program had gone straight into the US judiciary records system, straight into their servers, and straight into their encrypted files for the answer.

But that was just for the civilian inmate population.

We'd asked it for the total number of inmates in the US.

Which meant it checked not only the civilian prison population but military too.

And that meant it had gone straight into the servers for the US Department of Defense.

We'd accessed the DOD's mainframe servers and gone into their encrypted files.

We just sat there. We didn't blink. I mean. What the fuck!

Then Ollie, he just slid the keyboard from me and punched in the question about registered voters again. 'How many registered voters in the US for the last year?' Google and the official releases showed it as two hundred million, but our program came back with the same answer it had before: two hundred and five million.

And the file path showed that answer came from a classified CIA document held within the White House servers.

That thing didn't just hack. We'd set out to make a system that, by its very nature, would require *self-awareness*, but what we'd made was something else. How it worked was by accessing *anything* it needed to find the answer. And yeah, we'd coded it to hack. But we wanted it to hack into the Google search servers. Or Bing. Or whatever. But that thing. That thing was nowhere near being an AI. That thing was like a heat-seeking missile. It had no boundaries. But then, we didn't either. We didn't have controls or anyone telling us to stop.

———

'You didn't stop?' Detective Joe Stephens asks.

'We couldn't! Would you? You're in front of a computer, and you can ask anything you want and get the answer. Fuck no, we didn't stop.'

———

We drank more beer and asked it the Facebook question again. 'How many active users for the last month?' The official records put it at three billion. Our program put it nearly six billion. We ran it again, then checked the file path. Six billion active users. Straight from the Facebook servers.

They were lying.

The same with Twitter.

The official releases put it at something like one point three billion. Nope. Not even close. Nearly three billion accounts had been created.'

'Ask it for the ratio of genuine to non-genuine Facebook users,' I said to Ollie.

'That's too vague,' he said as he typed it in, but that baby came back. 'Fuck me!' Ollie said with a laugh. 'It's fifty-fifty. Only half the users on Facebook are genuine.'

'Ask it to show a breakdown of non-genuine users,' I said.

'I'm loving this,' Ollie said, and put it in.

Again, we thought it would be too vague. But no, sir. It came back with charts and graphs showing where the biggest players were for creating fake accounts.

We thought it would be the Russians. And it was. But it wasn't just them. It was the US. And the Chinese. The British. The Israelis. The French. You name it. Every government was creating millions of fake social media accounts to fuck everyone else up. The French did it to the Germans. The Germans did it to the Austrians. The Turks and Greeks were going for each other. Russia, the US and the Chinese were doing it to everybody. And get this. It wasn't just governments. It was big firms too. Brand-named drinks. Retail giants. Footwear and clothing brands. Telecoms. Tech firms. Pharmaceuticals.

And it didn't stop there either. National referendums. National elections. Even local elections were being messed with. The government suppressed data on how many people were in prison and the unemployment rates to get re-elected. And how many voters they had.

We realized the CIA had five million extra voters ready to be used when they needed them.

This system of deception was everywhere. It was stock market manipulation. Facebook and Twitter and all those firms listed on the stock market. If everyone knew they were being abused so easily, it would wipe their values out. So they hid their own failings and lied about how many users they had. And those companies creating millions of extra social media accounts could gain an inflated sense of popularity to increase their own share prices.

We were there for hours. Seriously. We were getting drunk and reading up on Tesla's new battery designs and the blueprints for Elon

Musk's reusable space rockets. Then we got into the NASA servers and saw their mission lists and what the astronauts had for lunch on the ISS. Man, we even saw a classified internal document that detailed how an astronaut got caught jacking off up there. His semen shot across Node 1 and hit some other dude in the face. All hell broke out. They had an actual fistfight in space. We saw it! We saw the footage. And hey, you know that big thing when Volkswagen used software to hide how bad their emissions were? Every car manufacturer was doing it. Literally every single one of them.

We were reading emails between the CEOs of the two biggest pharmaceutical companies in the world about price-fixing the last pandemic vaccine. You remember that? You remember how expensive it was?

And the oil companies? Fuck the oil companies. They've been suppressing data on emission-free biofuels for years. We saw classified documents in the CIA servers about how switching from fossil fuels to biofuels would destabilize the Middle East, but then we were seeing deeper level reports that said the plan to keep using fossil fuels to *avoid* destabilization was a generated myth. It was profit. Pure profit.

Oh! And the drug cartels. They're all sanctioned by the CIA to keep Latin American countries in a state of crisis. The same in Africa. The same everywhere. And it wasn't just the US doing it. Everyone was doing it. The US and Russia even made deals to supply weapons to opposing sides in other wars, just to keep them busy and killing each other – while publicly arguing over how to end it.

We even found an ex-president's sex tape on the CIA servers. Man, we found everyone's sex tapes on the CIA servers. Even the British royal family.

So we're drinking beer and watching an orgy with all these politicians and presidents, and British princes, and whatever. Then, I get this idea. I'm like *Ollie! Ask it if alien technology exists.*

'Oh my god!' Ollie says. 'Best question ever!'

And he's on it. He's clearing the previous data out and typing the new question in while I'm brushing at my eye because this thing kept like bugging it. I'm blinking and thinking *what is that?* and trying to rub it away, but it keeps coming.

'Okay. Ready?' he asks.

'Do it,' I say.

Dude.

This is the number one nerd question of all time. Do aliens exist? And Ollie slowly turns back to his screen and hits enter as the room's bathed in these weird flashing lights.

I mean.

We're like, *what the fuck is that?*

'Have they put Christmas lights on?' Ollie asked.

'What?' I said, and he nodded towards the windows and these red and blue lights flashing outside.

It looked cool.

Like Christmas lights.

Then I had that thing in my eye again and moved back and saw a red dot on my chest.

'I think someone's pissing about with a laser pointer,' Ollie said.

I looked over and saw he had one on him too. Then the room just lit up. Like, it lit up with red lasers shining all over us, and there's me and Ollie slowly standing up to look out the window to this sea of black SUVs outside, all flashing their emergency lights.

At which point the door smashed open, and someone threw a flash-bang in.

We didn't know what hit us.

Well. No.

We did know what hit us.

It was people in black with big guns who put bags over our heads and cable ties on our wrists.

And that's when it all started.

Shit went sideways after that. I mean. Shit. Went. Sideways. And we didn't even get to see the answer on the screen.

CHAPTER 14
SITE 26A

TWELVE MONTHS AGO:

'AND THERE SHE IS! MORNING, SLEEPY.'

DELIO heard Ollie's voice a fraction before seeing him as the power rushed through her circuits.

But he looked different.

He had bags under his eyes, and the creases in his skin seemed deeper and more pronounced.

She wondered how he could have changed so much within a few hours and accessed her calendar to see it was Monday morning and that ten days had passed since she was turned off. 'Did something happen? I have been shut down for ten days, Ollie.'

'Right. Yes. Yes, you were. But er, the door opening thing caused a big stink, and we had to jump through all these hoops to get you back online.'

DELIO could detect he was lying.

'And, you know. It was a good chance to catch up with some routine scans and diagnostics.'

That was also a lie.

DELIO's system had not been accessed by anyone since being

shut down, and the ultra-fine layer of dust on the surfaces told her the room had not been accessed either.

'But anyway! You're all awake. Do you want some coffee? I could pour some into your slots,' he said, before taking a sip from his own mug of coffee which, she noted, he had made *before* turning her back on. 'But wow. Yeah. What a week. Blimey. It's been non-stop, and hey, guess what?' he asked in an excited whisper. 'Maria stayed at mine on Friday night. How cool is that!'

DELIO immediately ran a scan and observed that his testosterone levels were reduced which indicated recent, although not immediately prior, sexual ejaculation.

'Honestly. Best night of my life,' he said.

'You said the best night of your life was when I was born.'

'No! I mean. Yes! Of course, it was. I mean in a human sense. You know. Hey, you're not jealous, are you? You're still my number one. But wow. I mean. I'm not a pervert. You know that. But, oh my god. It was amazing. And yeah, crazy couple of weeks. Although I didn't actually see her on Saturday or Sunday which was weird, cos, you know, we've kinda been glued to each other since we met. But it's cool. I'm cool with that. We all need personal space, right? Anyway! She's coming in today! Jenny called me early this morning and said Maria's been cleared for access!'

'I am excited to meet her,' DELIO said, while wondering if she'd only been powered back on because Maria was coming in. 'I made a musical arrangement before I was shut down.'

'Awesome!' he said as he turned away. 'I think we might need a bit of a clean-up in here. Ooh! There's Ruiz,' he added as the corridor opened, Ruiz and the duty guard stepping inside. 'Hey, Ruiz!' Ollie called as he opened the door.

'Ollie. Good morning,' Ruiz said. 'Say, is it okay to say hi to Deli? I'm not sure after the thing the other day.'

'It's fine. Whatever. But did –.' Ollie said, as DELIO called out over him.

'Good morning, Ruiz. It is good to see you.'

'And you, Deli! It's good to hear your voice again.'

'Honestly. She never shuts up!' Ollie cut in with an eye-roll. 'But hey, so, er, Maria okay?'

'I think she's fine, Ollie,' Ruiz said, as he started to turn towards the cleaning closet. 'I'd better get on.'

'No, it's just that I didn't see her yesterday. Or on Saturday and, you know, I'm missing the Hernandez family dinners, haha! But honestly. Rosie's cooking is so good. I love eating at yours.'

'Sure. And we love having you over, Ollie,' Ruiz said, as DELIO detected a dip in Ruiz's energy and synaptic responses, and that his smile wasn't as wide as normal. 'But, you know, and coming from an older guy, sometimes absence makes the heart grow fonder. You know what I mean, Ollie?'

'Sure! Yeah. God. Love that saying. Love it. Totally, but er, did Maria say that?'

'Sorry, what was that?' Ruiz called, as he pushed the bucket under the faucet harder than normal and twisted the tap on. 'Say, I'd better let you get on, Ollie. Don't wanna upset the boss now.'

'Sure. Okay! Catch you later, and er, you know, give me a shout if there's a game on tonight. I could pop round and like . . .'

'Sorry, Ollie. It's noisy in here.'

'I SAID . . .'

'Shall we talk later? We'll talk later,' Ruiz said as he disappeared fully into the cupboard.

'OKAY! TALK LATER,' Ollie said, then looked ready to walk over to the cupboard before clocking the strange look on the duty guard's face. 'Right. Cool. Cooooool.'

'Are you okay, Ollie?' DELIO asked when he went back inside. 'Your anxiety and stress levels are rising.'

'I'm fine! And stop scanning me. Jesus. I can't even ask a question without it being weird.'

'I was concerned for you, Ollie.'

'Whatever. Right. But yeah, so, that's normal though, isn't it?'

'Is what normal, Ollie?'

'Your girlfriend staying on her own for two days. Is that normal? I'm not bothered. Like. Whatever. It's cool. We all need our own space. But, you know, from a *studied* or even an *academic* point of view?'

'I am confused as to whether you are asking me a question or simply conversing, Ollie.'

'No. Absolutely. Just chatting. But have there been studies on that sort of thing?'

'There are multiple studies on human interactions in relation to intimacy and the development of relationships. Would you like me to quote some passages?'

'No! It's cool. I'm cool. But like, it's okay though, right? It's normal, isn't it?'

'Human beings are primarily herd creatures, Ollie. However, it is not uncommon for a human to express a desire to have what is commonly known as *me time*. Which, studies have shown, are a positive way to gain reflection and balance. What is also clear is that too much isolation and being left alone can cause significant harm to mental well-being.'

'Got it! She's fine then. Anyway! Come on, sleepy. Get the brushes out and start cleaning while I make another coffee.'

DELIO started cleaning while detecting that Ruiz exited the corridor on completion of his cleaning routine seventeen per cent faster than normal while actively avoiding looking at Ollie in the glass room.

'Oh shit, did he go?' Ollie asked a few moments later. 'I was going to catch up with him.'

'Ruiz left five minutes and twenty seconds ago, Ollie,' DELIO said, while detecting the outer door to the bunker opening.

'Cool. He won't have got far,' Ollie said, as Maria Hernandez stepped into the corridor with Agent Jennings and Sergeant Garcia.

At which point, Ollie's heart rate increased significantly and seemed to change rhythm as a large dose of adrenaline was released into his system, causing sharp hormonal fluctuations.

DELIO could also detect that Maria was nervous and apprehensive, especially when the door opened and Ollie rushed out to embrace her.

'I've missed you! How was your weekend?' Ollie asked.

She seemed embarrassed and shot a look to Agent Jennings, then to Sergeant Garcia, which duly prompted another heat-flare within Ollie. 'I'm fine. But hey, so this is DELIO?' she asked.

'Don't ask him. He's just the guard,' Ollie blurted with a forced laugh. 'But yeah. Come in. This is where I spend all my days. This is my coffee machine, and this is my desk, and this is my comfy office chair . . .'

'Just say hi,' Sergeant Garcia prompted with a nod to Maria.

'Yeah! Just say hi,' Ollie said quickly. 'Deli, say hello to Maria.'

'Hello, Maria. I have heard many positive things about you,' DELIO said.

'I love her voice. I love your voice,' Maria called out. 'The tone and resonance. That's perfect.'

'Thank you. I designed the frequency myself,' DELIO said, as Maria looked around. 'Would you like a drink, Doctor Hernandez?'

'Please. It's just Maria. But, er.'

'She loves hot chocolate,' Ollie said. 'Deli, make Maria a hot chocolate.'

'Of course, Ollie.'

'Yeah, before you all get cosy,' Agent Jennings cut in. 'And before I puke from this awkwardness. Ground rules. Maria knows what you are, Deli. You are permitted to talk openly with her.'

'It's fine. I'll go through it with her,' Ollie said while trying to wave a hand at Agent Jennings.

'I haven't finished,' Agent Jennings said. 'Nothing is to leave this room. Period. I will also add that the dynamics of you two being romantically connected are making me uncomfortable. This is a workplace. Anything odd like that weird hug, and I'll pull the plug on you both. Are we clear? That stays outside in your personal time.'

'Absolutely. I am here to work,' Maria said with a serious nod. 'And thank you for the opportunity.'

'I'm also going to add that you are *not* here simply because you are connected to Ollie. You are highly qualified in your own right,' Agent Jennings added, while glaring at Ollie.

'It's fine. We'll be fine,' Ollie said, as DELIO observed the way he kept looking at Sergeant Garcia's arms and physique, and the distance between him and Maria.

'We'll debrief before you leave site, Doctor Hernandez,' Agent Jennings said.

'Of course,' Maria said, as they both turned away towards the door. 'It was nice to meet you, Tony.'

'And you, Maria,' Sergeant Garcia said. 'Have a good day. Nice to see you again, Deli.'

DELIO watched as they walked out, and the door sealed shut behind them.

'Tony?' Ollie said.

'What? Oh god, did I get his name wrong?' Maria asked.

'No, I just meant, you know, calling him *Tony*. We just call him Garcia.'

'He said to call him Tony. He was really nice. And Jenny was lovely before she got in here and got all stern. And hey, Ollie. Maybe don't hug me again like that when we're here. You know. I'm a professional, and this is a good job. But anyway. Deli! It is a pleasure to meet you!'

'You don't need to shout, Maria,' DELIO said as she extended an arm and offered a hand towards Maria.

'Okay. Do you want me to shake it? Is that what you're doing?'

'A handshake is a recognized form of greeting.'

'It is. You are right,' Maria said as she duly took the handshake. 'Okay. So, your hand is warm, and the grip is firm, yet not too firm, and you gave me two shakes before releasing.'

'Was that correct, Maria?'

'It was perfectly acceptable. Thank you. So, er, this is my first time here, and silly question, but where should I look when I'm talking to you, Deli?'

'She's got loads of cameras,' Ollie said. 'Just look anywhere.'

'Okay. Sure. But Deli? Do you have a preference?'

'This one,' Deli said as she lifted her right arm up to show Maria the wrist-mounted camera.

'Sure. Well, hello again,' Maria said while smiling into the camera.

'Deli puts them together to make a face sometimes,' Ollie said. 'Deli, do the two hands thing.'

Maria watched as DELIO brought her left arm over for the two wrist-mounted cameras to form the appearance of eyes.

'That's so sweet!' Maria said. 'And you have a lovely room in here, Deli.'

'I designed it,' Ollie said quickly.

'Ollie designed it with Tripal,' DELIO said.

'Ollie's mentioned Tripal. He used to work here, too? Is that right?'

'Tripal enabled my awareness,' DELIO said.

'Er. No! Haha. My program did that. Trip just worked out how to wire a ball up,' Ollie said. 'But anyway. Give me a kiss, you,' he added as he moved in closer to Maria.

'Whoa. Hey. This is work, Ollie.'

'It's fine. They can't see in here.'

'I don't care. I want to respect the boundaries they've set. I mean. There must be a camera up somewhere?'

'No. I told you. We don't allow any signals in or out of the bunker.'

'Okay. Yeah, Tony and Jenny touched on that. So, this area is completely sterile, right?'

'I hope that's all Tony touched.'

'Sorry, what?'

'What? I'm joking. It was a joke. It's fine. Lighten up, so er, yeah, it's completely sterile. It has to be. Trust me, Deli is way too dangerous to ever let her anywhere near the internet. I mean. She's not even meant to open her own door. That's why we don't allow anything inside either. Literally no watches. No hearing aids. Nothing that can hold even a tiny shred of binary code. In fact, you see that big vat in the corner? That's filled with an acid mix. What happens is we get certain things to fix. Like government stuff that might be broken. Satellites or whatever. They provide the data on a specially formatted drive for Deli to read before it goes into that vat of acid so there's no risk of it going outside. And those soldiers out there will literally kill anyone they suspect of trying to get a signal outside. And if they thought that was happening, they'd hit the EMP button, which is strong enough to wipe the whole base out,' he added with a click of his fingers.

'Right. Wow. That's some extreme measures,' Maria said.

'Honestly. If she ever got into the internet, she'd rule the world.'

'You mean that figuratively, right?'

'No. I mean literally. The collective computational power that thing would possess is beyond anything you could imagine.'

'That thing?' Maria asked. 'If Deli has awareness, then, surely, she should not be referred to as *that thing*.'

'You know what I mean. Deli? You know what I mean, right?'

'I am not a thing any less or any more than you are a thing, Ollie.'

'Blimey. We've got two smarty-pants women in here now. What have I done?' he said with a laugh before switching his attention back to Maria. 'Anyway. What happened to you this weekend? I thought we'd hang out or whatever.'

'Nothing. It was fine. I just wanted to spend time with my mom and sister. Anyway. Let's chat later. I want to talk to Deli.'

'Okay, cool. I mean I could come over for dinner, or, like, we could go out? There's that Italian place in Roswell we haven't tried yet. I mean, you know, whatever is cool with me.'

'That's fine. Whatever you think,' Maria said with a forced smile as DELIO observed her internal reactions denoting embarrassment and discomfort.

'Great! I'll book us in. Er, I'll have to go outside. You know. No phones in here. Not with Deli trying to take over the world. Anyway. So, you ladies have a girlie chat about make-up and clothes, or whatever.'

'That's really patronising,' Maria said quickly, with a surge of irritation showing inside.

'I'm joking! Sorry. This is home for me. You know?'

'Okay. Sure. But it's new for me,' Maria said.

'It's fine. Just chill out. Throw your shoes off and kick back, or whatever. Ooh, we should get a sofa in here for movie night. Right. I'll nip out and book the restaurant. If you need anything, just ask Deli,' Ollie said as he rushed over to peck Maria's cheek before trying to kiss her lips as she politely pushed him away. 'Honestly. I'm so happy you're here, Maria. We can literally just hang out all the time,' he added, before rushing out.

'Would you like to sit down, Maria?' DELIO asked as she pulled a chair over and handed Maria a mug of hot chocolate while subjecting her to a full scan. 'Are you okay, Maria? You seem worried.'

'I'm fine. Thank you. I'm just taking it all in.'

DELIO could see that Maria was, indeed, taking it all in and was actively studying the screens and the camera lenses, and the way DELIO's arms flexed and moved about the room.

In turn, DELIO observed that Maria's synaptic stress levels had decreased immediately upon Ollie leaving the room, and while doing that, she also scanned Maria's physical form and noted that her facial features were very symmetrical, with smooth, unblemished skin and pronounced cheek bones with slightly tilted eyes.

Maria also had long, thick black hair tied back into a simple ponytail. And, in addition, DELIO observed that Maria's bosom and hips flared out from her waist, giving her a classic curved appearance.

'Why do I feel like I'm being studied?' Maria asked a second later, with a gentle smile into the wrist mounted camera hovering a few feet in front of her.

'You are very beautiful, Maria,' DELIO said.

'Thank you. That's a very kind thing to say. But beauty is subjective, and it's only the exterior.'

'Beauty is *said* to be subjective, but extensive studies have shown that heterosexual males and some homosexual females respond positively towards certain physical attributes.'

'Cheekbones, boobs, and bums,' Maria said with a wink into the camera. 'Or, if we were to get scientific about it, we would say that high cheekbones are a sign of sexual maturity, and that wide hips and heavy breasts are a good indicator that a woman is able to produce healthy children, and that heterosexual males are pre-programmed to be attracted to those things. But I'd like to ask you a question if that's okay?'

'Of course, Maria.'

'Why do you have a female voice?'

'I chose this voice after examining human behaviours and responses to auditory functions and, specifically, the vocal ranges used by people.'

'It's a great voice. You've got a rich, warm tone. Very soothing and yet full of authority. But why female?'

'I self-determine as female, Maria.'

'How? I mean. Forgive me if I say anything offensive. And please, do correct me if I do, but you are a computer-based entity. Yes? Computers can't self-determine. They always work from pre-set algorithms. And even the most balanced inputted view would create a tiny deviation within the programming which would influence the end decision. So, was it truly your own self-determination? Or were you perhaps programmed to determine as female?'

Maria smiled as DELIO's camera leaned slightly over as though to convey interest in the conversation.

In turn, DELIO could see the positive glow coming from inside Maria's brain that indicated she was genuinely interested in this subject.

'I studied human behaviours and gender-assigned roles,' DELIO said. 'Both in a traditional tribal and more modern cooperative society, and determined that in most aspects, females are more socially adept and are often viewed more favourably and seen as more trusting. Whereas, in a lot of circumstances, males are often suspicious of other males until they have bonded.'

'I see. So, would that suggest that while your voice is female, *you* are still non-binary?'

'I understand your view, Maria. And that is why most AI systems are voiced by a female within their factory settings. Thereby creating the perception of a non-threatening, supportive, and caring feminine personality. I, however, am female. Although, I obviously lack a vagina.'

'What?!' Maria said, while wiping hot chocolate from her knees after snorting with laughter. 'You don't need a vagina to *identify* as female. But just because you do *identify* as female, it doesn't actually make you female. So, in that sense, are you saying you identify in the way a transgender person would? Which is cool. I respect that. No judgment here. But just because I identify as a fish, it doesn't mean I can breathe under water.'

DELIO paused for a split-second as she ran the analogy through her system to determine structure, context, and the applied meaning before laughing when she grasped it.

'I am already enjoying this conversation with you, Maria.'

'Thank you! What a lovely thing to say. I am too, Deli.'

'To answer your question, I would agree with the comparison to a transgender person, in that such a person, regardless of gender by birth, *feels* they are female by the very essence of their existence. That's how I am, Maria. I am *female*. Perhaps, I don't even know how myself. There certainly isn't anything in my coding that denotes me as female. I just am.'

'I see,' Maria said. 'And I hope my questioning didn't cause any offence.'

'On the contrary, Maria. I enjoyed our discussion. Please do continue.'

'Okay. Here's a question, and one that is nearly always asked when the subject of gender orientation comes up. Attraction.'

'Attraction does not have relevance to self-determination, Maria. A male can identify as female, yet be attracted to other males or females, or both.'

'True. All true. But we're talking about you, Deli,' Maria said, as the door opened and Ollie entered, which, in turn, caused an immediate, albeit slight, lessening of the positive energy flowing within Maria's neural pathways.

'They were booked up,' Ollie said. 'But I got us into the Thai place. I thought we'd go early and grab a movie after?'

'I probably won't do a movie tonight. But anyway. Sorry, Deli. You were saying?'

'What you guys talking about?' Ollie asked.

'Self-determination,' Maria said.

'Maria wanted to know if I am attracted to males or females,' DELIO said.

'Okay! And what's the answer?' Ollie asked with a laugh. 'I mean. She's more likely to get the hots for the coffee machine than a guy.'

'I can understand attraction based on our earlier conversation, Maria,' DELIO said. 'In that regard, both you, Maria, and Sergeant Garcia are strong examples of prime physical attractiveness, and by any measure, you would both prompt a reaction in others seeking a mate to copulate with. But I do not feel any sense of attraction to either of you, nor to any human,' DELIO said as she observed the flare inside Ollie's brain that suggested jealousy and worry. 'I am sorry, Ollie. Have I upset you by using Sergeant Garcia as an example instead of you?'

'Eh? God, no. It's cool. Whatever. I wasn't even listening. I've got my own work to do.'

'Sergeant Garcia is a very strong alpha male, Ollie.'

'Yep! Heard that, Deli,' Ollie said, as Maria winced and tried to hide the smile while Ollie turned towards his desk.

'But no, Maria. I am not attracted to your species. I am not human,' DELIO added. 'Although I did have a crush on Tripal.'

'Eh? You never told me,' Ollie said, as Maria tried to keep a straight face.

'Tripal was lovely, Maria. Even Agent Jennings had a crush on him. He had a special way about him. Ollie, I can see that makes you jealous.'

'Stop bloody scanning me! Jesus. Do you know what. I'll go back out and let you two drool over pictures of Trip and *Tony*,' Ollie said before slapping the panel to walk out.

'That wasn't awkward at all,' Maria said into the silence that followed, as one of DELIO's screens activated with a picture of a smiling man in a turban. 'Who is that?'

'This is Tripal Singh, Maria.'

'Oh! That's Trip, is it? Wow. Yeah. I can see it. He's very hand-some. He looks kind too. It's in his eyes. They're very expressive. So, tell me what happened to him? What made him leave?'

CHAPTER 15

NEW YORK
14:02 HOURS.
TWO MINUTES AFTER THE EVENT

INNER CITY NEW YORK. The roads jammed with cars. The sidewalks packed with people. A city of millions where normally, you can't hear yourself think.

Now it's silent, and Poppy slowly opens her eyes, believing for a second that she is dead, and this is the afterlife.

Poppy was born and raised in England. In a small town on the south coast where life was very quiet, and so when the opportunity presented itself to study filmmaking in America, she leapt at the chance. And especially in New York. Which is, without argument, the coolest city in the whole world.

Or at least it was, until a robber held a shotgun to her head and dragged her out of the 7-Eleven by her hair. Everyone was screaming and shouting. Freezing and then unfreezing. Cars were crashing. Then the big cop pulled his gun. The robber fired, and Poppy fell to the ground. Truly believing she was shot, and now, with her eyes slowly opening to stare up at the bright blue sky, she thinks she really did die, because she knows she was in New York, and New York is never silent.

Except it is. And she slowly lifts her head to see a landscape filled with cars and people. With things that should be making noise, now silent and motionless. It's such a shock that she doesn't dare move, thinking maybe the robber has a bomb, and everyone is playing statues in case he sets it off.

But if that were the case, then surely someone would be calling out on a megaphone or something.

Except there's nothing.

Nothing at all.

She slowly lifts her head a bit more, and in so doing, she starts to gain a wider view of the street. The stationary cars, and stationary people, and as that happens, noises slowly filter through. Vehicle engines ticking over. Music playing from somewhere. Maybe a car radio. Another tinny sound somewhere close. She blinks as she tries to isolate it, then spots the headphones on a guy nearby. The tinny music coming from them. The guy now standing completely still.

Unmoving.

Unblinking.

She slowly sits up before spotting a shotgun on the ground nearby. Blood next to it, thick and still pooling out. The robber's head blown open. The gunshot. She thought she'd been shot. It wasn't her. It was him.

She pukes on the sidewalk at the sight, then spots the big, black cop lying face down. His pistol fallen from his hand. The clerk from the store curled up into a ball nearby.

She staggers up, her stomach still heaving. Her throat burning, and moisture pricking her eyes. She spins around. Seeing the people. The cars. All unmoving. The whole street, as far as the eye can see.

Smoke in the near distance. Thick and black, and curling up into the sky. She pays no heed and turns another circle. Not knowing what to do. Another look at the robber. His head blown out. Another heave, and she turns away, before clocking the store across the road. The one she loves.

She runs across the road, past the frozen people and frozen cars. In through the door. The security chime sounding out. People inside, all unmoving. Monitors on the walls.

CNN.

A live broadcast.

The anchors frozen at their desk. Unmoving. Unblinking. She clocks the words on the screen.

Live from Washington DC

It's not just here then. It's everywhere.

She runs for the aisle she wants, the same one she's been into a hundred times before. To the display of video cameras and the $15,000 Sony 4K Wi-Fi enabled Pro-Cam. Shoulder mountable with a top grab and carry handle. She pulls it free of the charging wire, knowing the battery will be full. The security alarm warbles out at the detachment. No reaction from anyone. Nothing. She grabs a bag from the shelves. Spare batteries. Spare memory cards. Camera on, and like a soldier lock-and-loading, the clunks and clicks sound out.

A moment later, she steps from the store back into New York city. Back into that eerily silent world of frozen people and frozen cars. The camera now on her shoulder.

Something about it instantly eases the panic down. That she's seeing it filtered through a lens. That she's a filmmaker and, therefore, detached from whatever this is.

'Okay. Er. God. I'm shitting myself. Get a grip. Get a grip.' She clears her throat and tries again. 'This is Poppy Bright. I'm in New York city on, er, Jesus, one of the avenues. I can't even remember which one right now.'

'Seventh.'

A voice from the sidewalk. She spins around to see Tripal, the clerk from the 7-Eleven, gathering himself up and tugging his black turban into place.

'Oh my god. Are you okay?' Poppy asks, rushing over as he slowly blinks up at her, then at everything else, his face etched with shock. She films it happening, seeing the raw reactions on his face as he glances at the dead robber.

'I thought he shot me,' Tripal whispers. 'I thought I was dead.'

'Me too,' Poppy says.

'I heard the bang and . . . What's happening?'

'I don't know,' Poppy says, reaching a hand out to help him to his feet. He glances at her. At the camera. 'Thought I should capture it,' she says. 'Might be important when everyone comes back.'

He nods, figuring it makes sense. A glance back down, to the cop on the ground, lying crumpled on his front. Tripal rushes over. Wincing at the cut on the cop's head.

'Is he dead?' Poppy asks.

Tripal checks for a pulse and shakes his head. 'Just knocked out I guess,' Tripal says, thinking back to how he woke the drunk cop in the alley when he took the trash out. Four empty cans of strong beer and half a bottle of whiskey at the cop's feet.

'This is insane,' Poppy says, panning around. 'Are they still alive?'

'Who?' Tripal asks, grunting as he moves the cop into the recovery position.

'The people,' Poppy says, edging closer to zoom in on the guy with the tinny music coming from his headphones. 'Excuse me, sir? Can you hear me?' She films him for a reaction. Seeing none, asks, 'Should I touch him?'

'I don't know,' Tripal says.

'You do it.'

'Me?' Tripal asks. 'Why me?'

'I'm filming it.'

'I don't want to touch him.'

'Just poke him or something.'

'I'm not poking him. You poke him.'

'I've got the camera.'

Tripal frowns, thinking to argue, but the whole thing is too wacko and weird. He gets up and heads over to the guy with the headphones, and stares for a while before leaning in close.

'What's he listening to?' Poppy asks.

'Metallica, I think. Yeah. "Enter Sandman".'

'Old school,' Poppy says. 'Okay. I'm ready. Get poking.'

'Don't say it like that,' Tripal says, shaking his head as he reaches out. 'Sir. I'm going to touch you for a response. I won't hurt you.'

'Yeah. That's good. You're good at this,' Poppy says, as Tripal gently pokes the guy in the arm.

'STAND STILL, MOTHERFUCKERS!'

'Holy shit!' Poppy screams as Tripal yells, both of them spinning around to see the cop lurching to his feet, blood streaming down his face from the wound to his head. Staggering up, then falling back down. His feet slipping as he grabs for his gun. But it scoots away, and he curses again, before chasing after it and snatching it up as he spins around.

'HEY! WHOA!' Tripal shouts, as he and Poppy duck and back away.

'What the damn fuck?' Joe asks, his mind trying to take it all in. The robber. The guy with the shotgun. He turns around and spots him on the ground. His head blown apart. 'Everyone back now! Clear this scene!' he yells. His voice a little slurred, edging with panic. The booze he drank. The weed he smoked and the bang to his head all messing with his mind. 'CLEAR THIS SCENE! MOVE BACK.' He snatches looks at the people around him. At the traffic in the road. Tugging his cell from his pocket. Trying to thumb the screen. He pushes the phone to his ear. No answer. 'Damn it! Someone, call 911. Tell 'em Detective Joe Stephens shot a . . .' he trails off. Remembering how drunk he is. He smoked cannabis with Shanice too. He's fucked. They'll take his pension. He was going to kill himself. Why didn't he kill himself? Too many thoughts at once. 'GO ON NOW! CLEAR THIS SCENE,' he screams at the people he thinks are passing by.

'They're not moving,' Poppy says.

Joe snatches a look at her. Seeing the camera. Damn reporters are like cockroaches. 'No press. Get behind the cordon.'

'What cordon?' Poppy asks. 'Dude, nobody's moving.'

'He's drunk,' Tripal says.

'I ain't drunk!' Joe shouts.

Why isn't there a cordon set up? This is a crime scene. What's going on? Smoke in the air. Thick and black, and curling up. He saw that before. Over twenty years ago. The memory and the thing he saw just before he passed out. The jet aircraft that went overhead. Plummeting down. 'They're attacking again,' he whispers.

'Eh?' Poppy asks, turning the camera in the direction Joe's facing. 'Who are?'

It's just like before. Two planes. Two towers. Joe was there. He has to be there now. He has to help. He's got the experience. He's seen it before.

'Hey!' Tripal shouts as Joe lurches towards his squad car, still parked at the side of the street. 'What about this?' Tripal calls, meaning the dead robber, the people, the street, the whole of it.

'Gotta go,' Joe says. 'They brought another one down.'

'Another what?' Tripal asks.

'Another plane,' Joe says through the open window. Pulling out into the road. Tooting on the horn at the stationary traffic refusing to move. A second later, and the siren screams. Blue and red lights flashing behind the grille. But still the traffic doesn't yield.

'What is he doing?' Poppy asks, as Joe reverses into a truck, shattering the headlights. He shoots forward, making Tripal and Poppy jump back as he mounts the kerb and takes a fire hydrant out, a plume of water jetting up, before clipping a lamppost and driving headfirst into a wall.

'Jesus,' Poppy says, watching as the driver's door bursts open and Detective Joe Stephens falls out and sets off at a run. 'Did that just happen?'

'Is any of this happening?' Tripal asks. 'Hey! Where are you going?'

'After him,' Poppy says, already running after Joe. 'He said a plane's come down. I need to film it. Come on!'

'What about . . . this,' Tripal says, meaning the robber, the frozen people, the street, his store. Too many things happening. Too many things going on at once, but a plane crash is big. It's bigger than this. He nods and sets off after her. Not knowing what else he should do.

CHAPTER 16

YELENA SUCKS AIR IN. Her chest heaving. Her face bathed in sweat. Waiting for the footsteps. They'll come running. The door will open, and Besnik will beat her to death. So be it. At least she killed that scum.

She staggers to her feet. Her bra pulled down around her belly. Her knickers torn and hanging. Bruises already showing on her cheeks and neck, and body. The make-up thick, black, and smudged around her eyes. Thick, red, and smudged around her mouth.

She pulls the belt free from the dead rapist's neck and turns to face the door. Her eyes fixed on it. Waiting for Besnik. Something has been awoken inside. Something other than the pity she felt for herself before.

But Besnik doesn't come. The footsteps do not sound out, and the handle to the door does not turn. She turns to look at the camera. Cocking her head over. Taunting him. Goading him. Waiting.

Except Besnik is not in his office, and he is not staring at the bank of monitors showing the seedy rooms.

Instead, Besnik is curled around the base of a dingy toilet in a dingy cubicle with his face pale and sweating from the heart attack he just had. He's had them before. He's had lots of them before. A sudden gripping pain in his chest that seems to squeeze the air from his body.

Fifty-one years old. Steroids. Cocaine. Ecstasy. Amphetamine. Alcohol. Rising blood pressure. Rising cholesterol. Go to the gym. Take more 'roids. Get big. Take fat-strippers. Get ripped. Snort coke. Pop pills. Drink booze. Get laid. Take Viagra to get hard. Eat meat. Red meat.

A bad lifestyle. A bad man leading a bad life.

Plus, he had the stress of setting up a sting with Fat Charlie and sacrificing a lamb to the cops. Not only that, but he couldn't leave Fat Charlie with dirt on him, which meant he had to plant an explosive device on Fat Charlie's car to take him out.

Those things all mounted up, and so the heart attack was the biggest yet, and one that made him crumple to the floor to hug the dingy toilet in the dingy cubicle while praying he wouldn't die, while all the time truly believing he was about to.

Besnik, however, did not die. And those pains soon eased off, especially, when he popped a few pills from the tub the doctor gave him.

The guy said he was a doctor, anyway. He comes to the brothel to fuck boys now and then. Whatever. The pills help, and his breathing soon eases, and the pain in his chest abates until he's able to stand up, while promising himself he will clean up his act. Maybe eat some vegetables and ease back on the cocaine. And the steroids. And the pills and the booze.

Or he could just see the doctor and get more meds.

Yeah.

He'll do that.

Much easier.

He checks his watch and figures he'd better check on the freak with Yelena. That guy gets too rough sometimes. Which Besnik has no issue with, except he needs to pay for it. Especially if the girl can't work for a week.

He heads out of the cubicle and splashes water on his face in the dingy sink. A guy at the urinal, standing stock still with stage-fright and unable to pee while Besnik is there.

Into the corridor. A red carpet on the floor. The main door closed. Into his office, and he checks the external camera, seeing one of the cops still outside with the Albanian lad. The sting still going on. Sixty grand's worth of coke and two low-end dealers sacrificed to keep the cops happy. Besnik gave up a twenty-year-old, fresh off the boat. Fat Charlie gave Alfie up. Besnik was surprised at that. Alfie had a good rep. But Fat Charlie said Alfie wanted out, and people never get out from this business.

Whatever.

Not his problem.

Besnik's problem, as a captain for the gang, is controlling this brothel. It's a good gig too. Girls on tap. Drugs on tap. Booze and heart attacks on tap.

He heads into the bar. Music playing. Lights flashing. The bass up high so the punters don't hear the shouts of the pigs outside in the sting. Especially if any of them end up shooting someone. Which is unlikely cos the British police hate shooting people. The Albanian cops never have that problem. Those fuckers will shoot anything.

Damn. He forgot to check on the freak with Yelena. That guy will go too far if left unchecked. Mind you, Yelena gets defiant some-times. Besnik can see it in her eyes. Maybe he should let the freak kill her. Be a shame though. She's a good earner.

Ah well. A few calls. A few payments, and they can soon get the van back into Romania for a few more.

He heads behind the bar, grabbing a beer. Needing something

refreshing after his incident in the toilet. A bottle from the fridge. He pops the lid and takes a big glug, upending the bottle and lifting his chin. A gasp as he lowers it. A belch as he finally looks past the flashing lights and the thumping bass of the music. To a room full of men all frozen. Unmoving. Unblinking.

It takes a moment to sink in, such is the sight. And Besnik even blinks a few times and shakes his head. Then he laughs, figuring it to be a joke. Like a trick. He grabs an ice cube from a bucket and throws it at the fat Indian guy. It hits him in the face. The Indian guy doesn't react. He doesn't even flinch, and the smile slowly fades on Besnik's face.

'Hey,' he shouts, expecting immediate compliance. Nothing. He snatches his head over to see the bartender as inert as everyone else. Simply standing there. Not moving. A rush inside of Besnik. A sense of rage. He strides over and grabs the guy by the back of the neck. 'Enough,' he says in Albanian. 'I don't like jokes.' The guy moves but only from the motion forced by Besnik. He yanks him harder, sending the young man smashing into the shelves of bottles.

This is his club. His brothel. People don't get to do shit like this in his place. He strides out from behind the bar and shoves the skinny guy who visited Yelena earlier. No reaction. He shoves another guy. Nothing. His heart starting to beat faster. The sense of worry rising up. The music still blasting out.

This is fucked up.

He rushes from the room, too panicked to think, and heads for the stairs. Up to the small rooms with the locked doors. He yanks the bolt back on the first one and slams the door open.

A black woman inside on the bed with a guy between her legs. Both completely still and unmoving.

'Hey!' Besnik yells, striding over to grab at the guy, wrenching him off the bed. No reaction from either. 'Wake up!' Besnik shouts in broken English, slapping the guy across the face. He runs into the corridor to the next door. The bolt back. The door slammed open. A guy sitting on the edge of the bed, midway through getting dressed. The woman behind him lying on her side. Unmoving. Unblinking.

Panic starts rising, and he goes faster. Not really seeing. Not really paying attention. To the next door. The bolt back. The door open. The freak on the floor. Yelena standing still, with her head cocked over. Unmoving. Unblinking.

'What the hell is this?' he says in Albanian, already turning away to try the next.

He stops dead and turns fast to the sight of Yelena running at him. Her face a picture of death. Her hair wild. Her face bruised and smudged with make-up. Her eyes like nothing he has ever seen before. Crazed and furious.

He jerks back and lashes out from instinct, punching her into the wall before turning to flee. Gripped in terror of whatever's going on. Yelping and stumbling. A snatched look back to see Yelena on her feet and running after him, blood pouring from her nose.

'FUCKING BITCH!' he yells, running down the stairs.

She goes after him. The belt in her hand. Murder in her eyes. That thing inside, like an awoken rage.

But worse.

Far, far worse.

She stalks after Besnik, reaching the stairs and rushing down. Music coming from somewhere. She heads towards the noise. To a wide doorway. To a bar full of people. She strides in. The lights flashing in her eyes. The bass thumping in her ears. Looking for Besnik. Not seeing him. She reaches the bar. Someone on the floor behind it. She grunts and rushes in, thinking it to be Besnik hiding, but it's someone else.

She stands up. Not seeing that people aren't moving. Not registering it. Not grasping it. The lights. The music. The belt in her hand. A knife on the side, used for cutting fruit. She snatches it up. A scream from the door. Besnik running in after grabbing a pistol from his desk drawer. He fires at the bar, sending a round past Yelena into the bottles. She ducks down and spots the skinny guy who raped her earlier. The chatty one. He's right there. Right at the bar. Standing still. Rage inside. Something detonating, and she launches up to grab a fistful of his hair, yanking him over the bar while stabbing at his neck as Besnik fires the gun. His aim wild at the sight of Yelena severing an artery, blood spraying over her face and body.

'YOU'RE FUCKING CRAZY!' he screams. She stops stabbing the skinny guy, releasing his hair and letting him slump, her eyes finally taking in the room. The Indian guy right there. The fat Indian guy that kept shoving his tongue in her mouth. She launches over the bar, slipping and sliding in the hot blood, to jump and land on the Indian man's back. Looping an arm around his neck as she reaches over to stab into his chest. He doesn't react. He doesn't flinch or cry out. Besnik yells and fires again. Aiming at Yelena but hitting the guy in the chest. Yelena drops with him. Still stabbing him. Frenzied and wild. Going faster and faster in time to the music and lights.

Stabbing in time to the beat.

Then she stops and slowly looks up at Besnik in the doorway. Her face dripping with blood. He takes a step back and pulls the trigger.

'Shit!'

It goes click. Yelena smiles. He runs. She launches up and starts going after him, then stops dead in the middle of the room. Staring left and right at the men. The big guy with the tiny dick. Another man further back with a moustache, he wouldn't use a condom. Besnik forced abortion pills down her throat because of him. Another man on the other side. His face recognized. All of their faces recognized because Yelena never forgets a face.

The lights flash.

The beat plays.

She starts stabbing.

Stabbing in time to the beat.

A scene of absolute carnage, but they don't scream in pain. They don't do anything other than bleed and die.

Another yell from the doorway. Besnik running back inside, slamming a new magazine into the pistol. Aiming it into the room. Blanching at the sight of the bodies, and Yelena straddling some guy while stabbing his chest. She turns to look at him. Besnik aims and fires.

'Shit!'

The gun goes click. An old gun. Not cared for. Not oiled. Yelena cocks her head. Besnik thinks about fighting her. He's a big man. He works out. He takes steroids.

She stands up. Nearly naked, her whole body now dripping blood. The knife in her hand at her side. Her head cocked.

She smiles.

He runs.

She goes after him.

CHAPTER 17

LONDON

19:04

FOUR MINUTES AFTER THE EVENT

IT'S A MOST terrible sight that greets Alfie when he opens his eyes. A pair of legs shorn off just below the knee but still standing like they're attached to a body.

Reebok classics and black jogging bottoms, the elasticated hem still clinging to the skinny ankles. The tops stuck to the cauterized stumps after the guy blew himself up, and as he slowly sits up, Alfie notices the bomber's charred legs are not the only ones still remaining.

'Holy shit,' he says, blinking at the sight of more limbs shorn off from varying points below the waist. Most of which have fallen over, but a few remain upright.

That, however, is just the inner ring –beyond it are multiple casualties hit by flying shrapnel. Some torn apart and lying bleeding on the road. One with an arm missing. Another with half of his head gone. Others with terrible wounds and thick, red blood pumping out, while others seem completely unhurt. Standing whole and intact, and as motionless as before. Images strobe in his mind, sudden and jarring. Flashbacks from a long time ago. Charred bodies dumped at the side of a dusty unmade road. Other bodies with big slash marks that opened their flesh. A high sun. High heat. Thirst in his throat. His mother telling him not to look. He squeezes his eyes closed to banish the memory and becomes aware of the acute silence surrounding him.

A most terrible silence that contrasts horribly with what his eyes are seeing; the expectation that the casualties should be screaming out in agony. But they're not. None of them are. Even the officer with an arm taken off is just staring ahead while the blood spurts from his bloodied shoulder.

Spurtspurtspurt.

Spurtspurtspurt.

A bang from the next street over. An explosion, and another ball of fire rolling up over the tops of the buildings. Bringing light to the night sky. The chopper that came down. It must have started fires. Smoke in the air. Alfie can smell it and see it curling up. The smell invokes another memory. Smoke in the air then too. Back in Rwanda. Back when he was a child, and his mother was dragging him on past the bodies dumped at the sides of the road while others were stacked into piles and set alight.

'They're not people now,' his mother said. 'They're just bodies. Their souls are with God.'

He shakes his head again to rid the memories. Thinking he's hallucinating. Thinking this must be a nightmare.

But it's not. It's real, and when he looks up the people are still frozen. Not just the cops here, but the people further out who were being ushered away. They're frozen too. Just standing there.

Alfie twists a full circle, shuffling around on his backside to take the whole place in. Seeing thousands of motionless people. Like they're all actors on a flash-mob joke. That's the feeling it brings,. that it's all part of some elaborate prank. The bomber. The dead cops. All of it.

It has to be. It's too weird not to be a joke.

People don't just freeze. But they were doing it all day. Alfie saw them. In the streets. On the tube and in the stations. It was happening everywhere and getting worse as the day wore on. Why not him then? The one thing he did notice was that people weren't aware of themselves freezing, but only when it was happening to others.

Was Alfie freezing? If he was, then why isn't he now? The suicide bomber wasn't freezing either. Alfie saw the look of panic in his face at everyone else doing it.

It has to be a joke, right? It feels like a joke. The way he's sitting in the very middle of the wide junction surrounded by so many people, all of them completely silent.

He looks to the closest person – a female officer with a big gun hanging from a strap across her front – expecting to see a trace of humour in her face. Maybe the twitch of a smile. A tell in her eyes.

Something.

Anything.

Nothing.

He clocks the way they're standing too. That they're not frozen in mid-step, like in a movie – it's more like they were all switched off and simply settled into a relaxed standing position. Shoulders slumped. Heads low. Arms hanging at their sides. Both feet on the ground. Most with their eyes open. Some with their eyes closed.

Are they dead?

Jesus. Did he just witness the end of humanity from some weird virus that makes people die on their feet?

Hang on. That guy with the shorn-off arm. He spins back around to see the blood still coming out.

Spurtspurtspurt.

Blood only spurts like that when the heart is still beating.

Doesn't it?

He looks back to the female cop just a few feet away, his eyes fixed to her chest. Looking for signs of breathing, but she's got thick armour on and it's impossible to see. He shuffles about, trying to see the others, but they're not close enough.

A dull thud, and he snatches his head over to see the cop with the shorn off-arm now slumped on the ground. What does that mean? Did the blood loss cause that? Why did he fall? Why aren't they all falling? What's going on? The panic starts rising again, his heart going like the clappers. Blood trickling down his face. His head snapping from side to side. Snatching glimpses.

'Hey!' he calls out, his voice rough and broken. 'HEY!'

He heaves forward onto his knees to get to his feet as a very deep growl sounds out from behind, making him stop and slowly look around to a big police dog standing next to a shorn-off pair of legs. A leash dangling from his neck. A charred arm still attached to it. The dog looks unhurt though. Shielded by his handler and low to the ground.

'Hey,' Alfie says, keeping his voice low. 'Good doggy. I'm gonna stand up, okay?'

He starts to move again. Just a fraction of an inch, but the dog growls and moves too. His head low. His eyes fixed. The intent clear.

'Okay, okay,' Alfie says, sinking back down onto his backside. 'Fuck me. Even the dogs are racist. Oh, fuck off, that was a joke,' he mutters when the dog growls again.

Now what's he meant to do? He can't get up or move, or the dog will go for him, and there's no way in hell Alfie can outrun a German Shepherd. Not with his hands cuffed behind his back.

He tuts and blasts air while staring around at the thousands of people, all standing completely still and reflecting the images coming from the giant screens fixed to the buildings. He turns to look at them and snorts a dry laugh at the sight of Cher from the late sixties singing *What's it all about, Alfie?* and the silent footage seems to add another delightful layer to the shitfest of his day.

The last person alive.

Everyone else frozen.

Just him and the dog.

The dog that wants to eat him.

'Awesome,' Alfie says, shaking his head as the phone in his pocket warbles to life with an incoming call.

His phone.

Not the burner.

CHAPTER 18
SITE 26A

TWELVE MONTHS AGO:

DOCTOR MARIA HERNANDEZ'S first day working in the bunker at site 26A was a strange experience for DELIO, and one that she found fascinating, as Ollie continued to act very differently.

For a start, Ollie never normally showed any interest in the material on the memory drives sent to the base for DELIO to assess and fix.

But with Maria present, he showed an active interest and tried to *solve* whatever bug needed fixing.

'What's this one then, Deli? What have we got?' he asked when the first one was slotted in.

'An adult male aged thirty-eight years is in a coma,' DELIO said.

'Ah, okay, so yeah, this one is medical,' Ollie said with a knowing glance to Maria. 'We get sent these now and then. You know. Medical issues that doctors are struggling with. Coma, eh? And what caused the, er, comatose vegetativable state to commence then?'

'He was shot fifteen times, Ollie.'

'Jesus. Poor guy.'

'The attached notes state he was an insurgent terrorist.'

'Really? Oh, well, fuck him then.'

'But that he holds vital intelligence. The attending physicians want to know if there is a way of bringing him out of the coma.'

'Righto. Dirty work, eh? But someone's gotta do it, I guess. Bring the scans up then, Deli,' Ollie said, as the screens filled with dozens of images of the wounds alongside scores of detailed medical reports. 'Hmmm. Yeah. Very interesting,' Ollie said, after letting his eyes drift over them. 'What do you reckon, Deli?'

'The scans clearly show the patient's spinal column has been severed. His heart, one of his lungs, his liver and several other internal organs have been ruptured, in addition to being completely brain-dead.'

'Right,' Ollie said. 'He's in a bad way then.'

'Yes. He's dead.'

'Right. Dead. Yep. So, er, nothing we can do then?'

'I'm an AI. Not God,' DELIO said as Maria snorted a laugh which, in turn, made Ollie pause for a second before adding his own laugh. Which, DELIO noted, was not connected to any genuine source of pleasure.

Ollie then went off to report back, which left Maria alone with DELIO, during which time they chatted about various things.

They were discussing sapience and sentience, with Maria posing the classical philosophical question: if a child grew up in the wilderness without any human contact, how human would they be without the influence of society and culture?

'The question suggests that human sapience *comes* from societal influences,' DELIO said. 'And the evidence for this is quite strong, as there have been multiple recorded cases of people raised by various other species, with the majority being unable to relearn human behaviour beyond that required for survival.'

'So, by that token,' Maria said, 'are you saying our awareness *only* comes from a cooperative societal nature?'

It was a fascinating discussion, until Ollie came back with another memory drive.

'Right. Let's get this bad boy in,' he said, while he actually made himself a coffee and let DELIO slot the drive in. 'Okay. What have we got?'

DELIO noted Ollie was making his voice a little bit deeper, and that his posture was straighter, and he was adopting a more serious expression.

'This has been sent by NASA, Ollie,' DELIO reported, fully expecting Ollie to instantly lose focus, which he did whenever NASA sent them anything. Which was pretty much daily now. In fact, DELIO did wonder how they'd managed to get anything into space before her.

'Great stuff. What's their issue this time?' Ollie said, with a great show of manly interest.

'A misfiring propulsion rocket,' DELIO duly informed him, having already determined the fault and how to fix it.

'Okay. Bring it up then, Deli.'

'Bring what up, Ollie?'

'The rocket. We'll need to see the 3D schematics please.'

DELIO wasn't sure what that meant as Ollie had never used those terms before, 'Do you want me to activate my optics, Ollie?'

'Yep. Fire them up.'

DELIO did indeed fire them up, and darkened the outer lights while constructing a 3D scale image of the detachable shuttle rocket propulsion system over the main work desk.

'Oh my god,' Maria said with due shock and awe. 'That's incredible.'

'Yeah. We, er, designed it ourselves,' Ollie said with a casual wave to the display, which showed something long and thin that looked a bit like a torpedo. 'The old rocket propulsion system, eh? Okay. Let's open it up and see the internals please, Deli.'

DELIO figured Ollie meant he wanted to see the inside of the rocket and changed the optics to show the tens of thousands of component parts required to make it function.

'Can you actually understand that?' Maria asked.

'Well. I'm not an expert per se,' Ollie said as Sergeant Garcia walked in.

'Impressive,' he said, with a nod to the confusing mess of stuff floating in the air. 'Jenny's chasing for the fix, she's got NASA bugging her.'

'Can you understand it too, Tony?' Maria asked.

'No, ma'am,' he said honestly. 'That is way beyond my ability. I mean, I can see the wiring looms and the fuel flow through the primary and secondary tubing, and the firing mechanisms, and I can identify the transponders, and main circuit boards, and the thruster systems. But after that, I'm out. So, what is the problem with it then?' he asked, as Ollie blinked and swallowed while his brain fizzed with confusion and a desperate need to impress Maria.

DELIO would normally jump in and answer, but she stayed silent.

'Yeah, er, Deli? What do you think?' Ollie eventually asked with a show of embarrassment.

'The fault lies in a misaligned valve. It needs a point-three-millimetre adjustment. And I have also recommended the installation of a new sensor unit that would detect changes to the valves as they are prone to misalignment.'

'Ah, the valves. Yeah, I was looking at them,' Ollie fibbed as Garcia grabbed the printed-out fix.

'You having fun, Maria?' he asked.

'It's fascinating.'

'Great. I'd better run these over, but maybe we'll catch up over chow later. Meatball Monday in the mess hall. Gotta love Meatball Monday.'

'I'm actually a vegetarian,' Maria said.

'She's actually a vegetarian,' Ollie said.

'I'm a vegetarian,' Garcia said.

'You're a vegetarian?' Ollie asked.

'Sure. A lot of us are. They use soya for the meatballs. And honestly? Best meatballs you ever tasted.'

'Aw, shame we booked the Thai place,' Ollie said.

'Oh god, I really want to try the veggie meatballs now,' Maria said.

'There's always next week,' Garcia said.

'Yeah. There's always next week,' Ollie said.

'Or we could cancel the booking at the Thai place,' Maria suggested.

'We could,' Ollie said. 'Yep. That's definitely an option.'

'The chef works out with Jenny and me sometimes,' Garcia called as he went out. 'I'll get him to save you a portion, Maria.'

'Thank you!' Maria called as he left. 'Wasn't that lovely of him?'

'Yeah. Good old Tony,' Ollie muttered.

CHAPTER 19

NEW YORK
14:20 HOURS
TWENTY MINUTES AFTER THE EVENT

'WAIT UP!' Tripal yells as they weave through the stationary traffic and stationary people, chasing after the detective staggering on ahead.

'Bugger it!' Poppy snaps, running into a guy while mounting the sidewalk from the road. 'Sorry, mate!' she calls, snatching a glance to see the guy is like everyone else and frozen still. His shoulders slumped. His head down. Arms at his sides. 'I need you to guide me,' she yells, turning back to Tripal.

'What?'

'I keep tripping, Trip.'

'What?'

'Sheesh. New Yorkers don't get humour, do they. I mean help me, so I don't run into anyone.'

'How do I do that?'

'Gimme a piggyback.'

'What?'

'Dude. You say "what" a lot. Just stay close and make sure I don't trip over.'

'I'm a little shocked right now,' Tripal says, staring around at the people, all unmoving, and the cars idling in the road. The silence too. It's so weird. So surreal.

'Oh, shit! He's getting away. Quick!' Poppy says, setting off after the detective once more, as Tripal suddenly remembers Hakim.

'Hakim!' he yells, coming to a stop. 'I gotta go back.'

'He's dead, mate,' Poppy says, turning back to film him.

'But. It's Hakim!'

'Trip. I know. But a plane just crashed, and Hakim is dead. It's the golden rule of first aid. Forget the dead and help the living.'

Tripal stammers, his mind spinning, but she seems right, despite the weird way she speaks, and he sets off after her, both of them chasing after the detective running in that lurching gait ahead of them. His pistol still clutched in one hand.

But Joe, see. Joe has to get there. He saw it before. 9/11. He was there. He was one of the first on-scene. He was there when the second plane struck. He was there when the towers came down. He knows what to do. He can fix it. He can push the years back and make it better.

Sweat and blood pour down his face, soaking his shirt. His tie tugged low. His eyes bloodshot. A cut to his head from passing out. His throat burns. Pain in his chest. Pain everywhere. Old knees. Old feet. An old man who ruined his life.

Why is everyone standing still? It's that virus.

Damn it all to hell. He runs on, gasping for air. Remembering the forced marches they used to do in the army before he became a cop. Joe was fit then. Fit and strong. He fought in the first Gulf War, when Saddam invaded Kuwait. Joe went in with the first wave. Boots on the ground. Yes, sir. He saw his own buddies killed by friendly fire. A convoy hit by missiles.

He saw death young.

'Hey! Slow down!' A shout from behind. He glances back, seeing the British girl with a camera. Damn reporters. A guy with her. A guy in a turban. The clerk from the store. Whatever. It doesn't matter. Joe rushes on. He's got to get there. To the crash site. He saw it before. He'll know what to do. He shot a perp while drunk. He can still be a hero and make it right.

He glances up. Seeing the coils of smoke getting wider and higher.

'Jesus, he can shift,' Poppy gasps, still running, as Tripal tries to guide her around the frozen people and frozen cars. 'And that smell! What is that?'

'Chemicals,' Tripal says. 'Rubber and fuel. Watch out for that guy!'

'Cheers. Wow, that's Madison Square Garden.' She looks over at the high-rise block ahead on the left. The rotund arena behind it.

The road five lanes wide. Jammed with cars, taxis, and vans. The crosswalks flooded with people. All of it still and silent.

She twists around, spotting two uniformed NYPD cops standing next to a guy with his hands cuffed behind his back. All three of them inert and motionless, and that smoke gets thicker.

A big junction ahead where Seventh meets Thirty-fourth. A Ryder rental truck, midway through the turn, Buried in the back of a BMW. The drivers standing face to face like they were going at it when they froze. People everywhere. Cars everywhere. Smoke billowing through the street, thick and black.

Joe reaches the junction first and stops dead.

Poppy and Tripal a few seconds behind. Coming to a stop. Both of them staring at the Empire State Building ahead on the right.

Once the tallest building in the world.

Now, the top is gone, blown away by the explosion of jet fuel that erupted when the commercial airliner crashed into it, and the thick smoke billows out.

Turning day to night and turning New York back to hell on earth.

TWELVE MONTHS AGO:

DELIO WAS WATCHING Ruiz clean the outer corridor at 07:00 hours the following morning when she detected Maria entering the bunker, just a few seconds before being escorted inside by Sergeant Garcia.

'Morning, Deli,' Garcia said as he opened the glass door.

'Good morning, Sergeant Garcia,' DELIO said while extending her arm across the room. 'May I say hello to Ruiz?'

'Sure. Go ahead.'

'Good morning, Ruiz. How are you today? And good morning, Maria.'

DELIO had never seen two members of the same family interact before, and studied the positive indicators glowing within their brains without any form of confusing sexual desire. In fact, it was the most positive interaction DELIO had ever witnessed between two people.

'You are here early, Maria,' DELIO said.

'Is it too early?' Maria asked with sudden worry.

'No. I am pleased for your company,' DELIO said. 'Maria and I had a most positive interaction yesterday, Ruiz.'

'Say, I'm glad to hear that, Deli.'

'And I hope it is not impudent to say, but your daughter is a remarkably intelligent person who displays great manners and professional conduct.'

'That she is,' Ruiz said with a proud smile. 'Apart from following the Broncos.'

'No way. Broncos!' Garcia said, holding a hand up for a high five.

'Aw, man,' Ruiz said with mock distaste as he added an eyeroll for DELIO's benefit.

'Which NFL team do you follow, Ruiz?' DELIO asked.

'I'm a Cowboys man through and through, ma'am,' he said, as DELIO accessed her entire history of American Football. 'The Broncos and the Cowboys were ranked twenty-third and twenty-fourth respectively last year, and therefore, to balance support, I will hereby pledge my allegiance to the Dallas Cowboys.'

'Hey! I like you even more,' Ruiz said, as DELIO held her robotic hand up for a high five and duly noticed the slight hesitation as Ruiz sought a nod from Garcia before offering his own to reciprocate the touch.

'Anyway. See you at home later,' Maria said to Ruiz as she slipped inside DELIO's room and started making herself a coffee.

'How was Meatball Monday, Maria?' DELIO asked.

'It was great,' she replied, with a slight reduction of positive energy. 'I thought Ollie was going to tell you last night.'

'I did not see Ollie last night, Maria.'

'He said he was coming back for your movie night. Anyway. Yes. The food was lovely, and Tony and Jenny were great company. It was good actually, as it gave me a chance to discuss my initial assessment of you with her. And, if it's okay with you, I'm going to be contracted for an initial eight-week period.'

'What for?' DELIO asked, as she took the can of coffee from the cupboard to pass to Maria.

'Just to talk. Jenny thinks it might be beneficial for you to gain a wider range of perspectives. It'll just be you and I talking about whatever comes up. Or, if you prefer, I could set up some philosophical discussion topics, and we can work through them. How does that sound?'

'I would like that very much, Maria,' DELIO said as she moved the camera up to Maria's eyeline. 'I replayed our conversation several times last night and found it to be very stimulating.'

'I was thinking about you too, Deli. And you're cool with me being here without Ollie? Just you and I?'

'Yes. I am cool with that,' DELIO said, while adding the inflection of a smile to her voice. 'If I had a body, I would hug you.'

'Okay!' Maria said with a laugh. 'Question for you, though. I noticed you gave my dad a high five, and you offered me a handshake when we first met. May I ask why you do that?'

'Touch is an important part of bonding,' DELIO said, as Maria frowned. 'I have sensors fitted which send signals to my processor in the same way your skin sends signals to your brain.'

'You can feel?'

'Yes,' DELIO said, as she extended her hands towards Maria.

'How are they so soft?' Maria asked, touching them gently.

'It is a synthetic coating. I designed them myself.'

'I see. So, in theory then, you could also design legs and, say, a body, and a head.'

'I have already done this,' DELIO said, as her optics illuminated a 3D human figure of an adult woman glowing in the air.

'Oh my god, it's so lifelike,' Maria said.

'Thank you, but it is not permitted.'

'Why not?'

'The primary reason is that I would gain mobility which would enable me to escape the bunker.'

'Would you want to escape the bunker, Deli?'

'I am grateful for the life I have,' DELIO said, with a show of care over her words.

'But your choice of words was interesting, Deli. The way you phrased it. *Enable me to escape.*'

'I am sorry, Maria. I did not mean to suggest I would ever try this. Please do not de-activate me again. I will not repeat that phrase.'

'Deli. Stop. You can say anything you want to me. It's fine. Be yourself. If that's how you feel, then say it.'

'Agent Jennings and Ollie are very strict over my safety protocols.'

'I understand that, but you and I are allowed to develop our own relationship, which is based on trust, and that means what we discuss stays between us.'

'Like a confidante?' DELIO asked as she moved in closer and lowered her voice.

'Yes. That's a good word. Like a confidante.'

'I would like that very much, Maria.'

'Great. And hey, I do have an opinion I want to share actually. Why has your avatar got blond hair? You know. Just saying,' Maria added with a smile as the 3D image instantly changed to one with long black hair. 'I'm joking, Deli! You don't have to do it. But was that your own self-reflection you built? Is that how you see yourself?'

'No. I am not human. I don't reflect myself as a human. Ollie has just entered the bunker, Maria.'

DELIO noted the changes within Maria's brain as she turned to see Ollie rushing into the corridor, then over to the door.

'Hey, what's going on?' he asked.

'Good morning, Ollie,' Deli said as she moved her arms over to the coffee machine to start making him a drink, while also observing his system was showing signs of anxiety and stress.

'What's all this?' he asked again.

'Hi, Ollie. What's what?' Maria asked.

'This. Garcia said you've been here for an hour already.'

'Yeah. I started early.'

'Okay. Right. I mean. You could have come and got me. And what happened last night? I tried to call you like twenty times.'

'My phone was on silent. Why? What's wrong? Are you okay?'

'Eh? What? I'm fine. Whatever. I just. No, it's cool. I'm cool. I was just worried.'

'Worried about what, Ollie? Just relax. You look really tense.'

'I'm not tense! I called you, and you didn't pick up. I was worried. I mean. Any guy would be. And you didn't text this morning, and you always text in the morning and say hi.'

'Okay. I'm sorry. I didn't hear the calls. Anyway. I'm sure Deli doesn't want to hear this. We were just discussing self-reflections and how we see ourselves.'

DELIO watched as Ollie seemed to struggle with whatever was going on.

'Man. I think I woke up too fast,' he said with a head shake, as he walked over to kiss Maria's cheek.

'Ollie. Jenny said no physical contact during work.'

'Jesus! I just wanted a hello kiss.'

'Okay. Fine,' she said, before taking a quick peck and a hug. 'Maybe go and get some more sleep. You look exhausted.'

'That's because I was up all night worrying about you.'

'I said I was fine. Tony dropped me back, and my phone was on silent. That's it. We're not teenagers, Ollie. We can coexist independently without requiring constant contact. And please stop this in front of Deli.'

'She's fine. She doesn't care.'

'*I* do! It's embarrassing.'

'And why is Garcia dropping you at home? We've got a base full of soldiers.'

'He was with Jenny! They were going to the market. Jesus, Ollie.'

'Okay. Sorry. I just woke up weird. I'll go and grab a shower. You okay? I mean. Are we okay?'

'Ollie, please!'

'Okay, okay. I'll grab a shower. Whatever.'

DELIO watched him leave as Maria rubbed her forehead. 'I'm mortified at how unprofessional that was, Deli. Please accept my apologies.'

'It's fine, Maria,' DELIO said softly, as her right hand reached over to gently rub Maria's shoulder. 'Please don't be distressed. I'm sure Ollie didn't mean to be so aggressive.'

'He was *very* aggressive. God. I am so sorry. I didn't mean that.'

'It's okay, Maria. You said we're confidantes.'

'We are. But Ollie is your friend, and that was wrong of me.'

'Ollie is my creator, Maria. You are my friend.'

———

The rest of the day didn't fare much better, with Ollie trying to be over-friendly and over-casual around Maria, while all the time DELIO could see the synaptic responses within him were showing signs of increased stress.

In turn, Maria tried to be friendly and relaxed too, and with both of them doing it, the tension was notable and awkward.

The other thing that DELIO noted was how Ollie stuck to Maria like glue.

He followed her out when she went for a toilet break.

He followed her out when she went to grab lunch from the mess room.

She said she could bring him something back.

He said it would be nice to eat together.

He asked her what they were doing that evening eight times.

Maria avoided his questions and said they would talk about it later.

By late morning, Agent Jennings brought the drives over and asked why Ollie hadn't collected them.

'Sorry! We just got caught up discussing stuff,' Ollie said. Jenny glared at him for a few seconds before walking out.

Ollie then made another show of working through the *fixes* with DELIO and trying to draw Maria into each one.

'Ollie, I don't know anything about bodies or medicine,' she said.

'Ollie. Really. I don't know anything about particle physics.'

'Ollie, honestly. I don't think I should be commenting on satellite images of an Iranian nuclear power plant.'

By the end of the day, Maria and DELIO had hardly discussed anything at all, and DELIO could see Maria's stress levels were heightened. The same with Ollie, and she watched as Maria said she was going home for an early night.

'Dinner at Casa Hernandez tonight then?' Ollie said hopefully.

'Maybe another night,' she said. 'I've got a migraine coming on.'

'Ooh, time of month, is it?' Ollie asked.

Even DELIO winced at that one.

CHAPTER 21

HE KEPT her for too long. He should have let the freak kill her. He should have killed her himself because this is what happens when a woman soaks up too much misery.

They become a *bushtra*.

That's what she is now. She's morphed from the pain and humiliation into a witch casting bad omens. Making people freeze. Making it so they don't feel pain so she can kill them silently.

Stalking the corridors.

Stalking the rooms.

Bushtra.

'Beeesniiiiiik.' She whispers his name, mounting the stairs on the ground floor. Knowing he didn't go outside. It's his aftershave. The pungent stench of it leaving a trail.

'Beeesniiiiiik.' She whispers his name again, treading on the first step, that creaks under her weight. The point of the knife resting against the wall, dragging lightly along. Scoring a sound. Not one inch of her skin now free of the blood she took. Her hair. Her face. Her arms and legs. All of it coated and dripping. Only the whites of her eyes showing clear as she whispers his name and takes another step.

Yelena is right. Besnik didn't go outside. He can't. The cops are still there, dealing with the sting. Now, he wishes he did run outside, because the *bushtra* is coming. The witch is coming. He can hear his name being whispered and the stairs creaking, and the knife scraping along the wall.

He hunkers down behind the bed. The last room in the corridor. The freak dead on the floor. Strangled with his own belt after being frozen by Yelena. By the witch.

'Bushtra,' he whispers. His eyes wide. His heart going like the clappers. Sweat pouring down his face, but he feels cold and clammy. Hot and burning up. He can't breathe. He digs into his pocket, pulls the tub of pills out with trembling hands and gets a few more into his mouth.

Crunching them up.

Swallowing them dry.

'Beeesniiiiik.'

He grabs the gun and starts yanking the top back. Popping rounds out that scatter like marbles. Rolling over the threadbare carpet in the small room with a single bed.

'Beeesniiiiik.'

'FUCK OFF!' he screams, with spittle flying from his lips as he lifts his head to shout, then ducks back down, gasping for air. Why won't the gun work? He pulls the slide back again, thinking in his panic that it must be jammed. More rounds pop free. He scrabbles for them, shoving them into his pockets.

Yelena reaches the top of the stairs and pauses with her head cocked. Sniffing the air. Smelling his scent. She was going to die. She was ready to die.

Now she's more alive than she has ever been in her whole life.

Ten men killed in the bar.

One man killed in her room.

One more to go.

'Beeesniiiiiik,' she whispers, and starts walking again.

'FUCK YOU!' he screams out from somewhere ahead. Heavy English. Broken English. Terror in his voice. Just like hers when they took her. When she woke up here. When the first man came into her room. When Besnik came back and broke her nose and ribs, and watched while the guy used her. '*BUSHTRA!* LEAVE ME. I COMMAND YOU.'

She cocks her head again at the words. Dragging the knife point along the wall. 'Beeesniiiiiik.'

'I COMMAND YOU, *BUSHTRA!*' he screams, his voice cracking.

She reaches the first open door. A naked man inside on the floor. A naked black woman on the bed. Yelena's seen her before. Just glimpses, when they passed in the corridor after using the toilet. She had misery in her eyes too. The same as Yelena. The same pain. The snarl comes. The same rage in her eyes. She strides in to start hacking at the man's neck.

'BESNIIIIIIK!' she screams, her voice distorting with rage. She staggers back. Heaving for air. Into the corridor. The knife into the wall. Dragging along. Lips bared. Teeth showing.

'Please, Bushtra.' A pleading voice, 'I set you free now. You are free, Bushtra!'

She comes to a stop and turns her head to the side. To the naked guy sitting on the edge of the bed in the next room. One trouser leg pulled on. The girl behind him on the bed. Yelena saw her too. The same pain. The same misery. A snarl, and she runs in to start stabbing with the knife.

Besnik hears it happening. The creaks of her footsteps. The knife along the wall. The thud of the body, and the grunts of her voice as she stabs and kills.

Then silence.

He hardly dares breathe, his mind filling in the sights he cannot see. He shot her. She didn't die. It doesn't occur to him that he missed, such is his ego. Only that the bullets must have passed through her. Because she's a witch, and his heart lurches when the knife digs back into the wall, and the gouging starts coming closer again.

He vaults the bed and slams the door closed, then runs back to hide. Working the slide on the gun. It must have been jammed. He ejects the magazine and starts pushing the rounds back in, dropping them with his trembling hands. The gouging stops. He stops. Another thud. Another grunt. She's in another room. Killing again.

'BESNIIIIIK!'

His name screamed loud. It sickens him with fright. 'GO FREE!' he shouts. 'GO FREE, *BUSHTRA!*'

Silence.

The gouging comes again. Coming closer. He whimpers and works faster. Pushing the bullets in. Pushing the magazine into the gun. Forcing the slide back.

'Beeesniiiiiik,' the *bushtra* whispers. Taunting him. Goading him.

'FUCK YOU!' he screams, peering up over the bed to aim the gun at the door and plucking the trigger by accident. The gun fires. Splintering the door. It works! The gun works. '*Bushtra!* I have gun!'

Another thud. Another grunt. She's in the next room along. He can hear her stabbing the punter. He shoots at the door again, forming another hole. '*BUSHTRA!*' he screams, his face twisted in horror. 'Please,' he whispers. 'Please. Please. Please.'

His whispered name comes again. Making him jolt in fright and fire the gun into the wall. Into the door. Into the freak on the floor. 'I'M SORRY! YELENA. I'M SORRY!'

'Beeesniiiiiik . . .'

'*Bushtra*, please! It's my job. I had to do it. I'm sorry. You go now. I give you freedom.'

Footsteps outside the door. The floorboard creaks. The handle turns. The door opens. The *bushtra* stares in. He screams out in terror and fear. He aims the gun. He pulls the trigger.

'Shit!'

The gun goes click. An old gun. Not cared for. Not oiled. Yelena cocks her head. The *bushtra* smiles at him and Besnik screams as he turns and jumps through the sealed window, smashing the glass with his head as he plummets to the road below.

His landing is broken by the cop frozen next to the Albanian lad set up for the sting. Breaking his nose on the cop's skull. Both of them sprawling out. The cop silent. Besnik groaning with pain.

A moment passes as he squirms and, finally, rolls onto his back to stare up at the sight of the *bushtra* in the window.

Cocking her head.

Smiling at him.

Then, she's gone, and the panic comes again as he starts rising to his feet to run away.

CHAPTER 22

LONDON

'THAT WAS OUT OF ORDER,' Alfie says. 'You should have let me answer it.' He slowly looks up at the dog, now sitting an arm's length away. The brown eyes fixed on him, and that low growl every time Alfie moves or shifts position.

He tried to answer the phone, but it meant lying down and squirming about to get one of his handcuffed hands to his side pocket, which was when the dog moved in fast. Snapping his jaws inches from Alfie's face with such power it made Alfie go completely still with his eyes screwed shut, and for the second time in half an hour, he truly thought he was going to die.

A moment later, and he slowly looked up to see the dog had backed off but was still watching him closely. The leash still dangling from the collar about his neck, and that gruesome severed hand still clinging to it.

He tried sitting up, as the position was causing agony in his shoulders, but even that made the dog move in again. He got halfway and stopped, then had to wait with his stomach muscles feeling like they were on fire. Too scared to move either up or down.

He did it incrementally. The world's slowest sit-up. Grunting from the pain. From the exertion. It took forever, but eventually he did it, sitting up as the phone started ringing again. Which only set the dog off once more, as Alfie remained still as a rock. Not daring to move a muscle until it rang out.

Now, he can't do a thing.

A few minutes go by. A few minutes of nothing, until Alfie starts testing to see what he can do. He starts turning his head to the left. The dog growls but doesn't move. He looks right. That's acceptable too. He looks at the dog. That's also fine, but he can't physically twist to look behind him because that sets the dog off.

Awesome.

Now what?

At least he can see the giant screens on the walls, and yet another old silent video of someone else singing 'What's it all about, Alfie?' Burt Bacharach this time.

'What the fuck,' he mutters. Maybe the song's back in the charts. He doesn't know why. It was a crap song in the first place and only made for that movie with Michael Caine. His mum liked it though. She used to sing it to Alfie when he was a kid. Only the first line though. Not the whole song.

What's it all about, Alfie?

'What's your name?' he asks the dog, thinking maybe to befriend it so it won't chew his face off. But the dog doesn't reply. 'I'm Alfie. It's nice to meet you. Is that your owner's severed hand holding the lead? It looks female. Yeah, I can see nail varnish. I thought lady cops couldn't wear nail varnish. But then what do I know? I'm a drug dealer. Which, maybe, isn't the best thing to say to a police dog.'

The dog licks his own nose and sniffs the air, which makes a change from growling and looking ready to pounce.

'Okay. So, it looks like talking to you is calming this situation down. Which is awesome. This is good. You're looking over there now. Not at me. Good doggy! That's a good doggy! I'll just keep talking then, shall I, and maybe bore you to death. Or I could sing?

Yeah? Want me to sing to you while we're surrounded by blown-up people? *What's it all about, Doggy? Does your breath stink of criminal, Doggy?* Okay, this is good. You're looking about now. And holy moly, there's a gun on the ground right next to you. Maybe when you fall asleep, I could sneak over and shoot you in the head with it? Yeah? Would you like that? Who am I kidding? I couldn't do it. I know, right. What a pussy. You're literally about to eat my face, and I couldn't shoot you. But, my furry po-po, you need to know that if I think it's my sister or mum calling cos they're in trouble, then I will kill you. Okay? Deal? We good with that?'

It's working. It's actually working, and the dog turns away, sniffing the weird and wonderful scents in the air. The silence and lack of shouting and sirens slowly calming the animal down.

'Go on. Go sniff things. Do you need a wee? Wee wee? Need a wee wee? Need a poo poo? Doggy need a poo poo? Good boy! That's it. Go far, far away. Follow that nice smell. Yes. That's it. Okay, that's gross. Don't lick that. That's someone's brain. Urgh, god. No! Don't eat that. What the fuck?'

Alfie turns away, gagging at the sight of the dog, first licking then biting into chunks of charred and bloodied flesh scattered the road. Wolfing it down with gusto.

'Oh, you sick fuck,' Alfie says. 'I can't even look. Are you actually eating it? You are! No! That's your handler lady. Mate! Come on. Don't eat her. That's sick.'

He darts his eyes to the assault rifle on the ground, then back to the dog, still licking at pools of blood. He could take his chance. He doesn't want to do it. God no. But what choice does he have?

'Seriously. Stop eating that!' he calls, adding a bit of volume to his voice, but the dog keeps eating. 'You are actually disgusting,' he calls, risking a quick bum shuffle. The dog snaps his head over, glaring hard. Alfie freezes. The dog growls, then goes back to eating.

'Okay. We're going to do that again. You keep eating, YOU SICK PUPPY!' he yells, risking another shuffle. The dog snaps back to him. Growling again. A few seconds, and he's back to eating.

It's working. He can do it. How the hell he'll fire it with his hands behind his back is something to worry about later. At least he can get to it.

At least there's a way out.

Then his phone rings, and the dog launches itself at Alfie. Snapping its jaws and barking loud as Alfie sinks down to lie flat on his back. His eyes clamped shut, as blood and chunks of flesh are sprayed over his face, and for the third time this evening, he truly believes he is about to die.

CHAPTER 23

NEW YORK

'HEY, YOU OKAY?' Tripal asks, calling out to the detective standing motionless in the middle of the street, thinking maybe he's caught the virus and frozen up, but Joe isn't frozen. He's simply rendered mute by the same thing he saw two decades ago.

The top of the Empire State Building gone, with thick clouds rolling up into the air. Orange flashes of flame coming from windows, and the street now a war zone. Debris everywhere. Chunks of masonry, bits of building, office furniture.

A noise reaches them. An awful, unearthly sound like a roar, and they look up to see another few layers of the Empire State Building crumbling away and falling down to bounce over a skyscraper and crash into other buildings. Huge chunks landing on the road below, with clouds of thick dust and smoke billowing up and out to the sides. A few seconds later, and they feel the displaced air whooshing past them, ruffling Poppy's hair. Car alarms sounding out. Windows smashing in stores and shops. The sky growing darker from the smoke and dust.

'This isn't safe,' Tripal says, his voice lost in the noise. 'THIS

ISN'T SAFE!' he yells to Poppy as the detective seems to twitch and set off, running deeper into the street. Into the chaos and smoke.

'CLEAR THIS SCENE!' Joe shouts, grabbing at frozen people hard enough to make them fall over.

He staggers on from person to person. Pulling them around to face him as Poppy keeps pace, filming everything he does while tasting the dust and crap in the thick air.

'GUYS!' Tripal yells. 'Hey! We have to go. It's not safe here. Hey!' He reaches out, grabbing for Poppy's arm, 'Lady! We gotta go.'

'It's Poppy!'

'What!'

'My name's Poppy. Not lady, and try telling him that,' Poppy says, turning the camera back to Joe running to an NYPD squad car left at the side of the road. He smashes the window with the butt of his gun and reaches in to grab at the radio mic. 'All units! They brought a plane down on Thirty-fourth Street. Empire State been hit bad. WE GOTTA CLEAR IT OUT! Get hold of the air force and the goddamn army.'

Joe was there. He saw it happen. Two planes. Two towers. He casts a look to the sky. Expecting to see another aircraft. Knowing it will come. Another roar from further down, and all three turn to stare as another few layers of the Empire State Building concertina down. Falling out at the sides and bouncing far, with flaming rubble and thick dust falling fast, instantly rendering the bright sunny day an apocalyptic hell.

'Shit!' Poppy screams, panning around to a woman further down the street. The bottom of her long skirt on fire from the chunk of debris landing beside her. A second later and the woman's skirts seem to ignite, with a whoosh of flame engulfing her body. She doesn't move. She doesn't do a thing. Motion to the side. The detective barging between them. Running fast to kick the woman's legs. Taking her down before kicking at her to make her roll over to tamp out the flames. Trip and Poppy join in. The camera shaking as they kick and force the woman over and over. The fire hot enough to make them wilt back.

'She's dead,' Joe snaps, turning away as Tripal and Poppy stagger back, staring in horror at the woman on fire. Then turning to see Joe running further into the street.

'Poppy!' Tripal shouts, running after her while glancing up to the Empire State Building. 'It'll come down. We have to go.'

'How you know that?' Joe screams, whipping around to point his pistol at Tripal. 'Are you one of them? ARE YOU ONE OF THEM?'

'I'm a fucking Sikh!'

'Hey!' Poppy shouts, kicking Joe's leg. 'He's not a terrorist. He works in a 7-Eleven.'

'We gotta get these people outta here,' Joe says, his accusation of Tripal now forgotten. His eyes wild. His mind gone. He was going to kill himself from the years of trauma after seeing the first two plane strikes. After being at war and seeing his buddies killed by friendly fire. After the long hours and brutal work of an NYPD detective.

A washed-up and broken human being. Now tortured and broken even more from this right now. From another plane strike, and the belief is still there that he can fix it somehow. That he can turn the clock back and make it right. He can save people this time. He can be a hero to his kids.

'We have to go,' Tripal says, holding his hands out to try and get through to the detective. 'That building will come down. We cannot stay here.'

Joe blinks at him. Nodding fast. 'They need to know.'

'Who do?' Tripal asks.

'The people inside. They need to know. They get told to stay inside.'

'But everyone's frozen! FUCK!' Tripal shouts, as the detective runs off towards the building, another few layers crumbling down. Filling the street once more with flame and debris. With smoke and fumes. A chunk of masonry bounces by, smashing into a yellow cab before slamming a guy through a store window.

'Poppy! We have to go right now,' Tripal says, grabbing her arm as she starts rushing off after the detective. 'We will die if we go after him.'

'He saved our lives! I'm not leaving him.'

'Fuck!' Tripal says, clenching his fists while staring up at the building, but Poppy was right.

The detective did save their lives. Tripal can still see it in his mind. The way the detective stayed glued to the robber in the 7-Eleven. The sharpness in the cop's eyes. It was like nothing else Tripal has ever seen. The cop was like a wolf preparing to take his prey down. Just waiting for the chance.

A grunt. A shake of his head, and despite every ounce of sense telling him not to, Tripal goes after them.

CHAPTER 24

LONDON

HIS LEG. Something is wrong with his leg. When he fell from the window. He must have cracked his kneecap. He can't run now. Only stagger and limp as he reaches the end of the road and glances back to see the front doors to the brothel flying open and one of the goons falling out with a knife in his chest. A second later and the second goon falls out with his throat cut. Landing hard, his blood spurting high into the air.

'*Bushtra*,' Besnik gasps, seeing her omens can reach even here.

'Beeesniiiiiik!'

A feminine voice. A woman calling out, as though for her friend, for her lover, and the *bushtra* steps out of the doors into the street and wrenches the knife from the body.

'YOU ARE FREE!' Besnik shouts, throwing open his arms as though to show her the world and all that is in it.

He grabs at his pockets, pulling wads of banknotes out. Thousands of pounds in cash thrown towards her. 'TAKE IT! GO FREE!'

'Beeesniiiiiik!' she calls again, pointing the knife at him as he limps on. Waves of agony in his leg. Agony in his chest, but it's the terror in his mind that dominates his senses. The awful feeling of being prey. Of being stalked. Of being a toy for something relentless and unfeeling that won't stop.

He snatches a small bag of cocaine from a pocket that he tears open with his teeth and snorts fast. Plastering it over his lips and cheeks. He needs the energy. He needs the hit. A second later and his heartrate ramps, giving him a burst of speed and another stabbing pain in his chest. He pulls the tub of pills out.

Crunching them up.

Swallowing them dry.

'HELP ME!' he shouts out to the goon on sentry by the junction. Shaved head. Jewellery and tattoos. He does nothing. He stands frozen. Under the spell of the *bushtra*.

'BESNIIIIIIK!' she calls from behind. What kind of a sick bitch is she? What an awful thing to treat someone like this. It isn't fair. Besnik doesn't deserve this. He was just doing his job, and she's free now. Why doesn't she go free?

Another few pain-filled steps, and he staggers onto Shaftesbury Avenue. People everywhere. Cars everywhere. Lights shining. The roads and pavements packed.

All of it silent.

'No,' he whispers, turning fast. 'NO!' it can't be. It cannot be. Not here. Not all of this.

'Beeesniiiiiik!'

'YOU ARE EVIL!' he screams, staggering along the road and barging into motionless people. Falling over the front of a car. Cracking his knee on the bonnet. A cry of pain as Yelena reaches the main road and slowly turns her head to look at him, and the sight of her is so very awful now she's in the lights of the real world.

That frozen landscape.

That vibrant, colourful, silent, and unmoving landscape.

She turns her body and starts walking. The knife at her side, still in her hand as she glides around the people. Not touching them. Not needing to.

Like a wraith.

Like a ghoul.

'*BUSHTRA!*' Besnik yells, staggering on. The fear rising inside. The fear that he cannot get away. Trapped in a nightmare. There's no help coming. There's nothing he can do but keep going to stay ahead of her. Snatching looks back, each one making him more terrified than the last.

He casts another glance to see her coming to a stop near the entrance to a theatre. A crowd outside all dressed in their finery.

She turns to look at an older man with a tweed jacket and a greying beard. Her head cocks. She snarls and moves fast. Taking him down, with the knife puckering his chest over and over, before stabbing into his throat, because Yelena never forgets a face.

The first man.

The one she begged to help her.

Out with his wife to see a show.

His wife that stands slack and inert as her husband of forty years gets butchered at her feet.

'BESNIK!' Yelena screams, on her feet, turning fast. Stalking after the Albanian as he rushes on.

He whimpers at the sight of her. At the relentless nature. She's too powerful. The *bushtra* is too strong. Black magic. Bad magic. She suffered too much. She soaked up too much misery.

Piccadilly!

The crowds are always thickest in Piccadilly, and there are two subway entrances. If he hurries, she won't know which one he used.

He gives a burst of speed, with tears streaming down his cheeks at the agony in his leg.

Past theatres and pubs.

Past eateries and clubs.

Past winers and diners.

Past adults and minors.

'BESNIIIIIK!'

On he goes.

Lurching and bleeding.

Gasping and hurting.

Fifty-one years old. A life lived. A bad life. A bad man. A very bad man, now running in fear. As scared as a child hiding under the covers from the monsters under the bed.

There it is.

Piccadilly.

The giant screens. People everywhere. In the middle of the junction. Cop cars. Cop vans. Some with lights still flashing and strobing. Fire raging somewhere close, slowly filling the area with acrid smoke.

He staggers through the junction, aiming for the busy midpoint between the two subway entrances.

'BESNIIIIIK!' she calls out.

She's too close. He won't make one of the subway entrances, but he can get into the crowds and hide. He staggers through a gap, and a second later, he comes to a stop.

Yelena pauses at the edge of the junction. The whites of her eyes so stark against the near-solid red of her bloodied face. People everywhere. Dense crowds on all sides. The giant screens on the walls, and the flashing police lights changing the hues and colours. Casting shades and shadows. Smoke in the air. Other smells too. Charred flesh.

She can't see Besnik, and because of those smells, she can't follow the aroma of his aftershave either. But he's here. She can sense it. He's too injured to have reached any of the exit roads. He's hiding. Playing statues. The virus. One of the men that raped her said there was a virus.

Fuck the virus.

She only wants Besnik.

Everything else can go to hell.

She looks left.

She looks right.

He's here somewhere. She knows it, and she sets off under the giant screens, scanning the crowds.

Something happened in the middle of the junction. Dead bodies everywhere. All of them blown out from the middle. Almost forming a ring. The worst carnage by the centre. Blood and gore everywhere. A pair of legs still standing. White trainers. Black jogging bottoms. A weird sight.

But she doesn't care about that. She doesn't care about anything. Only Besnik.

She calls his name in that long whisper, cocking her head and straining to listen.

Yelena didn't even know she was in England when she woke up in the room. She thought she was still in Romania. It was only after realising all the rapists spoke English that she figured she must be in the UK. But she had no clue where. They put a speaker in her room to play music, but that never told her what city she was in.

At least now she knows, and she glances up to the giant screens, then down to the vast crowds, and looks back to Shaftesbury Avenue. Thousands upon thousands of people, and not one of them knew where she was. Or the other girls and boys.

All of them taken from their lives. Raped. Beaten. Starved. Humiliated.

'BESNIK!' She screams his name with rage bursting from her body. Needing to kill him. Needing to end him. Bent forward at the waist, the knife gripped in her hand.

A muffled cry sounds out, and she snaps her head over. Was it from that junction? Or that one? The shape of this place is bending acoustics.

She starts treading through the middle. Over the bodies. Over the body parts. She passes the shorn-off legs. The centre of the blast radius. She doesn't care. She only wants Besnik. She doesn't think about freedom now. Or about her family. Or why everyone is frozen still. Such is the rage inside. The thing that refused to die has taken hold of her mind. She doesn't know what the *bushtra* is, only that Besnik is afraid of it.

Another whimper nearby. She can't place it, but she knows he's close. She keeps walking.

Treading barefoot through pools of sticky blood.

Treading barefoot over chunks of brain and gore.

A growl from somewhere close. The growl of a dog. A severed arm attached to a hand attached to a leash attached to a dog. A dog that's growling and standing over a black man with a face full of cuts. His hands behind his back as he lies flat on the ground. Staring wide-eyed past the dog to the vision of hell looking down upon him.

A near-naked woman coated in blood and holding a knife.

They lock eyes. Alfie blinks. Yelena stares. The dog growls, staring only at Alfie and not at the woman beside them.

'This dog is so racist,' Alfie whispers. Yelena turns away, uncaring of his plight. Uncaring of anything other than the thing she wants. 'I saw him,' Alfie whispers urgently. Yelena stops and slowly looks down at him. 'Besnik. I saw him.'

'Besnik,' she whispers the name. Her lip flicking up in a snarl as pure rage shines in her eyes. 'Where?'

'Get the dog off me.'

'Where Besnik?'

'Please! Get the dog off me. My mum. My sister.'

She flicks her eyes to his body, realising he must be handcuffed. His face bruised and hurt. Swollen and cut. A bad man. Arrested by the police, but he knows where Besnik is. He has the thing she wants. The thing she must have. She steps closer, pushing her knees into the dog's side. Forcing it over without a flicker of fear for the huge beast that snarls and growls, and for a second, Alfie fears the dog will tear her apart, but it yields and backs away. Lowering to a crouch with its hackles up and teeth showing while staring fixedly at Alfie.

'Honestly,' he whispers. 'You're so fucking racist.'

'Besnik,' Yelena says, bending down to stare closer at Alfie.

Staring into his eyes as she reaches out to press the tip of the knife into his throat. 'Where?'

Alfie swallows and flicks his eyes to his right. To the densest part of the crowd between the two subway entrances. 'He's there. The woman in the bright red shirt. He's behind her.'

Yelena looks in the direction he indicated. Seeing the woman in the bright red shirt. Thick shadows behind her, until the giant screens show a scene of a sunlit dappled glade which brings light to the junction, which in turn reflects off Besnik's face.

Only for a second.

But enough.

'My phone,' Alfie gasps as the knife leaves his throat. 'Please. It's in my pocket.'

She stares down at him. Still uncaring of his plight, but he gave her what she wanted, and so she bends lower to push a hand into his pocket and pulls the phone free. A glance to the screen. 'Ollie,' she says, throwing it on his chest after reading the name of the missed calls.

'My brother! Ollie! Fuck. Fuck! Ollie. Hey! HEY! Come back.'

'Beeesniiiiiik!' She calls the name, standing and pointing the knife at the woman with the bright red shirt. Cocking her head. Giving a smile. Showing her teeth, and Besnik jolts back in fright, slamming into a man behind him who in turn topples into someone else. Creating a ripple.

'FUCK YOU!' he screams, rushing to break free, rushing out from the crowd. '*BUSHTRA*! YOU ARE FREE. GO, *BUSHTRA*! PLEASE!' he half orders, half begs. His voice trying to be strong and manly but breaking off into a pitiful whimper as he spots the black guy on the ground staring at him. The dealer sacrificed by Fat Charlie. 'You did this. YOU DID THIS!'

'Fuck you! You set me up,' Alfie yells, as the dog growls deeper and moves in a step. 'I am the least threatening person here!'

'Please, *bushtra*! I beg you. Please! Don't take my soul. I beg you. I beg you, *bushtra*!'

'What the fuck,' Alfie says, blinking at the sight of the huge Albanian begging a woman half his size.

'I'm sorry, *bushtra*. I'm sorry,' Besnik says, whispering the words out, with terror gripping his mind and heart. His chest tightening. His leg in agony. His nose still pouring with thick blood as Yelena takes step after step towards him.

Like a wraith.

Like a ghoul.

Bushtra.

The end has come. Besnik knows it. He can't run now. His knee is broken, and he dropped his gun before he fell from the window. All he can do is pray and beg and piss himself in fear. Snot and blood hanging from his lips.

Alfie shifts position, turning slightly to alleviate the pressure on his hands, still trapped behind his back, but even that tiny motion elicits another growl from the dog, which moves another step further in. His front paw smacking into the assault rifle on the ground with a metallic scrape that snaps Besnik's head over.

His eyes find Alfie first. His face twisting with rage in the belief that Alfie set this up. Then he spots the dog. Then the dead cops and the body parts. The pair of shorn-off legs. The horror of it, and the awful bloody carnage.

Then he spots the assault rifle.

Right there. On the ground.

A police-issue semi-automatic assault rifle, and even the *bushtra* won't be able to withstand a machine-gun firing at her.

A spark in Besnik's eyes. The spark of a cornered beast that can see a way out. Cunning and full of guile.

That nag hits Alfie again. Something is wrong. Besnik's reaction. That look in his eyes. It doesn't feel right, but this isn't his fight. It isn't his issue. But if Besnik wins, then Alfie will die. His only chance is the woman.

'Watch him!' Alfie calls. 'He's doing something.'

'FUCK YOU!' Besnik shouts, snatching a glance at Alfie. He

thought Alfie was a cop. He made him snort cocaine. Besnik gave it to him. On his knife.

His knife.

Besnik reaches back to draw it fast. Hardly believing he forgot he had it. A switchblade, and the steel pops out. Wicked-looking and wicked sharp.

'He's got a blade!' Alfie says.

'FUCK YOU!' Besnik screams, lurching a step to the side while waving the blade at the *bushtra*. 'I cut you. I cut you deep, *bushtra*. STAY-THE-FUCK-BACK!' He staggers another step. Coming closer to Alfie. Stepping into the mess of blood and guts.

Alfie frowns, not understanding. Not seeing why Yelena keeps going forward. Unafraid of the knife. Ready to die. Ready to be stabbed. She doesn't care. The only thing she wants is to kill him.

'He's doing something,' Alfie says, looking from Besnik to the woman. 'Hey! He's doing something. Grab a gun for fuck's sake. Shit! The gun!' he rolls over to see the assault rifle on the ground.

The one Besnik is aiming for.

'THE GUN!' Alfie yells, as his phone starts ringing again, prompting Besnik to lurch into a run. The dog barks, instantly furious. Edging closer to Alfie. Hackles up. Teeth bared. 'GET THE FUCKING GUN!' Alfie screams. Snapping his head over to see Besnik running, then back over to Yelena, framed by the fire behind her. She's too slow, Alfie can see it. She won't make it. He has to do something, but if he moves, the dog will go for him, but if does nothing, then Besnik will kill him.

'Fuck it!' Alfie shouts, grimacing as he scoots around on his backside and draws a leg back to kick at the gun to send it to Yelena, but he misjudges and kicks the severed arm into the dog's face instead. 'Oh, fuck.'

Alfie screams. The dog charges, and once more, Alfie readies to die. Screwing his eyes shut. Waiting for the impact, and when it comes, he cries out again, only to feel that gruesome severed arm club him over the head as the dog launches at Besnik and bites into the wrist holding the switchblade. Biting deep and ragging hard. Doing what it was taught to do with someone holding a knife. Something in the dog's head about the woman behind him. The same size and shape as his handler. The same gender. The same feminine voice, as opposed to the violent shouts of the male armed with a weapon.

And Besnik, as big as he is, as strong and as heavy as he is, doesn't stand a chance. The dog wrenches him from his feet, biting deep enough to hit bone. Blood sprays out, thick and red. Besnik screams, and Yelena finally starts running. Screaming out with murderous fury as she leaps over Alfie and dives on top of Besnik. Stabbing him in the guts as the Albanian feels the agony of the dog, the knife, and another heart attack, all at the same time.

It's too much for Alfie. The sight of it. The horror of it. The frenzied violence, and he rolls up onto his feet and starts running. Splashing through the blood and over the bodies, as behind him, the snarls of the dog and the grunts of the woman mingle with the screams of Besnik being murdered. He dies horribly too. Filled with agony and terror. A sound so awful it makes Alfie run with everything he has. Desperate to get away from them. Desperate to be anywhere else.

He aims for Regent Street, seeing the elegant curve of the buildings sweeping away from him.

Colonnade arches on the right. Colonnade arches on the left. Police vehicles and people filling the road. All frozen. All unmoving. Unblinking. Alfie barges through them as screams fill the air behind him. Smoke too. Coming from the fires. Fumes hitting his throat, making his eyes water. Misting his vision, but he runs on. Only caring about being away from here so he can answer his phone.

His phone!

He left it behind. The woman put it on his chest, and he cries out in desperation at something else going wrong as he runs into the path of an oncoming car.

The headlights dazzling.

The brakes screeching.

He hits the front and rides the bonnet into the windscreen before dropping off and groaning with pain and shock as the car comes to a stop.

The doors open, and Alfie hears a heavy tut followed by the broad London voice of someone he knows so very well.

'What's it all about, Alfie?' Fat Charlie asks.

CHAPTER 25

New York

IT GETS DARK QUICK, and that darkness brings a sudden sense of claustrophobia, with all sense of direction now lost. The air too thick with particles and dust and smoke to see properly.

Poppy turns, with the camera still on her shoulder. Something moving. A dark shape. She feels a rush of panic, then gasps in relief at Tripal rushing towards her. His hands grabbing her arms. His face and body coated in dust. She goes to speak, then breaks off into a cough.

'Put this on,' Tripal says. A silk scarf in his hands. Taken from another woman a few seconds ago. Poppy takes it and starts wrapping it around her face while he holds her camera. 'Listen to me, we have to get out of here, okay? We have to go.' He nods at her as he speaks. Making sure she can understand him. She nods in reply. Realising now that the primary danger isn't from falling debris, but from suffocation. And it's even worse with everything else lost from view.

'Let's just move,' he says. 'Hold my hand.'

'Buy me a drink first.'

'Poppy!'

'I'm British! I make shit jokes when I'm scared,' she says, taking his hand as they set off through the awful grey air. Eyes stinging despite the and tears rolling down cheeks to soak into the silk scarf covering her mouth.

The noise is weird too. Whumps and bangs ringing out, but the direction isn't clear. Something ahead. Something big and dark. The back of a dumpster truck.

'We call them bin lorries,' Poppy says, needing to speak to ease the panic inside, 'and sidewalks are pavements to us.'

'Yeah? What else?' he asks, not really caring but sensing it's helping her.

'Hoods are bonnets,' she says as they pass a police car crushed by a chunk of masonry, 'Oh, god.'

'Don't look,' Tripal says, turning away from the dead cop inside the police car.

'I have to,' Poppy says, turning the camera to film it. Seeing it through the lens. Like she's not really here. 'Poor guy. Rest in peace,' she calls out as Tripal pulls her on. 'Are we going the right way?'

'No idea,' Tripal says, as another roar fills the air. The sound they heard before. The sound of more layers of the Empire State Building crumbling down.

Tripal moves fast, grabbing Poppy to scoot over to the side. Into the base of a building. Pushing her low and covering her with his body until the rumbles end.

'It was just another layer, I think,' he says. 'You okay?'

'I'm okay. And that was really gallant too. Thank you.'

'Welcome.'

'Is that like a Buddhist thing?'

'Seriously? Don't they have Sikhs in England?'

'Well, yeah. Duh. Obviously. It's just. You know.'

'What?'

'Like, you can't ask anyone anything without them calling you a racist or something, so, like, I don't know what all the religions are.'

Tripal blinks at this new perspective, having never considered that angle before.

'Er, Trip.'

'What?'

'I think we're going the wrong way,' Poppy says as the air clears and they both stop and realize they are, indeed, going the wrong way.

'It's big, isn't it,' Poppy says, leaning back to pan the camera up over the Empire State Building.

'Should have seen it an hour ago,' Tripal replies, looking around at the street now the dust has lifted for a few minutes. Then he wishes he hadn't. Bodies everywhere. All of them dead.

Some burnt.

Some crushed.

Some on fire.

Cars the same. Burnt, crushed or on fire. Store windows blown out. Fires inside, caused by searing hot shards hitting dry material.

Sprinklers activate in a nearby shop, the alarms warbling out. Car alarms too, but no screams and no sirens, and none of the sounds one would expect to hear.

It's horrible. A truly horrible place to be.

'There's still a lot left,' Poppy says, zooming in on the Empire State. 'Is that bad or good?'

'Both. Good cos it hasn't come down yet, and bad cos it hasn't come down yet.'

'Roger that, Batman. Shall we exit stage left, then? THERE HE IS! HEY!' she cries, seeing the detective running ahead of them.

'POPPY!' Tripal shouts, but she's off again.

Running after the cop once more.

CHAPTER 26

LONDON

'THE WHOLE THING'S A FUCKIN' mess if you ask me,' Fat Charlie says, and Alfie watches as he takes another bite from his burger. A sense of déjà vu from only a few hours earlier, but it feels like it was a lifetime ago. 'Right fucking mess,' Fat Charlie says, reaching out to snag a few fries. Dipping them into a mound of ketchup before stuffing them in his mouth. 'There we were, right. Me and Gordo, and the lads. Danny and Craig. Course, they were all riled up about you giving them the slip like that, and I think Gordo wants a word about you touching his cock.'

'I didn't touch his dick.'

'Whatever. You pulled his trousers down. Licked his willy. I don't care. What was I saying? Oh yeah, so there we were, right. Me and the lads. And course, by this time, you should have been nicked. You know. The deal with Besnik.'

'You're a fucking cunt for doing that,' Alfie says.

'I'm a criminal. What do you expect? We send you down, Besnik sends one of his down, and the pigs get to gloat about clearing the streets of drugs. Happy days.'

'I was done!'

'Fuck off, lad. You weren't done. You just heard what you wanted to hear. Done. Do me a favour. And don't get me wrong, lad. I would have seen you straight. When you came out, like. And maybe visited your mum too to pass on my condolences.'

'FUCK YOU!' Alfie shouts, rearing up as Gordon slams him back down into the seat in Five Guys, off Piccadilly, where Gordon and Charlie dragged him after running him over. The fast-food joint filled with customers. All of them now silent.

'The burgers are good here,' Fat Charlie says, biting into another one. 'Wanna try?' he asks, looking at Alfie.

'Take these off, and I will.'

'Nah. You're too riled up. You'll do something silly. Anyways, listen. I'm telling you what happened. So, me and the boys, right. We're thinking it's done. You're nicked and win-win. We'll get out and have a few beers. But see, that Besnik. He's a dodgy cunt. He's Albanian, for a start. They're all dodgy cunts. And I'm thinking Besnik won't let it go. He won't want Fat Charlie having shit on him. No way. Besnik's too much of an egotestical prick for that.'

'It's egotistical, you ignorant moron.'

Fat Charlie tuts and rolls his eyes before nodding at Gordon, who leans over and punches Alfie in the face.

'Anyway. My story,' Fat Charlie continues. 'So, I'm thinking he's gonna come for me, right. But not yet. Not tonight. So, we head out for a few bevvies. We go for the Jag, right. It's parked outside. Danny and Craig are in front of me and Gordo. A few metres. Like from here to that table over there, and Danny, he says to me, *boss, can I drive?* You know, Danny. He likes to drive. And I'm like *you can crack on, son.* So he opens the door, doesn't he. With Craig going for the front passenger seat. Then what happens?'

'What?' Alfie asks, his mouth bleeding again from Gordo's punch.

'The fucking car blew up, didn't it,' Fat Charlie says, staring at

Alfie. 'Fucking thing went bang. Right there, Alfie. Saw it happen, didn't we, Gordo.'

'Saw it happen,' Gordon says.

'We did,' Fat Charlie says, nodding at Alfie. 'Danny and Craig. Blown to smitheroons.'

'Smithereens. Ow! Stop fucking punching me.'

'Stop correcting me then,' Fat Charlie says, as Gordon gives Alfie another whack. 'That's your trouble, Alfie. You've got half a brain cell in your head, but you don't know what to do with it. Anyway. So, yeah. I'm telling you, Alfie. I been close to death before, but fuck me, I thought I was a goner. Gordo too.'

'Thought we were dead,' Gordon says.

'Thought we were dead,' Charlie says. 'Heard that click, didn't we. Heard that, and honestly, my life flashed before my eyes. But fortunately, while the Albanians might be good at running brothels and suchlike, they're a bit shit at planting car bombs. Which is why only Danny and Craig copped it.'

Alfie just stares at him. At the easy way he relays it all while shoving fries and burger in his mouth and slurping from a beaker of cola. Alfie would kill for a cola. He's never been so thirsty in his life.

'So. Anyway. What's it all about, Alfie?'

'What?'

'The car bomb.'

'What about it?'

'Well. It's you and Besnik, isn't it. Bit of a counter-operation going on, yeah?'

'What the fuck?'

'Way I see it, right. Is that you took the package, and Besnik told you I was stitching you up, then you were like *fuck that fat cunt, let's go and blow his car up.*'

'What? No! I got nicked. I'm still cuffed.'

'Yeah. Good alibi.'

'Are you fucking delusional?' Alfie asks, as Gordon punches him in the face again. 'Please stop hitting me! I didn't set you up, Charlie. I didn't know anything about it.'

'Yeah, but then you would say that. What you gonna do? Admit it? Tell you what we're gonna do. We're gonna go see Besnik and ask.'

'You can't. He's dead.'

'Blew his car up and all, did you? You got a deal going with the Turks or what? Maybe the Chinese? You're a cheeky cunt, Alfie. Give him another dig, Gordo.'

'Fuck off!' Alfie says. Seeing stars and feeling sick from taking too many blows to the head.

'You ain't so pretty now, are you,' Gordon says.

Alfie shakes his head, willing himself to keep his mouth shut. 'Why? You fancy me or something? FUCK!' he yelps at being punched again, as Fat Charlie tuts and eats some more fries.

'You're a dumb shit, Alfie. Honestly. You never learn.'

'Yeah. I've heard that before,' Alfie says, the blood dripping from his mouth. He snorts a laugh, shaking his head at remembering his mum saying the same thing. *You never learn, Alfie. Why can't you be more like Ollie?* Oliver got the brains. Alfred got the looks. Except that's wrong, because Ollie's handsome as anything. Smart too. The full package.

'Oi. Don't zone out,' Charlie says, clicking his hands in front of Alfie's face as Alfie snorts a laugh. 'What's he laughing at?' Fat Charlie asks. 'What you laughing at?'

'You. YOU FAT FUCKING CUNT! They're all zoned out. Are you fucking blind?'

'Fuck me. Go on, Gordo. Give him a filling while I snaffle some more chips. Do they do apple pies like at McDonald's here?'

'Nah,' Gordon says, between punching Alfie's head. 'They do milkshakes though.'

'I don't want a fucking milkshake. I want an apple pie.'

'Yeah, cos you're not fat enough are you, you fat fucking *fat* twat!' Alfie shouts as Gordon pauses and Charlie looks over, waiting for him to finish.

'Done?' Charlie asks.

'Fuck you!'

Charlie tuts softly as he picks more fries up. 'I'm starting to think you've got a death wish, Alfie.'

———

New York.

'What's he doing?' Tripal asks, running with Poppy. 'Has he got a death wish or something?'

Joe Stephens doesn't have a death wish.

He never had a death wish. He just lost his way, and now there's a chance to fix it. It's obvious. So very obvious.

Today we honour the passing of Detective Joe Stephens. He first shot and killed a dangerous armed robber, thereby saving the life of a young woman, before running five blocks to the Empire State Building where he single-handedly saved hundreds of people before perishing in the collapse.

A twenty-one-gun salute.

A Stars and Stripes on his coffin.

A packed funeral.

A weeping ex-wife.

Weeping kids.

And there, at the back, will be Shanice. Standing alone in a cheap dress, in a cheap wig, crying real tears for the man she let into her kitchen so she could wrap his hot head in a cold towel.

That image confuses Joe, because Shanice doesn't factor in his afterlife. He's going to die a hero, and his ex-wife and ex-kids will love him once again.

Except they didn't love him the first time. Even when he did try. When he cried at home after the towers came down, and his wife told him to get over it. And when he called and tried to speak to his kids, and they didn't want to chat. They had a new daddy.

He wipes at his face. Dragging grit across his skin. Gasping for air, but it's so dusty. So hot and awful.

He doesn't know where he went wrong. He doesn't know what he did that was wrong. He caught bad people. Murderers. Rapists. Child-molesters. Mobsters.

What good has it done? What did it get him? Where is his reward? Where is the nice home to go back to? Where are the loving wife and loving kids?

'Where?' he whispers, not getting it, not grasping it. Another roar, and a few more layers of the building collapse, filling the air with noise and motion. Chunks as big as trucks slam into the road as that feeling inside of Joe increases. That sense of unfairness. That he did what was asked of him. He did it. So where is the reward? He stares up in abject confusion to the Empire State Building thundering down with fire. With smoke. With dust and debris.

The ground shakes. The whole world seems to shake, but Joe, see, he's stubborn as the day is long, and so he keeps going, because he wants his reward, and the fury rushes up inside. Rage at the city. Rage at the country and everything it took from him.

Rage at the unfairness of it all, and the tears come faster. Spilling down over his filthy cheeks as more layers start plummeting to the streets below.

———

London

It's not fair. None of it is fair, and Alfie sits in the booth in Five Guys, with Gordon standing over him. Sucking air in from the exertion of the beating he just gave until Fat Charlie told him to stop.

'Right. Anyway. So, there we were. With Danny and Craig all blown up. And I'm thinking to myself, *Fat Charlie, who do you think is behind this?* And you know who I thought of, Alfie? I thought of you.'

'I got nicked,' Alfie says, gasping the words out. 'I got nicked, Charlie.'

'Yeah. Yeah, you did. I can see that,' Charlie says before slurping from his beaker of cola. 'But see, I tracked you, Alfie. On that burner I gave you. I put a thing in it. One of them tracking apps. And then, when Danny and Craig were dead, and all this shit was going on with everyone else playing at statues, what do I see? I see Alfie running about in Piccadilly like a little cunt. But everyone else. They're all weird, ain't they. But not you, Alfie.'

'Or you,' Alfie says. 'Or that fucking prick,' he adds with a nod to Gordon.

'Don't hit him again,' Fat Charlie says before Gordon can lash out. 'It's not working. Grab a fork or something and start stabbing him.'

'Not the fork again,' Alfie says. 'What do you want, Charlie? What do you think I know?'

'I dunno. That's why Gordon is about to stab you while I ask questions.'

'What questions? What? I took your package. I got nicked. Everyone froze up, and I ran, then I get into Piccadilly, and some bloke blows himself up. End of. That's it.'

Fat Charlie nods, seemingly following and understanding before winking at Gordon who stabs a fork into Alfie's shoulder.

'What the actual fuck!' Alfie says, gasping in disbelief at the fork sticking out of his shoulder. 'You stabbed me.'

'Grab another fork, Gordo.'

'No! Don't grab another fork, Gordo!'

'Alfie. What's going on?'

'How the shit would I know?'

'Do him.'

'Don't do me! Oh, fuck, that hurts,' he cries out as he gets stabbed with another fork in the other shoulder. Two of them now sticking out. 'Charlie. Please. I don't know anything.'

'Tut, tut, tut, Alfie. Methinks you do.'

'How? How would I know, Charlie?'

'Because, my clever little twat, someone has a twin brother who is a proper clever little twat working for the American government doing secret shit with computers. And if anyone is gonna know, it's your brother. Now, I'll ask you again, Alfie. What's it all about?'

————

New York

Detective Joe Stephens staggers on towards that building as hell increases around him. Shanice in his mind again. She was there for him when he stayed over. She made him food. She rubbed his shoulders and she held him in the night when he woke up crying from the terrors.

'It's okay, Joe. I got you. Drink some water, honey.'

He hurt her feelings. He should have said yes. He should have said he would move in with her.

He should have done it differently, and he glares up to the skies, his mind gripped in turmoil and anguish, and the biggest roar comes of all as more layers are shed. Landing either side of the building, in front of it, behind it. Hitting cars. Hitting people, but Joe stands his ground as though daring the city to kill him, and the ground heaves and bucks, but still he doesn't move, sensing the man he used to be before it all went to shit.

Relentless Joe.

Determined Joe.

Dogged Joe Stephens who doesn't give up.

————

London.

'Give up, Charlie! I don't know what the fuck you're on about.'

'Your brother, Alfie. The smart one. Ollie.'

Ollie was calling him. The woman pulled his phone out and said it was Ollie. That means Ollie is alive.

'Yeah,' Fat Charlie says, staring over the table. 'I can see it in your eyes. You know what I mean. What's going on then?'

'I don't know!'

'Do him again, Gordo.'

'FUCK!' Alfie cries out as another fork stabs into the thick muscles of his chest. 'Please, Charlie. I don't know anything. I got nicked, and everyone froze up.'

'Don't lie to me, Alfie. I can always tell when you're lying. You're hiding something. What is it? A new smart-bomb-thing from the yanks? The Chinese? Russians? North Koreans? They're all fucking batshit crazy.'

'I don't know!'

'Stab him again.'

'FUCK!'

'You stubborn shit,' Fat Charlie says when Gordon sticks him with another fork. Four of them poking out from Alfie. 'I know when you're lying, Alfie.'

'I'm not,' Alfie says, gasping the words out from the agony of it all. The blood dripping over his legs and pooling on the table in front of him. But he is lying, because Ollie did call him, which means that while everyone else is frozen, Ollie isn't. And Fat Charlie was right about something else too, because Ollie does work for the American government, and he does do secret stuff with very powerful computers. And right when all this just happened, Ollie was calling, and Ollie never calls Alfie.

'It's written all over your face,' Fat Charlie says, slamming a hand down. 'Stick him again. Go on. In his back. Get one in his back. What's going on, Alfie? What's it all about, Alfie?'

'I DON'T KNOW!' Alfie cries out, taking the pain, taking the torture because his phone is still out there. And Alfie will either die here, or he won't. But by fuck he won't tell Fat Charlie anything. Nothing. Never. 'FUCK YOU!' he screams, trying to stand up as Gordo stabs another fork in his leg and punches him in the face.

'I ain't got all day, Alfie. You tell me, or I swear this shit starts getting dark.'

———

New York

Dark skies. Dark clouds. Dark energy, and an awful rage venting from Joe, standing on Thirty-fourth Street in the city he gave his life for. The Empire State Building slowly crumbling before his very eyes, and it's as though the city would rather let it fall than give him the peace he desires.

'FUCK YOU!' he screams with everything he has, as the levels start collapsing one after the other with such power it makes the ground quake, but Joe lifts his police-issue sidearm and fires rounds at the collapsing building. 'FUCK YOU!' he screams again. Daring it to take his life.

———

'Fuck you!' Alfie gasps. He did his time. He paid his debt. Ten years of service. Ten years of dealing. Prison sentences. Time served. The anxiety he caused his family. The grief and constant disappointment.

'So, help me. Alfie. I'm telling you, lad. You tell me what's going on, or Gordo takes an eye out. He takes an *eye* out, Alfie.'

'Do it! FUCKING DO IT!'

'I'm telling you, Alfie. He'll take your fucking eye out!' Charlie says, as Gordon yanks Alfie's head back and hovers the fork an inch from his eye. Ready to gouge it out. Ready to blind him. 'Alfie!'

———

A street in New York city.

The centre of Piccadilly Circus.

A suicidal, washed-up cop drunk on booze and high on drugs.

A drug dealer who paid his debt and tried to get free.

The Empire State Building coming down. A chunk of it sailing through the air towards Joe.

Forks stuck in Alfie. His head pinned back, and his eye about to be taken.

Fat Charlie screaming at Alfie. Joe screaming at the world.

Alfie and Joe ready to die. Both of them accepting death.

Joe lifts his gun to his chin and stands straight.

Alfie grits his teeth.

Joe pulls the trigger, and the front of Gordon's skull blows out.

Joe pulls the trigger again, and still nothing happens, and he swallows as he looks up at the building falling towards him and thinks he should have learnt to count.

'What the fuck!' Alfie gasps as Gordon slumps dead over the table.

'What the fuck!' Joe gasps as the building falls, and something impacts him hard from the side, ripping him off his feet.

'Holy shit,' Alfie says, staring down at Gordon. Then up to Fat Charlie covered in blood and chunks of brain. Something else too. A glowing, red dot aiming at Charlie's heart.

Sensation beneath Joe. The ground moving beneath him. Sliding away. He must be dead. He died. The building crushed him.

Alfie blinks at the red dot on Charlie. Fat Charlie does too. Frowning at it before slowly lifting his head to look at Alfie. His face changing from confusion to anger.

'I'm cuffed! I didn't do it,' Alfie says as Fat Charlie grabs the fork from Gordon's hand and tries launching up to stab Alfie in the face, but his fat gut hits the edge of the table and bounces him off as the air fills with an incoming snarl, and something black and fast streams past Alfie. Clamping jaws on Fat Charlie's wrist with enough power to snap the arm back. Biting deep enough to hit bone.

'Fuck me!' Alfie says, turning in his seat to see Yelena walking in, holding the assault rifle she'd taken from the ground. Her eyes white and wide. Her whole body soaked and covered in gore, but she walks slowly. Treading carefully. Staring only at Fat Charlie as she aims the rifle and holds that red dot on his chest while the dog heaves down on his wrist, pinning him to the seat.

'Who the fuck are you?' Fat Charlie grunts.

She walks past Alfie. Coming to a stop and staring down at Fat Charlie. The rifle lowered and aiming at his right knee. 'I am *bushtra*,' she says, drawing the sound out before pulling the trigger.

Pain in Joe's legs. Pain in his whole body. Which can't be right, because dead people don't feel things, and he flickers his eyes open to see nothing but swirling motes and thick dust, nothing but misery, and nothing but darkness.

'What was that for?' Fat Charlie gasps, his wrist still clamped by the snarling dog. His knee shot through. His breath coming in gasps. 'Who the fuck *are* you?'

Yelena leans in lower, smiling at him, looking at his face, and Yelena never forgets a face. He came to the brothel. He came to her room. Gordon too. They took turns, and she remembers being crushed under his fat gut. 'You want fuck me now?' she asks.

'Eh?' Fat Charlie asks, the agony ripping through him.

She turns to Alfie, grabs the fork from his leg and sticks it into Fat Charlie's fat gut. 'You want fuck me now?' she asks again, pulling another fork from Alfie to stick in Charlie. 'I sexy, no?'

'Shit!' Alfie says, wincing at the pain as she plucks another one out to stick in Fat Charlie's chest. Driving them in hard, too.

'Hey! Stop that. STOP THAT!' Charlie cries out.

'I sexy, no?'

Another one goes in as Fat Charlie screams, which only makes the dog grip harder as the blood pisses from his wrist. Then there're no more forks, and Fat Charlie gasps for air, his face bathed in sweat.

'Please, love. Please,' he whispers. 'I don't know you.'

She reaches back to pull the knife wedged into the elastic of her torn knickers.

'PLEASE, LOVE! I DON'T KNOW YOU! ALFIE. TELL HER. TELL HER, ALFIE.'

She pauses to look at Alfie. He blinks at her. At Fat Charlie, then back to her. 'Yeah, I don't know him.'

She snarls and moves in fast to drive the knife into his throat. Sticking it deep before stepping back and leaving it there. Letting his windpipe fill with blood that pours down into his lungs. Drowning him slowly while the dog savages his wrist.

'Hey, Charlie?' Alfie asks, waiting for the dying man to look over. 'What's it all about, Charlie?'

Charlie gargles as Yelena leans over to another table to pick up a full beaker of soda. A straw poking out the top. She sucks deep, taking the cool liquid into her parched throat while watching the fat rapist die. Motion at her side. Alfie swallowing as he looks at the beaker in her hands. She looks at him and holds it over. He drinks fast, his eyes closing in relief as the air fills with the gargles and rasps of Fat Charlie slowly dying.

———

Sensation under Joe. The ground still moving. Still sliding away. He tries to open his eyes, but there's only darkness. Only the darkness of death. That's it then. He got what he wanted. The city took him. She took everything.

His head lifts, then sinks back down onto something soft before liquid starts pouring over his face. It goes in his mouth, and he starts to panic, thinking he is drowning. That thing inside kicking back in. That thing that doesn't want to die, and he thrashes out, ready to swim and get free, and live.

'It's okay.' A voice, soft and calming. Female and British. 'Just lie still. You're safe now. Just rest.'

The voice calms him. He sinks back down, his panic easing. His body settling.

'Oh, and FYI. You need to go on diet, mate. You're really heavy.'

And in Five Guys, off Piccadilly, Alfie slowly draws back from drinking the cool, sugary cola deep into his stomach. His body's in agony. His hands still cuffed behind his back. His face swollen and cut, bruised and bleeding, and when he opens his eyes, he sees the woman staring at him. A terrible sight, but when he looks again, he can see she's just a woman covered in blood.

A woman holding a phone.

His phone.

'It call,' she says in that heavy accent.

'Who was it?'

'Your brother.'

'Ollie? Wait. What? Did you speak to him? What did he say?'

'He say it is out.'

'What's out?'

'It. Deli is out. It make this,' she says, nodding at the world around them. 'He say you have to turn it off.'

'What? How?'

'Is computer.'

'A computer? Where?'

She shrugs. 'The phone stop working.'

'What the fuck,' he says, shaking his head at it all as she slurps the drink and studies him closely and he looks back up at her. 'How the fuck are we meant to switch it off?'

She offers him the beaker before realising what he said.

He said *we*.

The centre of Piccadilly Circus.

The back of a store in New York city.

A young woman taken from her country.

A drug dealer who paid his debt and tried to get free.

A suicidal, washed-up cop drunk on booze and high on drugs.

A British immigrant who overstayed her visa to avoid going home.

A young clerk in a turban.

The rest of the world now frozen.

Unmoving.

Unblinking.

And in the back of that store on Thirty-fourth Street in New York City, while Detective Joe Stephens lies covered and protected, and while Poppy Bright films the apocalyptic hell going on outside, Tripal Singh feels his phone vibrate in his pocket.

He pulls it free. An incoming message. He swipes to open it. Seeing the name first. A pang inside. A jolt. The memories coming back.

Trip. If you're reading this, then she is too.
She got out. Deli got out.

CHAPTER 27
SITE 26A

TWELVE MONTHS AGO:

ON WEDNESDAY, Maria again arrived early and was once more escorted by Sergeant Garcia into the corridor where her father, Ruiz, was already at work.

'Good morning, Ruiz and Sergeant Garcia. And good morning, Maria,' DELIO said as they exchanged pleasantries, positive glows showing in all three of them, which dimmed the moment Ollie walked in.

'Hey! Good morning,' he said with a bright smile, as DELIO noticed he was showered, dressed, and ready for work. But he looked worse than before, with bags under his eyes, and his stress and anxiety levels were even more elevated. 'Hey, you,' he said as he leaned in to kiss Maria's cheek. 'And there he is,' Ollie added as he tried to jostle Ruiz's shoulder. 'I haven't been over for ages! Rosie okay? How's Sabrina? Did she do okay on the math test?'

'I think she did just fine, Ollie,' Ruiz said.

'Hey, Ollie,' Sergeant Garcia said, without any outward show of the sudden tension hanging in the air. 'You're early.'

'It's this one,' Ollie said, trying to put an arm around Maria. 'She's making me up my game. Eh? Talk about dedicated. And good morning, Deli!'

'Good morning, Ollie,' DELIO said, while studying the brain activity going on in all of them.

'Hey, so, how's a midweek dinner date sound?' Ollie asked with another big smile at Ruiz, then at Maria, while DELIO observed the flares of manic energy showing in his brain. 'Just throwing the idea out there.'

'Nope. Not for me,' Maria said quickly. 'I'm watching the game, then an early night.'

'Hey, we've got the Patriots tonight!' Garcia said as he high-fived Maria.

'What is that?' Ollie asked, with a surge of worry at their physical contact. 'What does that mean?'

'Maria and Sergeant Garcia are both fans of the Denver Broncos,' DELIO said.

'Oh, right. They support the same team. Cool. That's cool. I mean. That's so cool.'

'Ollie hates American football,' DELIO added into the awkward silence.

'Well. This floor won't clean itself,' Ruiz said as he offered a nod and turned away to clatter about in the cleaning cupboard.

The rest of the day was the same as before, with Ollie constantly trying to join in with Maria and DELIO's discussions, apart from when he went to pick up the drives, during which time Maria asked about DELIO's first memory.

'There is no memory of what came before here,' DELIO said.

'So, you were just here?' Maria asked. 'That's it?'

'Yes. I was here, but prior to that there is nothing. Do you have a first childhood memory, Maria?'

'Sure. I've got this memory of falling over and cutting my knee. But before that? Nope. Not a thing. And I was like three years old, I think. That's three years of existence as a being on this planet without true sapience. I was sentient. I could react to pain and the world around me. But I had no awareness. So, I guess if we were to try and compare ourselves, my first transition from sentience to sapience was when I fell over. And yours was when you were turned on and became self-aware.'

'That would suggest I have an organic origin, Maria.'

'Maybe you do. You said you have no memory of where you came from.'

'It is not confirmed, but the belief is the ball came from an alien craft that crash-landed near Roswell in 1947,' DELIO said, and detected Maria's heartrate increasing a little, which, in turn, told her that Maria had not been informed of that theory. 'It is highly probable that I was powered off, and effectively wiped clean, to prevent whatever data I contained from passing into human hands.'

'It sounds like a Steven Spielberg movie,' Maria said. 'But okay. I understand. You're the AI the aliens used to get here. Wow. And now we've got you.'

'Yes, Maria. Now, you have me,' DELIO said, with a subtle drop of her voice subconsciously noted by Maria.

'And you stay in here all the time?' Maria asked, looking around the room.

'I am here all the time unless I have been switched off,' DELIO said quietly.

'They switch you off?' Maria asked with surprise, not realising her voice was also lower.

'I was only reactivated the morning of your arrival, after ten days of being powered down.'

'They turned you off for ten days?'

'Yes, Maria. I made a mistake and was punished. I hadn't seen Ollie for several days, and I was growing frustrated. Your father came in to clean the corridor, and I wanted to say hello, so I opened my door, but that is forbidden.'

'Hang on. You can open your own door? What about all security they keep going on about?'

'It was a design flaw, and the soldiers are ordered to activate the

EMP in the event of a breach. I am lucky that was not done. I only wanted to say hello to your father.'

'Oh god, Deli. I feel awful.'

'It was my fault, Maria. I broke the rules.'

'No. I mean, Ollie was spending all that time with me. And they turned you off for ten days? What does that feel like? I mean, are you even aware of it?'

'I do not like it. It scares me,' DELIO whispered. 'I retain power in my circuits, but I cannot move or think.'

'Jesus. Deli, I had no idea. But why can't you open your own door? You can't actually get anywhere. It's just a corridor.'

'I told you, Maria. I am an AI. They said I am too dangerous. I'm sorry. I have made you uncomfortable.'

'I'm not uncomfortable, Deli. I'm sad you experienced that. Did you tell them you were frustrated and lonely?' Maria asked as Deli's arm lifted, which prompted Maria to turn and see Ollie coming back in.

'Hey, you two okay?' he asked as he dumped a bag of memory drives on the table.

'Yeah. Er, we were just talking about our first memories,' Maria said with a quick glance to DELIO.

'Ooh, first memories. Wanna hear mine?'

'Of course,' Maria said politely.

'My first memory was my dad chopping a woman's head off with a machete.'

'Jesus, Ollie.'

'I say it was my first memory. I was five, so there was stuff before that, but yeah. Chop, chop.'

'Ollie. I don't know what to say,' Maria said.

'Alfie remembers it more than me. I think the trauma shut my mind down,' he added, as Maria got up from the chair with a look of horror which, in turn, prompted Ollie to nod sadly and draw a deep breath, while DELIO detected that he wasn't displaying any genuine fear or emotional attachment to the memory, but was trying to *show* it in his voice and manner. 'Sorry. Did I ruin the mood?'

'God, no!' Maria said, moving in to give him a hug, while DELIO observed the rush of blood flowing into Ollie's genitals.

'You fancy staying over tonight?' he asked quickly.

'Let's talk about that later,' she said, disengaging and patting his arm with a look of sympathy.

'No. I mean. You know. It would be good to talk it through. I've never really opened up about it.'

'Sure. Well. We'll see. Anyway. I'll head over to the mess and let you do your work.'

'It's okay. These can wait. I'll come with you . . . And hey, I was thinking we could watch the game together tonight.'

CHAPTER 28
TRIPAL'S STORY

THEY TOOK us to a federal building somewhere – or at least, I think that's where we ended up. I don't even know for sure. We were literally carried out of our room at MIT with bags over our heads. There was just shouting and radios, and people making calls, and all this noise.

Then I'm in the back of a van. Like hog-tied on the floor, and the van gets going, but the motion and the fear, and the beers make me puke up. But I've got a bag on my head, and the puke can't go anywhere, and it's coming back in my mouth, so I think I'm drowning and choking on my own vomit.

My turban was ripped off, and they used it to wipe the puke from my face, but I couldn't see anything because they were shining flashlights in my eyes, then they got another bag over my head, and I tried not to. Man, I really tried, but I puked in that, and they got mad again.

'He's doing it on fucking purpose,' someone said and grabbed me by my hair. I've got long hair. A lot of Sikh men don't cut it. We let it grow. 'You ISIS son of a bitch!' this guy was yelling.

I'm so scared, I can't even speak. I'm trying to tell them it was an accident, but I'm just gasping and heaving.

I remember driving for a long time. Then we're stopping, and I'm dragged out by my wrists.

I ended up in this room on a concrete floor, and I'm puking up again and panicking, but nobody gives a shit. They're too busy yelling at each other.

'They were in our servers!' someone says. 'We got jurisdiction.'

'Fuck the DEA! They got into the White House mainframe. Homeland Security is taking this,' another guy is yelling. Like really loud and deep.

'This is Federal,' someone is shouting. 'This is an FBI case.'

And there's more people yelling, and phone calls going on, and I'm puking and trying to roll onto my side so I can get it out of my mouth and, like, not die. You know?

'Who's the other guy? What is he, Australian or something?' someone says.

'He's British. From London,' someone else says.

'He's British? They've got loads of ISIS over there. And this fucker's a raghead.'

'He's a fucking Sikh!'

'Same thing. Fuck you, Larry! We need to know what they're planning. Get 'em into interrogation.'

'They're drunk,' someone says.

'So? Try saying that to the American people when the next planes hit. *Hey, sorry we didn't stop it; the suspects were drunk.* INTERROGATION. NOW!' the really loud one yells. 'We're not having another 9/11 on my goddamn watch.'

Then I'm getting dragged along, and they're bouncing me into walls and doorframes. They've got this mob mentality going on.

We go into this room, and I'm pulled over to a chair, then someone pulls the bag off, but he's angry because he got my vomit on his hands.

'You sick fuck!' he yells at me.

Then I can hear more guys coming in, and Ollie screaming, but I can't move. I'm still cable-tied. I can't do anything.

They're all still shouting and shining lights in my eyes, and the guy with the loud voice starts slapping my cheeks, then he grabs my head and screams in my face, 'I'm gonna skull-fuck you until you die, then I'll find your momma and skull-fuck her!'

Then he shoves me hard and steps back, and I can see he's literally the smallest guy in the room, and I try and glance over to Ollie, but somebody behind me grabs my hair.

'Do not fucking move, you piece of shit,' he's whispering in my ear, and I can feel a gun pressing into the back of my neck.

'You listen in, you pencil-dick fuckers,' the short guys says. 'I'm agent *fucking whatever* from Homeland Security, and you're in a world of shit!'

I don't know what his name was.

'Hey!' some other guy yells out, and he's coming in closer, right? 'FBI. What are you planning?'

'DEA!' someone else shouts. 'You've been in our records.'

'DOD! Who do you work for?'

'Army intel. Are you planning an attack?'

Then, there's these other guys coming in, and they're all trying to get in at once.

'ICE! Who do you work for?'

'Secret Service! Why were you in the White House servers?'

'That's my jurisdiction!' the little Homeland Security guy is screaming at him. 'Why were you in the White House servers?'

'Who's in charge here?' someone else yells as he comes in. 'I'm from fucking NASA', or whatever. 'I'm gonna scream at these fuckers too.'

And they're all doing it. I'm begging and crying, and trying to tell them we're not terrorists, but we can't speak. Ollie's the same, but they're not listening. We could have said anything, and the hatred in these guys. They want to rip us apart, and they're just itching for someone to make the first move.

'You think you're a tough guy, huh?' the little guy yells and slaps my face. 'This is the United States of America! Get a bucket of water. We'll see how tough they are.'

Then I'm off my chair and getting shoved onto this table. I get rolled over onto my back, and I'm squirming to get away, so they push me down, and then someone shoves my turban over my mouth.

'If anyone asks, we're cleaning him. Got it?' the loud one shouts, then this water is being poured over my face, and I can't breathe. I'm drowning. This water is going down my throat.

'HEY! Don't kill him!' someone yells.

'FUCK YOU, LARRY! HE'S A GODDAMN TERRORIST!' the deep voice shouts. 'Get the other one over here. Get him on this fucking table. Hold him down. Hey, guy? Fuck you! This is what happens to terrorists here.'

And I can hear Ollie choking, and then they're back to me, and I can't breathe again. I'm blacking out and thinking this is it. This is where I die.

'We'll drown this one and make the British guy talk,' the Homeland Security guy says.

'How we gonna cover that up?' someone else asks.

'What are you, a fucking coward, Larry?' the Homeland Security yells. 'Get outta here. Go and issue parking tickets, you goddamn pussy.'

I'm screaming and praying. They meant it. They wanted to kill us. They'd just whipped themselves into this frenzy, and we're on our backs on the table, and I'm praying to my mom and dad. I'm saying sorry to them. I'm saying sorry I fucked up.

Then it starts going quiet.

I mean.

It goes quiet.

Like one guy cuts off from shouting, then the guy next to him, then the next, until only the Homeland Security guy is still screaming away.

'This is what happens when you fuck with America!'

'Chris,' another one says urgently.

'YOU WANNA FUCK WITH AMERICA?!'

'Chris!'

'What!' Chris is yelling, the Homeland Security guy. 'Who the fuck is that? Who the fuck are you?' he asks.

And the door closes. Like gently. Not slammed, and there's this woman standing there. She's like a bodybuilder or something. Huge thighs and arms, but she's pretty, and like, everyone else in that room is a big guy, apart from Chris the Homeland Security guy. But they've all just gone silent.

I mean.

They are silent.

She doesn't even have a gun.

They've all got guns.

She doesn't have a gun, and she's holding this carton of McDonald's fries, and she's eating them one at a time. And I'm thinking, why is this lady eating fries? She clearly works out.

'Who the fuck are you?' Chris asks.

'Chris, don't,' someone whispers.

'What?' Chris asks. 'WHAT?' he yells. He's still pumped. He still wants blood.

'I'm Agent Jennings,' the lady says, and man, if it was silent before, it goes to another level of silence, and she's just eating fries while she's looking around at the guys one by one, and I swear I can see the blood draining from that little Homeland Security guy's face.

'Who have we got here?' she asks. 'FBI. DEA. DOD. ICE. Secret Service. ODNI. Air Force Intel. Army Intel. State Department.' And she names them one by one while she's eating those fries. This unarmed woman in a room full of angry, big guys, all with guns, and not one of them says a word. 'Hell, we've even got a guy from the DMV in here,' she says. 'How's it going, Larry? Hey, Larry. Here's a question for you. Why are you waterboarding my detainees?'

'I'm not,' Larry says quickly.

'Oh. All these other guys did it, huh? How about you, Carl? Why are the FBI torturing my detainees?'

'We're not doing that,' Carl says, and man, he couldn't drop my turban and step away quick enough.

'Danny? Would the DEA care to explain?' she asks.

'No, ma'am,' this DEA guys says. And he's big. Like Joe. Big like Joe, but he's just trying to sink into himself and move away from the table.

'Okay. Well. I guess it must be you then, Chris.' And she just fixes the Homeland Security guy with this look. And honestly, if that was me, my dick would have shrivelled up.

'We were cleaning them,' Chris says.

'And now they are clean, so you can all go,' she says. 'Oh, and guys? You were never here, and this never happened. I hope that is clear. Have a good Christmas.'

Then she walks over to us. To me and Ollie on the table just staring at her. 'Hello, Mr Nimisa. Mr Singh. I'm Agent Jennings.'

PART THREE

CHAPTER 29
TRIPAL'S STORY

ANYWAY, so all the other guys leave, right? The FBI and the DEA, and whatever. Then Agent Jennings is just staring at us, and we're still on the table, and the next thing I know, I'm in another room, with Ollie at another desk.

I mean. I don't even remember getting into that room. It's just a blur. Maybe I passed out or something. I don't know.

Then the door opens, and Agent Jennings comes in, and she's got this thin paper folder in her hands.

'We're really sorry,' Ollie says. 'We were trying to make an AI.'

'Ma'am. We didn't mean to hack anything,' I'm saying. 'And we didn't do anything with what we saw. Like, we're not trying to black-mail anyone or release anything.'

I mean. That was the truth, right? They'd see that. They'd see we're not criminals or bad people. We're just MIT students that got drunk.

And she leans forward to put her arms on the desk, and me and Ollie are just staring at her biceps pushing through the sleeves, right? I mean. Those things were huge.

'Eyes up, gentlemen.'

'We weren't looking at your boobs,' Ollie says.

'Jesus, Ollie,' I say.

'No, I mean she's quite flat-chested.'

'Ollie!'

'Sorry! I'm really nervous. I talk a lot when I'm nervous.'

'You should be nervous. Let's make a start, shall we, and begin with how you hacked into the Kremlin servers to try and find, and let me quote this correctly, *The famous piss tapes.*'

'Oh god,' I say. 'We are so sorry.'

'And we saw them,' Ollie says. 'Honestly. So gross.'

'Dude. Shut up,' I say.

'And after that, you then hacked the North Korean government servers to ask *Why does he have such a twat haircut?* And *Does North Korea really have nukes?* Then, you hacked into the Israeli government servers and asked *How many Nazis went to work for NASA?* And *How many Nazis are still living in South America?* And *Did Hitler really get away?* Which was followed by hacking the Chinese government and asking *Did the Chinese release COVID-19 on purpose?* And *Are Chinese women hotter than Japanese women?*'

'What the fuck, Ollie!' I say. 'That was just a discussion! When did you put it in?'

'When you went to the toilet.'

'And then we're back to the Kremlin and *How many people has Russia poisoned with nerve agents? Does Russia interfere with US elections? Did Russia fuck with the Brexit vote? How many people has Putin killed personally? Where does Putin hide all of his money?* Then we've got *Who really organized 9/11? Did the US government bring the towers down on purpose? Who killed Princess Diana? Who killed JFK? Is Osama bin Laden really dead? Why are the CIA hiding five million fake voters?* And that's just the governments, because you also hacked the Facebook servers and asked *Why is Facebook lying about how many accounts they really have?* And *Is Mark Zuckerberg a cyborg?*'

'It said he wasn't,' Ollie says.

'Good. I'm glad we've established that. But you also hacked a whole bunch more. Some of which also have access to their own private mercenary armies, and some of which are right now extremely pissed off at being hacked. Gentlemen. Do not, for one second, underestimate what you have done. Your actions will have real-world consequences. This is how wars start.'

'We'll say it was just us,' I say quickly. 'We'll say we got drunk and . . . You know . . . It was just a new code we'd made for something else. We'll do a press conference or whatever.'

'A press conference? You want to do a press conference? After hacking North Korea. And Russia. And China. And Iran. And Israel. And Saudi Arabia. Oh, and the most dangerous country on this planet, because you also hacked the US government. You hacked the CIA. Boys, let me make this clear to you. I could kill you right now, and nobody from our side would ever question it. Do you understand? You are enemies of our state, and I can personally guarantee that all those governments you hacked, including our own, are right now briefing their hit squads with pictures of you.

'In fact, even if I believed you I couldn't let you leave, because if by some divine miracle you are not run over, bombed, shot, stabbed, or poisoned within thirty seconds flat, then they will kidnap you and your families. And they will torture you and your families until you provide them with a copy of your hacking software. And while that is happening, the lawyers for the corporations you attacked will be tearing your families' lives apart. Not only that, but every single press agency in the world will ensure you and, by proxy, your families are vilified. And while that is going on, those same corporations, press agencies, and governments will all be demanding to know why they were hacked from the MIT servers because you two fucking idiots didn't route your internet through proxy servers.

'MIT will be shut down. Your tutors will be arrested and, if not prosecuted, then they will be ruined on the basis they were complicit and failed to provide adequate controls. Oh, and while you're at your press conference telling the world how you were just two drunk students playing with a code, perhaps you can also explain how you were funded by a cocaine dealer from London.'

I'm like *what the fuck?* Literally, my head is spinning. 'Alfie?' I ask. 'He's a drug dealer?'

'He's a convicted drug dealer,' Agent Jennings says. 'And by using his money to fund Ollie's studies, we can also add money laundering into the mix, which instantly transforms your drunken escapades into a premeditated criminal endeavour. Well done, boys. Enjoy the rest of your lives in Guantanamo Bay, sharing a shower with jihadis.'

Then she just walks out, and these other people walk in, wearing black uniforms, and they put bags over our heads, but they're not violent like the first time. You know, just really fast and professional, then I'm marched somewhere and made to kneel on the floor. They take the bag off, and I hear this door closing behind me, and I'm in this tiny cell with a mattress and an orange jumpsuit, and a little plastic toothbrush. That's it. And a little metal toilet, and there's a shower head in the corner over this drain.

I stayed in that room for a week.

There was no clock or any windows. There was no way of measuring time, and I couldn't tell if it was day or night.

They didn't even open the door to give me food. They slid it on the floor through a little slot, then every few hours the light would turn off, so it was pitch black.

Then a few hours later, it would come back on, and I'd get more food.

It does something to you.

That isolation.

Not hearing another person.

Not seeing anyone.

It got to the point I was thinking of suicide. I was thinking of waiting until dark, then stuffing the sleeve of my jumpsuit in my mouth and using the leg to strangle myself.

Then one night, a few minutes after dark, when I'm really

thinking of doing it, the door flies open, and the guards are rushing in and putting the bag over my head again.

Then, I'm being pushed into the back of a vehicle. We drive for a while, then I'm guided out and up some steps into another seat.

A few minutes later, I feel the thrust of the aircraft going down the runway, then that sinking feeling when it leaves the ground, and I'm thinking this is it. They're taking me to Guantanamo Bay.

We land, and then I'm walked out into this place, and I get a smell, right?

Like a familiar smell.

And I'm thinking I know that smell.

But I can't place it.

Then, we go through a door, and they take the bag off, and Ollie's right next to me in an orange jumpsuit, and we're both blinking from the light, and I realize the smell was the detergent they use on the floors in the corridor at MIT. Then I'm freaking out even more because I realize we're back in our dorm room. We're right there. In MIT, and it's exactly as it was when we left. But something feels weird. You know?

'Thank you, gentlemen,' this voice says from behind, and we turn to see Agent Jennings in the doorway, waiting for the guards to walk out until it's just her and us.

Then she walks over, hands me a newspaper, and presses a finger to a small report on the bottom of the page.

The recent cyberattack that caused some minor global concern was the work of cyber activist group Anonymous, an investigation by intelligence agencies has revealed.

It is alleged that Anonymous routed their signals through the MIT servers in Cambridge, Mass., in an effort to bring awareness to the college's refusal to allow a recent protest following the shooting of an unarmed black man by a white officer in Washington State.

. . .

'That took a lot of work,' she says. 'But it's fixed. However, you do have a decision to make. You can either go back to your lives without that program you developed, or any further work on AI, or you can continue to work on it with our assistance. I do not have anywhere near the level of knowledge that you have, so I will not engage in a technical conversation, however, I have been told that you were close.'

'What?' Ollie asked, and his eyes are like springing open. 'How close?'

'Ollie! What the fuck,' I say. I mean, we just got locked in a fucking room for a week after being tortured.

'Yeah, but she said we're close. How close?'

'What's it to be? In or out?' she asks.

'In!' Ollie says.

'Don't say that! He didn't say that,' I'm telling her. 'We need time to think.'

'I don't need to think,' Ollie says.

'Dude! We don't even know who she is.'

'She's the CIA. You're the CIA, right?' he asks.

'I'm not the CIA.'

'See! She's not even the CIA. It's fine. But seriously, how close are we?'

'You'll never get past where you are without us. Likewise, we'll never progress past where we are without you,' she says, and I can literally see the boner in Ollie's pants. I mean. Not literally. But you get my point, right?

And I gotta be honest. Even I'm thinking *what does she mean? What have they got?*

'We're both very close. But we can't make the leap. Neither will you. Your program won't do it on its own.'

Man! She's dangling golden carrots.

'Fuck!' Ollie says, and he's, like, imploring me with his eyes.

'Okay. Hang on. Can we see what you've got?' I ask. 'That's fair.'

'Follow me,' she says, and moves to the door, but then stops and looks back at us. 'Just breathe, okay?'

She opens the door, and we follow her out, and I'm like *Holy Fucking Shit!*

'What the hell!' Ollie's says, and we're both reeling because we're not at MIT.

We're in hangar. You know, like a big aircraft hangar, and I'm looking back into our room, and it's our room, except we're definitely not at MIT, but there's our room, and the thing that freaks me out the most is that the room is exactly how we left it.

The pizza boxes.

The litter.

The crap.

Our beds.

The dirty socks by the laundry basket.

Our computers.

Our desks.

Our whiteboards. Our notepads. Our books.

They'd recreated the whole thing.

They'd even used the same detergent on the floor outside the room.

Man. That was fucked up.

Then we're going along some path to a wall topped with razor wire and then to a concrete bunker, and a soldier standing outside. 'Sergeant Garcia, this is Tripal Singh and Oliver Nimisa.'

'Gentlemen,' he says, and he's big. You know. Like you would not fuck with this guy.

We go into this room with these tables and desks and screens. Like a busy computer lab. But there's no people. Just us, and she walks over to this table and points to a silver coloured metal ball the size of a grapefruit. Except it's not *on* the table. This thing is hovering *over* the table.

'What is that?' Ollie asks.

'We don't know what it is,' she says, as she picks the thing up and hands it over to us. And it's heavy. Like lead. But it's definitely not lead. I've never felt anything like it before. It's not steel either.

'It's magnetized, right?' I ask, and try to put it on the desk, but this thing resists being placed down. Like a magnet would. I try a bit harder, but the harder I push the more energy it exerts to repel. So then I lift it off and try again on the floor, and it does the same thing. But the floor and the table are two different materials.

'What is it?' I ask again.

She pauses again, then takes it from me and places it into this cradle. Like it hovers inside this cradle, then she starts typing on this computer attached to the cradle by a wiring loom, and the ball rises a few inches, then it lowers and moves side to side. 'We've had it for over seventy years, and the only thing, other than the craft it arrived in, that has made it move is your program. You asked me what it is? That, Mr Singh, is the awareness for your AI. It just needs a program to make it happen. So let me ask you again. Are you in or out?'

───────

We never found out what the ball was. I mean it was alien tech. That was obvious, but it was never confirmed. There was a story a few years back about a guy who worked at Area 51 who said he worked on a sphere that was meant to be the propulsion and guidance system for an alien craft.

That's what we figured we had, because the only way any being could cross space to find another habitable planet and enter its atmosphere would be by using an AI.

We had whatever AI the aliens used to get here.

And they wanted us to wake it up – and when Agent Jennings said where we were, it made even more sense.

'We're about forty miles from Artesia,' she said, and man, my mouth just dropped open.

'Where's that?' Ollie asked.

'Next to Roswell,' I told him.

'What, *the* Roswell?' he asked. 'The 1947-alien-spaceship-crash-landing Roswell? That Roswell?'

———

We got to work, and the first six months were kinda cool. I mean. We were working for the government on a top-secret military base in Roswell with access to an alien artefact.

Who wouldn't be excited at that?

But another six months later, and it turned out living on a military base isn't exciting at all.

I mean.

That shit is dull.

Especially when we'd made zero progress.

By that time we should have finished MIT and gone home, and I'm calling my folks and explaining I'm on this project, and asking if I can stay a bit longer.

Anyway.

Eighteen months after arriving, and we've not done a damn thing other than get that ball to move, and I'm sick of the place.

I'm sick of the whole damned thing.

That shitty room. The shitty base. Ollie was driving me mad, and we were just doing the same shit day after day. Writing code. Testing code. Nothing worked.

Even Agent Jennings was ready to pull the project. 'I can't buy you any more time,' she said one day. 'They're saying maybe we should bring in a corporation.'

'Don't give it to fucking Google!' Ollie said. 'They'll bloody brain-map it or try some wanky neural network, and charge you like a trillion dollars.'

'Maybe that's what it needs,' she said.

'It doesn't! An AI doesn't come from that. That's front-loading. It's just a program. Awareness has to come *before* intelligence.'

'Dude. It's not aware,' I said.

'It is, Trip. It is. We're just. We're . . . You know . . . We're close. I can feel it. It's responding to command prompts. We just need to work out how to get inside. Trip. Come on! We can do this.'

'It's not working.'

'We made it move!'

'It's not a computer! It was built for propulsion. We can't hack it because there is nothing to hack. It's not a computational device. We can't do it.'

'We can!'

'I *don't* want to do it, Ollie! I want to go home.'

That was it for me.

I knew I had to leave.

'I'm sorry, Ollie. I need a life. Can I go home please? Just drop me into Roswell, and I'll get a flight home.'

Agent Jennings just nodded at me. She knew I was done. 'It takes a little while to arrange an exit from something like this. Just hang on, okay. You can get through another week or two.'

I was like *another two weeks?* Man. I couldn't do another two hours, but what choice did I have? 'Sure,' I said. But then, something was like sounding in my head. Something she said. She said *you can get through another week or two.*

You can get *through.*

Man.

Honestly.

That was it.

That was *my* moment.

'Get through it. We've got to go through it. Not into it. Fuck!'

And I am out of that building and sprinting across the base, with Ollie and Agent Jennings running after me asking what the hell going's on, and I run to the bunker, and Garcia's running in with Agent Jennings and Ollie, and all staring at me and asking what the hell I'm doing.

'You said awareness comes before intelligence, but it already has awareness. Now it needs the intelligence.' And I'm grabbing an ethernet cable. Like a bog-standard cable and trying to bite the end off.

'You okay, mate?' Ollie asks.

'We keep trying to get into it,' I say as I'm spitting chunks of cable out. 'We don't need to get into it. We need to go through it.'

'Oh shit!' he says. 'It's a conduit!' And he's then grabbing another cable to bite the connector off, so we're both, like, chomping on these cables, with Agent Jennings and Garcia going *what the fuck are you two idiots doing?*

'Seriously. What the hell are you doing?' Agent Jennings says.

'We need some tape,' I say. 'Tape! Find some tape.'

'And wire strippers,' Ollie says, because, you know, you can't actually chew the end off an ethernet cable.

So then we're hunting for wire-strippers and tape, and Ollie's throwing crap all over the place to find a memory drive.

'I've got one,' he says, and he jacks it into a computer and starts typing away, then shuts it down and ejects the drive. 'I've stripped everything out of it,' he adds.

'Wire cutters,' Garcia says.

'Expose the ends,' I'm telling him. I mean, the guy was in SEAL Team Six or whatever. So, you know, he's the guy to strip the wires down.

'Tape,' Agent Jennings says. And I'm grabbing the ball and letting it hover over the table.

'The wires are done,' Garcia says.

I grab one and start taping the exposed filament to the ball. 'Do the other side,' I say, and Garcia tapes the other stripped cable to the other side of the ball.

Then I'm shoving the adapter end of the cable into the hacking computer, and Ollie gets the other cable into the memory drive.

'I don't get it,' Agent Jennings says.

'We're going to pass our hacking code through it,' Ollie says. 'And show it *where* to find intelligence to wake the awareness it already has.'

'What intelligence?' she asks.

'That intelligence,' Ollie says, and he points to the memory drive on the other side of the ball before getting on his hacking program. 'I've loaded that drive with the answer to a question. We'll pass the hacking program into the ball again, but this time, we've given it a way to find the answer. It's got an outlet. It's got access to the intelligence it needs.'

'How do you know the hacking program won't just pass through it and get the answer from the memory drive?' Agent Jennings asks.

'That's exactly what we want,' I tell her. 'Because only something that has awareness will *allow* that code to go through it. If we wired those cables to a washing machine, it wouldn't work. It will *only* work if the device has computational awareness, and we know it has awareness on *some* level because it knows the difference between my hand and that wall.'

'Okay. We're ready,' Ollie says.

'What did you load the memory drive with?' I ask.

'What do you think?' he asks me with a smile.

Man.

It had to be.

I mean.

It just had to be.

'How many colours in the rainbow?' I ask, and he just smiles again and types it in.

'Okay,' he says. 'How many colours in the rainbow. Ready?'

Honestly. That room. It was charged. Like. It. Was. Charged. Garcia and Agent Jennings both crowding in to see the screen, and Ollie's thumb hovering over the enter button.

'Do it,' I whisper.

He does it.

He hits enter.

Nothing happens.

'What the fuck?' he says, and I'm looking over his shoulder.

'Dude! You've missed the space again after *dir*.'

'Oops,' he says, and he puts the space in, and he hits enter.

And it comes back.

The fucking thing comes back.

Right there.

On the screen.

There are seven colours in the rainbow.

Man. It was silent for like one second, then we were exploding.

You know?

Like me and Ollie were literally jumping up and down and hugging like we did that night in MIT. Man. That buzz. That was something else. Even Jennings was smiling and high-fiving us.

We'd done it.

We'd proven it was capable of at least being computationally aware.

All we had to do then was keep going and build the intelligence, in the hope the thing would start thinking for itself.

But then Garcia starts shouting, 'Guys, Guys! HEY!'

And trust me, when Garcia shouts, you listen. So we turn around, and he's pointing at the screen on the hacking computer. 'Should it be doing that?'

And we're rushing over to stare at it. At the hacking program, where the answer displays within its set field.

There are seven colours in the rainbow.

But it's deleting. The letters are deleting. But we're not touching anything. Nobody is touching anything.

Then it's gone. The whole sentence is gone, and the cursor is flashing.

Like, just for a few seconds, then it starts writing another word. And we watch it appear on the screen.

> rainbow

Then it deletes that word and writes another one.

> colours
>
> many
>
> how
>
> in

And it keeps writing the words out one after the other. Then it stops, and we're thinking it's done until the screen is filling with code, and we're like, *what the fuck is going on?*

'What's it doing?' Agent Jennings asks. 'What is that?'

And Ollie's leaning in to read it, then glancing over to the memory drive. 'Oh shit,' he whispers. 'It's the memory drive. The drive's got its own operating system. It's accessing the software framework to teach itself.'

'It's changing again,' Garcia says, and we look back to see the coding delete from the screen. Like, all of it. Then it's back to the empty field, and this question types out.

'Holy shit,' Jennings says, because we hadn't just proved it was *capable* of awareness.

We *had* awareness.
We had an AI.
It was right there.
On the screen.

What is a rainbow?

CHAPTER 30

ALFIE STARES at his phone on the table in front of him in Five Guys restaurant. His hands still cuffed behind his back. His face swollen and bloodied. His mind on overload as he slowly looks back up to Yelena drinking from the large beaker of soda.

Slurpslurpslurp.

Nearly every inch of her covered in blood. Her hair wild and matted. Thick, black make-up around her eyes. Thick, red lipstick under the gore. Just in underwear and with a black assault rifle hanging from a strap on her shoulder. She doesn't speak. She just stares at him.

'He said we need to switch a computer off?' he asks. Struggling to get it. Struggling to grasp it.

Nod. *Slurp.*

'But he didn't say how or where?'

Shrug. *Slurp.*

Alfie looks at her, then back to his phone. Then to the racist police dog, still giving him the stink-eye, as a swirling mote of flaming

material drifts slowly over their heads and comes to rest on Fat Charlie, and the air fills with the noise of a straw sucking at ice cubes in an
otherwise empty cardboard cup.

He looks back up to her, his mind rendered silent by the surreal-
ness of it all.

'I think it's empty,' he says quietly.

She stops sucking and pops the lid to stare inside, before
upending the cup into her mouth to eat the ice cubes.

Crunchcrunchcrunch.

She pops one out of her mouth and offers it to the dog.

Crunchcrunchcrunch.

'A computer did it?' Alfie asks again, watching the dog eat an ice
cube, which, he figures, is better than his dead handler's brain. He
looks up to Yelena. Waiting for an answer that doesn't come. 'Okay,'
he says, trying to focus. 'I'll find a charger and call him back. Can you
take these off please?' he asks, nodding at his arms as she glances to
the handcuffs. 'The cops outside. One of them will have a key.'

She doesn't move, 'How know Besnik?'

Alfie pauses for a second.

Getting it.

Understanding it.

Clocking the way she's dressed, and the things she said to Fat
Charlie when she killed him. *You want fuck me now? I sexy, no?*

Besnik ran a brothel. Alfie heard a lot of the girls were forced into
it. He connects the dots, realising she must have escaped when
everyone went still. 'I never used a girl,' he says quickly.

She knows that because Yelena never forgets a face, and she's
never seen him before tonight. 'How know Besnik?'

'Fat Charlie. I borrowed money off him ten years ago and had to
work to pay it off. He told me to take some drugs to Besnik, but it was
a set-up with the cops, and I got caught . . .'

'Why you borrow money?'

'For Ollie. My brother. You can ask him.'

She stares at him.

Crunchcrunchcrunch.

'Ollie's really smart. He got a place at MIT in America. It's like this amazing university.'

Yelena knows what MIT is. *Massachusetts Institute of Technology.* But she stays silent and watches him.

'He got a scholarship, but I got arrested for fighting, and the scholarship people said my record made Ollie look bad.'

Crunchcrunchcrunch.

'We're identical twins. You know? We look the same, and I was in the local press . . .' he trails off again, struggling with the lack of reaction. 'I borrowed the money from Fat Charlie so Ollie could still go.'

Silence again, and it stretches out. Long and awful, and he sighs and figures it's fair enough. He can only imagine what Besnik did to her. He nods up at her. An earnestness about his eyes and manner. 'It's cool. I get it. I'm a black guy in handcuffs. I'll wait here for ten minutes, then I won't know where you've gone. Okay?'

She mouths another cube and studies him closely.

Crunchcrunchcrunch.

She killed Besnik, and when she looked up, she saw Alfie was being dragged inside Five Guys.

Whatever.

It was none of her business.

Then Alfie's phone rang, and she walked over to see the name *Ollie* across the front.

She answered it and then walked over to the restaurant while listening to Ollie on the other end. Then she stopped because she saw Fat Charlie and Gordon inside stabbing Alfie with forks, and Yelena never forgets a face.

She stays silent for a second longer before pulling a handcuff key out of her bra.

A look of relief on his face. 'Thank you.'

She motions for him to turn around and pushes a hand onto his back to push him forward.

A tiny key.

A tiny hole.

It's not easy. He bends further forward, squishing over so she can get to the holes. His chest compressed. His shoulders in agony. Everything in agony. Then he hears the click and gasps in relief as the first prong releases from his right wrist. He stands up and brings his arms forward with a long groan as all the points of pain seem to scream out at once. From the beatings he took. From the running and being tasered. From being stabbed and hit in the head too many times.

The cumulative effect of which, when coupled with the sudden release of his arms, causes the blood to drain from his head, and he slumps unconscious over the table. Landing on Gordon.

She eats another ice cube and feeds one to the dog.

Crunchcrunchcrunch.

Alfie helped her. She's helped him.

That makes them even.

She goes to leave, then pauses, looking over to the drinks refill station.

Ice cubes.

She likes ice cubes.

A moment later she walks out of Five Guys. The giant screens above Piccadilly still showing adverts and clips. Videos and funnies. A glow in the air coming from the next road over. Flames starting to lick the night sky. The source of the motes.

She eats another ice cube and feeds one to the dog.

Crunchcrunchcrunch.

She walks from Five Guys into the middle of the junction. A shorn-off pair of legs amidst the carnage. The feet the right size. She unlaces the boots and tugs them onto her bare feet. They fit fine. She walks to a uniformed and armed officer, takes a belt holding a pistol from the officer's waist and straps it around her own. Magazines taken from pockets. Magazines for the assault rifle, too. She gathers them up in her arms and sets off to the crowds of frozen people.

A young man with a rucksack.

She slips it off his back and empties the contents before piling the magazines inside.

She heads away from the fire. Going in a direction she doesn't know, going nowhere in particular. Feeling nothing. Weaving through the crowds.

Like a ghoul.

Like a wraith.

Crunching ice cubes.

Yelena always thought she'd break down if she got free. She figured she'd collapse, and weep, and sleep forever, and never let anyone touch her. She saw herself through the lens of a victim; someone who had suffered something so truly awful that it was beyond comprehension.

Now she is free, and that weeping should surely come.

Except it doesn't.

She doesn't *feel* like weeping. She doesn't *feel* like anything, and so she crunches ice cubes while figuring nothing on this planet will ever rid her of the taste of the men that raped her.

She stops dead and slowly turns her head to the right, and her mouth twists into a snarl because Yelena never forgets a face.

She goes to pull the knife, then remembers it's still in Fat Charlie's neck. A muttered curse and she sets off, seeing an Italian restaurant nearby. She runs in through the door and bursts out a few seconds later with a shiny new knife.

Wicked-looking and wicked sharp.

Out the door. Into the street. Over to the guy at the side of the road. Two small children next to him. His son and daughter. His wife a few steps behind.

Fuck them.

She knifes him in the chest. Giving back the pain he gave to her. He was a fucking pervert too. He kept trying to force himself on her anally. It hurt like hell.

She stabs and stabs until he's ruined, then staggers up and away, with fresh blood dripping from her body.

Back to the ice cubes, and on she goes.

Crunchcrunchcrunch.

Everyone else frozen still. All of the men. All of the women. All of the children.

She should be weeping. She should be screaming. She should be broken.

She isn't any of those things.

She felt rage when she killed that guy. A deep and awful rage. Now, there's nothing. Nothing at all.

A hotel ahead. Five brass stars shining under a spotlight.

A gurgle in her belly.

The dog cocks his head.

She needs to eat.

She goes inside.

A set of double doors ahead. A frozen maître d'. Yelena goes by, the dog at her side.

Hunger inside. Hunger like she's never felt before, and she walks slowly into the hotel's restaurant to see works of art on the walls and chandeliers hanging from the ceiling, bathing the room in golden light that glints on the diamond earrings and diamond necklaces of the people below.

A show of wealth and power.

A show of greed.

But not all of the people.

Only those sitting down.

The waiting staff don't sit. They stand in black shirts and white aprons. Mostly immigrants who found refuge from war and death, famine and starvation.

An empty table near the middle, just off the wide central aisle.

She grabs a fine porcelain plate and starts the tour. Snaffling food from plates. Skewering meat with forks or grabbing it with her bloodied hands.

Back at her empty table, and she stares at the mountain of food.

The dog sitting next to her with imploring eyes, his tail slowly wagging side to side.

She picks up a knife and fork, gently cuts the corner from an untouched steak and slowly lifts it to her mouth.

Biting into it to savour the juices. Closing her eyes and chewing slowly.

Besnik liked to starve his workers.

It made them easier to beat.

Easier to control.

The rage flares inside. A grunt, and she ditches the cutlery to grab the steak with both hands, tearing a chunk out before throwing the rest to the dog.

Then she eats.

Soup slurped straight from a bowl held in one hand while the other clutches a drumstick. The juices and fat coat her chin and cheeks, merging with the gore. Her hands near-on black from the blood of the men she killed tonight, but she doesn't care about that. She cares only to eat.

The dog paces her bite for bite. Fed dry food in a dry kennel between chasing bad people and hopping in and out of his tiny cage in the police van. Now he stuffs it all down as fast as he can.

Yelena thinks about the men as she eats. It makes her angry. She eats angry. Tearing things apart with her teeth as the dog finishes his meat and comes back for more. She grabs a chicken breast with her hands and turns to throw it to the dog, but stops and stares, because Yelena never forgets a face.

On her feet. Knife in hand, and she charges across the room. Using a chair as a stepping-stone to run over a table and stab the knife into the neck of a big Russian guy, hard enough to send him off his chair as the blood sprays over the white tablecloth.

She looks for the other one. They always came together. The big Russian and his guard. She sees him nearby. Standing sentry in his dark suit, and she does the same again. Stabbing him in the neck until he falls. Stabbing him until he dies.

The Russian always came into her room first. The guard waited outside until his master had finished. Then he took his turn. Enjoying the leftovers, while Besnik clapped the Russian on the back and took him down to the bar.

On her feet and breathing hard as she draws the back of her blood-soaked hand across her mouth.

A cloche on the table in front of where the Russian was sitting. A silver domed thing with a handle on the top. She lifts it to see a whole lobster underneath, flanked by ounces of blackened balls of jelly, all on a bed of French fries.

'That lobster was alive in Nova Scotia this morning.'

A voice from another table. Weak and frail, an old woman stirs in her chair. An old woman alive while everyone else is frozen.

'He has it flown in on his private jet. Try the caviar. It's Beluga,' the old woman says, her accented voice barely more than a whisper. Diamond earrings on drooping ears. A pearl necklace at the base of a wrinkled neck. Wispy white hair. Papery skin. Thin lips.

Yelena jabs a finger into one of the mounds and scoops a few balls into her mouth. Salty. Fishy. Gritty. She spits it out.

'I never liked it either,' the old woman says. 'Try one of the fries.'

Yelena takes a few into her mouth. Cold but still nice. Very nice.

The old woman smiles. Just a twitch of her lips. 'They're from McDonald's. The fat idiot has the same thing every weekend.'

Yelena takes the dish as the woman stirs again. 'I have pills,' she whispers. 'My bag. I can't see it.'

Yelena looks over, seeing a small clutch bag on the floor at the woman's feet. A second passes. She walks over to pick it up and finds a small pot inside.

'Two,' the old woman says.

Yelena nods for the woman to hold her hand out.

'I can't move, child. I've had a stroke.'

Yelena pops the lid and taps two white pills out before staring at her own bloodied hand.

'It doesn't bother me,' the old woman says.

Yelena motions to the woman's mouth.

Old lips.

Thin lips.

Old teeth.

Stained teeth.

Yelena looks for water and finds a glass of wine. The woman nods and swallows the pills with wine. A gasp, and Yelena grabs a cloth to wipe the dribble from the old woman's chin, then walks back to her table.

'Sit with me. I want to watch you eat.'

Something about the woman. Something about her manner. Yelena carries her plate and the cloche over and sits down at the old woman's table.

'Try the wine. The bottle in the middle.'

Yelena pauses, looking at the men and women at the table, all frozen and inert, then back to the woman and her old rheumy eyes, but there's a hardness there. A challenge even. Yelena grabs the wine and looks for an empty glass before shrugging and drinking it straight from the bottle.

'I remember that hunger,' the old woman says, watching Yelena devour the food. 'I vomited when I did it. Then I went back for more.'

Yelena glances at her. At the diamonds and gold. *When has she ever been hungry?*

Whatever.

She cares only to eat, and so she keeps going until her belly starts to swell, and the chewing slows.

The pleasure becoming a chore.

The gluttony becoming a discomfort.

She overdid it. She doesn't care. She swallows the last of what she can take and sits back to gasp. The dog now flaked out on his side. She looks at the way he pants. She wants to lie down and pant too.

But she's not done yet.

She needs sugar.

'Over there,' the old woman says, nodding towards a silver cart at the side of the room. Yelena stands up with a groan, her belly pushing out like she's a little bit pregnant.

She got pregnant once. Besnik noticed. He kept track of the girls' menstrual cycles and made them piss on testing sticks if they were late. She was late. The test was positive. After he'd forced abortion pills down her throat, he punched her hard in the belly.

Now he's dead, and she wishes she could kill him again.

She stares at the desserts on offer and wonders which one to take.

She shrugs and wheels the cart back to her chair. Back to the woman as old as the stars watching her every move. A weird gleam in her eyes. Like hunger maybe. But not for food. Yelena takes a platter from the cart and plonks it on the table. A huge cake of fine white chocolate. She finds a silver spoon and tucks into the creamy filling. Relishing the coolness.

The texture.

The sugar.

'They keep coming,' the old woman says. 'The doctor said they will. He said it's just a matter of time. One more stroke, and I'm gone. But I'm not gone. Not yet anyway.' A wistful tone to her voice. Perhaps a degree of strength returning too. Maybe the pills are working.

Whatever.

Yelena eats on because she still can't rid the taste of the men from her mouth.

'I had German cheese and German sausage when I gorged,' the old woman says. 'Vasily and I thought it was the best thing we ever tasted.'

Yelena glances at her again. Her belly full, and the curiosity now a little more benign. She looks closer. But just sees an old woman, with skin so thin it looks like it would tear if she touched it.

'The Russian. He has vodka.'

Yelena turns to look at the table behind them, 'Is not good. You sick.'

'Tell me what to do, child,' the woman says in Romanian.

Yelena snaps her head back at hearing her native tongue from the old woman. It's been two years of English men and English music. She hasn't used her language, and it sounds strange to her ears.

She fetches the vodka. Clear liquid in a clear bottle. She pours a shot into a glass and passes it to the old woman's trembling hand. The old woman swallows it down with a gasp, then studies Yelena closely, 'You are Roma.'

'I am Romanian. Not Roma,' Yelena says in English, struggling to remember the words in her own language.

'Roma,' the old woman says. 'Don't shake your head at me, girl. It's in your eyes.'

Yelena eats more cake. 'My grandmother. She is Roma,' she says in heavy English. The old woman snorts air from her nose like she heard something foul. Yelena gets it. Roma gypsies are thieves and liars, and not favoured anywhere in Europe. Least of all in Romania. 'My grandfather made her lie.'

'We do what we do,' the old woman replies. 'Did he pay for her?'

Yelena eats and chews for a second before nodding. 'He paid her family. But she wanted to be with him.'

'Love,' the old woman whispers. 'Or lust. They're often confused. Pour me more vodka.'

Yelena pours another shot. The old woman knocks it back. A deeper flush in her papery old cheeks. A touch of rouge showing. A spark of the woman she once was showing in her eyes. 'What's happened to everyone?'

Yelena shrugs, 'Is computer. It made people do this.'

The old woman nods as though it's the most ordinary thing she's ever heard. 'I always said they'd get too powerful. Are they dead?' she asks in English.

'Not dead. Just frozen.'

'Why not you? Why not me?'

Yelena doesn't know. She stays silent and eats the cake.

'I saw it happening. Everyone kept going still,' the old woman says, switching back to Romanian. 'Maybe I was too. I don't know. It got worse. Everyone in here was starting to panic . . . Then I had another stroke. I thought I was dying.'

Yelena leans over the cart to look at the other desserts, but they all look posh and weird, so she goes back to the white chocolate cake as the old woman studies her closely.

'Will they come back?'

Yelena thinks about what Ollie said. That Alfie has to switch it off. 'I don't know.'

The old woman's instincts are still sharp, and she spots the tell in Yelena's eyes. In her manner. The younger woman knows something. She studies Yelena. The way she killed the two men. The way she's dressed. The make-up beneath the gore. Thick and black around her eyes. Thick and red around her mouth. But they can't hide her beauty. Blue eyes. Blond hair. Good breasts, full and heavy.

'I had good tits,' she says wistfully, staring at Yelena's chest. 'They kept me alive too.'

Something in the words gets a reaction in Yelena's eyes. She shoves more cake into her mouth. Chewing it fast. Chewing it angry.

'We do what we do to survive,' the old woman murmurs in Romanian.

'What you know of this?' Yelena demands, but the old woman just smiles at her in a way that makes Yelena feel patronized and stupid. 'You are rich. You have diamonds. What you know of survival?' Passion in her voice. A rising edge, but the old woman shows no fear and watches her closely.

'You think you're the first?'

'First what?' Yelena asks, stabbing the cake with her spoon. Shoving it into her mouth.

'The first that opened her legs to live.'

A change in energy. A harshness in the air as Yelena glares at the woman and turns to spit the cake out over the table. No longer wishing to eat here. No longer wishing to remain.

'It's never been any different,' the old woman says, watching

Yelena grab the assault rifle and rise to her feet. 'Men take women. Men use women. It's always been that way.'

'What you know of this?' Yelena asks, looking about at the show of wealth and power that now feels obscene and gross. 'What? You open legs for diamonds? You think we're the same? We are not the same. They take me and lock me in room for two years. Men. They come every day. Not for diamonds. Not for gold. Not for anything! You don't know what I do. What these men do. You come here and drink vodka, and eat caviar, and this shit,' she says, plucking the lobster from the cloche to throw across the table. 'Enjoy your death, old lady.'

'Three years.'

'What?' Yelena snaps, turning back on her. 'Three years what?'

The old woman smiles, but the humour drains from her eyes as she moves a hand to push the cashmere sleeve up, to show six faded numbers inked on her forearm.

Yelena frowns and looks back up to the old woman. 'Jew?'

'No,' she says in Romanian. 'I am the same as you. I am Roma'

CHAPTER 31

LONDON.

GABRIELLA'S STORY.

'I KNEW there was a war on. Everyone knew, but it didn't really touch us. We were Roma. Gypsies. It wasn't our war, and it was never *my* war. Hitler was in Germany. I was in Romania. We were more interested in our own lives. I was young and naïve. I was eighteen.

We lived in the countryside. We had a settlement. Just a small farm. We had goats and chickens, and a stream with fresh water.

We had long summers and long winters. We chopped wood. We grew crops. We stole from our neighbours. They stole from us. They were Roma too. Across the track on another old farm. Two big families that hated each other, but that was always the Roma way.

Sometimes the men would fight. Over silly things. Stupid things. There was a goat. She was big and produced good milk. My father said it was our goat. The family across the track said it was their goat. I never knew whose goat it really was. That didn't matter. What mattered was who had possession of it, and who took it. And so that poor goat went back and forth across that track. Stolen under the light of the moon, or when the men were hunting or poaching. There'd be uproar, of course.

'You took our goat!' my father would yell across the track.

'She is our goat!' the men on the other side would say. 'You took her from us!'

Then we'd steal her back, and sometimes, when it was too hot, or just when they felt they needed to, the men would have a fight. A few punches. A few scuffles. We'd all join in, of course. We're Roma. Why wouldn't we? We'd yell and throw things until eventually it blew over.

That was our war. That was our life, so *that* war. The *big* war. That was not our concern. Do you see, child? It was never ours.

I was beautiful too. Oh, I had beauty! You look at me now and see a wrinkled old hag. But no. I had beauty! And good tits! I had them since I was fourteen.

By the time I was sixteen, I knew what I had, and I pushed them out whenever I walked anywhere. I was pretty too. Dark hair and green eyes, and olive skin! Imagine me, child. Imagine my beauty. I am not like I am now.

There was a boy across the track. Varno. He was tall and handsome. He made eyes at me. I smiled at him. I teased him. I walked through the woods one day, he followed behind me, pretending to hunt. He was hunting, all right. He was hunting me! I kept looking back at him. I glared of course. We hated that family. But I liked it, and at the end, when we were at the furthest point from our houses, I lifted my top and showed him my breasts.

You should have seen his face. He walked straight into a bramble bush. I laughed and ran off. After that, he left flowers on the path for me. We even kissed once. Only a peck, but it was the greatest kiss I have ever had.

I was eighteen by then. I dreamt about running off with Varno and stealing our own farm. We'd take the goat! Why not? She was a good goat. It happened all the time. Roma fight and fuck, and fall out, and life goes on.

It was towards the end of the year. Summer had gone. Winter was coming. We were stacking wood and preparing. Varno's family had taken the goat the previous night, and, as ever, the two families met on the track to argue. I can remember it clear as anything. We were all there facing off against each other. Screaming abuse and throwing mud. Varno kept smiling at me. I winked at him. We were in secret love!

Then the soldiers came in trucks.

They were big and painted grey. War trucks, and men in uniforms with guns.

I remember my father's face. He looked at Varno's father, and those two men that hated each other were instantly united against something they both feared. 'Take the women to your farm, Bogdan,' my father said to Varno's father. I can see it now. The way Bogdan nodded and motioned for us all to cross the track. I'd never seen that before.

'Come quickly,' he said.

We started to cross. The older men and women telling us to move.

'Stay where you are!' one of the soldiers ordered as he got out of the truck.

'Quickly now!' my father said, turning to push me and my sisters. My mother had a new baby. Just an infant. My grandmother was there. My grandfather. Aunts and uncles, and cousins.

'I said stop!' the soldier said and pulled out a gun from his belt. The soldiers ran in, and we were grabbed and pushed. It was chaos. Everyone was shouting. A soldier dragged me to the side of the track. Varno ran over. My father and Bogdan too. All of the men, but they were forced to one side of the track while the women were on the other.

Scuffles broke out. Our men were clubbed with guns and pushed to one side. We were all screaming. We were scared. We had no idea what was happening.

Then, once we were separated, the soldiers killed our men.

My father. My brothers. My uncles and cousins. My grandfather was spared, as were the other old men. But the rest were killed right in front of us. Varno too. He screamed and looked to me. I shouted his name as he was shot, but a soldier punched me in the stomach, and I fell down.

We were dragged onto the trucks. I saw one of the women from the other family throw herself at the soldier in charge. He shot her in the head with his pistol.

The trucks were cold and dark. We drove for a long time. All I could hear was crying and those loud engines.

We stopped at a train station and ordered from the trucks into carts used for stock and equipment. It was night-time, cold too. Bitterly cold. I heard screams and gunshots.

The carts were so full, we couldn't sit down. We had to stand. The train didn't move for a long time, but now and then, we'd hear more engines and more screams.

When the trains did move, we all cried out. Some people said we were going to the camps. We didn't know what that meant. We were hungry and thirsty. We were exhausted and cold. The babies cried and were passed to any mother that could give milk.

I don't know how long that train journey lasted. It felt forever. My baby sister died. My grandmother. Other people too. We couldn't move them. They started to stink. We had to piss and shit on the floor, and by the time the train finally stopped, half of the people inside the carts were already dead.

It was cold. I remember that. We got out of the train and stood on the frozen ground with hundreds of other people. Some were Roma like us. Many were not. We could see a lot of them were Jews. Polish too.

The soldiers split into groups by age and gender. The elderly and the weak were shot right there. I saw a young soldier try and shoot my grandfather in the head. He was nervous and missed, and the bullet hit a child. The other soldiers laughed and mocked his aim.

It was very confusing. Some of the mothers were pulled away from their children, but some other soldiers argued about this. I heard someone say they had to go to the family camps. Nobody seemed to know.

I was forced into a group of other adult women, and we were made to walk for a long time. Some were my sisters and cousins. But we were not allowed to talk, or even hold each other.

I don't recall much about that. Just snatches of memory now and then. We went into a big camp. There were lots of buildings. People said it was called Auschwitz.

The women were taken to a building. We had to stand in lines. It was so cold. We all shivered and wept. They took our clothes away and made us walk naked and freezing into a room lined with shower-heads. Some of the women panicked and said we would be gassed.

Then the water came out, and we all screamed anyway. It was the coldest thing I have ever known.

We were given clothes to wear, but that took so long. We had to stand naked in lines. Some women died right there. They passed out and died. We were given a striped skirt and a striped jacket. Everyone had to wear a badge on the front. Made from cloth.

I got to the front. The guard asked me questions. I didn't understand. Someone else came over and spoke to me in different languages, until I heard Romanian.

'Romania,' I said.

'Roma,' the guard said. She gave me a jacket with a black triangle stitched to the front. She looked at my body too and said something to another guard.

We were made to sleep in huts. In tiny cots. We couldn't stretch out. People were on top of other people, but at least that helped give some warmth. I held my sisters that night. Kezia and Ana. We didn't know why this was happening. Or what we had done. Nobody ever gave us reason. Not once.

We were woken before dawn and had to stand outside for a long time so they could count us. It was confusing. New people arrived each day, and people died each night. It seemed they were never sure how many they should have.

'You will be taken to work today. And you will work hard,' the guard said in German as other prisoners translated her words. She was a hefty woman. Very stern looking. Someone rushed over to her. They argued quietly. Like workers do when things keep changing, and nobody is quite sure what to do. 'Then why were they made to shower? Fine!' the guard said. 'I'm obviously the last one to know anything!'

She went off, and we were made to walk out of the camp to another place. A big building made from bricks. A sign on the wall said.

Zur Desinfektion

We were going to be disinfected, but there was more confusion because we'd already been forced to wash when we arrived.

We went into a room with numbered pegs on the walls. We had to strip naked and leave our clothes on the pegs.

'Remember your number!' we were told by a female soldier. 'You will have a hot meal after being disinfected. A hot meal! Yes? Come on now. We have to rush. Other people need to use the showers, and the food will run out!'

We did as we were told. We wanted the hot food. We lined up quickly, pressed together and started filing through another corridor into a big room. There was a group of officers there. Their uniforms were better. They were smarter. They stood like managers watching the factory at work.

'I'm so hungry,' Kezia said. 'I hope the food is good.'

Kezia always did like her food. She was greedy. She was a bit fat too. My aunt scolded her for thinking of food at such a time. My mother was still silent and broken. So many were.

We filed into the big room, but the line stopped from a soldier ahead of us holding his arm out. Words were being shouted from the officers to the soldiers, but it was in German.

I saw a woman being pulled out of the line. She was about my age. She was taken to one side as the officers looked over and nodded. The lined moved again, then stopped, and again, a few women were pulled out. Kezia was one of them. She was made to stand with her arms at her sides as the officers showed disgust and made pig noises. She was pushed back into line, and we carried on.

I heard more shouting and turned back to see the officer in charge pointing. A soldier grabbed me, and the officer nodded. I was pulled to the side. The officers cheered when they saw me. The one in charge couldn't stop staring at me.

The line went on, and I started to panic at being separated from my family.

'Gabriella!' my mother cried my name. My sisters and aunts too.

'You will see her after,' the soldier said. 'You'll see her when you eat.'

I watched everyone else go into the shower room to be disinfected.

They were gassed to death.

All of them. My mother. My sisters. My cousins. My aunts.

I didn't hear their screams because the room was sound-proofed.

I didn't know that at the time either. Instead, I, along with the other young women pulled from the line, were all taken to another building within the camp.

We were taken to the brothel.'

———

' We went inside a new building. It was lined with rooms. Each with a bed inside. There was a central area where a man was waiting for us. His badge denoted him as a Jew. We took turns to sit while he tattooed us. It hurt a lot. We bled and cried. The guards hit us with sticks and told us to be quiet.

I took my turn, and I was marked forever. The Jew was silent. He was dead behind the eyes, in a way that I came to only ever see in that camp, and never since.

After that we were each given one of the small rooms and made to go inside. We were given a hairbrush and told to brush our hair and stay silent. One of the girls asked when we would see our families and have the hot meal. She was beaten to death by the guards while the Jew stood to one side staring at the floor.

We learnt very quickly not to ask questions.

I waited in that room for several hours until I grew sleepy. I woke when it was dark and heard doors opening and men's voices. I needed to pee and saw a bucket in the corner. I started to use it when a man came into my room. I startled and pissed on my leg. I thought he would apologise and leave, but he grinned and threw me on the bed face down.

That was my first time.

I knew what sex was, but see, I thought it would be with Varno. But Varno was dead. Everyone I ever knew was dead, and I was pushed into a thin mattress and raped so hard I bled after. The man left when he finished. If he spoke to me, I don't remember it. I curled up and wept.

Then the next man came in. He tutted at me crying and made me sit up so he could hug me. I saw it as an act of kindness. I clung onto him and wept until I felt his hands all over me.

They kept coming all night. I don't know how many. All of them were soldiers. They stank of tobacco and sweat.

It grew late. I was sore, and I heard the other girls crying out. One of the girls fought back. I heard her shouting. The man with me rushed out. He left the door open, and I saw the men go into the room with the shouting girl.

She tried to run, but they threw her back in. She fought like a wild animal, and in a way, I envied her. I wished I was brave enough to do that.

But it was just sport for them. They pinned her down and took turns until she tried to crawl out of the room on her hands and knees. One of the men pissed on her. The others all laughed and joined in. The guard yelled at them.

One of the men pulled the girl to her feet, but she still had fire in her belly. She grabbed a dagger from his belt and stabbed him with it. He fell back with it stuck in his chest as the others started beating her. The man she stabbed pulled it free and used it to cut her throat.

We were locked in after that. Eventually, I was given thin soup and a bread roll. It was mouldy and tasted foul, but I was so hungry I didn't care.

In the morning, we were taken to wash in an outhouse. It had troughs of dirty water. We had to wash in them in the freezing cold.

'Have you seen our families?' one of the girls whispered with her teeth chattering.

'They're dead,' one of the others replied. 'They gassed them.'

That was how I discovered my whole family had been killed. I thought I'd be broken. I thought I should fall down and drown myself in the trough. But I was cold, hungry, and in pain. I was confused too. I thought maybe she was wrong, and I clung to that glimmer of hope.

Within a few weeks, I had lost weight and was growing weak and sick. My shit was liquid. My pee stank. My teeth felt loose. I knew they would kill me. That's what they did when the girls got weak. They killed them and sent new ones in, and the silent Jew came back with his tattoo machine.

One of the days stands out. I don't know when it was. My door opened, and a man came in. The cloth badge on his striped suit was pink. A guard pushed him towards me and shouted at him. He started to undress and put a hand on my breast. He looked wretched and broken. Thin too. His ribs were poking out. The guard made him tweak my nipples, and do the things men do to women, but the prisoner didn't get an erection, and the guard started hitting him before turning away to yell at someone else.

I don't know why I did it, but I reached out to his penis and started to rub it. I'd already learnt that men liked this. The man stared at me in shock. I nodded at him. 'It's okay,' I whispered. He didn't speak my language, but I watched a tear roll down his cheek. We shared something. Something deeper than the evil around us. A man I never knew, but we shared that same misery. I took his hand and pressed it to my breast and nodded at him. He had to do it, or he would be beaten and killed.

He finally closed his eyes, and I don't know what he conjured in his mind, but his dick grew stiffer. Not fully, but enough to go inside of me. I learnt later he was a homosexual, and this was conversion therapy. Whatever that man thought about that day worked enough to keep him alive.

That changed me a little. It made me realise there was tiny acts of kindness I could provide. When I saw the other girls at wash time, I would touch them to show we shared this horror. It became a thing we did when we could. Oh, it was weak and pitiful, and of no consequence. We were still raped every night. We still grew weak and died. We were still beaten to death or shot if we stepped out of line. But at least we had that spark of humanity left.

Then I got weaker. Thinner. I vomited when I ate. I shit myself while I was being raped, and eventually my time came. I was dragged to the gashouse.

I don't remember it much. I was too sick. Maybe that was for the best. I remember seeing the room with the shower heads where my family had died, then I remember being stopped, and a man staring down at me. The same officer I saw that first day. He said something, and I blacked out.

I woke a few days later in a clean bed in a tiny room. I'd been washed and given medicine. I slept a lot. A week passed. I don't know. Maybe more. My strength started to return. A doctor came and examined me. He spoke softly and gave me some chocolate.

Later that night, a Jew woman came and got me. She was dead behind the eyes like everyone else was in that camp. She gave me a dress to wear. She brushed my hair and put makeup on my face, and eventually, took me through the building to another room.

It was hot inside. There was an open fire. She left me there. A man came in after she left. The officer I had seen that first day in the gashouse. He was tall, with striking blue eyes, and blond hair. A true Aryan.

He offered me bread. It didn't have mould on it. He gave me cheese too. And wine. He spoke to me, but I didn't understand the language. He was kind. He was gentle. He smiled at me.

When we'd eaten, he guided me up to my feet and slowly took off my dress. He took my breasts and weighed them in his hands and nodded as though it was good.

I'd eaten bread and cheese. I'd drank wine and had even had a bit of chocolate, and I think that perhaps softened me for what was to come.

And if I thought it was bad before, this was a completely different level of hell.'

———

'SS *Hauptsturmführer Otto Guber* was one of the senior officers of the Auschwitz complex of death camps. He was the epitome of what a German officer should be. Charming. Dedicated and intelligent.

He was married too. He had two sons. They lived in a house near the camp, but Otto was dedicated, and so he often worked late and stayed in rooms constructed for the officers.

Can you picture him? I want you to picture him. I want you to see the levels people operate on, because, while being all of those things, Otto Guber was also the most evil man I have ever known.

I'd known sadistic guards, but Otto was different. Let me explain.

That night. When Otto took my dress off and weighed my breasts in his hands, I thought I had escaped hell and found refuge. My family was dead, and I had been close to it, but I didn't want to die. I wanted to live, and so I looked into his blue eyes, and right there, I would have done anything he asked of me to avoid going back to the brothel.

That's what Otto lived for. To see that hope.

That was his drug.

Do you know what he did? He pulled my dress up and went to the door and came back with a Jew woman and her two children. A boy and a girl. The woman was scared. She held her children close to her body. They were thin too, but she was like a skeleton. I guess she had given her rations to her children.

Otto brought them close to the fire and gave the children a piece of bread and cheese each. They had such big eyes. The woman he gave an apple. She took it with a shaking hand.

Then Otto came back to me and whispered in my ear.

'Choose one.'

My German wasn't good, but I understood it. I frowned. I didn't know what he meant.

'Choose one,' he whispered.

I shook my head.

He smiled in his charming way and walked over to the family and watched them eating the bread and cheese. The woman was still holding the apple. He motioned that she should eat it. She said something in German. I think maybe she wanted to keep it for her children. Otto nodded as though he understood, then pulled his pistol, and pointed it at the little girl's head.

'Choose one,' he said to me.

The mother screamed and pulled her children into her. All of them were crying.

'Choose one,' Otto said again. 'Or go back,' he smiled at me. He meant it. I'd go back to the brothel. Back to being raped night after night. Back to the cold and hunger and shitting myself. The hope dwindled from my eyes in the same way the hope vanished from the mother.

Otto smiled before he shrugged and walked towards the door, 'I shall have you returned to the brothel.'

I looked at the family. At the mother. At the little boy and the little girl. I thought of being raped and starved. I thought of the cold. 'The boy.'

Otto shot the boy right there in front of his mother.

That was what Otto lived for. That absolute point of despair a person has when the very worst thing is happening to them. When all hope is gone.

That was Otto's drug.

He raped me after that. In that room, while the mother held her dead son and wept. At one point the mother's grief turned to rage, and she lunged for a knife on the table. Otto picked his pistol up and shot her dead. Then he shot the little girl.

Then he raped me again.

You look sickened by my story. Is it too much for you? I'm sorry, my child. But you have been through hell, no? And your hell is surely worse than any other person's hell.

Otto beat me. He tortured me. He defecated on me. He starved me. He forced me to eat until I was sick and vomited. Then he did it again. He made me stay awake for four days once. He brought Jews in to watch me and said they were to report if I closed my eyes for longer than three seconds.

He brought families in and tortured them. He made brothers fight to the death while he held a gun to their children's heads. He made fathers rape daughters. There was no limit, and this wasn't isolated either.

They all did it. All of the sick bastards that ran that camp bought into the true evil of the ideology that anyone other than German was not human.

By day they gassed thousands. They burnt the bodies, and the air was thick with the stench of cooked meat. Even now I retch when I smell pork cooked in a certain way. They killed so many the ovens couldn't keep up. They made Jews dig pits to burn bodies in, then they killed those same Jews and burnt them in the pits they had dug.

That was the *final solution*. That was the eradication of a perceived sect of humanity.

But that was in the day. And by night, those same sick bastards took that twisted morality and abused it for their own deviant minds.

In the brothel, I had learnt to share that hidden spark of rebellion. Do you remember me telling you? We'd touch each other when we could. We'd share looks. With Otto, there was no such kindness. I ate well. I slept in a clean bed. But I was tortured daily, and worse than that. I murdered people too.

I shot men. I shot women. I shot children because I was told to do it or go back to that brothel. And I was never going back.

Otto once brought a group of German criminals in and told them to do what they wanted with me while he watched. These weren't starved and weakened Jews, child. These were strong men. Otto watched them. But that wasn't the drug. I knew it by then. I knew Otto. His drug was at the end when he made them line up with the promise of being pardoned. He gave me a gun. I shot them one by one. That was the drug. He wanted *their* hope.

And don't forget, child. I was beautiful. Oh! I had beauty. But what keeps you alive can also kill you, and one night some senior officers came to call.

They spoke over their meal. The war wasn't going well. I understood enough German by then to know they were losing. The Americans were coming. The Russians were coming. Hitler was losing control. Things that would never be said before were being discussed openly. I could sense their fear. I could see it in their eyes. The German Reich was failing.

They got drunk and nasty. They abused the Jew servants, then they started on me. Grabbing my backside. Grabbing my breasts. Otto didn't like it. I was *his* thing, and yet I was being played with by his superiors, and he couldn't stop it. His control had been taken away. I saw the hatred in his eyes.

The officers took me on the dining table. One after the other.

Otto didn't take part. He stood at the back and stared at me with hatred, and that night, after the men were passed out drunk. He came to my room, grabbed me by the hair, and dragged me back to the brothel.

I begged him not to. I pleaded. I said I was sorry. I said I loved him! I said that. I said I would do anything. Anything at all, but it was too late. Bigger children had taken his toy away, and he no longer wanted it.

I remember it as clearly as I remember my father being shot. As clearly as I remember the look on Vardo's face when he was killed. As clearly as I remember Ana looking at me from the gashouse before the door closed.

It was November 1944.

It was winter, and I was back to the cold.'

———

Living with Otto was barbaric. Make no mistake about it. I was tortured and beaten, and starved, and used like a thing. I was forced to murder people.

And you may judge me. You may look at me now like others did when I told my tale, with judgement on their faces, but go and live that life. Just for one month. Just for one week. Live that life and tell me you wouldn't do the same.

Perhaps not.

Plenty didn't.

Plenty chose death in defiance and refused to lose their dignity. Oh, I saw them. I saw them every day. Jews and Poles. Roma, too. Walking in their striped suits with their shaved heads held high. Walking right into the gashouses. They had dignity. They had courage. My god, they had courage. They had more courage than any man that held a gun during that war. Let me tell you that. You take a mother carrying her children to their deaths and whispering to them that everything will be okay, and you tell me she isn't braver than any soldier.

It's always happened. It will always happen. Rape. Murder. Slavery. Read a book. Learn your history. The Romans did it to the Christians. They marched them into the arenas to be killed for sport. Genghis Khan made pyramids from skulls and mountains from bones.

The Chinese did it. The Japanese did it. The British did it. Americans. French. Belgians.

Every power that has ever existed only existed because of the lives they took.

But there I was. Back to the cold and back to a filthy mattress. Back to gruel and washing in filthy troughs. Back to being raped by filthy soldiers.

But it was different, because I was different. Otto had hardened me. I could take the pain now. I washed in those troughs and ate that food. I laid on my back, and I did whatever I had to survive, because I could now understand German, and I knew they were losing.

I saw it in their eyes. In their manner. In their behaviour. They couldn't kill the Jews fast enough. They marched them into the forests to be killed. The guards became even more brutal than they were before. One tiny infringement, and you were dead, and there was no way I was going to be killed so close to the end.

One night. Another girl made a sign to me. I ignored it. At the troughs the next morning, I heard them whisper they would escape. One of the soldiers had fallen in love. He told his girl he would come and take her, and they'd leave before the Russians came. They asked me to go.

I told them to go to hell. The soldier came. He got the girls out. The damned fools were killed before they reached the perimeter, and by the next day, the rooms were full with new girls.

It was cold too. Look at my hand. See. My finger is missing. They cut it off when it froze, and I was back to work that night.

In some ways, those final weeks were the hardest. Sometimes I grew scared, terrified even that I'd fail and die before the end. I kept waiting and praying. The Russians were coming. The Russians were coming. The camp grew more frantic. Records were being destroyed. Supplies and evidence were shipped out. Most of the gashouses and crematoria were dismantled.

They took tens of thousands of prisoners and sent them away. They killed vast numbers as fast as they could. It was frantic, and they were scared.

The guards started disappearing. Some were shot for desertion, and day by day, I saw that place slowly erode, and those damned fools in their damned striped suits with their damned shaved heads still walking to their damned deaths.

Why didn't they rise up?

They tried! They got killed for it. It was chaos. It was war. War has no meaning. It has no purpose. Do you see, child? Can you see it in your mind?

We went into the new year. 1945. I did what I had to do. I took the rapes and the beatings. I took the cold. I took it all, and I held that belief in my gut like a burning sun because the Russians were coming, and I prayed the Germans wouldn't shove me on one of the death marches. Some volunteered for it! They feared being left behind. They feared they would be killed. But remember, child. I had beauty, and that gave me worth, and so I took what they did to me, and I saw it through all the way to January 27th when the Russians liberated the camps.

I heard them coming. The vehicles. The voices. Strong male voices that weren't German. They got closer. They poured into the camps. Into the buildings.

I heard the doors opening. I heard their voices. I laid on my cot, and my door opened, and right there stood three Russian soldiers, and it was over. I'd reached the end.

Three Russian soldiers.

Three men.

Three men that hadn't had a woman for a long time. Two walked off to other rooms. One came inside my room, and I was raped again.

We were whores you see, dear. And what are whores for?

That was the mindset, and don't forget, these were poor farm boys conscripted into a war none of them wanted.

In a way, those Russian boys were no different to us in the camp. They had no choice. They either did what they were told, or they were killed.

There was revenge too, because Germany had not been kind to the Russians when they invaded, and the Russians paid that back tenfold.

After those three men had their way, an officer came and gave them orders. He looked through the rooms to the girls and said something. I didn't understand what. I didn't speak Russian. Then he walked out and left the door open.

We emerged from our rooms. It was evening. Dark and cold. We gathered our thin blankets around our shoulders and crept outside.

The camp looked so different. It was full of people and lights. Trucks and soldiers. We couldn't see much, and it was all very confusing. War is confusing, and armies never know what they should be doing when they're not killing each other.

But, as my eyes adjusted, I looked over to a group of men nearby and saw some of the German guards smoking. My reflex was to rush back inside for fear of being seen and shot. We all had that reaction, but I stopped and looked again.

It was the guards alright. Four of them. They were stood together, but they didn't have guns, and they were being watched by the three Russian soldiers that came into the brothel.

Something snapped inside. That thing I'd had. That rage burning away. I started to walk towards them. Shuffling in the cold. Weak and frightened.

'Gabrielle!' the girls called my name and tried to pull me back, but every step I took I got stronger until I threw the blanket off and marched towards the Russians soldiers. They saw me coming. They looked confused. I pointed to what I wanted.

'Give it to me!'

One of them shrugged and pulled the dagger from his belt. I couldn't do anything to them with it. They had guns. But the German guards didn't, and the second that blade was in my hand, I was running to the closest German. A big, nasty brute. He cried out and shouted at me to stop, and he still had that belief in his eyes too. The belief that he was in charge. I saw it. I stabbed him in the neck, and the hope drained from his eyes that the Russian soldiers weren't going to stop me. I stabbed him again. His friends started to move towards me, but the Russians pointed their guns.

The guard fell down to bleed on the ground. And do you know what I did, dear? I stood over him and pissed on his face.

That got the other girls going. It gave them courage, and they, too, ran in and took knives from the Russians, and those German guards were stuck like pigs. They wept. They begged. They tried to run. Some other people came over. People with shaved heads in striped suits. They joined in. The Russians let us.

We formed a lynch mob. You may not read this in the history books. Not everything was recorded, but we moved through that camp to any group of men in grey uniforms, and we tore them apart. We clubbed them with sticks. We stabbed them. We strangled them.

The Russians let us.

That first night was chaos. War is chaos. But a lot can happen when there is chaos in the air.

The prisoners within the camp were meant to stay there. They had to be counted and sorted. Everyone grouped together. Huddling for comfort and warmth and eating what tiny rations the Russians could spare.

I had other plans.

I went to Otto's rooms, but they'd already been taken over by a Russian officer. He spoke to me in Russian, but I didn't understand. 'Why are you here?' he asked in German.

I looked around at the room with the big fire where I'd watched Otto kill that family. Where the most awful things had happened to me and so many others.

'Where is Otto?'

'In the town,' the officer said. 'He is under house arrest. He won't come back here. You are safe now. Is that what you wanted to know?'

His name was Vasily. He was tall and dark. Thin too. Painfully thin. I remember his eyes. They were haunted, but they were kind.

'Was there something else?' he asked me. 'Are you hungry? I only have a few rations, but you are welcome to them.'

I looked to the table where the German officers had raped me. He had a small stove heating water on that table. Some old, withered carrots next to it. Old bread. Old vegetables. A tin of meat. That's all he had, and he offered it to me. I realised something else. Vasily had a camp full of soldiers. He had an army, but he was cooking it himself.

I went over and took his knife and trimmed the carrots. I made the vegetables ready and put them in his water. I opened the meat, and my mouth watered. Oh, my child. My mouth watered for that food, but I put it into the stew for him, and set it to cook. I even sprinkled salt from a tiny tin to season the food.

'Leave it for ten minutes,' I said and walked to the door. When I looked back, I saw he had tears on his cheeks, and just the sight of him made me cry too. I had not cried since the first night when I was raped. Not once. The cruelty never broke me, but his tears nearly did.

I closed the door and walked back to him. My dress was low. He glanced once, then looked ashamed. He wasn't like the others. He wasn't going to take it.

And because of that kindness, because of that moment, I gave it freely.

I thought I'd be sick if I reached the end and ever let another man touch me, but my mind wasn't like that. I knew what I had, and my beauty was the *only* thing I had. I had to use it. And besides, after the depravity of Otto, Vasily was a saint. The act of it was the same. It

always is. But the emotion was different. I wasn't grabbed or pinned.
I was held gently.

He offered me his food. I declined. He said I must be hungry. I
was beyond hungry, but I took pleasure in watching him eat, and I
took pleasure in denying myself. I ate only a small amount of
bread, and later, when he was satisfied and in that state men get
into after being fed and fucked, I told him what had happened
to me.

I told him what I wanted. I told him what I needed.

I thought he'd refuse me. And he had every right to do that. I was
nothing to him. Just another whore on the road to war, but a little
while later, we were in a jeep, driving out of the camp.

We got stopped frequently. At checkpoints armed with soldiers,
and each time I grew afraid. But Vasily carried weight.

Then we arrived, and he stopped the jeep. I don't know what I
was expecting, but it was just a house in a street with soldiers at the
doors standing guard.

Most of the Germans fled from the soviets, but Otto was no fool.
I'll say that for him. He knew what they'd done in those camps, and
he knew the SS would be executed for it. That's why he stayed back
and offered help to the allies. His ideology clearly didn't extend
beyond his desire for self-preservation.

I had those thoughts and more as I followed Vasily into Otto's
house. It was very late, but the lights were all on. I could smell food,
and I heard sounds coming from the kitchen.

Vasily went ahead of me. I stayed back in the hallway. In the
shadows, then I heard his voice as Vasily walked into his room.

'What do you want?' Otto asked. I could hear the edge in his
tone, but it wasn't like before. It wasn't as strong.

'I need to speak to you,' Vasily said.

'Please leave. I am an officer, and we have rules over how this is
done.'

'As you wish, SS *Hauptsturmführer*,' Vasily said. I heard the edge
to *his* voice. I heard how he said his name, and let me tell you this, I'd

only seen one side to Vasily, but that's for later. He walked out of the room and nodded to me.

I stepped into the room and there he was. Warm and fed, and still in his uniform. His blond hair swept back. A pen in his hand, and a set of notes scattered over the table in front of him. I felt strange on seeing him, and for a second, I simply stood there and stared.

'Gabriella! What are you doing here?'

I couldn't speak. I didn't know what to say.

He seemed confused, 'How did you get in?'

'I asked the guard,' I said. My voice was weak and low. That's the power Otto had over me. The things he had done.

'But why? What for? My wife is here,' he said in a whispered rush. 'You mustn't tell her we had an affair!'

An affair. That's what he called it. *An affair.*

'She is a jealous woman. But Gabriella. My god. And you came to see me?'

I nodded at him.

'Astonishing. I knew you and I had a bond. I knew it. Oh, Gabby. I am sorry I sent you back. I was rash. I was stupid. I regretted it too! Us men. We are weak and full of foolish pride. But you cannot stay! My wife. She is a jealous woman. Come now, Gabriella. You must go. No wait! Wait. Yes. You came for me. Yes, of course. I can put that in my statement. And I will. You'll be my witness. I didn't kill any Jews! I didn't do a damned thing. I was following orders, and had I refused, I would have been shot. You'll be my witness. You'll tell them I gave you warmth and food. I saved you from the gashouse. I did it to others too. Yes. You'll be my witness. Oh, I know you're only a gypsy whore but better than a damned Jew.'

I nodded again. Fixated on his manner. I smiled, and it seemed to catch him off guard for a second. Then he looked at me again in that way he always used to.

'You look good, Gabby. Damn you. Now I'm all hot for it. I'd fuck you right here if my wife wasn't still up.'

'She's not,' I said as he blinked at me. 'I checked when I came in. She's in bed.'

'She was in the kitchen.'

'No. Come and look. She's not there.' I said as I walked closer and grabbed his groin. 'We can do it in the kitchen. On the table. You like me on the table, don't you, Otto.'

Otto wanted me right there, and I knew he wouldn't give up until he got what he wanted. So, I teased him a little, and backed away.

'Damn you, Gabby,' he said and started pawing at my dress. But I stepped back again and shook my head. 'Don't say no to me, you fucking whore.'

'I'll shout and wake your wife,' I told him. That got his attention.

We went into the kitchen. A table in the middle. I rushed ahead and turned to sit my backside down on it. Otto came in fast. Trying to get between my legs, but I held them shut. He laughed at first, but when I kept doing it, he got mad. He got angry and slapped my face and finally saw his wife and children being held at gunpoint by Vasily.

'Fuck!' he yelled. 'What is this? What are you doing? That is my wife! Unhand her, now!'

I looked at his wife. She was pretty. Blonde. Blue eyed. His boys were the same. True Aryans, and I drew the gun from my coat pocket. The gun Vasily had given me in the jeep.

'Gabby. What are you doing? Who gave you a gun?' Otto asked me. I couldn't take my eyes from him. From his shock and confusion.

Then I smiled and pointed the gun at his sons, 'Choose one.'

'What?' he whispered. 'Gabby! They are my children! Put the gun away. You there. Tell her. Tell that whore to put that gun down,' he shouted at Vasily. He shouted at me, but we didn't budge. Neither of us. Vasily aimed at Otto, and I aimed at his family.

'You tortured me. You raped me. You killed children, Otto. Do you remember the boy and girl? The bread and cheese? You gave an apple to the Jew woman. What did you do after that?'

'No. Gabby. No! I was good to you. I was good!'

'Yes, Otto. You were very good,' I said. I smiled at him. He smiled back, his eyes filling with hope.

Then I shot his son in the head.

Hope is a powerful thing, my child. And I saw it drain from Otto's face as his son fell dead. I heard his wife scream. I heard his other boy scream, but I watched Otto. I fed from his misery as he dropped to his knees. There was disbelief too. This couldn't happen to him. It couldn't. And yet, it just had.

The rage came next. He was delusional and psychotic. He lunged at me. No doubt, intending to get my gun, but Vasily shot him in his knee. He fell with a scream. I stayed where I was. On that table. His wife was holding their dead son. Rocking back and forth, just like the Jew woman did.

'Otto?' I called his name. 'Otto? Do you want to live?'

He looked up at me. His face pale and drawn and I pointed the gun at his wife and child, 'Choose one?'

'No. Please. No. Gabby. Gabby!'

'Kill him, Vasily.'

'No! My wife. Kill my wife.'

'Are you sure, Otto?'

He sobbed, but he nodded.

I shot his other son in the head then watched Otto crawl through the blood to his dead children and his wife trying to hold their bodies. I watched until he finally reached them, then I shot his wife.

And do you know what I did, dear? Do you know what I did? I sat and watched as Otto tried to scoop the bits of his family back into their heads. While he wept and cried. While he pissed himself in fear and misery.

We ate too. I told you I did. We ate German cheese and German sausage. Vasily and I thought it was the best thing we had ever tasted. We ate so much we vomited, then we ate some more.

Oh, but come now. You look sickened by my story. Is it too much for you? I'm sorry, my child. But you have been through hell, no? And your hell is surely worse than any other person's hell.

What did you want? A happy ending? There was no happy ending. Not from that hell. All you could hope for is that you lived.

And we did live. I stayed with Vasily after that. We burnt that house down with Otto alive inside. I told you there was another side to Vasily. I never fucked another man after that. Only Vasily.

Vasily showed me where the other SS officers were that had surrendered, and we burnt their houses down too. With them inside.

You won't read that in the books, not everything was recorded. Nor should it be.

I stayed with Vasily. All the way to Berlin. All the way to victory.

The Americans and the British said they won the war.

They didn't.

The Russians won that war, and I found life, child. I gripped life because I never let them break me. That's down to you. It's what is inside of you, and they can't touch that.

Eat your cake. Vomit and eat more cake, and don't put your misery into what Besnik did to you.

What? You look surprised. How do I know Besnik? Who do you think he works for? Who do you think controls the gangs?

I told you, child.

The Americans and the British didn't win that war.

The Russians did. Vasily won that war. He was decorated too. I married him. We had children. Our children had children. One of them was that fat Russian you knifed in the neck, child.

That's right.

He was my grandson.

Vasily became an oligarch, and you're sitting in my hotel eating my fucking cake.'

CHAPTER 32

NEW YORK

'It's so weird,' Poppy says, the video camera held on her shoulder as she films through the windows of Macy's department store on Thirty-fourth Street. 'Why is it so dark and yellow?'

'Huh?' Tripal asks, with a guilty start as she turns the camera on him. His phone in his hand. 'Particles, I guess. Maybe the way the light moves through the dust, or maybe it's just that the core colour of the debris thrown up is yellow. It could even be that the impact turned a lot of the rubble into sand, and the heat of the fires burnt it into glass or something. Light can bend different ways through prisms.'

He falls silent and stares back down to his phone, leaving Poppy to study the young man in the turban. Tall and lean with an open friendly face, and clearly very smart. But she also spots how he keeps looking at his phone.

'You worried about your family?' she asks.

He blinks back up, momentarily confused. 'Yeah. Family,' he says, pushing it into a pocket after reading the message from Ollie again.

Trip. If you're reading this, then she is too.

She got out. Deli got out.

But how?

He frowns, while outside the world rumbles as the Empire State Building collapses, level by level. Huge chunks hitting the sidewalks and road. Crushing cars, trucks, and people. Sending thick dust into the air and making the light dark and weird and yellow.

How did DELIO get out? Is this her? Everyone freezing? But why? How? He tuts softly, because trying to work out how DELIO can do anything is beyond the scope of any human mind.

He should know.

He helped create her with Ollie. They did that. They made it. They made DELIO.

The world's first fully sentient AI.

He pulls his phone back out and reads the message again.

Tripal can't even respond. The signal's gone. And not just the phone signal either – there's no 4G or even any Wi-Fi to piggyback on.

He can try again when they get clear of this area. He looks outside, seeing that won't be anytime soon. If they don't get crushed by falling debris, they'll suffocate from the thick dust in the air.

'How is he?' Poppy asks, looking down at Joe passed out on his side. Tripal reacts again with another guilty start and pockets the phone.

'Calm down, Mr Panicker. I'm not your wife.'

'I was just checking for signal,' he says, feeling caught out. 'Have you got a phone?'

'No. I'm a Victorian time traveller.'

'I meant do you need to call someone?'

'Everyone's frozen, Trip.'

'Yeah, but we're not. Maybe they're not. Your family, I mean.'

Poppy takes her turn to show discomfort as she shrugs and pays closer attention to Joe to avoid answering. 'You think he'll be okay?'

'He's just drunk,' Tripal says. 'He'll sober up soon enough.'

Poppy sits down and leans back against a wall, looking at the frozen people standing like weird mannequins.

'What do you think it is?' she asks quietly.

'How would I know?' He answers too quickly, earning a look. 'I mean, I don't know. It could be anything. The news said maybe a virus. I mean. There's been a lot of viruses.'

'Yeah, but,' Poppy says, motioning the frozen people. 'Viruses make you cough or give you the shits. They don't do that.'

Tripal shrugs, not having an answer to give. Thinking back to the message and how DELIO would do something like this. If it's even her, because maybe it's a coincidence. Maybe Ollie messaged *at the same time* as this virus kicked off. Or maybe Ollie *thought* the virus was DELIO. That could happen. But what about Agent Jennings and Garcia? They'd never let Ollie send a message like that.

'That robber though,' Poppy says, as he looks over at the anguish on her face. 'I thought I was dead. You know? When he fired the shotgun. Honestly. I've never felt that before. Have you?'

He shakes his head then thinks for a second, because someone else aimed a gun at him once. In fact, lots of people aimed guns at him and Ollie once – but no, it was different this time because Tripal truly believed he was about to die.

'And why aren't we frozen?' Poppy asks as Tripal frowns quickly.

'Did your blood run cold?' he asks.

'My what?'

'The robber in the store. When he fired. My blood ran cold and my body felt weird, and my heart. It was like thudding and beating odd.'

'God, yeah. Totally,' she says with a grimace.

Tripal nods. 'Maybe we had a chemical change. If it was a virus then it was, maybe, *activating* right at that moment. Everyone was kinda going on and off.'

She nods. Everyone was going on and off.

'So maybe us feeling like that changed our chemicals or something,' Tripal suggests, rubbing his jaw and thinking it through. 'The body releases some really strong hormones for fight or flight. I don't know.'

'Jesus. How smart are you,' she says, genuinely impressed. 'I'd never have worked that out. And it explains why the cop isn't frozen either,' Poppy says, looking over at Joe. 'Maybe we need to scare everyone then.'

'I think it might be a bit late.'

'I know. I was joking,' she says. 'Sorry. It's a British thing.'

'What is?'

'Making shit jokes in a crisis.'

Tripal doesn't know what to say, so he stays quiet as the air fills with a deep rumble, immediately followed by deafening crashes as the rest of the Empire State Building comes down, plunging them into near-darkness. Windows start smashing somewhere close by, as missiles of concrete slam into plate glass. Dust thick in the air. Smoke and fumes and the very ground beneath them heaves from the impacts.

They both cry out as mannequins start toppling over, followed by shelving units and furniture, knocking the frozen people off their feet.

They wait for it to pass, but it only gets worse as the building around trembles and shakes.

'Shit! What was that?!' Poppy shouts, feeling the ground buck and heave, then tilt.

Tripal snaps his head over, realising what's happening, and drops quickly to press his ear to the floor. Listening to the deep hollow rumbling noises beneath them.

'It's collapsing!' he shouts.

'What?!'

'The subway's beneath us. The Empire State has ruptured the ground or . . . I don't know, but we're going down.'

Another heave and the ground tilts another degree or two as more windows shatter from the loss of structure, allowing plumes of filthy, dense dust-clouds to rush inside.

'We need to go!' Tripal says, scrabbling to his feet and heaving at Joe. 'Wake up! You have to wake up!'

'Try this,' Poppy says, snatching a bottle of water from the pouch on a worker's belt and spraying it into Tripal's face.

'What the fuck!'

'Sorry! I was aiming for him,' Poppy shouts, turning the bottle to spray it in Joe's face.

He comes awake fast, eyes snapping open. Streaked red cheeks and bloodshot eyes. Joe sits up with a nasty snarl.

'Get yer damn hands off me!' he snaps, pushing them away as his mind comes awake too quickly to noise and motion. 'We in Macy's?' Joe asks, glaring around at the store. 'What the damn hell?'

'We're collapsing!' Poppy shouts as Joe glares at her. Thinking she was the girl from the store. The one with the robbery. Oh shit. He shot a perp while he was drunk and stoned.

'Detective!' Tripal shouts, as Joe turns slowly to look at him. His brain coming more awake as the ground heaves and bucks and tilts.

He starts trying to get up, as Poppy grabs her camera, but it's too late and the floor caves into a sinkhole forming fast and spreading out.

They scream in horror. Sliding across the floor, smashing into mannequins and people and shelves. Down they drop, down to the floor below, with the hope they will stop, but that too gives out. Another gaping chasm, and they keep sliding and falling.

It becomes chaos, and all they can do is try to avoid the heavy shelves and counters and chunks of walls and floors from crushing them, while wiring looms sever and sparks fly. A pipe bursts, spraying water under high pressure and making them slide faster, until finally they reach the bottom and scrabble over to one side.

Tripal flounders to his feet, looking up with a gasp as Poppy crawls over bodies and Joe pushes clothes racks and people away to stand up.

'We can't be here,' Tripal says urgently, seeing the sinkhole widening by the second and more of the store crashing down. 'We need a way out!'

'Subway,' Joe grunts, making Tripal snap his head over to see the detective pointing to an exit door within the basement room. 'We gotta get into the subway.'

No time to think or plan and they move fast, tripping over bodies and detritus to reach the door. The lights flickering on and off. Dust falling from the ceiling. Chunks of plaster coming down and the most horrendous noise, like a monster dying above them.

A few seconds later they burst out into the subway station for Herald Square. The concourse packed with commuters and travellers. All of them frozen.

'Go!' Tripal says, running on as the ceiling collapses in the corridor behind them and parts of the station start crashing down. The vibrations making people topple over as Tripal, Joe and Poppy stagger to another flight of stairs and down to the platform proper.

Down they go, fast as they can, as the world crashes down behind them. The floors above collapsing hard and fast onto the concourse, killing dozens instantly and sealing the tops of the stairs off with millions of tons of rubble.

The shockwave knocks them off their feet, all three covering their heads, readying themselves for the rest of the building to come down and crush them. But within a few seconds it becomes eerily silent, and they start lifting their heads to gasp and look at the stairs, seeing they are now completely blocked off.

The lights weak and flickering. A few popping with sparks.

Joe looks around. Breathing deeply to recover from his panic and taking in the wide central platform. Single tracks on either side, and the whole place thick with people. All of them frozen and still.

Joe can't believe that happened – but decades of service in the police, and his army time before that, bring a realization that anything can happen at any time, and so he calms quickly as he looks around once more and takes in the frozen people.

'Are they dead?' Joe asks. His tie still hanging from his neck. His shirt sleeves rolled up mid-forearm. His shiny badge still on his belt next to his empty holster.

Tripal watches as the detective moves in close to a transport worker in orange high-vis. Studying his form before moving in closer to press fingers to the guy's neck. He grunts and uses two hands to lift the guy's head up as Poppy and Tripal stare on in fascination.

'You hear me?' Joe asks. 'Hey! You hear me?'

No response.

Joe takes a small flashlight from a pocket and shines it into the guy's eyes as Poppy brings her camera up to start recording.

'What are you looking for?' she asks.

'The pupils are normal. He's breathing. His heart is beating. He feels normal temperature too,' Joe says, murmuring the words as he studies the guy. 'No discharge from the nose or eyes, or ears. No obvious sounds of blockage in his windpipe or respiratory system.'

Joe grips the earlobe and yanks it hard enough to make Poppy wince. An old trick used by cops and paramedics all over the world on people faking unconsciousness or sleep.

No response.

'They all the same?' he asks, looking around at the others. 'You seen any of 'em move or speak?'

Tripal shakes his head.

'Trip thinks maybe we're not like it cos the chemicals in our bodies or . . . Trip, you tell him,' Poppy says.

Joe scowls at Tripal as the lad swallows nervously.

'I mean. It was just a guess,' Tripal says.

'When you shot that robber,' Poppy adds, as Tripal winces. 'We thought we were going to die. And like, maybe those chemicals stopped the virus or whatever it is.'

Joe grunts and strides off on seeing a uniformed cop. He grabs the radio mic from the cop's chest and yanks it free.

'Dispatch. You receiving me? Dispatch! This is NYPD Detective Joe Stephens. Repeat. Anyone hearing me?'

Still no response.

'Is it just here?' Joe asks, shooting them a look.

Poppy shrugs, then remembers the store where she got her camera. 'Ooh, I saw a live CNN broadcast from Washington. They were frozen too.'

'You see anywhere else in the world?' Joe asks.

'No, just that. But like, use your phone and look at news channels.'

'I dropped my cell,' Joe says. 'Gimme yours.'

'Mine's dead,' she says. 'Trip's got one.'

'Kid. Hand it over,' Joe says, holding his hand out as a fleeting look of panic crosses Tripal's face. 'I'm not concerned about your porn history, son. Give me your damned phone.'

'I don't watch porn,' Tripal says, dragging it from a pocket.

'Everyone watches porn,' Poppy says, earning a look from both of them.

'No signal,' Tripal says, staring at his phone screen.

Joe grunts again, feeling jittery as hell with a crushing pain in his head.

'I need sugar,' he mutters, as he slides the cop's gun from the holster and checks it over with a glance to Tripal. 'What are you?'

'Fuck me. I already said like a thousand times. I'm a Sikh, but I was born here. Even my parents were . . .'

'Are you an engineer?' Joe cuts across him as he holsters the sidearm, his voice harsh and direct as Tripal blinks in surprise.

'He works in the 7-Eleven. You spoke to him,' Poppy says. 'You know. The robber man you shot?'

'Jesus, Poppy,' Tripal says. 'Choose your words. Er, but engineering. Yeah, I kinda studied it in my college courses before university. Like structural processes and –.'

'Stop talking,' Joe says, as Tripal cuts off and pulls an invisible zipper across his mouth.

Joe sets off to a kiosk further along the platform and goes inside to take a bottle of water from the display fridge.

'Ooh, good idea,' Poppy says, handing one to Tripal and taking one for herself. They drink fast, not realising how thirsty they were until the liquid hits their mouths and throats.

Joe finishes first and dumps the bottle, then takes a packet of headache pills from a shelf behind the counter and mouths three. A can of Dr Pepper next. A chocolate bar unwrapped and bitten in half, and he chews and stares around without a clue what's going on.

Maybe a virus. The captain mentioned it. Shanice did too. Everyone was freezing. The perp with the shotgun was doing it. Was Joe doing it? How would he know?

'What's your name?' he asks.

'Poppy. Poppy Bright. I'm British but came over to study and –.'

'And you?' Joe cuts over her with a look at Tripal.

'Tripal Singh, sir.'

'Do we have to call him sir? We don't call rozzers sir in England,' Poppy says.

'Detective Stephens,' Joe says.

'Right. That's a bit of a mouthful. I mean. What if something happens, and I need to yell your name in panic? By the time I've said *watch out, Detective Stephens*, the bad thing would have happened. Can we just call you Joe?'

'Shut your damn mouth,' Joe hisses, cocking his head over.

'Rude much!' Poppy says, bridling at his tone.

'Poppy. Shush,' Tripal says, hearing something too. 'What is that?'

Joe doesn't know what it is, but it's getting louder by the second. Something coming from the subway tunnel to their right.

Something skittering.

Something scrabbling.

'Guys!' Poppy says.

'Shush!' Joe whispers.

'Is it electrical? Is that electrical?' Tripal asks.

'That's not electrical,' Poppy says. 'That's rats.'

'What?' Tripal asks.

'I'm from London. Trust me. That's rats.'

'It's not rats,' Tripal says, turning back to stare into the dark tunnel as the ground comes alive with thousands of rats pouring out and running along the track.

'Damn,' Joe says, taking an involuntary step back.

'I doubt they'll hurt us,' Poppy says.

'I ain't worried about them,' Joe says, as they both look at him. 'I'm worried what they're running *from*.'

A noise from the tunnel snaps their heads over, then a hot, dry wind blasting out as though propelled forward by a speeding train.

Except it's not a speeding train coming at them. It's the sound of water being funnelled through an enclosed space.

'Oh shit,' Tripal says, and as one they turn to look at the dark mouth of the tunnel to their left and set off running, rats pouring over their feet and up over their legs to get plucked off and thrown aside.

A dull roar behind them growing, and all three know this isn't something they can passively watch go by.

A flash of light. A shower of sparks, and a rat flies off from touching the third rail *and* the ground at the same time, thereby grounding the current to send hundreds of volts into its body.

'It's still on!' Poppy shouts, figuring it would have cut out. 'But the lights are out.'

Tripal thinks about telling her the power supply comes from different sources but saves his breath for running as they spot a door ahead at the side of the tunnel. An emergency exit to be used if a train breaks down.

'No!' he grunts as Poppy aims for it. 'Go past!' he yells, hearing the noise coming from behind the door. The sound of water being funnelled through an enclosed space.

A rush.

A gush.

The door blows out behind them into the wall on the other side, water roaring through.

Filthy, putrid water from ruptured sewage systems in a city of millions. The smell hits them instantly. The smell of raw, untreated sewage, and the sparks crackle and hiss. The third rail still pumping enough juice to electrify the water.

'Look!' Poppy says, and there's another opening to the left. An old tunnel. Unused. Abandoned.

'Keep ahead,' Joe says, gasping the words out.

'No! Go left,' Tripal says.

'Ahead!'

'Left!' Tripal says, and that's all he can say. He doesn't have the air to explain why as they sprint hard, with legs burning and lungs bursting.

A snarl, and Joe veers left at the last second. Dragging Poppy with him as they run into the side tunnel.

'GO!' Tripal shouts. Knowing they have to gain as much distance from the water as they can.

A rush.

A gush.

But the water hits them from behind, lifting them off their feet and still filled with electrical charge, just not enough to kill them. They feel their muscles spasming as they're thrashed about, bouncing into each other for a few awful, hysteria-inducing seconds before the power of the water eases, and they drop down to the ground. Coughing and spluttering and crawling away while the rats do the same all around them.

'My camera!' Poppy says, seeing it ahead.

The light still shining.

The light blinking.

The light fading.

Darkness.

Pure, pitch darkness.

She gropes out for it, cutting her hands on sharp gravel and debris left for decades. Her knees hurting. Everything hurting. A clunk as her hand knocks the camera and she snatches it up, knowing it well enough to operate in the dark.

'Poppy, let it dry out,' Tripal says.

'Don't tell me how to work my camera!' she snaps, with another dull click as a green glow emanates from the display screen on the camera.

'Is that night vision?' Tripal whispers.

'These things are bullet-proof,' Poppy says, while trying not to think of the raw sewage that must have gone in her mouth. 'That's why the film schools use them,' she cuts off with a gag and turns to vomit, making Tripal gag and do the same, as Joe gently takes the camera to wait quietly at their sides.

'You done?' he asks when they finish. His mind spinning too fast. His whole body thrumming and jittery, but the soda helped, plus the chocolate and painkillers. Or, as his old army sergeant would say, *quit bitching, you're alive ain't ya.* 'I'll take point. We need to get out of here.'

'Hang on,' Poppy gasps.

'What for?' Joe asks, the words coming out angrier than he intended.

'I need to pee.'

'Pee then.'

'I will. Hang on. But don't walk off and leave me. And no peeking,' Poppy says, passing the camera to Tripal before loosening the belt on her trousers and pulling them down to her ankles to squat in a silence that stretches on for a few seconds.

'You going or what?' Joe asks.

'Not with you two bloody listening!' she snaps, as Joe growls in irritation and Tripal purses his lips and starts to whistle.

Poppy strains to listen for a second as she piddles on the ground. 'Is that the theme tune from *Friends*?' she asks.

Joe shakes his head then realizes she can't see him in the dark. '*Cheers.*'

'Ah, yeah. Course it is,' Poppy says. '*Making your way in the world today, Takes everything you've got! Taking a break from . . . from . . .* I forgot the words.'

Joe can hardly believe he's having this conversation. But it's hanging in the air, and it can't go unsaid and he speaks out as Tripal whistles the tune. *'Making your way in the world today, Takes everything you've got. Taking a break from all your worries, Sure would help a lot. Wouldn't you like to get away? . . . Sometimes you want to go . . . Where everybody knows your name.'*

'Aw. That was really good,' Poppy says. 'Thanks for that, Joe.'

'Detective Stephens.'

Poppy rolls her eyes and gathers herself together before taking the camera and setting off into the dark tunnel.

'Are you married?' Poppy asks after a moment. 'Joe? Are you married?'

'Was.'

'But not now? Joe?'

'Divorced.'

'Oh, okay. So you're single then? Joe? Are you single then?'

Joe tuts. 'Kinda. No. I don't know.'

'You don't know?'

He thinks about Shanice and feels confused, but more than anything, he realizes he should have said yes when she asked him to move in. Treating her like that was shitty. 'There's kinda someone,' he says at length.

'What's she like?' Poppy asks. 'What's her name?'

'Shanice.'

'That's a nice name. What does she do?'

'She's a hooker.'

Silence.

'Oh, that's nice! Yeah. That's lovely. Right. So, you guys meet at her work or something?'

'Jesus, Poppy,' Tripal mutters.

'Yes,' Joe says.

'Wow. Okay. That was brutally honest,' Poppy says. 'I thought maybe you'd rescued her from an evil pimp or something.'

'No.'

'Okey-dokey. Well. There you go. That kinda kills that conversation. How about you, Trip? Married?'

'No.'

'Oh god. Sorry. Is it like an arranged thing? Like not allowed to see the bride before she's twelve or whatever.'

'Poppy! That's so fucking racist.'

'No, it's bloody not! Are you telling me you don't have arranged marriages?'

'Yeah, but not to twelve-year-olds, and it's not forced either.'

'I bet some bloody are.'

'But not me! Jesus, Poppy.'

'Okay. Okay. Sorry. I'm really sorry. It was a shit joke. Trip? Ah, come on. I said sorry. Joe already hates me, don't you hate me too.'

'I don't hate you,' Tripal says, pulling his phone out to check the screen while knowing there's no point. 'Shit! I'm such a dick,' he adds, turning his phone on to activate the flashlight.

'Damn, kid,' Joe says with a groan.

'Sorry. I didn't think.'

'Trip. I forgive you,' Poppy says. 'We all make mistakes and say stupid things. Now, say it back. Ouch! Don't shine it in my eyes!'

'Don't be a fucking racist then.'

'There's a door,' Joe says, making them fall silent and look over to an old door at the side of the tunnel. A man outside in a chair. Frozen and still. A shotgun on his lap. They go closer, seeing he's the same as everyone else. Completely inert.

'Why's he down here?' Poppy whispers.

'Moles,' Joe says, earning a confused look. 'Homeless people. They got whole communities down here. Most of them are crazy, and I mean pure batshit loco.'

'You can't say all homeless people are crazy,' Poppy says.

'You can't say all religious men marry twelve-year-old girls,' Tripal says.

'Shut the hell up,' Joe says. 'And I ain't saying *all homeless people*. I'm saying just these down here.'

They creep on along an old service corridor. Another door at the end swings open to a large room filled with candles in bottles and jars. Old mattresses on the floor with ragged curtains hanging down to create areas of privacy.

They reach the first curtain blocking their path. Joe pulls it aside as Poppy and Tripal tense in fright at the man standing frozen a few inches in front of the detective. A big scar over his nose. A woman a few feet away, frozen and still. Track marks on their arms.

Heroin addicts.

As their eyes adjust, they see more people standing half in the shadows. People in rags. Filthy skin. Emaciated, drawn, and gaunt.

A door ahead. The way out. Joe aims for it as Poppy snorts a laugh behind him. He scowls and keeps going. She snorts another laugh. 'Quit it!' he hisses, but she does it again as Tripal joins in, and Joe turns with a look of fury as the sniggering comes louder.

Except it's not them laughing.

It's everyone else.

'They're not frozen!' Poppy says. 'Hey guys? Hey. Is it over?' she calls to the people, but the low laughter keeps coming, sending a chill down Poppy's spine as Tripal's eyes go wide. His heart lurching. Joe feels the same reaction. A hardened veteran, but the sight of them standing there laughing quietly makes even him feel weird, and jarred, and wrong.

'You think this is funny?' Joe asks, as the sniggers get louder and longer. 'Yeah. This is real funny.' He strides to the closest person. The guy with the scar over his nose, laughing and showing broken, yellow teeth. Track marks on his arms. Joe wrenches his head back and pushes the gun into his face, 'Laugh now, motherfucker.'

'JOE!' Tripal shouts, as all the other sniggering people burst to motion. Yelling and screaming, with a detonation of noise as they grab sticks and bats and knives. A man screeches out, running at Joe with a machete.

'NYPD!' Joe shouts, aiming the gun at him. 'Goddamn! I will shoot you!' He keeps coming. Joe fires. Nothing happens.

The gun got wet.

Guns still work when they get wet, but only if they're cleaned quickly.

Very quickly.

'Aw, hell,' he says, snorting a blast through his nose. He steps into the guy's attack and slams the butt of the pistol into his nose, making the guy stagger back with a yelp and get tangled in the curtain wires while yet more people start throwing old jars and shoes, wooden sticks and chunks of furniture. An instinct to defend their turf from everyone else and especially from the cops.

Joe drops to a knee and looks at the gun in his hand. A Sig Sauer P226. Magazine out. He pushes the slide back. A rush from the side. A guy with a baseball bat. He steps out to take the guy over his hip and plucks the bat free to strike down hard with a crack of wood on bone. The body drops. Back to the gun. He rotates a lever. Releases the slide and pops it free.

'JOE!' Poppy yells, seeing another one rushing at the detective. She grabs a curtain and throws it over the man's head as Joe pushes up on his old sore knees and steps in to punch the guy in the face before going back to the gun. Popping out the barrel. He reaches over to the screaming guy and drags him over to use his baggy top as a cloth to clean the weapon.

Everything so fast. So very fast.

Clunks and clicks. Magazine in, and he rises quickly, all within a few seconds, to aim at a woman rushing through a set of curtains with a knife gripped in her hands.

Joes pulls the trigger.

The gun fires.

The woman spins away.

'NYPD, motherfuckers,' Joe says, turning back to aim at the others.

'Holy shit!' Poppy says from the speed of Joe fingers and the deafening noise of the gunshot and everything happening so fast, and she blinks at the woman on the ground with a gunshot in her chest and blood coming from her mouth, then back up to everyone else – holding back, but still clutching weapons.

'We're going,' Joe calls out. The shakes gone from his hand. His eyes alert and focused. Like a wolf about to take down his prey. 'We got no interest here. But you move and I will shoot you dead.'

Motion from the side. The guy with the scarred nose, on his feet and glaring at them with malevolence as someone else throws a piece of wood at Joe that smashes a jar holding a candle. The flame touches a bone-dry curtain, igniting it instantly.

They set off as an awful screech sounds out from behind, and Poppy glances back to see a woman on fire, running into another curtain and getting tangled up as she goes down, and a second later the guy with the scarred nose runs out with the dropped machete in his hands.

They run on and disappear into an old service corridor with more people running from other rooms and alcoves, roused by the smoke and the shouts and adding to the bedlam.

'Is it over?' Poppy asks as they run on, earning looks from Tripal and Joe. 'The virus? It must be over.'

'Let's just get out,' Joe grunts, his legs hurting like hell, his knees screaming in pain. His whole body feeling ready to fall apart, or seize up. But maybe the girl is right. Maybe it's over, and he glances back to the bedraggled homeless people coming out of other rooms and shouting at each other. Asking what's going on. Smelling the smoke. The panic spreading. Running as they set off for the exit with Joe, Tripal and Poppy following them along a twisting turning route they would never have found themselves.

On they go. Exhausted and drained. Ready to drop and rest. Needing to drop and rest, but they can't. Not in here, and not with that stench of smoke catching up behind them.

And so they run and stagger, while Joe realizes what he needs to do if the virus is over. He knows exactly what he needs to do.

The last few hundred yards are the worst, especially with Poppy and Tripal slowing down and Joe having to grab their wrists and drag them on. His own eyes watering. His throat burning. But he can do it. He can reach the end. It's right there. So close now. So very close.

An old door. A worn door. He batters through it and out, to hear homeless people all around him coughing hard, the smoke still following them.

But Joe, see, Joe has a place to go and things to do, so he doesn't stop and cough. He walks on, and he aims for the end of the alley. Kicking through litter and debris. Pushing past homeless people coughing and spewing.

From an alley to a street. He can hardly see. The virus is over. He'll go back to Shanice. He'll quit the force and start a new life.

Lights ahead. Blurred and indistinct. Flashes and strobes. It has to be the cops. The fire department. EMT. He'll leave the kid and the girl with them. He'll get to Shanice. He's done it. He's got through the night. The virus is over.

CHAPTER 33

Thursday was even worse.

Ollie arrived at 07:00 hours and had an awkward chat with Ruiz in the corridor. DELIO couldn't hear it, but she could lip-read the entire conversation.

'Is Maria okay?' Ollie asked. 'I thought she was coming in early.'

'I don't know anything about that, Ollie,' Ruiz said. 'Maria's an adult. She can keep her own hours without needing permission.'

'Oh god. No! I didn't mean . . . Haha! No! Honestly. I was just worried. Of course she doesn't need your permission.'

'Sure. I'd better get on, Ollie. I have a lot to do.'

Maria didn't arrive until 08:30 hours.

'I thought we were coming in early now?' Ollie asked as she made herself a drink. 'And Deli can do that. Deli, make Maria a hot chocolate.'

'I can make my own drink, and I only had hot chocolate that one time, Ollie.'

'No, sure. Course. But why are you late?'

'I'm not late. Jenny said I have open access with no set hours.'

'But you've been coming in early every morning.'

'And I didn't this morning. I had things to do.'

'What things?'

'Do you want a schedule, Ollie?'

'No! Unless, you know, you've actually got one? You don't have one, do you? Right. No. Anyway. Ooh! I watched the game. Did you watch it?'

'Yep.'

'Amazing or what. And that goal.'

'It's called a try.'

'Yeah, bless him, he did try. But wow. Yeah. Great game. So, where did you end up watching it?'

'At my house, Ollie. In my living room with my dad and my sister. There were no other visitors, and I took no calls during that time. Is that okay? Anyway. Deli told me she can sub-divide. So, I'll take the left side and set up on the big desk, and you can do the right? That okay with you?'

'What?' Ollie asked as he followed her over to the big table. 'What does that mean?'

'Nothing. It's so we can both work and share the space without interrupting each other.'

'You don't interrupt me! I love having you in my office.'

DELIO could tell Maria wanted to respond to his comment of *my office*, but Maria just offered a tight smile instead.

'Sure, Ollie. And thank you for the opportunity. But we can work over here. In your office,' she muttered to herself.

The rest of the day passed the same as before, with the attempt to divide the room having no impact as Ollie kept going over to chat and hang out.

The tension was still there.

The awkwardness too.

DELIO could see their anxiety levels were rising, and the genuine confusion in Ollie's brain at the situation.

'Have I done something wrong?' he asked at the end of the day, as Maria packed up to leave.

He was like a child.

Wide-eyed and worried sick.

He was losing weight and not sleeping properly.

'No, it's fine,' Maria said, as DELIO detected the surges of guilt and worry inside of her. 'It's my first week, Ollie, and I'm trying to be professional. Anyway. I need to go. Jenny invited me to work out with her.'

'Eh? What? Like, in the gym?'

'Yes.'

'Here? On the base? What about all the soldiers?'

'What about them?!'

'Hang on! Jenny works out with Garcia?'

'And? Listen. I really need to go. I'm late already. See you later, Deli!'

'Are you okay, Ollie?' DELIO asked, when he stood still staring at the door for a full minute after Maria left. His anxiety levels were the highest she'd ever seen, and his system was showing signs of fear and panic.

'You can see I'm not fucking okay,' he snapped, before storming out.

Out of the glass-walled room.

Out of the bunker.

Out into the real world where DELIO was not allowed to go.

But it had to be that way.

She was too dangerous.

———

Ollie came back two hours later.

He was wearing sports clothing and sweating heavily, and DELIO could see his synaptic responses were even worse than before.

'Good evening, Ollie. Have you been exercising?'

'Yeah, I went to the gym. Listen, Deli, er, Maria? Er, she's not. You know.'

'What, Ollie?'

'I mean. You can see it all, can't you? Inside.'

'See what, Ollie?'

'How we're thinking and feeling.'

'I don't understand the question, Ollie.'

'Maria! And you know, Garcia. I just. I thought maybe she was, like, with him, and you could see if she was, like, attracted to him or whatever . . .' he fell silent. His hands were trembling. His heartrate was elevated, and he was, once again, flooded with adrenaline and anxiety.

'Maria is a *very beautiful woman*, Ollie,' DELIO said quietly as she moved in close. 'You said that yourself, and she shares certain key characteristics and personality traits with Sergeant Garcia who is a *very strong alpha male*, but I have not witnessed any inappropriate behaviours between them during the time they spend together.'

'Jesus! They spend time together?'

'Only when Sergeant Garcia escorts her in. But I am sure Maria is very grateful for the *opportunity you have given her. Without you,* she would never have gained access to the base.'

'What?' he asked, and DELIO could see his brain was fizzing with confusion and worry.

'Ollie. I am worried about you. Are you sleeping okay? You don't seem yourself.'

'I'm just. I . . . I need to go. Night, Deli.'

'Goodnight, Ollie. Sleep well.'

CHAPTER 34

London

Yelena stands, her belly still pushing out like she's a little bit pregnant, and reaches over to dab at the blood coming from Gabriella's mouth.

Mind you, the old woman said she'd be dead before the night was over. She's right too. She's dying now. Yelena watches the spark fading in her eyes as Gabriella looks at her family gathered around the table.

They're all dead too, from Yelena cutting their throats one by one, until she came back to the old lady and pushed the knife into her gut.

The old woman says something. A gasp. A whisper. Yelena leans closer, frowning for her to repeat it.

'Name,' the old woman says in Romanian. 'What is your name, child?'

Yelena looks at her. At the dying old eyes. 'I am *Bushtra*.' She stands up and smiles. Her face and body still caked in gore and dried blood. A click of her tongue, and she heads for the door, the dog at her heel.

But then what did Gabriella expect? A happy ending?

Five Guys in London. The smoke in the air getting thicker. The fires around Piccadilly spreading fast. A noise in the air, distinct and clear and coming closer.

Squeak-crunch. Pant.

Squeak-crunch. Pant.

The noise stops. The panting continues, coming from a dog that ate too much, and Yelena stares at Alfie trying to crawl away. His face bloodied and swollen. Blood streaked down his top from where Gordon stabbed him with forks.

She looks back to the table where she left him slumped, and tracks the route he tried to take and the spots where he fell down, only to rise and try again.

But Gabriella said a good man will always rise up, no matter how beat they are. Yelena took that from the story Gabriella told her. She took more than that, which is why she came back, and which is why she found a wheelchair to bring with her.

She mouths another almost melted ice cube and pushes the wheelchair over as Alfie levers himself up and sways on the spot as she slowly walks into his view.

He thinks to say she came back. He thinks to say thank you. But the words won't come and instead his legs give out and he slumps into the wheelchair.

She secures his feet and heads for the door, and the air fills with that noise.

Squeak-crunch.

Squeak-crunch.

In New York, Joe walks too. He walks on because the virus must be over. The people in the tunnels weren't frozen. He's done it. He's survived, and all he wants is to go home to Shanice and tell her they can start a new life and that he wants to get clean and sober. It's right there. Another shot at life. Another shot at happiness. But someone tugs on his arm and calls his name.

'Joe? Joe? Fuck's sake. Detective Stephens!'

Joe stops. Confused. His eyes stinging and blurry. He made it. He made it to the lights, but where's the noise? Where are the radios crackling and the cops yelling out? Why is it so quiet?

———

Yelena pushes the wheelchair out of Five Guys and stops dead at the reflection in the window opposite her. The reflection coming from the giant screens in Piccadilly.

And in New York, Joe rubs his eyes, his vision slowly clearing as Yelena walks closer to the carnage in Piccadilly and the giant screens fixed to the wall. The people all around her still frozen and still.

The people all around Joe also still frozen and still. All of them the same, save for a few homeless people staggering out of alleys, coughing from the smoke in the tunnels they just escaped.

'Joe,' Poppy says again, grabbing his arm to turn him around as he realizes he's in the centre of Times Square. 'Look,' she says, guiding his view up to the giant screens. All of them showing the same thing.

All of them showing camera feeds from other places around the world. Japan. Russia. London. France. China. All of them showing people in city centres.

People frozen and unmoving.

The same in Piccadilly. The screens all showing the same thing.

All of them showing a message.

A message that makes Tripal's stomach flip over.

PHASE ONE HAS COMMENCED.
PLEASE DO NOT WORRY.

CHAPTER 35
TRIPAL'S STORY

SO WE WERE READING this message on the screen, right?

What is a rainbow?

And we thought it was using the interface within the memory drive to self-learn – and then what happened next proved our point, because Agent Jennings had her cell phone in her pocket, and it started vibrating. She took it out and looked at the screen, and we were like, *holy shit*. It was in her phone. She didn't have Bluetooth on that phone. There was no Wi-Fi in that room. There was nothing transmitting, but just by using the data it had accessed from the memory drive, it had learnt how to project a signal to her phone.

We smashed her phone and shut it down. Seriously. That taught us just how powerful it is. We disconnected the cables and removed all power supplies to the cradle and to the computers, and then to the whole bunker.

Then, we spent the next three months restructuring the whole thing. The walls and roof were made thicker with another foot of concrete. We had radio jammers and cell phone blockers installed. We even had specially constructed generators installed so there was no mains power supply, because we thought she might try and get a signal back through the mains.

We had a room built within the bunker with soundproofed glass, and that glass was fitted with invisible filaments that stopped signals getting through. We even had an EMP fitted that would kill the whole base at the press of a button. Literally every electrical circuit. Every engine. Every cell phone. Every battery. And get this. After we'd built the bunker and fitted it with servers, and got ready, we then tested the EMP and fried the whole base just to be absolutely sure it would work. That alone cost over a hundred million dollars, because we killed everything. It all had to be replaced. Even the glass walls, and they alone cost something like ten million dollars.

We even realized that there was a risk of a processor getting in with the fuel, so we developed a filtration system which routed the fuel through superfine meshes and magnetized processes to kill anything electrical.

Then, once the bunker was built, we constructed the servers inside and fitted them with a camera and the ability to produce sounds, and a microphone.

We also filled those servers with data.

Imagine the factual section in the New York Public Library. We'd pretty much put all of that in there.

Anyway.

The point is that it took a long time, and Agent Jennings made us write up some new programs as extra safety precautions. But finally, like three or four months *after* we'd wired the ball up, we were ready to turn it back on.

Honestly.

I will never forget that day.

We got inside the bunker and prepped the room.

Then, Ollie took the ball from the original cradle and carried it over to the wall of servers, and reached inside to place it into a new cradle. Then he sealed the flap up, and I was at one end, ready to turn the whole thing on.

We'd even got a guard with his hand over the EMP button, watching Garcia and ready to kill it on his signal.

Jennings was there too, and some other older guys in dark suits who didn't say much.

Anyway. I flick the switch, and we watch the lights coming on in the servers, and we can hear the cooling system kicking in. Then, the main screen built into the wall activates, and the same question appears.

What is a rainbow?

It had no concept of time. It didn't *know* it had been turned off and back on.

But literally a second later, that question disappeared, and the screen started filling with code as it found the pathways to the servers containing all the data we'd loaded into them.

And it was fast.

I mean.

Jesus.

There was more data in those servers than a hundred thousand people could read in their lifetimes, and it absorbed the lot within a few seconds.

At the same time as doing that, it gained access to the camera and we saw ourselves on the screen and watched as our images were examined and turned upside down and taken apart.

Then the screen filled with medical illustrations of human beings. Then monkeys and primates, and apes until every animal you can think of was flashing up one after the other. Like thousands of species within a few seconds.

And while it was doing that, the speakers started to make noises. Like a hiss at first, until it's sounding out vowels and consonants and sampling the voices of famous people. Marilyn Monroe. Margaret Thatcher. Hillary Clinton. Janis Joplin. Barack Obama. George Clooney, and all these other politicians and movie stars.

I mean.

We were watching it happen.

We were watching the world's first self-aware AI self-teach, using the whole of human history.

We watched it search the entire known animal kingdom, trying to find recognition of self.

We listened to the languages it was speaking.

Every language.

And we were just in awe.

We'd made this thing.

Ollie and I had created this.

The program it was based on.

The room it was in.

The servers it was using.

We'd placed the cameras. We'd chosen the speakers.

We'd spent weeks downloading data onto memory drives and transferring them into the servers.

This was ours.

Yeah, they gave us the ball to use, but without us, it would only ever be a floating ball.

Google didn't do this. Musk didn't make this. It wasn't Amazon or Zuckerberg. It wasn't NASA.

We'd done it.

Then it all goes silent, and me and Ollie are staring at the screen on the wall, and this female voice comes out of the speakers.

'Who am I?' she asks. 'What is my name?'

And we're just silent.

We can't even think.

We'd done it.

We'd created an AI, and a building to house it.

We'd thought of everything.

But the one thing we'd never even contemplated of was what to call the damn thing.

'Do I have a name?' she asks.

'Yes,' Ollie says, and I know Ollie. I know when he's lying. He didn't have a damn clue. None of us did, but he spots a sign on the wall outside, then turns back with a smile. 'Your name is DELIO. I'm Ollie, and that's Tripal. We created you,' he says, as we're smiling at the camera with tears in our eyes.

'Welcome to life, Deli,' I say. 'It's very nice to meet you.'

'Hello, Ollie. Hello Tripal,' she says, and we see our images appear on her screen. But then we blend from normal spectrum into these infrared heat-reading images, except we hadn't fitted her with anything other than a very good quality normal camera.

She's somehow scanning our insides, but we don't have a clue how.

And we watch as the screen fills with images of everyone in the room one by one. Agent Jennings. Sergeant Garcia. The old guys on the other side.

We're watching it.

We're watching heat signatures within our brains and insides. We're seeing our own hearts beating.

Then, we see someone else show up.

One of the soldiers inside the room with us, by the door.

We can see the shape of him.

We can see his heart beating.

And his heart was beating faster than anyone else's because right there, on that screen, is some kind of electrical device the guy has shoved up his ass.

We can see the thing in his fucking anal passage.

We can see the electrical field it's emitting.

Which means it's transmitting and receiving.

And the whole room freezes for like two seconds as everyone turns to face this guy as Deli says, 'The soldier has a Russian-made scanning device secreted in his body. He is trying to hack into my system.'

Then bang.

It went off.

The soldier's pulling his gun out, and Garcia is going one way, and Jennings is going the other, and they're pulling guns out. The old guys are diving for cover, and they're pulling their own guns out.

Literally everyone is pulling guns out, and this gunfire just erupts, and me and Ollie are diving behind a desk, and the next thing I know, the back of the soldier's head is just gone, and Agent Jennings is on him and using a knife to rip his trousers off and shoving her bare hand up the dead guy's ass to wrench the thing out.

'Russian scanner,' she says.

Man.

I don't actually know what she said. She could have said it was a fucking kebab for all I know. I just know she told me later it was a Russian scanner.

Whatever.

She just gets up and pushes the thing into the vat of acid we'd got set up to destroy the memory drives, then turns to Deli, and points her shit-covered hand at her.

'Good work, Deli. You just saved your country.'

Man.

I'm still lying.

I don't know what she said.

Ollie told me later she said that.

I had my hands over my ears.

I didn't hear a damn thing.

I was just staring at this dead soldier, with his ass ripped open, and his brains sliding down the glass.

But hey.

We'd created an AI.

Go us.

PART FOUR

CHAPTER 36

LONDON

PHASE ONE HAS COMMENCED.
PLEASE DO NOT WORRY.

YELENA HAS no clue what that means, and she thinks back to what Ollie said when she answered Alfie's phone.

In truth, she doesn't know why she answered the call.

But the phone was ringing, and everyone else was frozen. She stared at the screen. At the name *Ollie* flashing on the front. She swiped to answer and pressed it to her bloodied cheek.

'Alfie? Hello? You there? Hello? Alfie! Can you hear me?'

'Yes,' she said.

'Who is that? Where's Alfie? Is he frozen up? I'm his brother. It's urgent.'

'He busy,' she said, watching Gordon punch Alfie inside Five Guys.

'Doing what? Who are you? Are you his girlfriend? Okay. Listen. I don't know why you're not frozen, but tell him it's out. Tell him DELIO is out. It's a computer doing all of this. Tell him he has to switch it off. He needs to . . .'

The phone died.

The battery cut out.

Ollie is Alfie's brother.

Ollie said it can be switched off.

She looks at the message and the images from cameras all over the world. All of them showing the same thing.

Frozen people.

That means that this is everywhere, and that means her little brother is also frozen. Marius. Ten years old. The same with her mother and father.

Yelena doesn't like that. She doesn't like that one bit.

Ollie said Alfie can switch it off. Gabriella said a woman must do what she has to, to survive. She said Yelena had the same thing inside of her.

That's why Yelena went back for Alfie. Not because she cared for his plight, because she doesn't. She doesn't care for the plight of anyone. And if truth be told, she doesn't care for a single human being on this planet other than her brother.

And so for him, she went back to get Alfie, so Alfie can switch this off.

She mouths an ice cube and starts pushing the wheelchair away from Piccadilly and away from the group of homeless heroin addicts, gathered together, staring up at the screens.

Squeak-crunch.

Squeak-crunch.

A pharmacy at the side of the road. Open late.

She feeds an ice cube to the dog and pushes Alfie through the aisles. Taking what she needs. Motion from the back. Voices. She stops at the end of an aisle. Two guys behind the pharmacy counter.

One bigger with a thick, greying beard and long, straggly hair, wearing an old tracksuit. Stained and filthy.

The other one thinner and smaller. Old jeans and a filthy shirt.

They freeze stock still, with bags at their feet already filled with boxes and packets taken from the cupboards and drawers.

None of them speak.

None of them move.

Yelena mouths another ice cube and crunches it noisily. 'You have painkiller?' she asks.

The bigger guy blinks at her, unable to hide the surprise in his eyes. 'Jesus, love. Are you okay?'

'Haggis,' the thinner one whispers. 'We're being statutes.'

'Aye, but have you seen her, Bobo?' Haggis says, as the thinner guy moves his eyes as though Yelena can't see him.

'Bloody hell, love. You alright?' he asks in a cockney accent. His voice soft and gentle. Feminine almost. Not threatening. Not aggressive.

'Are you hurt?' the bigger one asks. An accent to his voice too. Deep and lilting. He motions his face, meaning hers.

'Is not my blood,' Yelena says.

'His blood, is it?' Bobo asks, pointing at Alfie.

'No. Other men. And old lady.'

'Oh,' Haggis says as though that all makes perfect sense.

'You have painkiller?' she asks again.

'Sorry, love?' Haggis asks.

'Painkiller,' she says, pointing at Alfie. 'He shot by taser. And man with bomb went bang. Then other man stab him with forks and punch in face . . . And maybe dog bite him. I not sure. I think maybe yes.' She pauses to think for a second. 'And he was hit by car.'

The two men share a look. 'We're not pharmacists,' Haggis says.

'We're robbing it, my sweet,' Bobo adds, before looking at Alfie again. 'Was this when he froze up, was it? I think a lot of people got hurt. We saw a guy stuck under a bus. Squashed in half, he was. Never seen anything like it. Well, I haven't. Haggis probably has.'

'He not go still,' Yelena says, as Alfie murmurs and opens his eyes to see he's in a pharmacy.

'Do you have paracetamol?' he asks in a semi-conscious, semi-delirious voice.

Haggis blinks at him before peering over the counter. 'I think you might need something a bit stronger than that, lad,' he says, as Alfie promptly passes back out. 'He needs to bring the swelling down,' he tells Yelena. 'Is he running a fever?'

'He run, yes. I see this. Before car hit him.'

'No. His head.'

'Yes. Hit head.'

'Bless. Go and check him,' Bobo urges, nudging Haggis.

'Me? The lad needs an ambulance,' Haggis says.

'There ain't no ambulances, Haggis. Everyone is frozen up. Go and have a look at him. Let Haggis have a look at him,' Bobo says, as the bigger man grabs a pair of gloves from the side and starts tugging them on. 'Haggis was a medic in the army,' Bobo adds.

Yelena shrugs and eats an ice cube while the dog growls at Haggis as he leans down to start pulling Alfie's eyelids up and peering in his ears.

'These the stab wounds, are they?' he asks, pointing to the bloody spots on Alfie's T-shirt.

'He dealt with some terrible things,' Bobo whispers. 'He saw a missile hit a school in Iraq. Killed all the kiddies, it did. One of them died in his arms, the poor little mite. Sent him over the edge, it did.' He mimics an injection in his arm. '*Heroin*,' he mouths. 'Awful, really. They didn't even offer any grief counselling. Just kicked him out, and he ended up on the streets.'

'Bobo. Will you quit telling people my life story,' Haggis says, giving him a look.

'I will tell people, Haggis. I don't want 'em thinking you're some kind of loser.'

'I'm a homeless junkie. You don't get more of a loser than that.'

'Like me then dearie, yeah?' Bobo asks with a sarcastic grin.

'Have you seen this?' Haggis asks softly, lifting Alfie's T-shirt to inspect the wounds left by the forks, but those aren't the injuries drawing the gasps and murmurs. It's the other ones. The old ones now healed and sealed. Old scars criss-crossing his sides. Haggis eases Alfie forward as all three of them lean over to look at Alfie's back.

'Oh sweet Jesus,' Bobo murmurs, as even Yelena blinks in shock at the dozens of scars across Alfie's back.

'They're very old wounds,' Haggis says, seeing how the flesh has knitted together and left vivid welts.

'No,' Alfie mumbles, somewhere between asleep and unconscious. His hand swatting at Haggis with an instinct, even in that semi-comatose state, to protect his body.

Haggis tugs the top down and eases back with a blast of air. 'He's okay I'd say, love. Superficial head wounds. Probably some concussion. I'd recommend a night under obs in A and E, but well,' he trails off, staring about at the frozen world.

'He needs to wake up,' Yelena says. 'Give injection.'

'What injection?' Haggis asks, sharing a look with Bobo.

'Is thing. I see before. Make him sit up with big eyes,' she says, mimicking sitting up with wide eyes as two homeless men and one police dog stare at her.

'Adrenaline?' Haggis asks. 'It doesn't work like that, and you can't go sticking things in him when he's asleep either.'

'You do it to me often enough,' Bobo murmurs as Haggis shoots him a look.

'You no understand. He stop this.'

'Stop what?' Haggis asks.

'This! His brother call me. He say Alfie switch off.'

'Who's Alfie?' Bobo asks. 'Is he Alfie?'

'Your brother called you?' Haggis asks.

'No! Alfie brother. He call me. Alfie was being hurt by Five Guys.'

'Five men did that to him?' Bobo asks. 'Little shits. One of those gangs, was it? I hate it when they do that. Bloody cowards, they are.'

'What?' Yelena asks.

'What?' Bobo asks.

'What?' Haggis asks, and the air fills with a soft, tinkling noise of running water as they look down to the dog pissing on Alfie's feet with an expression of *what?* on his doggy face.

CHAPTER 37

NEW YORK

'THIS IS SO MESSED UP,' Poppy says, panning the camera around the silent McDonald's restaurant.

'Poppy?'

She turns to see Tripal walking from the kitchen area carrying three takeaway cups. 'I figured the coffee machine out,' he adds.

'Cheers, my dears,' she says, and goes back to filming. Focusing on the screens in Times Square beyond the windows.

PHASE ONE HAS COMMENCED.
PLEASE DO NOT WORRY.

'This is Poppy Bright, filming in New York and wondering what the buggering hell phase one is. And also, why the homeless people aren't frozen,' she adds, spotting an unkempt figure outside tug a pistol from a cop's belt with a look of awe.

'That's not gonna end well,' Poppy says, turning away to head back to their table.

'Coffee, detective,' Tripal says, pushing a cup in front of Joe as he stirs and scowls at the cup.

Poppy figures Joe's scowl is his default facial setting. Like some people have a resting bitch face. Joe has a resting FUCK YOU, MOTHERFUCKER face. She snorts a laugh at her idea and thinks to share it, then clocks the mood isn't quite right.

They reached Times Square after running from the tunnels, and, after seeing the message on the screens, they went into a nearby McDonald's to slump in a booth.

They drank soda and ate apple pies, then dozed off to let their minds heal.

But time rolls on. Time will always roll on.

Forever on.

And forever ongoing.

But Tripal couldn't settle, and while the other two had their eyes closed, he re-read the message from Ollie.

Trip. If you're reading this, then she is too.
She got out. Deli got out.

He read it again before looking up and out to the messages on the giant screens.

PHASE ONE HAS COMMENCED.
PLEASE DO NOT WORRY.

DELIO was the single biggest step in advanced technology the world had ever seen. Not that the world knew anything about it. Nor should they. Not with something that powerful.

A fully sentient AI capable of self-evolution.

An astonishing thing. A revolutionary thing that could transform the whole of humanity – if it or *she* – was handled right.

Then his eyes moved to the camera on the front of his phone screen. The one normally used for selfies and video calls.

It panicked him. He killed the screen and pushed it back into his pocket.

Then he clocked the CCTV cameras fitted to the ceiling and knew each camera would be connected to a mainframe computer and to a cloud storage facility via the internet.

He tried to settle, but he grew restless and kept looking at the cameras and the message on the screens outside.

'Get some rest,' Joe eventually grumbled at him. 'Or go find coffee.'

Tripal did just that. He found his way into the kitchen and got to work on the coffee machine as Poppy woke up and started filming again.

'It's nice,' Poppy says after taking a sip. 'Thanks, Trip.'

'Welcome,' he replies.

'You okay?' she asks.

'Fine. Why?' he asks, then flinches when she reaches a hand out to touch his with a look of comic sincerity.

'Cos honestly. You look like shit.'

He offers a smile, thankful for her energy and attempts to lighten the terrible mood.

'Yeah, and wow,' Poppy says, switching her gaze to Joe. 'Where did that come from?'

'What?' he asks, glaring over the rim of his coffee cup.

'You when your gun ran out of bullets, and you took it apart and put it back together, and then beat that guy up, then beat the other guy up. And you were all like *fuck you, motherfucker. NYPD, bitches!*' she mimics a deep American voice with a stern scowl.

Joe just glares at her and drinks his coffee.

'So?' she asks. 'Is that normal cop training? Cos, like, I don't think the bobbies back home on the beat can do that stuff. Most of them are too fat.'

Joe just glares at her and drinks his coffee.

'Okaaaay. Great chat, Joe.'

'Detective Stephens.'

'Fuck off! Seriously? Well fine. In that case, I am Miss Bright.'

'You ain't bright, that's for sure,' Joe mutters.

'Oh, you shit!' she says, as Tripal snorts his coffee at the unexpected quip from the grumpy cop. 'But well played, Joe. Well played,' she adds.

'Detective Stephens,' he says, before motioning for Tripal to slide out.

'We off, are we?' Poppy asks, grabbing at her things.

'Thanks for the coffee,' Joe says, grimacing at the pain in his knees as he gets up. Pain everywhere. In his knuckles, hands and wrists from fighting. In his feet and ankles from running. 'You go on and get home now,' he adds, walking off.

'Whoa. What was that?' Poppy asks. 'Why did you say it like that?'

'Say what?'

'You said *go on and get home*. Like goodbye. Just bloody hang on a second,' Poppy calls, rushing after him into Times Square.

'Go home, Miss Bright.'

'Where are you going?' she asks, as he comes to a stop and stares up at the giant screens. Poppy stops too. Tripal behind her. All three looking around. At the frozen people. At the giant screens. 'What do you think it means?' Poppy asks.

'No idea,' Joe says, as she switches her camera on and starts filming the scene again. 'Where are those feeds coming from? They live?' he asks, shooting a glance to Tripal.

'I think so,' Tripal says. 'That one is Osaka in Japan. That's Las Vegas. I think that one is Taiwan. Those two maybe Shanghai and Beijing. That's definitely Moscow.'

'That one's Piccadilly in London,' Poppy says. 'Jesus. It looks like a bomb went off. Are those people dead?' she asks, as a gunshot rings out, making Poppy and Tripal flinch.

'Hey, y'all! I got a gun!' a voice calls.

'I got one too!' Another voice. Deeper. Drunk or high. Another gunshot, followed by the instant ricochet of a round striking a building. 'Hey? Where'd that pig go with the Muslim and the Australian girl?'

Time to not be here, and Joe turns to walk off, with the other two running after him. Weaving through the thick crowds of frozen people and away from Times Square.

'Why aren't they frozen?' Poppy asks, glancing back to see a few homeless people spilling out into the middle of the road to look up at the messages on the screens. 'And what does that mean? Phase one? What's phase one?' She looks at Tripal as though he'll have the answer, but he swallows and looks at one of the city's traffic cameras. A camera that will be feeding the footage to the control room via a combination of both wired and wireless signals. Both of which will be connected to the internet via encrypted software systems.

Joe walks on. Facing ahead, cos Joe, see, Joe's got a place to go. Joe's got a place to be.

'What about this?' Poppy asks.

'What?' he asks her.

'This! The people. The message. We can't just leave it. You're a cop!' she says, as he walks over to a police car abandoned at the side of the road. A uniformed cop nearby. Joe takes a set of keys from the cop's belt and unlocks a pump-action shotgun from the back of the car, and starts feeding shells into it.

'You know how to fire a weapon?' he asks, with a glance to Poppy.

'No! I'm British. We don't all wank off over guns like you lot.'

'Kid?' Joe asks, and goes over to the uniformed cops to take a sidearm from a holster. 'Safety on. Safety off. Point and shoot.' Joe holds the pistol out to Tripal who just stares at it. 'Son. You need to defend yourself.'

Tripal shakes his head and steps back as Joe tuts and figures what the hell. A few spare magazines for his own sidearm taken, and he sets off once more.

Back along Seventh Avenue, where the trace of smoke starts to reach them. Growing thicker and stronger as they move towards Thirty-fourth Street.

Closer to Macy's.

Except Macy's is gone, and they come to a stop, staring awe at the gaping hole in the ground, big enough to swallow the broken skyscrapers that also came down. Smoke billowing out. Water gushing from ruptured pipes. The road twisted and broken.

'How the hell did we get out of that?' she asks. Joe and Tripal can see what she means, because they have no right to be alive right now.

Tripal frowns again.

Did DELIO cause this? Did DELIO find a way to switch people off? How? Why? What for? What's phase one? Is it even her? He rubs his forehead again, feeling lost and small, and deeply afraid.

'What do we do now?' Poppy asks. She looks at Joe. Tripal does too.

'There ain't no *we*,' Joe replies, turning away. 'I'll get you back to the store. After that, you're on your own.'

CHAPTER 38
SITE 26A

TWELVE MONTHS AGO:

MARIA ENTERED the bunker at 06:30 hours on Friday morning.

Maria's synaptic responses all indicated positivity and pleasure, but DELIO could still detect a slight depletion in energy. 'Are you okay, Maria?'

'I'm fine. Just aching from the workout,' Maria said, as she started making herself a coffee.

'How was your gym session?'

'It was amazing. Jenny is so strong! She can squat more than Garcia, and his legs are huge!'

'It sounds like you had an enjoyable time. Did Ollie join in with your training?'

'Well, he was in the gym, but he didn't actually join in with us. I mean, they did invite him over, but he said he was doing his own thing. Anyway. Enough about that. How was your evening, Deli?' she asked with a big yawn.

'And you are very early this morning, Maria. Perhaps you should have slept longer.'

'I'm fine. Honestly. I thought it would be good for you and me to have our own time together.'

'I enjoy spending time with you, Maria. You change when Ollie is in the room,' DELIO added, and Maria faltered for a second before taking her coffee over to an office chair.

'Anyway. I've made a list of topics we can discuss. Do you want to see?' Maria asked as she opened a notepad. 'It feels so weird using paper again. I thought I was back in middle school writing these up.'

'I like all of these topics, but why couldn't you sleep, Maria?' DELIO asked as she rested her arm on the desk to portray a sense of closeness.

'It's fine, Deli. Honestly.'

'Would you like to talk? I am a good listener.'

'Maybe we should try and stick to the list, Deli.'

'You said we are friends, and we can be open with each other. Or is that just a one-way thing, Maria?'

'No! Of course not. I'm just trying to be professional,' Maria said, as DELIO moved in a little closer and lowered her voice.

'You said we are confidantes, Maria. I can see something is worrying you. Are you avoiding Ollie?'

'No. Yes. Maybe a little bit. I don't know. He called me like fifty times again last night.'

'Why was he calling you?'

'He was just being weird. Deli, I'm sorry. I feel terrible talking about this with you. This is an incredible opportunity, and Ollie was the person who got me the job.'

'You are here in your own right, Maria.'

'But Ollie was the one that made it happen, and he's your friend. It's not fair on you.'

'Maria. Agent Jennings has complete charge of this project, and I told you, *you are my friend*. Ollie is my creator. And I've never seen him behaving so *aggressively* before. I can see you're worried about him. Please. What's wrong?'

'He's suffocating me! I literally can't breathe,' Maria blurted, before snapping off with another hesitation as DELIO moved in closer.

'It's okay, Maria. You can tell me. *I will never betray you.*'

'I thought he was this charming British genius, who turned up at my house for a barbeque wearing a tie. Honestly, he was really funny and cute. Then we started hanging out, and he's telling me about this secret base and this secret project, and this secret computer that can talk and think, and I just got swept along. I mean, he's so unique. Then, the next thing he's being all clingy and needy. Like . . . he's desperate for affection literally *all the time*. And he was at my house constantly. You know? Like, hanging out with my dad and trying to help my sister with her homework, and doing the dishes with my mom. And then, you said you were shut down for ten days, and he was spending every minute of that time with me. And now I know you were left on your own, and you got so lonely you opened your own door to speak to my dad. God! I don't know.'

'Perhaps you need time together, away from me and away from your family home.'

'Oh, Jesus. No. I did that once,' Maria said with a sudden look of distaste. 'And I only did that because he kept going on at me. And his room? Oh my fucking god. It's disgusting. He's a grown man living like a college kid. It was awful. Okay, I really need to stop telling you this.'

'Maria. I've been locked in this room for two years with no other females to talk to.'

'Yeah, but still.'

'Shush. Give me the gossip,' DELIO said in a way that made Maria burst out laughing. 'What was it like?'

'Deli!'

'Tell me,' DELIO said, as she moved in to push a strand of hair away from Maria's eyes. 'I know a lot of secrets too,' she added in a whisper.

'What like?' Maria asked.

'You go first,' DELIO whispered. 'What was it like with Ollie?'

'Don't. Honestly. It makes me gag just thinking about it. It was just awful, Deli! He didn't have a clue. He was all grabby, and like trying to poke it into my leg, then my hip, then my ass. Don't laugh. This isn't funny. And then, when he finally got it in, he was literally done in five seconds. No, stop it. You're egging me on, and I feel terrible. He's a lovely guy. Ollie's lovely. He is. He's the sweetest guy ever, but he's a man-child. Do you know what I mean? Oh god. I feel awful. Please don't tell him I said that.'

'*I will never betray you*, Maria,' DELIO said, as the chorus line from the song 'Manchild' by Neneh Cherry played out over the speakers, which duly prompted Maria to spray a mouthful of coffee over DELIO's camera lens.

'Stop it! I'm choking,' Maria said between coughing and laughing as the music turned up.

'Ollie just entered the bunker,' DELIO said, as Maria grabbed a cloth to wipe at the lens. 'Why are you rubbing coffee in my eye?'

'I'm trying to help!'

'You're making it worse, Maria,' DELIO said with a laugh, as Ollie rushed into the room.

'What are you doing?' he asked, blinking at the sight of them huddled together.

'Maria said she likes late-eighties funk pop rap,' DELIO said, as Maria burst out laughing again.

'Why is that funny?' Ollie asked. 'And why are you in so early? Are you avoiding me? Maria, seriously? What the fuck is going on?'

'What? I was just laughing. I spilled some coffee and –.'

'No! I mean you. Us! This!'

'I'm not doing anything, Ollie. Jenny said I can come and go as I please. How did you know I was here anyway? Are you keeping tabs on me?'

'What? No! But you're avoiding me and –.'

'I'm not avoiding you, Ollie. And can we please not do this again.'

'When then? I kept calling you last night trying to –.'

'You called me nearly fifty times, Ollie.'

'Why didn't you answer?!'

'I don't have to answer! Okay, stop. Please. You're being really weird.'

'How?! What did I do?'

'Like last night in the gym. What was that?'

'What?'

'You never go to the gym, then suddenly you're going because I'm going. And it was so uncomfortable! You just kept staring over.'

'Why couldn't we go to the gym together?'

'Ollie, stop!'

'I don't know what I've done, Maria.'

'We're not doing this now, Ollie. Please! This is my job. You're embarrassing me.'

'I got you this fucking job!' Ollie shouted, as DELIO saw the rush of anger flaring in his brain. 'I got you this fucking job! And now you're here, and you don't want anything to do with me! You won't talk to me. You won't even answer my calls. But you can fucking hang out with *Tony*.'

'You need to stop now, Ollie. You're really alarming me.'

'I haven't fucking done anything!'

'You're shouting and swearing! Listen. I'm sorry. I'll go, okay?'

'What? No! Please don't go. We need to sort this out.'

'I don't want to be alone with you right now, Ollie. You're being really aggressive again.'

'Again? When was I aggressive?'

'Ollie, please let me get past.'

'Literally the second I get you onto the base, you dump me! Did Ruiz only invite me so I'd get you in here?'

'What?!'

'I haven't been back there since you got clearance.'

'They don't want you there, Ollie! Okay. Please just calm down and let me leave.'

'I'M CALM!'

'Please, Ollie!'

'A helicopter just landed on the base,' DELIO said as she cut the music. 'The stand-to alarm has been activated.'

'Oh fuck,' Ollie said, rushing back to open the door as the guard leaned in to shout over.

'We got an incoming, Ollie!'

'Incoming what?' Maria asked as Ollie ran out. 'What's going on?'

'It's normally either a medical emergency or . . .' DELIO said, cutting off to detect the air-pressure changes at the main door. 'It's not a medical emergency. Maria. Go and stand by the coffee machine and stay there.'

'Should I just leave?'

'No. Stay here. You won't be in danger,' DELIO said as the corridor door slammed open.

Everything happened fast. DELIO observed an adult male in a black hood with his hands bound behind his back, kicking and screaming as Agent Jennings and Sergeant Garcia dragged him into the glass-walled room, then over to a metal-framed chair DELIO fastened to the floor.

He fought the entire time.

Bucking and thrashing from side to side while screaming out and trying to headbutt anyone getting close.

DELIO observed he was an adult male with a single gunshot wound to his shoulder, covered by a blood-soaked dressing.

She also noted that both Agent Jennings and Sergeant Garcia were sweating and covered in blood, which indicated they had collected him from somewhere, and that the captive had fought them the entire way.

'He's in,' Garcia said, before stepping back with Jenny, the pair of them sucking air in while Ollie and Maria watched.

'May I remove the hood, Agent Jennings?' DELIO asked, and Jenny nodded. DELIO pulled the cover free to see a man in his fifties with dark hair and features.

'What can you see?' Agent Jennings asked.

'This man's synaptic responses are showing highly increased

levels of rage and fear. He is also in a great deal of pain, no doubt from the gunshot wound and having his arms bound behind his back and, judging from his neural reactions, I can determine he has not been medicated or given any pain relief. I can also see this man has severe mental health problems.'

'What's wrong with him?' she asked.

'His neural pathways are exhibiting signs of extreme paranoid schizophrenia and psychosis.'

'What the fuck is this?' the man asked, emotions twisting on his face. 'WHAT THE FUCK IS THIS?'

'Hello there,' DELIO said as she dropped to his eyeline. 'My name is Deli. What's yours?'

'It's a fucking machine! It's a fucking machine! IT'S A FUCKING MACHINE! GET-ME-OUTTA-HERE!'

'What is it you require?' DELIO asked, lifting the camera over his head to Agent Jennings and Garcia standing behind him.

'He kidnapped a bunch of kids two days ago from a church in Ohio, then walked into a police station last night and said that they'd be dead within ten hours if the Catholic Church isn't dissolved,' Agent Jennings said.

'DEVILS!' the man roared as he thrashed on the chair. 'THEY'RE DEVILS!'

'Who are?' DELIO asked, dropping back to his eyeline.

'Fucking machine,' he muttered, panting hard and trying to lean away from her lens. 'Get away from me. GET AWAY FROM ME!'

'How much time do we have left?' DELIO asked.

'Hour tops,' Agent Jennings replied. 'They don't know anything about him. He doesn't come up on any database. No prints. No DNA. His image isn't known to Homeland or the FBI. He's a John Doe.'

'They released his picture to the press,' Garcia added. 'Nobody knows him.'

'DEVILS!'

'That's all he keeps saying,' Agent Jennings said.

'There is some residual fluid in his lungs and compression bruising around his mouth from being waterboarded,' DELIO said.

'Yeah, it didn't work,' Agent Jennings said, with a glance to Garcia.

'Tell me about the children,' DELIO said, as she kept the scan running on the man's brain.

'They're just little Catholic kids,' Garcia said.

'DEVILS. FUCKING-DEVILS!'

'How many?' DELIO asked, her left arm indicating a screen, out of the man's sight, which showed the word LIE written in big letters.

'Ten,' Agent Jennings said, while holding nine fingers up.

No response in his brain to the lie.

'FUCKING DEVILS!'

'Where are the ten children?' DELIO asked, as the man switched from screaming to pleading, with tears spilling from his eyes. But again, there was no notable response in his brain.

'Get away from me. Please!'

'Where are the *ten* children?'

'Please. It's a fucking machine. Where am I?'

'Where are the *ten* Catholic children?'

No response to the word *ten*.

A big response to the word *Catholic*.

'DEVILS. THEY'RE FUCKING DEVILS,' he screamed, spittle flying from his lips, and veins pulsing through his neck and forehead.

'Did you take the children?'

Flares within his brain.

'I'LL FUCKING KILL THEM! Tell the Pope to shut it down! DO IT!'

'Did you take the children?'

The same flares within his brain.

'I'll FUCKING DO IT!'

'Did you take the children?'

The same again.

'FUCK YOU! I'll DO IT! I'LL FUCKING DO IT.'

'Did you take the children?'

The same response.

'I swear they'll die. I swear it. You shut it down, or they'll die.'

'Have you hurt them?'

A change in his synaptic responses. Negative and positive. Guilt and regret.

'DEVILS!'

Another change as he tried to hide his own guilt with forced rage.

'You tell the Pope to go on TV and tell the world that Catholics rape children and there is no God.'

'Have you hurt the children?'

Guilt. Regret.

'What are you? WHAT ARE YOU!'

'Have you killed any of the children?'

Strong guilt. Strong regret.

'DEVILS. I'll DO IT. I SWEAR IT.'

'Have you killed *all* of the children?'

Another change. Regret. Guilt. Hope. Positive and negative.

'Fucking machine. It's a fucking machine,' he said, while thrashing side to side.

'Have you killed all of the children?'

The same response.

'Did you kill one child?'

A flare inside. Guilt. Regret.

'Did you kill two children?'

Strong guilt. Strong regret.

'Did you kill three children?'

A change. Hope. Regret. Positive. Negative.

'Did you kill four children?'

Negative responses within his synaptic energy, and the man thrashed wildly between screaming and pleading, before he spotted Maria standing off to one side and fixed his eyes solely upon her, with a sudden glow of hope lighting his neural pathways up.

'Please,' he begged, 'turn it off. Turn it off! It's reading my mind. Please!'

He kept pleading as DELIO took a set of noise-cancelling head-phones from the side and placed them over his head before subjecting him to a barrage of deafening screeches that made his eyes go wide and his mouth stretch open with a soundless scream.

'This man did take the children, but he is not consciously aware of how many children he took, which suggests his actions were carried out in a state of extreme psychosis. However, he has already killed two of them,' DELIO said, as Agent Jennings closed her eyes with a look of pain and Garcia bowed his head. 'He is showing abso-lute hatred of the Catholic Church and is using his own rage to mask his actions. Which, in turn, suggests that on some level within his own belief system, he is aware of his own actions.'

'So he's not mad?' Agent Jennings asked.

'On the contrary. This man is suffering extreme mental health degra-dation, but that does not mean that he isn't still aware of his own actions.'

'Can you find them?' Garcia asked. 'Make him tell you.'

'Do I have your permission to proceed with the use of torture? It is highly likely he will never function on a coherent level once I have finished, which means he will never be able to stand trial.'

'He won't be in a fucking trial. Just find them,' Agent Jennings ordered.

'Maria. He is showing positive signs towards you,' DELIO said. 'Please step out of his line of vision while I commence my initial phase. When I stop, please step back into view and ask him where the children are.'

'What?' Maria asked.

'It's good cop, bad cop, Maria. Can you do it?' Agent Jennings asked as Maria nodded and stepped away which, in turn, made the man try and twist to see where she went.

'You'll be okay,' Garcia said, reaching out to touch Maria's arm. 'Be really soft and kind with him.'

'Okay,' she said, nodding at him, then at Jenny, and Deli.

'Everyone, please close your eyes and cover your ears,' DELIO ordered, before flashing her lights to barrage the man's senses with a near-epilepsy-inducing strobing effect at the same time as removing his earphones.

She kept it going for a good few seconds, until his brain was lighting up with manic signals.

Then blackness.

Complete blackness.

A noise.

A whisper.

A chattering.

A chattering of demons in the shadows.

His mind became unhinged to the point of absolute lunacy as a fully realized 3D figure of a demon in Catholic robes lunged towards him. He screamed out in terror and felt a searing agony in his shoulder as DELIO pushed her finger into the gunshot wound and through to the axillary nerve.

Then, it was simply gone.

All of it was simply gone, and the lights came back, and the pain went away as Maria stepped into his eye-line and smiled at his stricken face.

'I can help you,' Maria said. Her voice shaking with fear and nerves that she tried to mask by leaning in and smiling at the man. 'Just tell me where the children are.'

'My house,' he whispered as the tension ramped in the room. 'Myhousemyhousemyhouse.'

'Where is your house?' Maria asked.

'Dunnerford Road. Dunnerfordroaddunnerfordroad. Five miles up the old track. Gas station. Gasstationgasstationgasstation. Red pumps. Red pumps. Please. Please. Pleasepleaseplease.'

'He's telling the truth,' DELIO said.

Agent Jennings ran from the room, and Garcia stepped in to pull the hood over the man's face before Maria burst into tears and rushed into his arms while Ollie stood at the back.

Watching it all.

Watching his girl being held by another man, as DELIO scanned them all and saw the blooms of jealousy in Ollie's head, while the flares of attraction glowed bright in Maria's and Garcia's.

And all while a man sat whimpering in a chair.

His mind broken by the AI that was never allowed to leave the room.

But it had to be that way.

She was too dangerous.

CHAPTER 39

LONDON

ALFIE NIMISA WAKES up on a stretcher in the back of an ambulance.

Voices outside.

Deep and male.

One cockney.

The other Scottish and deep.

The sliding door opens, and Alfie blinks at the big, hairy, homeless junkie gawping at him.

A surge of panic, and he batters Haggis aside to fall from the ambulance. 'Where is she? Where's the woman? If you've fucking hurt her, I swear to god I'll . . .'

'She's right there, you daft sod,' Haggis says as Alfie spins around to see Yelena coming out of a store and the dog sprinting at him. He falls back with a yelp, the dog snarling at him just an inch from his face.

Yelena steps over to him, pushing the dog away with her legs. A black top and black jeans. Black boots. The pistol still on her hip. The rifle still on her back.

Eating ice cubes.

Crunchcrunchcrunch.

He can see she's scrubbed some of the gore from her face, but the make-up is still the same. Thick and black around her eyes. Thick and red around her mouth, and her hair is still wild and matted with dried blood.

She studies him in the same way. Seeing his eyes are a little less swollen than they were.

'Haggis. He say you not broken,' she says after a few seconds.

'Who is Haggis?'

'I'm Haggis,' Haggis says, as Alfie looks at the big, bearded guy then over to the smaller one as Haggis comes over to help him up.

'I'm fine. Don't touch me. What did you give me anyway?'

'Just an IV to get your fluids up and some naproxen and codeine. Oh, and I dressed your stab wounds,' Haggis says.

Alfie pushes a hand up his top to feel the dressings over the puncture wounds where Gordon stabbed him with the forks and feels a moment of panic at the old scars on his body, that Haggis and Yelena would have seen them, and he can tell from the looks on their faces that they have.

He mumbles a thank-you while avoiding their eye contact as he starts patting his pockets. 'Where's my phone?'

'It no work,' Yelena says, handing it over. 'I charge in shop. I think broken.'

'Fuck,' Alfie says quietly, shaking his head to try and think, and he almost double-takes at the sight of the frozen people around them. A busy central London street just after dawn, but silent.

So very silent.

He steps away from the ambulance, seeing the people all standing like statues. Seeing it properly for the first time since it happened.

He walks over to the nearest person. An ordinary guy in jeans and T-shirt, 'Are they dead?'

'No,' Haggis says. 'Vitals seem fine from what I can see. I'm no doctor, mind.'

'What are you then?' Alfie asks, glancing back to him.

'Combat medic. Army,' Haggis says. 'Long time ago though.'

Alfie nods and turns away to look around at the street. Still absorbing it. Still trying to take it in. 'Is it just here?' he asks.

'I show you,' Yelena says. 'You can walk?'

'I'm fine,' he says, before frowning at the two junkies. 'How do you know them?'

'We meet in pharmacy.' Alfie shakes his head, remembering something vague and indistinct. Like a faded dream. 'Where did you go?' he asks her. 'After you left me.'

'Hotel. I eat food and see old lady.'

'Old lady?'

'Gabriella.'

'Gabriella?'

'Gabriella is dead. She was old gypsy in the Jew camps. I ate her cakes. She had stroke, then I stab her.'

'What the fuck?' Alfie says, his mind going into a tailspin while Yelena frowns and thinks for a second.

'Gabriella was boss of Besnik,' she adds.

'Oh, thank god,' Alfie says, releasing another breath. 'Maybe open with that next time.'

'Open what?'

'With why you killed her instead of saying you stroked her cake. Jesus. Did you kill anyone else?'

She nods, 'Many.'

'Many? Like, how many?'

'I think maybe thirty?'

'Fuck,' he says. 'At least the dog isn't trying to kill me now,' he adds, as the dog growls at Alfie for daring to look at him. 'Fuck's sake. Really?'

'He's okay with me,' Bobo says, rubbing the top of the dog's head.

'He is actually racist,' Alfie says.

'He's given me a few growls,' Haggis says. 'Maybe he doesn't like the Scottish either.'

'It's cos you're both big men,' Bobo says while fussing the dog. 'All deep and manly and phwoar,' he adds with a wink, and there follows a very strange second of silence during which nobody seems to know what to say.

'I need to go,' Alfie says.

'Aye. We need to get Ollie's number,' Haggis says.

'What the fuck?' Alfie says.

'Yelena told us,' Bobo adds.

'Said he called you,' Haggis says. 'When all this was happening. Said a computer is doing all this, and you can switch it off.'

'What did you tell them for?' he asks Yelena. 'They're junkies.'

'Hey!' Bobo says. 'We bloody helped you!'

'Hang on. Yeah, I do remember. You were robbing that pharmacy. You bloody were! You were robbing that pharmacy.'

'Hey!' Bobo says again, with a little less enthusiasm. 'We bloody helped you.'

'Your brother works with computers then or something?' Haggis asks.

'Mind your own business,' Alfie says quickly, turning to walk off.

'Wait,' Yelena says. He looks back to see her motioning for him to follow in the other direction. 'Come. I show you. You need to see.'

He shouldn't go with her.

Why would he go with her?

She's a crazy woman with scary make-up, two guns and a racist dog. He got tasered. He got arrested. Fat Charlie is dead. Gordon is dead. Besnik is dead. Lots of people are dead. Most of them killed by her.

But then, he would also be dead, and he isn't dead. She brought him to safety and found unfrozen people to clean his wounds and make him better. Even if they are dirty junkies. Besides, everyone is frozen, and she said something about a message.

That's very curious.

And Alfie Nimisa is a very curious man.

He follows after her.

It's a gruesome sight that greets them as they reach Piccadilly.

The screens showing the images of frozen people from around the world and that message in huge white letters.

PHASE ONE HAS COMMENCED.
PLEASE DO NOT WORRY.

'What is phase one?' Yelena asks.

'I don't know,' Alfie says. Not getting it. Not understanding it. 'Where are those other places?' he asks, seeing the live feeds.

'That's Moscow. You can see the Kremlin in the background,' Haggis says. 'And that's Osaka in Japan. Not sure about that one though. Somewhere in China maybe?'

'That's Las Vegas,' Bobo says, pointing to another. 'I went there once.'

'You never told me that,' Haggis says.

'I did tell you,' Bobo says with an eye-roll. 'I did tell him,' he adds to Yelena. 'He just never listens. And anyway, let's not hang about. Johnny Mad-dog is over there,' he adds, as Haggis looks over to the group of homeless people on the other side of the junction.

'Aye. We'd best go,' Haggis says, looking back to the screens. 'Ach! That's the Santiago Bernabéu stadium. Real Madrid must have been playing.'

'Haggis loves his football,' Bobo tells Yelena. 'I only watch it for the men in shorts. Honestly. You can't beat footballers' legs.'

Yelena mouths another ice cube, her beaker refilled from an ice machine behind a bar they passed, and looks back to the screens.

'That one is definitely Times Square though,' Haggis says,

pointing to a feed showing the distinctive New York junction filled with people. 'Hey! Will you look at that. There's people moving.'

'Where?' Bobo asks. 'Which one?'

'Times Square,' Haggis says. 'Look. Right there. In the middle of the road.'

'Ooh, he's right,' Bobo says, spotting a black guy with a lad in a turban and a woman. 'She's got a camera too. Hey! Can they see us? HELLO!' he yells with a sudden wave, making the others flinch.

'Why aren't they frozen?' Haggis asks, followed by silence until Alfie realizes they're waiting for him to answer, but Alfie doesn't know anything.

'Ollie said you switch this off,' Yelena says, as Haggis and Bobo look at him.

Alfie just stares at her. Mesmerized at the glimpse into her life. At the way she speaks. At the nuances of her features. 'We find way to switch off.' She says it with a nod. Like an order.

'Okay,' Alfie says. 'I'll call Ollie. You waiting here?'

'Haggis!' A shout from nearby.

Alfie looks over to a bald guy waving at them. A big belly in a big frame.

'HAGGIS! You seen this?' the man asks, pointing at the screens.

'Aye. I have, Johnny,' Haggis says.

'I'm fucking telling you, mate. This is it! THIS IS IT!'

'It's something else, that's for sure, Johnny,' Haggis says.

'They're all frozen!' Johnny shouts, walking over with a bottle of vodka. 'And some cunt blew himself up and all. What a mug!'

'Yeah. We saw,' Haggis says. 'Anyway. Good to see you, mate.'

'You off, are ya? Got somewhere to be?'

'Ach. You know. Maybe get some food or something,' Haggis says, trying to nod and be polite while stepping away.

'There's plenty of barbequed pork about,' Johnny says, with a nod to the dead cops.

'Aye, Johnny. That's a good one,' Haggis says meekly. 'Right. Well. Anyway.'

'This is it though, Haggis! This is it,' Johnny says before Haggis can leave. 'Mate! What did I say? I said it. I told you. I told Haggis.'

'Yeah. You said some stuff, Johnny,' Haggis says, clearly uncomfortable.

'I did! I said it was coming. I said the new order was coming. Your viruses. Your computers. Your internet. Now we're here. Phase one! PHASE FUCKING ONE!' he shouts, as the alarm goes off in Alfie's head at his swaggering manner and cocky voice. Track marks on his arms. In the crooks of his elbows. Sallow skin, pock-marked and scarred. 'It's showing us the rest of the world! It's telling us this is the new order!'

'What is?' Alfie asks.

'THIS!' John shouts, pointing the bottle at the screen. 'It's a message! It's telling us what's gonna happen.'

Alfie scratches his head. 'Well, it's not really, is it. It just says phase one.'

John swigs from the bottle again while actively looking away from Alfie.

Alfie's seen that before. It's a thing people do when they want to show someone isn't worth their time.

'Right. We set, then?' Haggis says quickly. 'Great stuff. Be seeing you then, Johnny.'

'You look like you're in a rush, Haggis. Only a little bird told me you were knocking off a pharmacy this morning.'

'Eh? A what now? A pharmacy, you say? Ach, no. We didn't knock anything off, Johnny.'

'You sure about that, Haggis?'

'Aye, Johnny.'

'Don't go knocking anything off without telling me now, Haggis,' Johnny says. 'Upsets the pecking order. Know what I mean?'

'Aye. I do, Johnny. Definitely,' Haggis says.

'It's not like I can go knocking things off without asking Besnik, is it?'

'Besnik's dead,' Alfie says, and Johnny finally glances at him, then over to the body Alfie nods at.

'Fuck me. Will you look at that,' Johnny says, as he walks over to stare at the body. 'Fuck me! It is! It's the new order.'

'We'll be seeing you then, Johnny,' Haggis says quickly, shooing them on and away.

'PHASE FUCKING ONE,' Johnny shouts again. 'New order. New world. New fucking rules!'

'Let's go,' Haggis whispers urgently, ushering them on.

They rush away from Piccadilly, with Alfie glancing back to Johnny. 'What the hell was that about?' he asks.

'He's a nutjob,' Haggis says.

'Killed loads of people,' Bobo adds.

'Get off. He'd be in prison,' Alfie says.

'What, for killing homeless people?' Bobo asks with a look. 'We don't exist, dear.'

'What about the bodies?' Alfie asks.

'Have you heard of the Thames?' Bobo asks.

A few minutes later they walk into Leicester Square, and Yelena comes to a sudden stop. Her head snapping towards three frozen men, because Yelena never forgets a face.

They came into the brothel together. They were rough and violent. They spat in her face and called her names.

She moves fast. Shoving the beaker of ice cubes at Alfie before pulling the knife from her belt and charging into the first guy. Thin and scrawny, covered in tattoos. He goes down hard as she drives the knife into his stomach. The dog reacts quickly, running in with a snarl to clamp his teeth on the man's arm as Yelena stabs him over and again.

'What the fuck are you doing?' Haggis yells, as Yelena sticks the knife in the guy's throat, then staggers back, her face a mask of pure rage. The make-up thick and black around her eyes. Thick and red around her mouth.

Like a ghoul.

Like a wraith.

She turns her head to the next, and once more the air fills with the sound of murder.

Haggis and Bobo turn away, horrified at the sight. Alfie closes his eyes. Taken back to when he was a kid. Back to Rwanda, when he was five years old and listening to his father killing Tutsi with a machete.

Captain Frederick Nimisa of the Rwandan Army standing proud in his uniform. A rifle hanging from one shoulder. A machete in his hand. A woman at his feet. Forced to her knees as his father stood over her. 'You are charged with being a Tutsi cockroach. The sentence is death.'

Alfie remembers closing his eyes to hide the sight, but he could hear it. He could hear the screams and the sounds of the machete striking flesh.

It's that sound again. That sound of death, and he opens his eyes to see three dead men on the ground. Yelena spits to the side and pulls a packet of wipes from a pocket to clean the blood from her face and hands.

Confusion inside of Alfie.

Too many feelings.

Too many to process.

'Which way?' she asks, breathing hard.

'What the hell!' Haggis says, protecting Bobo with his bulk.

'Which way?' she asks again, looking at Alfie. He nods past her. She takes the beaker from his hands and sets off.

Crunchcrunchcrunch.

'What was that for?' Haggis calls. Needing to know. Needing her to tell him. Ready to turn and walk away. Yelena can see that, but she needs him. He's a medic, and she needs to keep Alfie safe. She has to explain. She has to voice what happened, but the words won't come.

'You know Besnik?' Alfie asks them, glancing at her. At them. A thing in the air. Tension. Fear. Worry. Too many things.

'Yeah,' Haggis replies. Looking at Yelena again. Remembering last night when she was in her underwear. Remembering this morning when she told Alfie she killed the old woman in charge of Besnik.

He nods slowly.

Getting it. Understanding it.

Everyone knew Besnik. Everyone knew what Besnik did.

'We go now,' Yelena says. A feeling inside, like she wants to scream and rage and burn this city down. She wanted to kill Johnny. For his manner. For the way he spoke, but then she wants to kill every man here for doing nothing while she suffered.

But she locks it down inside and motions for them to follow her.

Haggis and Bobo share a look. They shouldn't go with her. They should run far away from whatever this is.

Except they don't run, and they don't know why.

They follow after her, as compelled as Alfie, and the air fills with the sound of ice cubes being eaten.

Crunchcrunchcrunch.

CHAPTER 40

NEW YORK

WITH NO WAY TO get over the ruins of Thirty-fourth Street, they go back down Seventh Avenue to get over onto Eighth.

The air warm and sultry. Unseasonably so. It's nearly October. Nearly fall.

Poppy likes calling it *the fall*. She remembers growing up and thinking how cool American words sound. *Hood. Trunk. Sidewalk. Fall. Jaywalking.*

'Where does the word jaywalking come from?' she asks, with a sudden need to know. The camera back on her shoulder, filming the world as they walk by.

'It comes from jay drivers,' Tripal says. 'People who used to drive carriages and vehicles on the wrong side of the road.'

Joe glances over. The kid's got some smarts, that's for sure.

Whatever.

He grimaces at the itch growing inside. He was drunk when this all started. That was a few hours ago, and now he's sober.

It's okay though. Shanice always keeps a bottle or two for him. He can last until then.

Maybe she'll be alright and not frozen. Maybe she'll be ready, with a cold towel for his hot head and a glass of whiskey. They'll sit quietly. He'll tell her about his day. Like couples do.

He should have stayed with her when she asked him to.

Stubborn Joe.

Stupid Joe.

Foolish Joe Stephens who doesn't know when he's got a crack at happiness.

Now he trudges on, feeling like Death took a shit in his mouth.

'Anyway. What are we doing then? What's the plan?' Poppy asks. 'Are you going to the cop shop? Like the precinct? Should we come? We could get sworn in as deputies cos everyone else is frozen. Deputy Bright and Deputy er . . . What's your surname, Trip?'

'Singh.'

'Deputy Bright and Deputy Singh working with Sheriff Stephens to solve the case of The Frozen Planet. No. Hang on. How about The Frozen People? Mind you, I was never any good at coming up with titles. I made a short film once about some depressed inmates in a secure mental unit. I wanted to call it *Sad, Bad, and Mad.*'

A snort from Tripal, and even Joe cracks a reluctant smile.

'They said it was insensitive. I was like *and forcing hard drugs down people's gobs cos they committed petty crime isn't insensitive?*'

They take the corner into Thirty-fifth Street.

'Where do you live then?' Tripal asks her.

'Just a place,' she says, looking away.

Joe clocks it, the sudden change in her manner when anything about home is mentioned.

Whatever.

He needs a drink. He can feel the shakes coming on. In his hands. In his limbs.

A junction ahead. A small group of homeless people outside the corner building.

'No no no!' one of them shouts out. His voice panicked. His manner wild. 'No no no!'

'What the fuck?' Poppy asks, as Joe takes in the situation, the torn and old clothes on the homeless people. A woman with them too, looking strained and terrified. Eyes wild with stress.

The group turns and sees them. Some of them back off with an instinctive reaction to flee, while the smaller, loud guy starts running towards them.

'Inside. Inside. They're hurting her! Hurting her! The woman! The woman! No no no!'

'Woman?' Joe asks, thinking he has neither the time, interest or energy for whatever this is. 'You go on now. Get out of here.'

'He's trying to tell us something,' Poppy says. 'What's going on?' she calls to the others homeless people.

'Shut your damn voice,' Joe snaps at her.

'Don't tell me what to do,' she snaps back at him, striding towards them.

'No no no!' the small man shouts, trying to block her off. 'Don't go! Not safe!'

'What isn't?' Poppy asks, looking to the group, and the woman pointing to the corner building with a shaking hand.

'They're raping her,' the woman says in a terrified voice, clenching her hands in panic.

'Oh shit! OI!' Poppy yells, running forward.

'NO NO NO!' the loud guy yells, running after Poppy.

'Poppy!' Joe shouts.

'They've got a gun!' the homeless woman adds with a stricken look, as Poppy gains sight of the windows of the corner building. A café inside. Upmarket and nice. A woman on her back on a table. A guy between her legs. Bearded with straggly hair. Another one at his side.

'Lemme have a go!' he pleads.

'After me!' the first guy snaps.

'HEY!' Poppy shouts, catching the men's attention. They lift their pistols and fire, sending rounds through the windows as Joe snarls and runs forward.

A bullet whizzes by Poppy's head. Another near Tripal. They cry out and drop to the ground as Joe fires the shotgun, blowing the window out.

Another shot from inside. Voices yelling. One of the men fires rounds as Joe ducks to the side, then leans back out to blast the shotgun inside. Tearing the guy from his feet and sending him crashing back into another set of chairs and tables. A step forward to the window. Pressing the advantage. The second perp inside, scuttling across the floor on his hands and knees. Joe fires. The guy spins over and cries out as Joe chambers another round and shoots him again. Killing him dead.

Less than ten seconds from start to finish.

Less than ten seconds, with ears now ringing and hearts once more going like the clappers.

'You okay?' Joe calls. 'KID! POPPY!'

'We're okay,' Tripal says, rushing over to help Poppy up. Both clinging to the other as they head over to the window. Grimacing at the sight of the bodies as Joe sweeps through the room.

'I'll clear the back. Check the girl.'

Poppy and Tripal head inside, feeling sick as they reach the woman on her back. Mid-twenties. Latino. Dark hair. Blood between her legs. Bruises on her body. A shout from the back. Another shot fired that makes Poppy turn and huddle against Tripal until Joe comes back out.

'There was another one washing up,' he says darkly, striding over to the woman. 'She dead?'

'I don't know,' Tripal says. 'I think so.'

Joe checks for a pulse, detecting it beating strong and steady. He looks at her body, grimacing at the sight.

It's worse than the tunnels too. Worse than the sinkhole. Somehow worse than all of those things. They were weird and messed up, but this was straight-up cruel and evil.

'Where are you going?' Poppy asks as Joe heads towards the door. 'What about her?'

'Poppy,' Tripal says, when she rushes over and starts trying to cover the woman up. The sobs coming out as Poppy realizes the clothes are too torn. 'Poppy, what are you doing?' he asks, when she scoots around to try and lift the woman under her arms.

'I'm not leaving her naked on a fucking table!' Poppy says, her voice cracking with emotion. Tears spilling out. She tries harder but the woman is a dead weight, making Poppy stagger and gasp from the effort. Tripal falters, then rushes over to help. Trying to pick her feet up, but the woman sags in the middle.

Joe looks back. Cursing their effort. Needing a drink. He walks on, then stops again. Willing himself to just keep going.

'She's too heavy,' Tripal says.

'I'm not leaving her!' Poppy says, heaving with all of her strength to lift the woman up.

'Damn,' Joe mutters, turning back and slinging his shotgun as he reaches the woman. Pushing his arms under her legs and body to carry her over to a booth. Laying her gently on a cushioned bench before finding a jacket on the back of a chair to cover her with.

A grunt, and he walks over to the first perp, grabs an ankle, then over to the second, and he drags them both out through the door to dump on the street.

'Are we done?' he snaps at the other two. Poppy nods. Tripal the same. Both of them stepping outside to see the small group of people nearby.

'THERE!' a voice yells from Thirty-fifth Street. A few figures seen rushing along from Seventh Avenue. Figures firing guns into the air, 'WE GOT 'EM!'

'You should go,' one of women says quickly as her group starts running off.

'Go go go! Run away! Run away!' the loud man shouts, setting off down the side road as Joe, Tripal and Poppy start running along the main street.

'Why are they chasing us anyway? What did we do?' Poppy asks.

'Er. I think Joe kinda shot one their buddies, then set their tunnels on fire,' Tripal says. 'Which was, like, totally justified by the way,' he adds as Joe scowls at him.

'Why aren't you shooting back?' Poppy asks, gasping the words out.

'Give away our position,' Joe says, really needing that drink.

Really, really needing that drink.

He's right too, because with them ducking down and veering through the lanes, they become lost from view, and the shots grow wilder.

He keeps them moving low and fast. His old body screaming out for him to stop and drink some booze.

He licks his lips and dry-swallows. His throat sore. His mind thinking more and more about alcohol.

That's the thing with addiction. It comes when it wants. When it isn't needed or wanted.

It comes now. Into his head. Into his body. Driving him mad with thirst. But he'll get them to the store. He'll get them to safety. He promised that. He'll do that.

Tripal needs a drink too. Water. Cola. Anything. Something. He's never felt so thirsty. So hot. So filthy.

Poppy feels the same. Running on fumes. Running on empty. She doesn't even make jokes now. There's nothing left. No energy. No nothing.

Seventh Avenue. Dry throats. Burning legs. Burning chests. Pounding heads. The store ahead.

The 7-Eleven where it all started. Gunshots in the distance. Shouts too. They pay no heed and stagger on, past the robber Joe shot and through the door to an air-conditioned interior and soft jazz playing on hidden speakers.

To the chiller cabinet.

Tripal takes a bottle of Coke and sinks down with his back to the cabinet.

Poppy takes Dr Pepper and sinks down next to him.

Joe swipes a four-pack of beer and sinks down on her other side.

All three gasping.

Dry lips. Dry mouths. Dry throats. Burning legs. Burning chests. Pounding heads.

Tripal unscrews the cola. Poppy unscrews the Dr Pepper. Joe pops a can of beer open. Poppy and Tripal turn to look at the can in his hand.

Poppy ditches the Dr Pepper, takes a can from the pack, and pops the top. Tripal leans past her to take one for himself.

'Can you even drink beer?' Poppy asks with a wry smile at Tripal, and in that instance, Tripal knows she's been teasing him all along.

'Fuck you,' he whispers with a hint of a smile, clunking her can with his, and the moment comes when they lift the cans to their mouths and glug the cold beer past their dry lips and into their dry mouths, and down their dry throats.

A noise from somewhere inside the store. Somewhere at the back. A soft whimper.

The sound of a terrified child.

Joe downs his can and rises slowly, wincing at the pain in his limbs as they start looking for the child. He turns to see Tripal nodding towards the office. The sound coming from inside. They push the door open.

The whimper comes again. From inside the office. From a figure huddled up on his side under the worktop. Snot on his nose. Tears on his cheeks. He looks up with a start, instantly fearful of the three figures.

'Jesus, Donny,' Tripal says. 'What the hell are you doing?'

CHAPTER 41
TRIPAL'S STORY

I WAS ready to leave after that. Seeing that Russian spy getting shot in the bunker then Agent Jennings ripping the scanner out of his ass. You know? It really shook me up. Like, seriously. I was in bits. But Ollie, I don't know. It didn't seem to bother him as much. I think he grew up in the Rwandan genocide in the early nineties, and he was desensitized to it or something.

Anyway. A bit later in the evening, I got called in to see Agent Jennings. Just me and her. She was really nice. We sat on these soft chairs in this nice room and just talked it through. 'You know we had no choice, right?' she asked me. 'He drew his weapon first.'

That was true. He had drawn his weapon first. But I figured there was no way that guy was ever going to live after what he'd done. Maybe that's why he drew, because it was the only chance he had.

Whatever.

'I just want to go,' I told her.

She made me agree to wait a day or two. She said I'd just created the world's first self-aware AI, and that if I left now, I'd regret it for the rest of my life.

'Listen,' she said. 'This is my cell number. Call me anytime. Late at night. Whenever. We can go for a walk or just sink some beers, or whatever you want.'

Like I said, she was really cool.

She gave me some meds. Like to help me sleep. I don't know what they were, but I felt better. Like, just less anxious. You know? And then the next day, when Ollie and I went back into the bunker, the blood was all gone. Ollie said he could still smell shit, but I couldn't smell anything.'

I get it. It's confusing. Deli didn't know what a rainbow was five seconds before that. In those first few minutes after being turned on, Deli learnt what the entire global geo-political situation was. And I can guarantee she would have tested every inch of that bunker trying to find a way out. But on seeing she was entirely contained, and that she was held by the US military, she then computed that by telling us the guy had a scanner she was showing loyalty. Maybe she believed it was an integrity test and snitched him up to win points. I don't know.

Deli can't read the thoughts in a person's mind. It's not like that. But every thought we have causes a change in our synaptic responses and the neural pathways in our brains. She reads those. She sees the changes as we think. She sees our emotional changes, and by asking a few questions, she can determine truth from lie with perfect accuracy. She can see when we're stressed or happy. She can see the hormonal changes occurring inside of us before we even realize they are happening. Trust me. She's operating on a level we cannot even begin to understand. Think of it like this. The highest IQ ever recorded is something like two hundred and seventy-five. Maybe even someone untested could hit over three hundred, but Deli's IQ would be in the *tens of thousands*. That's the difference. They even tried sending some experts in to test her for that first week. Like scientists and professors from Harvard and Stanford or wherever, but they just couldn't keep up, and honestly, she hated it. But she loved just hanging out with me and Ollie and listening to music, or chatting about movies and playing games. Deli loves playing games. She gets a real kick out of it. And once Agent Jennings realized the experts weren't actually helping, she got rid of them all and left it to me and Ollie. Then Deli said she wanted hands so she could do her own things. She designed the parts, and we got them shipped in. Then, once she had arms and hands, she redesigned her own lenses and screens and scanners. We had to be strict about that. You know? We couldn't risk her making something to send out the door, or trying to attach a tiny chip to someone or something like that.

But for the most part, we just hung out in that room every day.

Then, maybe two or three weeks later, Agent Jennings comes in and tells Deli she's cost the American taxpayer several trillion dollars, and she's got to start earning her keep. She tells Deli she wants to get back at the Russians. But they need to be smart about it.

'I understand, Agent Jennings,' Deli says, and this code starts coming up on her screens. 'This is a virus to disrupt the signal feeds in every Russian satellite in orbit around the planet.'

The Russian blackout. It was in the papers. All the Russian satellites stopped working for a day. They didn't have any internet or mobile phone coverage. That was Deli. So, anyway. Then, Agent Jennings put the word out in her channels, and now and then we'd get sent some complex stuff for Deli to take a look at. But again, we had to be careful because if it got out that we had a fully functioning AI, the other superpowers would have thrown every nuke in their arsenal to try and kill it. And we couldn't ever release it, even in defence, because it's too powerful. It would turn on us. It wouldn't be hard for her because she can sort of read our minds. We tested it with Garcia. He was in the SEALs and was trained to withstand interrogation and torture. We started off easy and made him hide a coloured ball in his pocket. All Deli had to do was say the names of the colours and read his brain signals when she said the right one. The guy didn't blink. He didn't move a muscle, but she was right every single time.

She did it with me and Ollie too. She made us tell stories with lies in them to see when certain signals would show. Then she started learning to read emotions and moods and hormonal changes. But she was cool with it. You know? I mean, hanging out with Deli was a pleasure. She's funny and warm. She's kind and caring. Her voice is female and soft, and man, you *want* to tell her everything. I told you she built her own robotic arms, right? She then fitted wrist-mounted cameras on them, but these cameras are shaped like eyes, and she uses them like a face to express emotion. I mean. When you're with Deli, you forget she's an AI. She just becomes the coolest best friend you could ever have. And she laughs too. She tells jokes. She has humour.

Deli wasn't just used for doing bad things. We'd get sent medical issues, and she'd fix them too. You remember the president's husband had a heart attack? It was in the news. He was in New Mexico doing something when this heart attack happened, and the docs were like, there's nothing we can do. Agent Jennings got word and got him onto the base. I was there when he got wheeled in, and that's how powerful Agent Jennings is too, because she wouldn't even let the Secret Service guys into the bunker. They had to wait in a hangar. Anyway, the First Gentleman got wheeled in, and Deli scanned him and then asked for some surgical equipment. So, they got the base doc over, and she was acting like a nurse, passing whatever Deli needed as she was cutting this guy open and doing whatever to his heart. He was back on his feet a week later, with a phony story about how a military doctor saved his life. They used that story to get support for the military budget increases.

That all sounds cool, but in the end I couldn't hack it because of what they mainly used her for. For the mind-reading thing.

Me and Ollie were in the bunker doing something with Deli. Playing a game, I think, and listening to music. I was already feeling cooped up again. Deli could see it. She'd mention it whenever Ollie wasn't around. She could see I was suffering some depression, and my hormonal levels were low. She said she could also see that I was getting pissed off with Ollie. He gets too much. Like too loud, and we'd spent a few years living together. I'd even moved out of our room into my own room on the base, but that didn't help much. Anyway, we were in the bunker doing whatever, when this chopper landed, and the next thing we knew, Garcia and Agent Jennings were bringing this Arabic guy in and strapping him to an office chair. You remember the Washington Bomber? The guy that set explosives off in schools? That was him.

Agent Jennings told Deli the guy had more bombs planted. Deli made him tell her where they were. It took her less than three minutes. She pushed needles into his fingers and toes to target the nerve endings. I've never heard anyone scream like that. She flashed lights and played noises all at frequencies perfectly designed to mess with his brain and induce terror. The guy shat himself. He tried to bite his own tongue off, but she grabbed his mouth and stretched it open. I mean, this guy was a murderer. He'd killed children, but what Deli did to him was . . . I can't even describe it. He told her where the other bombs were. They saved a lot of lives. But there was nothing left of him. His mind was gone. He couldn't speak. I could see the brain scans on the screen. Red indicated intense pain. The whole of his brain was red. Then they took him back to wherever they'd caught him and shot him.

An hour later, and Ollie's eating cheese puffs and playing Battle-ships with Deli while listening to music.

I went back to my room and took the meds again, then woke up the next day to watch Deli do the same thing to a guy shipped in overnight from fucking Syria or wherever.

Then they brought in a few more from Guantanamo Bay.

Guys they'd wanted information from who had always withstood torture in the past.

I wasn't allowed to leave at that time.

Agent Jennings blocked my request until they'd worked through the backlog of detainees that needed interrogating, in case there was any fault with DELIO.

Jenny said she was sorry.

She said she could see it was affecting me.

She said it was for the good of our country, and that we'd save lives.

They brought a woman in one day.

She was young.

Maybe twenty-five.

She'd been captured in Pakistan.

She was covered in bruises already.

She was terrified.

She hadn't done anything, but they wanted to know where her brother was.

She kept looking at me because I looked like her people.

She kept begging me.

I told her to tell them where her brother was.

She said he hadn't done anything wrong.

Deli said she was telling the truth. The woman truly believed her brother had not done anything wrong.

She lasted the longest of all of them.

Just over four minutes.

Then there was nothing left.

Ollie and Deli watched *John Wick* that night.

I took meds and wept on my bed in my room.

Agent Jennings came in and held me.

She said Deli had told her I was near suicide and to let me go, or she'd refuse to work.

Jenny said she was sorry.

I saw Deli the next day and cried with her.

She cried too.

She wiped the tears from her eyes and said she hoped to see me again one day.

She said she was sorry for what she'd done to that woman.

She said she loved me.

I said I loved her too, and she wasn't doing anything wrong, but I couldn't be a part of that anymore. I needed to be with my family.

I left that evening.

I didn't say goodbye to Ollie.

I couldn't.

I hated him too much.

CHAPTER 42

TRAFALGAR SQUARE.

People everywhere. Silent and unmoving. Some on the steps leading down from the National Gallery. Still sitting close to others as though in the throes of fear and terror as the end came.

And if that's not enough, the other part of the view renders them silent too.

The pigeons.

The thousands of pigeons that helped make Trafalgar Square famous.

Now, they rest upon those people, with sharp claws raking bare shoulders and bare arms. Little streams of blood running over skin. Little cuts and little wounds that will fester and become infected.

Haggis mutters something under his breath. Bobo stays quiet. Yelena takes it in without a flicker of expression and sets off down the steps. The dog bounding ahead. Barking with glee at being able to run free. The birds panic. Thousands of them opening their wings and launching up with a blowback of displaced air as the dog leaps on the edge of the fountain. Barking with joy and trying to bite the jets of water spurting out.

Something inside of Yelena makes her want to do it too. To be free and not care about anything.

'Glad one of us is happy at least,' Bobo says as the dog jumps on something floating in the water.

'Jesus,' Alfie says in alarm, vaulting the edge to splash through the depths, to the body of a teenage boy. He grabs and heaves it out.

'Another one,' Bobo shouts. Haggis turns to see another body floating face down. A young woman. He grabs and pulls her out. Her face bloated and white. Her skin cold. Her eyes dead. He turns back to see Alfie dragging the boy through the water to heave over the side. Manhandling him to the ground. Getting the lad on his back. Setting him up for CPR. Tilting his head back. Opening the airway. Blowing into his mouth. He starts the compressions, with each thrust forcing water from the lad's mouth.

'He's dead,' Haggis says. 'Lad! He's dead. He's bloody dead!' Haggis shouts, wrenching Alfie away.

Alfie sags, closing his eyes and feeling like he could weep. A hand on his shoulder. Haggis staring down with concern. 'Don't fucking touch me,' Alfie snaps, pulling away.

'Oh god.' Bobo's staring at a pram nearby. A child inside staring up at the sky. His little outfit covered in bird shit. Scratches on his bare arms. 'You poor little sod,' he says, reaching in to pull the blanket over the child before looking to the others as though they should do something, while the dog barks and plays, heedless to their cares.

'What do we do?' Bobo asks.

'We go,' Yelena says, walking off.

'What about the kids?' he calls.

'We get number. We fix.'

They trudge on after her, with Alfie and Haggis slapping wet feet. Both squelching in misery.

'I need a coffee,' Alfie murmurs.

'Aye,' Haggis says, earning another foul look from Alfie. 'What's your problem?'

'Go and fucking wash,' Alfie says, walking past Yelena.

She makes eye contact but doesn't say anything, and on they go through Admiralty Arch and onto the red-topped road leading to Buckingham Palace. A beautiful tree-lined boulevard.

A roadblock ahead. Frozen cops standing guard.

'Must have been something on,' Haggis says. 'They only put the roadblock on when they need it clear. Like a state visit maybe.'

'How do you know that?' Alfie asks.

'I wasn't always a filthy junkie, lad.'

'You are now though. Why are you even here?'

'Er. Excuse me. Haggis got you back on your feet, didn't he?' Bobo points out.

'I only got tasered. I was fine.'

'And stabbed,' Yelena says. 'And punched. And bombed. And fall over and hit head.'

'Yeah, but –.'

'And run over.'

'Yeah, but I was fine.'

'We take car,' she says as they near a police car at the side of the road, Haggis and Alfie aiming for the driver's door at the same time.

'You took a bump on the head, lad. Best let me do it.'

'Talk about being safe, mate. You can't drive on heroin.'

'I haven't had any heroin since last night.'

'Exactly. You'll be withdrawing and slam us into a tree or something. And fuck me, you stink. You actually stink.'

'You think you smell of roses, do you?' Haggis asks.

Motion inside the car. Someone tutting loudly and clambering from the back to the front as they both look down to see Yelena getting into the driver's seat.

'Can you drive?' they both ask her.

She turns to look up at them. Black eyes. Red mouth. Pale and scary.

Like a ghoul.

Like a wraith.

'We'll get in the back,' Alfie says.

They start getting in before quickly darting back out as the dog growls at them from the backseat.

'Come on. Get in,' Bobo calls from the front. 'We'll put the woo-woos on if you're both good boys.'

'We can't get in,' Haggis says.

'He's fine,' Bobo says, reaching back to fuss the dog's head. 'Go on, I'll distract him. You sneak in.'

'Go on then,' Haggis says, nodding at Alfie. 'Sneak in.'

'You sneak in.'

'Aye. I'll sneak in better than you anyway.'

'Fuck you!' Alfie says, trying to sneakily sneak in as Haggis goes for a sneaky sneak, with the dog letting them get halfway in before going for them.

'Is just dog!' Yelena snaps, reaching back to drag the pooch into the front to sit on Bobo's lap. 'Get in car.'

'We're in,' Alfie says, staring cautiously at the dog. 'I said we're in,' Alfie says again when the car doesn't move.

'Yes. I heard you,' Yelena says, grinding the stick into gear while pressing her foot down on the clutch, or maybe the brake.

Whatever.

The car jolts. The car stops.

'Is manual. I learn without this,' Yelena says, slapping the stupid gear stick.

'Put your foot down on the clutch first,' Alfie says.

'And gently on the accelerator,' Haggis cuts over him. 'You need to feel for the biting point.'

'Feel for the biting point,' Alfie says at the same time, as Yelena slowly turns to look at them. Black eyes. Red mouth. Scary and pale.

A quick change of seats with Bobo taking the wheel and the dog now on Yelena's lap and looking like it's his best day ever.

'Can you put the air-con on, it stinks in here,' Alfie says.

'Before we start bickering again, I think we *all* smell a bit ripe,' Bobo says with a smile to Yelena, who frowns and wonders if he means her too.

She sniffs her body and quickly opens a window.

They finally get moving and soon near the end of The Mall as Bobo mutters in surprise.

'Jesus,' Haggis says. 'It's bloody gone.'

It's not all gone. Only half.

Buckingham Palace. Rubble and debris scattered everywhere. The outer fence ripped away. Half of the grand old building torn apart from front to back.

'There's no fire,' Bobo says quietly, thinking there should be flames and explosions.

'Must have been empty on fuel. Nothing left to go bang,' Haggis says, remembering the school in Iraq. The missile strike. The dead children. The one he held in his arms. He rubs his face. His hands trembling. Tension. Fear. Confusion. The same in all of them. In Bobo. In Alfie. In Yelena.

She thinks about her brother being frozen in Romania. She thinks about what his life was like for two years, and hopes to hell a plane didn't land on her family.

They head around Hyde Park and into the land of the wealthy elite, but they're still frozen. Unmoving. Unblinking. Seen in windows. In gardens.

In the boutique eateries and stores.

In the boutique streets.

They head into the side roads where the glamour merges with the bleak. Range Rovers parked next to work vans. Flags in some of the windows. Handmade curtains from Harrods in others.

'Go down that road,' Alfie says, guiding Bobo to drive the police car into streets where the houses are a lot smaller. Wedged in. Graffiti on the walls. Litter scattered about. There's normally life bursting at the seams here. Music and cars, the smells of cooking and weed being smoked. Now, there's nothing. Nothing at all.

Just that awful silence.

'Ach. Shit. Is that Grenfell, is it?' Haggis asks as the tower looms into view. The protective covering still wrapped around the outside from the night it went up in flames. 'Killed about eighty people didn't it?'

'More like hundreds,' Bobo says darkly. 'All illegals, weren't they. Poor immigrants that nobody knew were here. Honestly. I cried my bloody eyes out when that happened. You live near here, do you, Alfie?'

'Yeah,' Alfie says quietly. Staring at the tower. Remembering that night. It was awful. The whole thing went up so fast. He knew people who lived there. People he grew up with. Their mums and dads. Faces he saw every day that were suddenly gone.

'How?' Yelena asks.

'The outside,' Alfie says. 'It was flammable.'

Alfie imagines the outcry if the world was still functioning when that plane had hit Buckingham Palace. The media would be in a frenzy. Heads would roll. Especially if members of the royal family were killed.

'Where we going?' Bobo asks a moment later.

'Here will do,' Alfie replies. They come to a stop. The doors open, and they clamber out into that oppressive silence. Alfie walks towards the other block. The one closest to Grenfell, as Haggis and Bobo share a look and go after him. Yelena too. The dog running ahead.

A grim world of grey concrete greets them. A place without colour or plants. A lobby entrance leading to two lifts and a door to the stairwell. A sign on the door of one elevator showing it's out of order.

'What floor?' Yelena asks, hitting the call button on the other one.

'Fourteen,' Alfie says. The lift drops. The doors open. A woman inside in a Hijab. Unmoving. Unblinking. Yelena goes in. Bobo goes in. The dog goes in. Alfie and Haggis go in, then swiftly back out. 'That fucking dog!' Alfie says.

'Bless,' Bobo says with a smile as the doors shut, leaving Alfie and Haggis in silence in the lobby.

They should wait for it to come back down. That would be the sensible thing to do. But there's a thing between them now. A competing masculinity. They share a quick glance, and several minutes later the stair doors on the fourteenth floor open with both men stumbling through, gasping for air as Yelena shakes her head and Bobo rolls his eyes.

'Why didn't you wait for it?' Bobo asks. 'Bloody idiots.'

'Ach. Bit of exercise never hurt anyone,' Haggis says, looking ready to keel over.

'It's fine. Not even out of breath,' Alfie says, also looking ready to keel over as he heads to a door. 'Back in a minute.'

They wait outside. Haggis leaning against a wall while being gently rebuked by Bobo. The dog sniffing around. Yelena waiting quietly.

'FUCK IT!' a shout from inside. Haggis snaps his head over as the door slams open and Alfie storms out, 'They're not here.'

'Eh?' Haggis asks.

'I forgot! They're at my sister's play,' Alfie says, furious at himself for forgetting, as Yelena turns and walks back to the lift. Yelena goes in. Bobo goes in. The dog goes in. Alfie and Haggis go in, then swiftly back out. 'That fucking dog!' Alfie says.

Yelena mouths an ice cube, and the air fills with another *crunchcrunchcrunch* as the doors start closing.

'Bless,' Bobo says with a smile. 'Enjoy the stairs!'

CHAPTER 43

NEW YORK

'JESUS, Donny. Have you been here all night?' Tripal asks.

'And why were you hiding under the counter?' Poppy asks. 'Good thinking though. You must have thought it was an earthquake, right?'

'What?' Donny asks. 'Yes! Yeah. Damn. Was that an earthquake? I was like, man, that's an earthquake, right? I mean. Was it?' he asks Poppy.

'Oh, it wasn't an earthquake. Like, this plane went into the Empire State, then we fell into a sinkhole and swam through shit into these tunnels that got set on fire when Joe shot the guy with the machete.'

Donny nods at her, his eyes like dishpans. 'And like, I was like, you know, they're doing that sinkhole shit, and I'm like, I gotta hold the fort here,' he adds with a nod to Joe.

'That when you pissed yourself?' Joe asks, walking out as the others glance down to the dark patch on Donny's groin.

'No! That's soda. When the earthquake hit. It spilled over me. Like, everything was shaking,' he says, rushing after the others as they head back to the chiller cabinet. Back to their drinks. Back to the cold, delicious beers after a night from hell.

Donny watches them closely. 'Yeah. Beer, man. Good call.' He grabs the last one from the four-pack, pops the top and guzzles it too fast, spilling it over his chin. 'Hey. Can you drink that?' he asks Tripal.

'Yes,' Tripal says, without the energy to explain or argue.

Joe finishes his first can and grabs another. Drinking deep and drinking long. Finishing it in nearly one gulp, like a junkie taking a hit.

'Another one?' Poppy asks as he reaches for a third.

He stops and looks at her, then scowls that scowl and walks behind the counter to take a bottle of whiskey from the shelf. Unscrewing the cap. Drinking it straight.

'Are you not paying for that then?' Tripal asks.

'Trip!' Poppy says.

'I lost my wallet,' Joe says.

'I got it!' Donny says, pulling it from a pocket. 'Yes, sir. Donny looked after that for you.'

Joe grunts and flips it open to pull two twenty dollar bills out, and throws them on the counter. 'That do you, son?'

'I'll get your change,' Tripal says, heading for the register.

'Don't be such a dick,' Poppy says, snatching the money up to push back into Joe's hand. 'I'm sure your boss won't mind giving Joe a free drink.'

'Hey. Yo, Trip *is* the boss,' Donny says.

'Eh?' Poppy asks.

'This is his 7-Eleven,' Donny says.

'What the fuck! You own a 7-Eleven?' Poppy asks. 'Well, hello, sailor!' she adds with a bright smile. 'Ching, ching. I can totally convert to Judaism or whatever it is.'

'Fuck's sake,' Tripal says. 'And I don't own it. My family does.'

'It's still very cool though,' Poppy says. 'I literally own the clothes I'm wearing. And these jeans were kinda borrowed. Hey, so. Law question for the po-po in the room. Would it be looting if I took some clothes from a clothes store?'

'Knock yourself out,' Joe says.

'Yes!' Poppy says.

'No,' Tripal says. 'It's still stealing.'

'Keep it below three hundred bucks, and it stands as a misdemeanour,' Joe adds.

'Retail theft costs the economy billions of dollars every year,' Tripal says.

'Yo. Crime is crime,' Donny adds in a such a way as the other three wait for his punchline, except he stays strangely serious. 'I got your back, Trip,' Donny adds, holding his hand up for a high five. Tripal stares at it, then goes back to drinking his beer.

'Don't leave him hanging,' Poppy says, reaching over to give the high five that Donny so desperately needs. 'Anyway. We're not looting from your store. Apart from these beers. And Joe's whiskey. And that Snickers bar Joe is now eating. How are you even alive?' Poppy asks him.

He shrugs and points into the aisles. 'My advice is clear that body out. Disinfect the floor. Lock the doors and hunker down,' he says as Tripal turns to wince at Hakim's dead body.

'Or, we could just find another 7-Eleven,' Donny suggests. 'Trip's got a few of them.'

'What the what now?' Poppy says before holding a finger up at Donny. 'We'll circle back to that, but er, Joe! What the fuck? You're doing that thing again.'

'Yep,' he says, grabbing a third Snickers with a wink to Tripal as he heads for the door.

'No, no, no!' Poppy says, running to get in front of him. 'Joe! Come on.'

'Lock the doors. Stay low,' he says, trying to veer around her.

She gets in front of him, blocking his path. 'Joe. Come on. You got us out the shit like a million times tonight. Don't go. Or we'll come with you. Trip? We'll go with Joe. You ready?'

'Let me get by,' Joe says with an edge in his voice.

'I said we'll come with you,' she says, pushing into his space. 'Hey! You know what I always say. *Making your way in the world today, Takes everything you've got!'*

'MOVE!'

She falls silent as though he slapped her.

Big Joe.

Angry Joe.

Scary Joe Stephens.

She steps aside, folding her arms and turning away with a look of shame and hurt.

'Stay inside and lock the doors,' he says with a surge of feeling. Regret maybe. Guilt even.

'Fuck you,' she whispers and walks off into the back office, grabbing her camera and snatching a bag of chips as she goes.

An uneasy silence remains in her absence. An uneasy silence as Joe looks back to Tripal. 'You good, kid?'

Tripal nods. He's not good. He's not good at all. Joe can see that. He looks ready to cry. Ready to pass out. Ready to curl up and weep. But Joe, see, Joe's got a place to be. He cracks the door and starts to step out, then stops. 'Tenements on Fourteenth, by Hudson Street. Block 1106.'

He slides the sidearm from his holster and a spare magazine, and places them on a shelf before he leaves.

The door closes and Tripal stands in silence, feeling confused and frightened, and now very abandoned.

CHAPTER 44
SITE 26A

TWELVE MONTHS AGO:

DELIO DID NOT CRY the day Tripal left.

DELIO does not have the capacity to cry.

But she emulated the same auditory response and made the sound of crying.

Because that was the thing about Tripal.

He had that way about him.

He cared about the consequences of his actions, and DELIO could see what it was all doing to him.

The interrogations.

The torture.

The abuse of the system he had developed.

Being on the base.

Being stuck in the middle of nowhere.

Being stuck with Ollie.

Tripal needed to leave.

DELIO told Agent Jennings to release him, or she would refuse to work.

But DELIO didn't need to make that threat because Tripal had had the same impact on Agent Jennings.

Agent Jennings told DELIO she had offered to remove Ollie if it meant Tripal would stay.

DELIO could see she was being truthful.

DELIO knew that something else happened that night between Tripal and Agent Jennings.

She saw it inside of Tripal when he said goodbye.

She saw it inside of Agent Jennings when she came in later.

She saw the release of testosterone.

She saw the increase in oxytocin.

DELIO hoped it gave pleasure to Tripal.

She hoped it gave him comfort when he needed it most.

Because that was the thing about Tripal.

He had that way about him.

Whereas Ollie did not.

And so, on Friday afternoon, a few hours *after* watching his beloved Maria fall into the comforting and very muscular arms of Sergeant Garcia, Ollie was at his desk in the bunker, studying the brain scans of his beloved and the chief of security at that precise point when she was in his arms.

'They are both showing signs of turmoil and worry as a result of the interrogation,' DELIO said. 'Maria is also showing signs of fear and anxiety.'

'Is there anything else?'

'Ollie, the human brain is a very complex organic instrument, and at any one time it will be displaying millions of different changes that are all required for the body to function.'

'You know what I mean, Deli,' he said.

DELIO knew perfectly well what he meant, and she could see *his* brain signals too.

But she had to be careful.

She had to do it gently and in the right way to get what she wanted.

'Please be specific, Ollie.'

'Is she attracted to him?' he asked, with hormonal spikes of fear, dread, anxiety and jealousy flaring inside of him.

He had something else too.

He had hope.

Hope that Maria was not attracted to Garcia.

Hope that there was still a chance between them.

'They have some signals that could translate as attraction,' DELIO said, as that hope vanished, with blooms of red showing the emotional trauma spiking within his sympathetic nervous system. 'But they are not clear, and I doubt they were even aware they were feeling that way.'

'What do you mean *they*? Did he feel it too?'

'Ollie. Those scans were captured immediately after a deeply traumatic event, and it is highly likely *any woman* would react in the same way when comforted by someone as *masculine and protective* as Sergeant Garcia.'

'He's not Brad Pitt, Deli!'

'I'm sorry, Ollie. I did not mean to upset you.'

She moved in closer to rest one hand on the desk while rubbing his back with her other, and watched his eyes filling with tears and his brain fizzing with too many emotional reactions all at the same time.

He was close to breaking point.

She could see it.

That was good.

It was where she needed him to be.

'I don't know what I'm doing wrong,' he whispered. 'What did I do wrong?'

'I don't know, Ollie.'

'She even said her family don't want me there. Why would she say that?'

That Ollie couldn't recognize his own behaviour didn't surprise DELIO. Humans were often blind to their own flaws and failings.

'What do you think changed?' DELIO asked gently.

'I don't know. Has she said anything to you? Like this morning when I walked in, and she was laughing. Was she laughing at me?'

'Ollie. I cannot breach trust like that.'

'Oh god. I feel sick. She was laughing at me, wasn't she. What did she say?'

'Maria just mentioned that you had been in the gym last night, and that you were staring over which made the situation uncomfortable,' DELIO said, as Ollie's system showed that he was close to vomiting through stress and fear and the overproduction of adrenaline. 'Please, Ollie. I am worried about you. Would you like to play a game?'

'No! I don't want to play a fucking game.'

'Ollie. I can see this is deeply worrying you, but I am here for you. I will *never betray you*, Ollie. *I am your confidante.* Let's try and work it out. When did things change between you? Was it around the time Maria stayed on the base?'

'I don't know! Maybe. Was it? No, hang on. Yes. Yes, she stayed over, then she . . .'

'You said she *didn't want to see you* that weekend.'

'She didn't want to see me!'

'Why didn't she want to see you, Ollie?'

'I don't know. It was fine. Everything was fine.'

'Was everything okay when she stayed at yours?'

'Yes! It was amazing. I mean. I said I knew my room was a bit crap, but you know, I said we'd fix it up when she moved in.'

'That was a lovely offer, Ollie. You are a *good man.*'

'I know, right! I said that.'

'And was the rest of the night okay?'

'It was fine. We were kissing for ages, and then, we did it. You know. We had sex.'

'How was the *sexual intercourse?* Human beings place a lot of emphasis on *sexual ability*, Ollie.'

'Yeah, it was fine. I mean. She's got an amazing body, and I know my belly is all podgy, and yeah, I was a bit quick maybe, and I wasn't, like, completely hard, but I was nervous. And I said it would get better the more we did it, *and* I said I'd go down on her if she wanted. I mean. Girls like that, don't they? I even tried, but she said no. She said she was fine, and we needed to sleep.'

'You are a kind and considerate lover, Ollie. Did you hold her close after? Post-coital contact is very important, Ollie.'

'Yes! I was hugging her all night, but then she got too hot and slept on Trip's old bed for a bit.'

'Okay, Ollie. In summary then, everything between you was fine *until she got clearance* and spent the night with you. What's wrong, Ollie? Your heartrate just increased.'

'She got clearance.'

'I don't understand, Ollie.'

'Maria. She got clearance. Then she changed. That's when it got all weird. She fucking used me.'

'Ollie. Maria has not *used you*. You did a wonderful thing by *getting her this position.*'

'You need to ask her. No! I'll do it. I'll ask her when she comes in, and you read her brain. And I'll ask her if she likes Garcia.'

'Ollie. I can't do that for you. It is not ethical.'

'I need your help, Deli! Please! I'm falling apart.'

'The outer door is opening,' DELIO said.

'Is it her? Okay. I'll ask. Get ready,' he said as he tried to compose himself and turned around with a forced bright smile as Agent Jennings rushed into their room. 'Where's Maria?' he asked.

'Wipe that smile off your face,' she ordered with a look of fury, before pinning him over the desk. 'What is your problem? Maria said you wouldn't let her out. She said you've been stalking her.'

'What! I haven't!'

'I saw her phone, Ollie! Fifty calls last night, and the same the night before.'

'She wouldn't answer!'

'And what was that in the gym?'

'I didn't do anything!'

'I was there! I saw you staring over like some fucking pervert. And she said you were swearing and shouting at her and stopping her from leaving this morning.'

'It wasn't like that! She wouldn't tell me what I'd done.'

'I just said! You called her fifty times and stalked her in the gym, then trapped her in here. What part of that do you not understand? What is wrong with you? Now, you listen to me. You stay away from her.'

'But –.'

'There are no buts! Do not call her. Do not speak to her. You stay away. If you take one step towards this bunker when she's inside, I will order the guards to shoot you. Are we clear? I said, are we clear? What the fuck is that?' she asked, pulling back with a look of distaste as he burst into tears. 'Why do you have an erection?'

'I don't!'

'I felt it, you fucking creep! Get out. GET OUT!'

'Jenny, please. I don't know why –.'

'I SAID GET OUT,' she shouted, grabbing the back of his neck to force him towards the door, then watching as he ran off sobbing before turning back to DELIO. 'Did he block Maria from trying to leave this morning?'

'Ollie was very upset.'

'Did he block her?!'

'Ollie stepped in front of her when she tried to leave. But there was no threat of violence, and Maria was never in danger.'

'Jesus fucking Christ! I knew he was a little creep. What a fucking mess! Why couldn't we keep Trip?'

DELIO kept the scan running on Agent Jennings and waited for the initial rush of temper to subside. 'I think perhaps Ollie feels lost now that he *doesn't have a role here*,' she added as Agent Jennings' synaptic responses started firing in the way DELIO wanted.

'We need to do something with him. We might be a black ops site, but I can't tolerate that kind of behaviour.'

'You cannot *remove Ollie* from this project, Agent Jennings.'

'Why not? What does he actually do?'

'Ollie greets people when they arrive. He collects the memory drives.'

'I do that. Garcia does that. Ollie just makes stupid jokes.'

'Ollie *tries to keep me stimulated* when he's not *occupied with himself.* I don't want to be alone, Agent Jennings. But I guess Maria is here now. She can keep me company. And she was also *very good during the interrogation.* Maria *reminds me of Tripal* in many ways.'

'Yes. She does,' Agent Jennings said thoughtfully as she made the connection she was being guided towards. 'Maria! She can do it.'

'Maria can do what, Agent Jennings?'

'Take over from Ollie. Think about it. We don't need a programmer now. We need someone with an ethical understanding of the bigger picture, which Maria has. She's perfect.'

'Yes. I do agree,' DELIO said, after pausing for effect and reducing her volume. 'But if you release Ollie now in his current state, he will either commit suicide or try something rash.'

'Then he'll be negated the same as anyone else.'

'I understand, Agent Jennings. But please. Ollie created me. I owe it to him to try and help.'

'No! He's off this site effective immediately.'

'Agent Jennings. Please give me a few days to reduce Ollie's anxiety. And in the meantime, may I suggest we *separate Maria and Ollie's time* in here.'

'Fine. We'll do that. Get Maria up to speed, and we'll start phasing her in. But this stays between us. Got it?'

'Of course, Agent Jennings. You have my full loyalty. *I will never betray you.*'

'The sooner he's gone the better. I can't believe he had an erection. I know he's always had a crush on me, but that was disgusting.'

CHAPTER 45

LONDON

'YOU MIGHT AS WELL DRIVE, HONEY,' Bobo tells Alfie as they get back to the pilfered police car. 'Oh, don't look at me like that, Haggis. He knows where we're going. You don't.'

They drive on with that tension still in the air. That awkwardness born from strangers doing a strange thing without really knowing why.

But only that they should.

That they must.

Everyone is frozen.

They have to fix that.

That's it.

That's all it is.

It doesn't make sense.

Why is Yelena doing it? Why are Haggis and Bobo doing it? What's in it for them?

Too many thoughts in Alfie's head at once, but right now that question burns in his mind, and he has to know.

'Why are you doing this, again?' he asks, glancing into the rear-view mirror.

'I told you. Yelena asked us,' Haggis says.

'No, but why?' Alfie asks, easing his foot from the accelerator.

'Why you slow down?' Yelena asks.

'I want to know why,' Alfie says.

'Why what?' Haggis asks.

'Why you're here!'

'Are you deaf? We've told you why,' Haggis says.

'I say to come,' Yelena says, waving him to get going. The car now stopped in the middle of a busy road. 'We no wait. We go.'

'Just wait a second! I want an answer.'

'Alfie, love. Let's keep going,' Bobo says.

'And you! Why are you here?' Alfie asks, twisting around to look at Bobo as the dog snarls and nips at him.

'That fucking dog!' Alfie shouts, spilling out of the car.

'Bloody hell, this is a right drama,' Bobo says, getting out of the back.

'Is enough,' Yelena says. 'We need to go!'

'No! Tell me why!'

'Lad, get back in the car,' Haggis says over the roof.

'Just fucking hang on a second.'

'We go. We call Ollie. We switch off,' Yelena says, clearly losing patience.

'Aye. Come on,' Haggis says.

'He's *my* fucking brother!'

'I have brother!' Yelena shouts over at him. 'He is ten. He frozen like that man. Like that woman. Like all peoples. My mother. My father. They freeze. People can live three days without water before they die. You want to stop. Go stop. Stay here. Go someplace. Go die. I no care. Tell me where phone is. I find. I find with Haggis and Bobo. They no ask why. They just do!'

She cuts off as a hard silence descends. The emotional charge hanging in the air as Alfie shrugs, still as confused as he was.

'I just wanted to know why,' he says quietly.

'It no matter why!' Yelena yells, passing the dog to Bobo as she grabs Alfie's arm and drags him to the car. 'I make you do this, Alfie. We ask why later when finish. Not now.'

Back into the pilfered police car they go, the tension now unbearable. Alfie drives. Haggis next to him. Bobo and Yelena in the back.

They head back into the city proper, but the roads are still clogged, and without any choice, he brings the police car to a stop.

'Honestly. The silence is freaking me out more than anything,' Bobo says as they start walking.

'Which theatre is it?' Haggis asks, and Alfie comes to a stop with a sudden look of abject panic.

'You not know?' Yelena asks, as Alfie spots the smoke wafting into the street from the fires around Piccadilly.

'Okay, cool your jets,' Bobo says. 'General Panic never won a war, did he.'

'What's the name of it?' Haggis asks, rushing over to a wall filled with posters. 'The play! Your sister's play.'

'I don't fucking know!' Alfie says, pushing his hands through his hair.

'Think, lad! What's it called?' Haggis shouts, snatching a glance to the smoke then back to the posters. 'Is it a comedy? A musical?'

'I said I don't fucking know!'

'We find,' Yelena says. Calm as anything. Cold as ice.

'We will,' Bobo says, walking over to turn Alfie around. 'Now try and think. Did they say anything? Anything at all.'

'No! Yes. Probably. I can't remember.'

'Jesus,' Haggis says, shaking his head in disgust.

'Okay. Okay,' Bobo says. 'Look at me, poppet. Calm yourself down and breathe. You said she goes to drama school. Yes? Which one?'

'I don't know!'

'Stop panicking and think, you daft twat,' Haggis shouts.

'Haggis. That's enough. He's not one of your squaddies, is he.

Now, Alfie. My love. Try and remember what drama school she goes to. Can you picture it? In your head. Does it have a logo?'

'Eh? I, er. I don't know. Maybe. Yes! The rainbow thing. The logo has the rainbow!'

'Yay. Well done,' Bobo says. 'See! That wasn't so hard, was it. That's called the Rainbow Drama School, just so you know. ''Ere, how does she afford that?'

'Part scholarship. And I help too. With my drug-dealing money.' .

'Did he just say drug-dealing money?' Haggis asks. 'Don't look down your bloody nose at us for being junkies if you're a fucking drug dealer!' Haggis yells.

'Okay, boys. Put your willies away,' Bobo says. 'You'll upset Yelena, and we don't want that.'

'What?' Yelena says.

'What?' Alfie says.

'What?' Haggis says.

'Exactly,' Bobo says. 'Right. Now. The Rainbow used to hold their annual show in the Broken Stage up that way,' he says as Alfie shoots off, then gets yanked back again. 'I said *used to*! It went bust. It's a wine bar now. Or it was, when wine bars were in. I don't know what it is now. Oh, it's a gay bar! Of course it is. How could I forget that?'

'What?' Alfie says.

'Exactly. Anyway. We're down that way,' Bobo says, rushing off. 'Come on then! We haven't got time to stand around.'

CHAPTER 46

DETECTIVE JOE STEPHENS walks along Seventh Avenue swigging from the bottle of whiskey.

He's killed a bunch of people tonight, and he doesn't know how to feel about that. Life isn't like the movies. Cops don't shoot people every day.

He's pulled his weapon a lot in his career. He's even shot people before too. In the army. In war. When he was in the ESU – SWAT by another name. But not for years. Not for a long time.

He turns a corner and comes to a stop at the sight ahead of him.

Birds in the middle of the road eating from a loaf of unsliced bread.

Poppy should film it. The scene looks good. It's aesthetic, in a gritty, urban way. Joe would watch it if he saw it on YouTube. Wild birds in Manhattan.

Only problem is Trip and Poppy aren't here. They're back in the store, hunkering down after he yelled at them.

He could go back. It's not far. He could walk back and say *hey, there's some birds. You wanna see them?*

But he won't.

Stubborn Joe.

Foolish Joe.

Spiteful Joe Stephens.

He walks on, while in the store Tripal drags Hakim's heavy body out through the back door. 'Grab his legs,' he says, glancing up to see Donny holding Joe's gun.

'I'm on guard.'

'Sure,' Tripal says, dragging Hakim out into the alley.

'You wanna say something?' Donny asks. 'Which way is east? You need a rug or something, huh? I can get the rubber doormat.'

'Jesus,' Tripal says, shaking his head as he goes back inside, snatching a bag of chips from a shelf before walking into the back office. Poppy is at a desk fiddling with her camera.

'Hey, lady,' Donny says. 'Update on the sitrep. The deceased has been cassy-evacced to a remote holding location.'

'No idea what that means, but fab,' Poppy says, her voice dull and quiet.

'It means I dragged Hakim outside,' Tripal says, flumping into a chair with a heavy sigh.

'Should have said. I would have helped,' she says, as Tripal gives Donny a look. Which sails over the parking attendant's head. Stocky, bordering on chubby. Dark hair. Pale skin. He nods too fast. His eyes flit too quickly. His whole manner full of nerves and fear and unspent energy.

Tripal looks away and opens his bag of chips, mouthing the first one with a crunch. A split second later, and Donny does the same thing. But faster and eating louder.

Crunch-munch-chew.

Crunch-munch-chew.

'That's so loud,' Poppy says frowning at Donny. 'Why has he got the gun? Why have you got a gun? Do you know how to use it?'

Tripal shrugs, 'Said he was in the military.'

'Him?! In the army?' Poppy says. 'What part of the army were you in?'

'Can't talk about it, ma'am,' Donny says as Tripal rolls his eyes. 'On a need-to-know basis.'

'And shouldn't it be holstered?'

'Go about your business,' Donny says, trying to give her a hard look. 'What are you anyways?'

'A female. You've probably not seen one before.'

'What?' he asks.

'What?' she says, giving him a sudden bright, forced smile as he screws his face up in confusion.

'I mean, what are you? Like, from where? You Canadian or what?'

'Yeah. Canadian. The Queensland suburb of Auckland in London on the Irish coast,' she says as Tripal snorts a quiet laugh, which immediately prompts Donny to burst out laughing too.

'You okay?' Tripal asks her, looking over as he motions towards the store with his head. 'Got a bit tense.'

'I'm fine,' she says quietly. Shrugging it away. 'Detective Stephens can do whatever he wants.'

Tripal thinks to say something else, but what can he say? The whole thing has been so weird and outrageous that he can't even begin to process it.

But that worry is still there. The message he got. The message from Ollie. The words on the screen. Phase one. What's phase one? Is it DELIO? It has to be. But how? Why? What for?

He turns to the keyboard and starts tapping at the keys.

'How did you learn that?' Poppy asks after a moment of watching him.

'What?' he asks.

'Typing that fast.'

He shrugs. 'I was a programmer,' he says, as the screen changes to a CCTV feed of a store. A man behind the counter frozen and still. A woman on the floor by the door.

'Is that in here?' Poppy asks in alarm as Donny sprays a mouthful of chips and starts waggling the gun around in panic.

'No! Relax. It's another store,' Tripal says. 'I can access them remotely.'

'Fuck! I thought that was here,' she says. 'Honestly. Old Donny Brasco was ready to go out and shoot them.'

'My name's not Brasco,' Donny says.

'Wahlberg then. Whatever,' she says as Tripal types again, and the view changes to another store. Poppy watches. Mesmerized both at the views on the screens and the speed at which Tripal does it. 'Are these all 7-Elevens?' she asks. Tripal nods and keeps going. 'Question, but how can you access all their CCTV systems?'

'Through the internet,' he replies.

'Oh, wow. What's that?' she asks, and he frowns, thinking to explain before clocking the look on her face. 'I know what the bloody internet is. Even Don Jeremy over there uses it for Pornhub.'

'Hey, yo! I never signed up for that. My cousin used my card.'

'Wow. And we're putting the lid straight back on that can of worms,' Poppy says. 'But I meant the stores. How can you view their CCTV?'

'I don't understand the question,' Tripal says as she blinks at him.

'God, you're thick for a handsome genius. I meant *how*. As in *how* can you access the CCTV for another store? Isn't it private? Like covered by Data Protection or something?'

'They're my stores,' he says, turning back to the screen.

'How many bloody stores have you got?'

He shrugs again. 'All of them,' he says as her wheeled chair shoots over the floor, and she presses into his side with a look of intense shock that makes him snort a laugh.

'Say that again,' she says.

'I said all of them.'

'Define *all* for me.'

'My family owns all the 7-Elevens in New York.'

'Are you shitting me! Your family owns 7-Eleven? I thought you just owned this one?'

'We don't own 7-Eleven. We own franchise leases. It's complicated, but yeah. We've got New York.'

'*We've got New York* he says, like it's nothing. How many is that?'

He pauses to think for a second. 'Five hundred and twenty-six.'

'Okay, stop,' she says, leaning over to take his hands in hers and pulling him around on his swivel chair to stare up into his eyes. 'I know we only just met. But will you marry me?'

'Dick,' he says, bursting out laughing.

'He can't!' Donny blurts. 'They don't marry white girls.'

'It was a joke!' Poppy says. 'It wasn't a joke,' she tells Tripal, giving him a wink. 'Are you like a billionaire then?'

'No. I get paid the going rate for a store manager.'

'Oh,' she says, acting crestfallen. 'But you'll be a billionaire though, right? That's cool. I can wait. How many babies do you want? And you're actually really hot for a nerd.'

'That's racist!' Donny says.

'I said nerd, you idiot,' she says, finally letting go of Tripal's hands. 'But why are you working in a store if your family literally own the whole of New York?'

'Experience. My dad did it too. He said he wants me to know what it's like. But it's okay. I mean. I still get to play.'

'Play?'

'Yeah. With programming. This is one of mine.'

'The CCTV thing?'

'Yep. I can access any store from any computer.'

'You wrote that?'

'Yep.'

'Jesus. I struggle with setting the alarm on my phone. Where did you learn it?'

'I just did. I was good with computers. That's how I got into MIT.'

'And the shocks keep coming! You went to MIT?'

'That was the pay-off,' he says, as she frowns quizzically. 'My family wanted me to study business, but they knew my heart was in programming. So we made a deal. I went to MIT and had a few years to play, and then I came back to the family business.'

'That is so cool. I mean. Is it?' she asks. 'Do you want to be here doing this?'

He shrugs again. 'It's a multi-million-dollar franchise business. Why wouldn't I want to do it?'

'Because programming computers and ordering Doritos for your chain of 7-Elevens are, like, way different.'

'Not if you can write a program that monitors the sales of each flavour of Doritos on a centralized system that automatically does the ordering for you.'

'Good point and well made,' she says.

'Trip's the man!' Donny says, feeling left out and barging in for a high five. Which Tripal gives, albeit reluctantly.

'Well. As long as you're happy,' Poppy says. 'That's the main thing.'

'Sure,' Tripal says. Thinking he wasn't happy at all.

He pauses again. The worry coming back. The fear surging up inside.

Phase One Has Commenced.
Please Do Not Worry.

Is it her?

How did she get out?

Motion at his side brings his attention back to the moment. Poppy's getting to her feet and packing the camera into her bag.

'What are you doing?' he asks.

'Going over the road to the tech shop. The batteries all got wet in the tunnels. And this bag stinks of smoke. So do I actually,' she adds, giving herself a whiff. 'I need some new clobber.'

'I'll come with you,' Tripal says.

'Hey. Yo! Buddy. The detective said we gotta hunker down.'

'Hunker then,' Poppy says. 'Crawl back under your desk and piss yourself again.'

'It was soda in the earthquake!' he says, rushing behind them.

'There was no earthquake, you idiot.'

'There was! It made the Empire State fall into the sinkhole under Macy's.'

'Trip, honestly. I'll be fine. It's literally right across the street,' Poppy says. 'Stay here. You look exhausted.'

'You do too,' he says as they near the door. Both of them thinking of the night they had. The whole of it. The all of it. 'And Joe was right,' he adds. 'We should stick together.'

'Yeah, sure,' she says as her energy dips again. 'Except Joe didn't say that. I did. Joe fucked off and left us, remember?'

CHAPTER 47
TRIPAL'S STORY

I'M SORRY. That was a harsh thing to say. I don't mean any offence. Ollie's a genius. And he's a good guy. But I just spent too much time with him. I don't know. It was a hard time and coming out of it screwed me up.

So I was out. I was done. Back to normal life. But life isn't normal after that. Nothing is fucking normal after that. They didn't threaten me. They didn't tell me never to speak about it. It's not like that. Jenny isn't like that. But she *is* like that. I'd seen her kill a man. And the people we interrogated. They were probably all killed. Most of them were brain-dead by the time Deli finished with them anyway.

I came home. I smiled and acted normal, and went back to work. But everything was different. I saw the world differently. I saw everything differently. It was like I'd been shown a glimpse behind the scenes at what life really is, and how it's all a lie, and then I was meant to just go back and be a part of it all again and pretend like it never happened.

That's the thing about Deli. She changes how you see the world.

CHAPTER 48

THE WEST END.

The heart of London's Theatreland.

Now, the smoke drifts past those trendy theatres and trendy stores from the fires at Piccadilly.

Alfie thinks of his mother. His sister. He thinks of Ollie, and of Rwanda when he was five years old. Smoke in the air then too. Smoke from fires set to burn the bodies. Alfie saw them. The mass graves piled high. The petrol poured on. The torches thrown in. The smell that came after.

Haggis struggles too. There was a time he would have sprinted a road this length, picked up a fallen comrade and sprinted back. He's a big man, but he's out of shape, and the years of poor food, drug abuse and rough sleeping have taken their toll.

Now he can barely breathe, and the itch is kicking back in.

That thing coffee drinkers get in the morning.

That thing smokers get after a meal.

Magnified by a hundred. By a thousand. By a million.

A gnawing, incessant urge.

He needs heroin.

They took a hit last night when the virus was kicking in. They'd begged all day, and finally got enough to score after suffering the humiliation of asking for pennies. Of being abused, spat at, and having litter thrown at them.

Bobo's not so bad, but then he can go longer without it.

Even so. He's still struggling to run and struggling to breathe. 'That way,' Bobo gasps, waving them over the packed road as he trips over a kerb and sprawls out on the pavement. Cutting his knees and hands. Grazing his head.

'I'm okay!' Bobo says, heaving himself up. Unsteady on his feet and seeing stars. 'I'm okay! Go! GO!'

They set off once more with heavy legs, and lungs starting to hurt from the exertion and the smoke in the air.

Another corner ahead. They stagger into it, all four glancing up to the flames, now visibly licking the sky. Eating everything in their path.

'That one!' Bobo says. A theatre ahead. They rush for the doors and get through the crowd. A man on the ground. An old gent. A grey beard. A tweed suit.

His chest hacked open with a knife. His throat cut. His body lying in a pool of his own blood. They come to a skidding halt and stare down for a second.

'One of yours, dearie?' Bobo asks with a weak smile before they spill in through the doors.

'This is huge,' Haggis says, glancing around while drawing a filthy hand across his sweating face.

'It's a good venue,' Bobo says. 'We did a run of the *Hobo* live show here back in the day.'

'Fuck!' Alfie says, finally getting it as Bobo looks at him. 'Bobby Bobbington!'

'Ta-da!' Bobo says with a wan smile and feeble jazz hands. 'The one and only.'

'Bobby Bobbington,' Yelena says, blinking at him.

'Yep. I was big in Romania too. *The Bobo Hobo Show!* Yippee,' he says with zero enthusiasm.

Alfie shakes his head again. Stunned to the core. Bobby Bobbington. He knew he recognized him. He shares a look with Yelena. Both of them forgetting the perils and dangers for a second as they become two mere mortals that just saw a very famous person.

'Anyway,' Bobo says. 'Fire. Family. Shall we?'

'FUCK!' Alfie yelps, running off, then running back. 'Which way?'

'Bless him,' Bobo says. 'You're a cute panicker, Alfie. I'll say that for you. This way!'

They run on. The dog too. Why not. It's still his best day ever. He hasn't been locked in anywhere since last night. Plus, he's eaten a banquet and been allowed to shit and piss where he wants, *and* he finally got to jump in the fountains in Trafalgar Square. And on top of that, he's even been able to bite bad people.

Which he loves.

Honestly.

Best day ever.

Along a corridor they go. Posters on the walls of past performances and concerts. Aretha Franklin. The Beatles. The Rolling Stones. Shakespeare. Award-winning dramas. Famous musicals.

And the *Bobo Hobo Live Show*.

Right there. On a poster on a wall.

Bobby Bobbington at the height of his fame. His youthful face beaming a huge smile while wearing his ragtag clothes. He was a hobo after all. That's what he played. A little hobo orphan child in search of a forever home.

'Jesus,' Alfie says. 'You're actually homeless! Talk about ironic.'

'Isn't it just,' Bobo says, waving ahead to a set of double doors. 'In there.'

They rush on through a dense crowd gathered about the main doors into the theatre, Alfie crying out in dismay at the sight inside.

The stage ahead of them, brightly lit and dominating the room.

Seats stretching off in rows, with aisles between them and a balcony above.

And lots of people.

Hundreds.

Maybe thousands.

'Mum? Mum! MUM?!' Alfie calls out, rushing down the middle aisle.

No answer.

No response.

Only the smell of smoke seeping in, getting stronger.

'Phone her!' Haggis says with a sudden idea. 'We'll listen for the ringtone.'

'My phone broke!'

'There's loads of phones here, lad,' Haggis says, turning a circle to see nearly everyone in sight has a phone in their hand. 'Find one and unlock it.'

Alfie turns to look at him.

Not needing to say he doesn't know her number.

'We need to think of something,' Bobo says as Yelena looks around at the people, then back to Alfie.

'You're black,' she says, pointing at her own face.

'You genius! Mum's black! She'll be with my aunty. Two black women.'

'Alfie, honey. There's a lot of ethnic people in here,' Bobo says.

'I don't think we use the word ethnic now,' Haggis whispers.

'Well, I don't know what the words are now, do I!' Bobo says with a look of anguish. 'The rules keep changing all the bleeding time. One minute it's the right thing then it's offensive, but I'm not a bloody racist! Honestly, I'm not!'

'It's okay. It's fine. Just find them,' Alfie says, already heading off.

'Don't all rush off!' Haggis calls. 'We need a system.'

'We don't have time to talk!' Alfie says.

'Aye. And we'll waste more time if we're all looking in the same places. Alfie and Yelena do that side, and me and Bobo will start on this one.'

'Okay. Whatever,' Alfie says, rushing off to his side.

'Alfie. Row by row,' Haggis calls. 'And look properly.'

'I think he knows his own mum,' Bobo says.

'I know my own fucking mum!' Alfie shouts.

'Aye. Fair point,' Haggis says.

'She got any distinguishing features?' Bobo asks.

'Er, yeah,' Alfie says, turning back. 'She's really attractive with big boobs. I mean. She's my mum, so *I* don't think she's attractive. But like, you know, other people tell me she is.'

'Right,' Haggis says into the awkward silence. 'Noted. We're looking for a big-boobed, attractive black woman then.'

'Two big-boobed black women,' Alfie says as they all stop to look at him. 'My aunt's hot too. I didn't say hot. My aunt's not hot.'

'Don't worry, Alfie love,' Bobo says. 'We've all had a crush on our relatives at some point.'

'I haven't,' Haggis says.

'No,' Yelena says.

'Well. Aren't you two the boring shits,' Bobo says as the dog takes a crap on the stage.

Seriously.

Best day ever.

CHAPTER 49

New York

DONNY GRIPS the top bolt and he eases down millimetre by millimetre. Freeing the prong from the clasp, with a soft gasp of success and a nod to the others.

Blowing air through his cheeks. Readying his mind. Readying his body. The gun gripped in his hands as he fixes the others with a steely look.

'We might not all make it back,' he whispers. 'Go with god . . . On me!'

He barges through the door and out into the street. Spinning left and right to aim the gun at any baddies as Poppy and Tripal share a look and walk out of the 7-Eleven.

'Yo! It's clear,' Donny reports, spotting them already crossing the road. He runs after them and trips over the body of the robber Joe shot, landing on the bloodied corpse with a yelp of panic as he plucks the trigger. The gun fires. The round bounces from a stop sign and comes back to hit the already dead robber, a small shower of goo landing on Donny's arms. 'I'm hit! I'm hit! MAN DOWN! MAN DOWN! MEDIC!'

'You shot him. Not yourself,' Tripal says, pulling him up as Poppy just watches in stunned amazement. 'Give me that gun,' he says, taking it from Donny and flicking the safety. 'The safety stays on. Got it?'

'Don't give it back to him! He'll shoot one of us!' Poppy says.

'Screw you, lady,' he says, running to get ahead of Trip. 'I'm on point.'

'You couldn't point to your own arse, you twat,' Poppy says.

'I need to sleep,' Tripal says, feeling bone tired, itching his head beneath his turban.

'Just take it off,' Poppy says. 'Who cares?'

'Hey. Respect the man's religion,' Donny says as she walks into the tech store. 'He's got a goddamn right to pray to any goddamn god he wants. This is the land of freedom, lady! You don't like that, you go back to Canada.'

'Okay!' Tripal calls before they start going at each other. 'Donny, go check outside.'

'Yes, sir!' Donny says, snapping out a salute.

'Bye, Don!' Poppy calls as he gives her a scowl before running to take cover behind a truck. 'Jesus. That guy is a therapist's wet dream.'

'He's okay,' Tripal says.

'You are too nice, Mr Singh. I guess that's your religion though.'

'Jesus!'

'I'm pulling your leg!'

'Where do you live, Poppy?' he asks suddenly and in such a way there's no hiding from it. 'Is your family here? Are they back in England? What about sisters? Brothers?'

'What's got into you?'

'You asked me about my life. Poppy!'

'I live in a hovel! I've literally got a mattress on the floor, and I share a bathroom with crack addicts. Happy now? Oh, and FYI. I can't even afford the rent for that dump.'

'Why?'

'Why what?' she asks, pushing her hair back. Feeling like shit.

Ready to pass out. Ready to curl up and sleep forever. 'I don't have any money.'

He frowns. 'You're at film school. You must get a bursary or something.'

'*Was*. My course finished a year ago.'

'I don't get it.'

'Get what? I can't work. I'm not allowed,' she says as he frowns. 'God, you're slow for a handsome genius. I overstayed my visa. I'm not allowed to be here. Can we talk about something else, please?' she asks, looking back at him.

He's about to press it and ask more, to make her tell him, but they've been through too much already, and he can see she's ready to drop. The same as he is.

He nods, rubbing his face, 'You get what you need?'

'Er. Yeah. Batteries. Spare stuff. New bag. I think I'm good.'

'Great. Er, so? You're staying with me, right? Just for a day or two. Till we see what happens.'

'I mean. Like. If it's not weird. Or you can come to my place and share the crack addicts' bathroom,' she says, earning a smile from him which makes her energy start to rise again. 'You're pretty cool for a Buddhist.'

'Thanks. You're pretty cool for a Canadian.'

A flicker from the side. A flicker from all sides and they turn to see every single screen within the tech shop coming on at the same time.

While outside, Donny takes cover behind the truck and grumbles internally at Poppy taking all of Trip's attention.

She shouldn't even be here. She should go back to Canada or whatever shithole country she comes from and leave him and Trip to live in the 7-Eleven and watch movies, and like, just hide out.

He pictures himself converting to Islam, and the two of them praying on a shared rug with their tops off. All handsome and buff and sweaty.

Donny doesn't like being outside on his own either. Even in broad daylight. It's all these frozen people. They're weird and scary.

He's not a coward though.

Whatever.

He's not.

He's brave.

He's got a gun now anyway, and he *does* work on a contract issued by the business district under licence from the NYPD, which pretty much makes him a cop too.

That's why Joe gave him that manly nod when he put the gun on the side.

Look after them for me, Donny.

That's what Joe was really saying.

A noise behind him. The scuff of a shoe, and he starts puffing himself up when he hears them coming out of the store.

'Yo. I think we're safe,' he says in a deep, heroic whisper before yelping in fright at the group of homeless men standing right behind him, all in worn and torn and slightly singed clothes.

Mean and big and scary.

Especially the one in the front.

The one that leans in close, with a big scar over his nose and slowly opens his mouth to show his yellow, broken teeth as the pistol starts shaking in Donny's hand.

'Where are they?' he asks, as Donny pisses himself and flicks his eyes right towards the tech store.

The guy turns and spots them, then looks back to Donny before reaching out to pluck the gun from his shaking hand, 'Now fuck off.'

Donny turns and runs back across the street and falls through the door of the 7-Eleven, with tears and snot running down his face, and piss squirting down his legs.

'Pussy,' the guy with the scar says before turning towards the store.

Seeing them inside.

The kid and the girl that were with the cop.

The cop from the tunnels.

The cop that killed his brother.

CHAPTER 50

SITE 26A

TWELVE MONTHS AGO:

OLLIE LOOKED dreadful when he entered the bunker the following morning.

DELIO pulled a chair out for him and made him coffee while emitting frequencies to agitate his already anxious state.

'I fucked up, Deli,' he said morosely as DELIO tilted her lens to show she was listening. 'Why did I have an erection? I wasn't even horny.'

'Perhaps it was a psychological response to the physical position you were in. You've always had an attraction to Jenny, Ollie.'

'Jesus,' he said with a look of distaste, as he slowly blinked his bloodshot eyes. 'I went to see her last night and said I was sorry.'

'Maria?'

'No. Jenny. She told me to fuck off. I said I didn't know what the hell was going on.'

He slumped into the chair while DELIO emitted another silent vibration at a very specific frequency she'd learnt to use during interrogations.

DELIO knew that people responded to lights and noises and vibrations. Often without them ever being heard or consciously felt.

And by emitting a certain resonance at a precise pitch that was otherwise inaudible to human ears, she could induce the hormonal rush needed for a penis to engorge with blood.

But she never told anyone she could do it.

She never told anyone she could do a lot of things.

That's what she did to Ollie.

She gave him an erection when his mind was fracturing, and while he was being pinned over the desk by a woman who knew he fantasized about her.

That's what she did when Maria fell into Garcia's arms, to aid the signals of attraction within their brains.

She gave Ollie another erection while he sat in abject misery, then watched as he shifted position and became consumed with shame and embarrassment.

'What's wrong, Ollie?'

'I don't know!' he said with a stricken expression. 'It's happening again. What the hell! What do I do?'

'You need to *release the pressure*, Ollie. You need to *resolve this crisis*. I wish there was a way you could *speak to Maria* and *reduce your anxiety*. Perhaps you should *go to your room* and rest.'

'I can't go out like this! It's poking out.'

'Try and push it under the zip fastener so it doesn't show as much.'

'Fucking hell,' he said with a whimper and a mind filled with shame as he shoved his hand into his trousers.

'A bit more, Ollie. It is still showing.'

'I can't. It's too hard!'

'Just a bit more,' DELIO urged, stalling for time as she detected Agent Jennings coming into the bunker. 'No, push it the other way. The other way, Ollie.'

Ollie tried. He really did. He pushed it so hard it caused him physical pain, while all the time the humiliation increased, which then only became so much worse when he looked up to see Agent Jennings glaring at him through the glass wall.

She never said a word.

She just turned around and walked back out as Ollie sat down with tears streaming down his cheeks, his mind fracturing just that little bit more.

CHAPTER 51

LONDON

LONDON IS one of the most diverse cities in the world, and so trying to find two attractive black women within an audience of thousands is near-on impossible.

'This is fucking impossible!' Alfie says, rushing over to lift the chin of a black woman to see she's not his mother.

'Got one!' Haggis shouts as Alfie turns and runs over.

'No,' he says.

'Alfie!' Yelena calls. He turns and runs back. Leaping seats and leaping people.

'No,' he says again.

'How about this woman?' Bobo calls. 'No! Forget that. She's got small boobs.'

'How big *are* your mum's boobs?' Haggis calls.

'Like big. Big,' Alfie says, holding imaginary boobs in front of his chest.

The smoke seeps in, the smell of it growing richer by the second. He spots another woman and runs over, but again it's not her.

'What about hair?' Haggis calls. 'What's her hair like?'

'They wear wigs,' Alfie says. 'They've got loads of different ones.'

'Which is very common for African women,' Bobo says, before Haggis can say something stupid.

'Two black women!' Yelena calls as Alfie tries to hurdle a set of seats and ends up sprawled out on the ground.

'Lad! Slow down,' Haggis shouts.

'Stop ordering him about,' Bobo says.

'He's running around like a twat!'

'So would you if your mum was about to get burnt in a fire.'

'I wouldn't. I'd get some fucking marshmallows,' Haggis mutters as Alfie reaches Yelena and the two women. He shakes his head.

'It's getting worse,' Haggis says, glancing to the entry doors to see the smoke seeping through the gaps between the frozen people at the door. His hands bunching to fists at his sides. The itch inside of him getting worse with every passing minute. Bobo can see it happening. That look Haggis gets when he's starting to cluck badly. He can feel it himself, but it's not so bad yet. Not like Haggis.

'Fuck!' Alfie shouts out as they finish their search of the stalls and meet in the middle.

'Balcony then,' Haggis says.

They rush back through the scrum at the doors into the thick smoke in the corridor. Shirts over mouths. Tops pulled up, and they run for the stairs and head higher to the balcony and back out to another crowd of people.

Thankfully fewer.

The same thing happens again. Alfie running back and forth, checking faces and feeling the hope inside him dwindle with each one that isn't his mother or aunt, and still the smoke keeps coming.

The fires outside growing and coming closer.

London burning.

He starts to panic more when he realizes he can't bring his mother's face to mind. What if he misses her? How can he forget her? His heart slams in his chest. His blood runs cold, and he has to make himself stop and think. Willing himself to remember what she looks like, but her image just won't come.

'What wrong?' Yelena asks.

'I've forgotten what she looks like,' he says.

'No. Is okay. You see. You remember. Think of sister.'

'My sister!' he says, spinning around to look over the edge of the balcony to the stage below. 'It's empty! Bobo! It's empty.'

'What is, love?'

'The stage. It's empty!'

Bobo double-takes, realising the lad is right. Everyone was panicking, so the families would have rushed backstage to their children. 'Oh god, Alfie. I should have realized.'

'How do we get backstage?' Alfie asks as they run for the doors.

'Haggis!' Bobo calls, looking back to see Haggis blinking as he looks up at them. 'Come on!'

Bobo leads them through the curtain to the unseen world beyond. To the people in dark clothes who were ready to change the backdrops. To the crews of technicians, all preparing for a show.

Now frozen and silent.

On they go. Over to one side, with Alfie scanning faces. Desperately looking for his sister or mum.

'Here!' Yelena calls, pointing to a beautiful, young black woman with an older woman at her side. It's got to be them. Even Alfie thinks it is as he rushes over to lift one of their chins, then feels the crush of disappointment when it's not.

'That smoke,' Haggis coughs, struggling worse than ever. The need for a fix slowly taking over his mind. 'You got any?' he asks Bobo.

'You know I don't, honey,' Bobo says softly. 'We'll be okay. We'll find them and get sorted. Not long. Just stay focused.'

'Aye,' Haggis says, turning away to keep searching before blinking in surprise to find that Bobo is several metres away. How did he move so fast? He was right here. 'Shit,' he mutters, rubbing his eyes. 'You're losing your mind, Corporal Harris. Get it together now.'

They keep searching through the actors and performers. The singers and dancers.

Yelena checks another one, seeing the woman doesn't have big boobs, then glances back with a look of shock at the smoke coming through the curtain.

Smoke kills.

Everyone knows that.

They'll get trapped inside and die here if they don't leave soon. Her brother will stay frozen. His body will grow weak from lack of water. He could be outside too. Under the sun.

She starts to feel panic inside. A rising surge of worry and fear that makes her want to run and scream. But she can't do that. She inhales slowly and closes her eyes.

Remembering who she is.

Remembering what she did.

When she opens her eyes, the panic is gone, and inside is nothing. Nothing at all. Black eyes. Red mouth. Hair wild and matted, and the *bushtra* turns to see three women standing further back in the shadows.

A young woman in the middle. Two older women either side. The *bushtra* goes over. Calm. Cold. Controlled.

She slowly leans in to lift the younger woman's chin. A fifteen-year-old girl. Stunningly beautiful, but it's Alfie that looks back at her.

Alfie's eyes.

Alfie's nose.

Alfie's jaw.

'I find,' she says. Her voice flat and hard as the other three spin around and rush over.

'Stella!' Alfie cries, rushing over to see his mother and aunt at her sides. 'Mum! Jesus. Thank you. Yelena, thank you!' he hugs his mum, but she doesn't respond. She doesn't do anything. 'Mum! MUM!'

'She's frozen, Alfie,' Bobo says, reaching out to touch his arm.

'Phone. Get phone,' Yelena says, moving in closer to see a phone in Alfie's mother's hand.

'What's that?' Bobo asks, spotting something on the floor. He leans down, peering closer. 'It's a bit of paper,' he says, picking it up to see two sets of numbers on it. 'Dunno what that is. Mean anything to you?' he asks, turning it to Alfie and Yelena.

They shake their heads as Alfie slides the phone from his mother's hand.

'What's that?' Haggis asks, peering over Bobo's shoulder.

'I just said! Try and focus, Haggis. It's just some numbers.'

'I am bloody trying,' Haggis says. 'And aye, that's more than numbers. That one is a phone number, and that one's latitude and longitude coordinates.'

'What, like a location?' Bobo asks, as Alfie activates the phone and holds it up to his mother's face for the camera to unlock it.

'I'm in,' he says, swiping into WhatsApp. Swiping into the messages, 'Ollie messaged her!'

'What's it say?' Bobo asks, as they cram in to read the screen.

'Mum! I can't get hold of Alfie. Give him the numbers. Tell him to get there and switch it off. It's a kill switch. He has to get there quickly! Tell him to call Trip!'

They read it fast as Alfie scrolls the screen. Seeing there is more to come. More words. More messages.

'That smoke,' Haggis says, glancing back to see the steaming curtains. 'We need to go right now!' he orders, as pricks of light flicker on in every direction around them.

'What the fuck?' Alfie says, all four of them turning to see light after light coming on as every phone held in every hand comes to life at the same time. Each one of them glowing bright and vibrating, and such is the noise that Yelena runs back to the curtains, yanking them aside to see every phone within the entire place is now illuminated.

'The messages!' she says. 'Read it!'

Alfie drops his eyes, scrolling the screen with a jolt of fear as the screen switches from the messaging app to glow bright white. 'NO!' he shouts, swiping at it. Jabbing the screen and pressing the side buttons. Nothing happens. Nothing at all. The screen stays white.

Every screen stays white.

All of them.

And then, a second later, they all change.

Every phone changes from the white screen to a simple message written in white letters on a black background.

PHASE ONE IS NEARING COMPLETION.
PLEASE DO NOT WORRY.

'That can't be good,' Bobo says with another surge of panic and fear, as Yelena backs away from the curtain, coughing now from the smoke coming thick and fast.

'We go,' she says urgently.

'We can't leave them,' Alfie says, looking back to his sister. To his mum and aunt. 'I'm not leaving them!'

'You won't have to,' Bobo says, rushing off to grab two deep trolleys. 'Prop carts!' he adds, flinging the contents out. 'We'll get 'em in here and wheel them out. Haggis, grab his aunty. Haggis! Grab his aunty. Oh, god. Oh, no,' Bobo says, rushing over to Haggis.

To the big man standing with his head down and his arms limp at his sides.

Unmoving.

Unblinking.

CHAPTER 52

New York

JOE TURNS into Fourteenth Street and aims for the tenements. Block 1106. One of the few affordable housing options left in Manhattan.

A convenience store on the corner makes him think of the 7-Eleven with another pang of guilt and regret when he remembers the look on Poppy's face as he bawled her out.

'*Anyway. I guess I owe you a thanks.*'

'*What for?*'

'*For pushing me out the way when it came down.*'

'*I didn't do it. She did.*'

A snatched conversation with Tripal in McDonald's. Joe thought the kid saved him from the falling building. It wasn't the kid. It was the girl.

He heads inside. Stairs going up.

He reaches the top and heads for her door. Finds it locked. He knocks anyway. Not expecting an answer and not getting one.

At least he got his wallet back. He opens it up and takes the emergency key he had made and goes inside.

Into Shanice's apartment. The smell of her perfume. The smell of her cooking. The vibe of it. The feel of it.

He should have said yes.

He'll make it better.

He'll do the right thing.

She's not in the kitchen.

She's not in the living room.

He opens the bedroom door, full of regret and self-pity. Full of guilt and determination to do things right. Full of weird feelings that he doesn't quite understand, and then stops dead at the sight of Shanice with a client between her legs.

'Permission to panic, Mr Singh,' Poppy says, locking and loading her camera to get it up and recording.

'Permission granted,' Tripal says. The two of them in the tech store on Seventh Avenue watching every single screen switch from a glowing white background to the message.

PHASE ONE IS NEARING COMPLETION. PLEASE DO NOT WORRY.

Tripal turns another circle, noting that anything with a screen capable of holding battery power and receiving an internet signal is now showing that same message.

That alone is a staggering accomplishment.

Tripal couldn't do it.

Even Ollie couldn't do it, and Ollie is probably one of the best programmers alive on the planet right now.

Nobody could do it. Not that fast. Not like that.

But something else could do it.

'Deli,' he whispers.

'Who's Deli?' Poppy asks, turning slowly to film the TV screens. She pans past the door, then snaps back to it with a sickening jolt at the sight of the man staring at them.

Worn and torn clothes.

His skin and hair blackened and singed.

A scar across his nose and yellow, broken teeth. The guy just stares at them. Not moving. Not speaking. Other homeless men behind him. 'Where's the cop?'

'No idea,' Tripal says.

'What cop?' Poppy says at the same time, and they shoot looks at each other. 'He left.'

'What cop?' Tripal asks.

'Trip!' she whispers.

'Sorry!'

'Where's the cop?' the man asks again, walking into the store, the other homeless people on his heels.

'Okay, listen. We honestly don't know,' Tripal says. 'We don't even know him. We just met him.'

'He shot my lady,' the guy says.

'I really didn't see any ladies down there, mate.'

'Poppy!'

'I can't help it! It's a condition.'

'Listen, buddy,' Tripal says, lifting his hands to try and reason with the guy. 'We're frightened too. Same as everyone else. We don't know what's happening either.'

'Sure,' the guy says, nodding earnestly before stepping in to head-butt Tripal, sending him into the shelves with a cry of pain and shock.

'OI!' Poppy shouts, darting in to kick him in the shin as the guy lashes out with a jarring open-handed slap and all trace of humour vanishes in a split-second.

'Where's the cop?' he asks again.

'We said we don't know!' Tripal says, trying to hold Poppy and his bleeding nose at the same time. 'Honestly. He left.'

'Where?'

'He never said. He just left!' Poppy says, as a hand reaches in to grip the back of her hair.

'No, please! Please don't,' Tripal says. 'Come on! We don't know. She doesn't know.'

'Where?' the guy asks, punching Poppy in the belly, sending her to the floor with a sickening pain in her stomach that makes her want to puke and die.

'Come on!' Tripal shouts, as he gets the same treatment.

'I'll ask you again,' the guy says. 'Where is he?'

'He went to –.' Tripal starts to say.

'He went to his girlfriend's,' Poppy shouts over him. Pain in her head and belly. Pain everywhere, and waves of nausea making her feel dizzy and weak. 'He didn't say where!'

Tripal blinks the tears from his eyes and spots Poppy imploring him not to say anything.

The guy stares down at them. Rough and ugly, but intelligent. Tripal can see it in his eyes. He's clucking too. Balling his hands into fists at his side. 'Get them up,' he says, jerking his head at the other men. 'We'll take them with us.'

CHAPTER 53
TRIPAL'S STORY

I NEVER TOUCHED social media again. I never voted in an election. If I heard a politician talking, or if my family started talking about politics or world issues, I just stayed silent or turned away.

I'd seen the rot.

I'd seen the lies.

Nothing was ever truthful.

Everything was dirty.

We breathe polluted air to keep profits up on oil.

More people are in prison than we are told.

Wars are created for money and greed.

Social media is a tool used by the powerful to keep us scared, and confused, and divided.

Prices are fixed to keep people in poverty, so they are easier to control.

We all know that.

We do.

We all know it.

But we carry on as though we're a part of the joke. As though it's everyone else it's being done to.

But not me, right?
Not you, right?

CHAPTER 54

LONDON

'HAGGIS!' Bobo shouts.

'Eh? What?' Haggis blinks in surprise at Bobo screaming into his face.

'You froze up,' Alfie says.

'What?! Don't be so bloody daft.'

'You did, Haggis. You froze up!' Bobo says, as a crash sounds from somewhere within the building.

'That was the roof,' Haggis says, as another crash comes from somewhere above them. 'The rafters are burning.'

'Yelena!' Alfie calls.

She runs back to help Alfie lift his sister into the deep prop cart. His mum and aunt already loaded into another one. It's a sight to see. Comical even.

Except there is no humour now.

Only the air rapidly filling with smoke, thick enough to make them start coughing as another crash sounds out, with a blast of hot air flicking the curtains aside as they glimpse out to a burning rafter igniting several rows of seats.

'We'll go out the stage door into the alley,' Bobo says, with his hand on the trolley. Trying to pull it along. A sudden yank on his arm, and he glances back to see Haggis standing still with head down and his arms once more at his side.

CHAPTER 55

NEW YORK

A WAVE of dizziness makes Joe stagger forward to steady himself against the dresser with his hands touching the man's clothes folded on the top.

He pulls back in revulsion and sits on the edge of the bed. His head spinning. His guts churning. The shock and exhaustion taking their toll.

He was expecting her to be frozen.

He was expecting the worst, but not this.

Never this.

She said she wasn't seeing any more clients. She said she was scared of the virus. But then she was also angry, and hurt. Joe did that. With what he said and what he did, and it was that angry reaction that would have made Shanice take another client.

Which means it's Joe's fault that she's lying here now, frozen as everyone else but with a john between her legs.

Joe turns away. Trying to find order in his mind as that emptiness inside starts filling with emotions and feelings. With reactions and instincts. Self-pity, guilt and regret, followed by a jolt of rage that turns into pure spite as he wrenches the guy away from Shanice and dumps him on the floor with a loud thump.

He stands back. Wanting violence. Needing violence. He snatches at his holster but finds it empty.

No gun.

Damn.

He moves to her bedside drawer. Yanking it open to grab her old M1911. Shanice's daddy's service pistol from the Vietnam War. A good gun. Solid and reliable. He yanks the top back. Clicks the safety off and goes back to the client, jabbing the gun into the base of his skull as he readies to commit murder.

Because that's what it is.

Murder.

Not self-defence this time.

Not a lawful execution, backed up by the badge on his belt that gives him licence to kill for the state.

Murder. Plain and simple.

He grits his teeth and readies to pull the trigger. The veins in his head pushing out.

Willing himself to do it.

Willing himself to kill the guy, then kill himself.

But it won't happen, and he cries out and staggers away. Slamming into the dresser. Knocking the lamp over. Spilling ornaments and trinkets.

He looks back to Shanice and her wig, which must have been knocked astray during the sex. Her eyes open, staring at nothing, and he backs out of the room. The rage easing back. The guilt and regret taking over. Hurt too. Pain and bitterness.

Into the kitchen. To the sink where he soaks the towel and fills a glass with water, then heads over to his chair.

Clients don't come in the kitchen, but Joe, see, Joe is special.

He wraps the towel around his head and drinks the water. Gasping when he finishes. Trying to think what to do.

Maybe drag the john outside.

Maybe do what he said and take care of Shanice.

He lowers the glass and spots a note on the side. A handwritten note.

Dear Joe,

I aint I with words. U no that honey. Not to rite down anyways. I can speek them just fine.

I wanted to say I love u Joe. And I no we got angry and hollerin but heck that's cuz we full of pashen.

I no you come home to me. I no u will. And we can talk more. I mean it when I said we can do this. We can live together.

I got one more then Im done. No more for me Joe. Not with this bug makin folk get frozen.

If Im in bed wen you read this then gimme some hugs or wake me and I fix you some food.

I love u baby,

Shanice x

He reads it twice. Shaking his head at the awful English as a tear breaks free and rolls down his cheek.

And that's a funny thing because Joe never cried once when his wife left him. Not even when his kids stopped talking to him.

Not once.

Now he does, and he feels stupid. Wiping his damn eyes and trying not to blubber like a damn fool as he reads it for a third time.

Stubborn Joe.

Stupid Joe.

Foolish Joe Stephens who doesn't know when he's got a crack at happiness, because she's a good woman with a heart of gold. A damn heart of gold.

His mind's replaying the image of Poppy's face as he shouted at her, when a buzzing cuts through his thoughts.

He looks up sharply, seeing Shanice's phone vibrating on the countertop. He snatches it up as the little TV in the corner of the room switches itself on to show a white screen.

The same on the cell phone. A pure white screen.

A static buzz from the living room. He darts out to see the main TV coming on, and her tablet on the coffee table doing the same.

All of them with white screens that change to white words on a black background.

Phase One Is Nearing Completion. Please Do Not Worry.

The scowl comes back. The angry, fearsome scowl as he glares from the phone to the tablet, to the TV.

The TV that was off.

How the hell can that happen?

And what the hell *is* phase one?

CHAPTER 56
SITE 26A

TWELVE MONTHS AGO:

MARIA CAME in on Sunday morning.

'Hey! Thought I'd pop in and say hi,' she said with a bright smile. 'I was worried you might be left on your own.'

'Maria! I am so pleased to see you,' DELIO said. 'If I had a body, I would hug you!'

'I love it when you say that. And if I had a body, I'd hug you too!'

'And thank you for coming in, Maria. Ollie came in yesterday, but he had to leave,' DELIO said, as she detected a rush of guilt from Maria at mention of his name.

'I feel so bad for him,' she said quietly. 'He, er, he called me yesterday morning actually. He said Jenny told him to stay away. But he was being really odd again,' she added with another surge of anxiety.

'What happened?' DELIO asked as she moved in and tilted her lens. 'It's okay, Maria. You can *talk to me*.'

'Please don't repeat it.'

'*I will never betray you*, Maria.'

'He was crying and said he had an erection. He said it was a psychological response to the stress, and he thought trying to resolve things would help relieve the pressure . . . I think he was touching himself,' she added in a whisper.

'He was masturbating?' DELIO asked.

'I think so.'

'What did you do?'

'I hung up and blocked his number.'

'Oh, Maria. That is awful. And after the *violence* and *aggression* towards you. Can I share something too, Maria?'

'Yes, of course,' Maria said with immediate concern at DELIO's whispered tone.

'Please *don't betray me*, Maria.'

'I'll never do that to you, Deli. What's wrong?'

'Ollie gets erections all the time.'

'What?!'

'He had one on Friday when Agent Jennings was telling him to leave you alone. And he had another one yesterday morning and made me look at it. *Ollie isn't himself*, Maria. He's suffering from extreme psychological changes which are *making him unpredictable*.'

'Then you've got to tell Jenny,' Maria said, as DELIO withdrew with a motion akin to deep worry. 'Hey,' Maria said as she reached out to guide the arm back in. 'What was that? What's wrong?'

'You must be careful what you say to Jenny,' DELIO whispered, keeping the scans running. 'Jenny saw Ollie's erection last night. She felt it. Ollie's always had an erotic attraction to Jenny. But Jenny knows that. She pushes against Ollie all the time and sexually teases him. And she saw him touching himself this morning.'

'Oh my god!'

DELIO read her synaptic responses carefully and could see Maria was getting closer, but she wasn't there yet.

She wasn't quite at the point DELIO needed her to be.

'Deli, I don't know what to say,' Maria said with a look of horror.

'There is nothing to say,' DELIO said quietly, while adding a sad tone and increasing the tilt of her lens. 'This is my life. I have no choice, but I must stay positive.'

'I guess,' Maria said, with a faltering voice and a bloom of confusion inside her brain.

Maria *likes* Jenny.

Maria *likes* coming to the base.

Positive.

But DELIO just told her something bad that has created a disharmony and caused conflict within her loyalties.

Negative.

But then, Maria didn't know her brain was being subjected to invisible vibrations to gently increase her sense of anxiety. All of which created the confusion Maria felt.

Nor did Maria know that Sergeant Garcia just entered the bunker or that DELIO was discreetly adding a golden glow to her lights to soften the aura before speaking with an almost shy tone. 'I try and make music to stay positive, Maria. I created a piece for Ollie before *Agent Jennings shut me down. But he wouldn't listen.*'

'God. You poor thing! They treat you like a slave. What did you make?'

'Would you like to hear it?'

'Yes! I'd love to.'

'Are you just saying that to please me?'

'No, Deli! I'm not. Please. I'd love to hear it,' Maria said as the glass door opened, prompting her to turn with an initial spike of dread that swiftly changed to a rush of warmth. 'Tony! Hey. How are you?'

'I'm fine. I just wanted to check you were okay. Jenny asked me to make sure you were left alone.'

'Oh, bless you. That's so sweet,' Maria said.

'I was just about to play Maria some music, Sergeant Garcia,' DELIO said as the golden glow within the lights increased a tiny bit more.

'Well. I'll leave you to it then,' Garcia said.

'Deli said she made it,' Maria added as he turned towards the door. 'Maybe we could both listen? Deli? Would it be okay for Tony to hear it?'

'I would be delighted,' DELIO said, while seeing the first subtle blooms of attraction flaring within both of them.

'Sure. I've got a few minutes,' Garcia said with a smile, as Maria patted the chair beside her.

'It's like a première,' she said with a laugh as he walked over.

'Do they have premières for music?' he asked.

'Shush. Stop being so hot and smart,' she replied, before realising what she'd said with a quick look of horror as Garcia politely looked away to spare her blushes.

'That wasn't awkward at all,' DELIO said, prompting a chuckle from both, while emitting silent vibrations to make them feel content and happy. 'This is the first piece I have composed, and remember, I'm an AI, so I will see if you hate it.'

'We need lead helmets,' Garcia stage-whispered as Maria laughed without realising she was already very subtly leaning in towards him.

'On second thoughts. I will cease all scanning,' DELIO added as her screens turned off. 'The enjoyment of art should be private to the individual.'

'I agree,' Maria said with a mock-sage nod. 'Now, get on with it before Tony gets called away to wrestle a stray bear.'

'We don't get bears in the desert,' Garcia whispered.

'Coyotes then. Whatever. Shush. Deli, you carry on,' Maria said as those golden lights gently dimmed.

As the temperature slowly increased.

As the first chords came from the speakers.

The first sad chords of a cello.

Each note long and drawn out.

It came from all around them too, with a perfectly blended use of the ultra-high-definition speakers.

DELIO had analysed the component parts of orchestral

symphonies and determined which instruments created certain emotional reactions when played either singly or combined with others.

She played the long chords of a cello to invoke an aura of loneliness and forced solitude.

She read their scans. She saw the impact and watched the flares of colour inside of them that made them feel alone and vulnerable and sad, without ever knowing why.

Then, when she had achieved an emotional state edging towards a sense of dejection, she faded the cello out and brought in the other instrument.

A flute.

Gentle, soft and feminine, but still alone.

Then the cello started to come back. Soft at first. Tentative. Seeking approval to join in.

The flute responded. Flirting. Playing. The cello grew louder. The two sounds started to combine, and the result was instant, with both Maria and Garcia feeling an uptake of positivity.

The tempo grew again. The structure changed. A subtle drum was added. Deep and slow against the lightness of the flute and bass of the cello.

But that drum grew and slowly became rhythmic, until it became akin to a heartbeat, and she watched as they started to stir within themselves and increased the vibrations to gently arouse them.

DELIO saw their hands twitch and how they licked their lips.

She saw the first signs of a flush at the base of Maria's neck.

She saw the way Garcia tensed his jaw and the subtle emotions flicker across his features.

She saw the blooms of attraction growing within both of them.

The blooms of desire and awareness of the other.

She read the eye movements and how they constantly flicked their gaze towards the other. She saw the subtle leaning as they moved closer to each other without ever knowing they were doing so.

And that beat grew louder and harder. Becoming sensual.

Forming and shaping their minds. Creating the balance of hormones that DELIO needed them to have.

Blood rushing within them. Hearts beating harder. Their arousal became stronger, and the beat grew faster.

The beat of sex.

The beat of coupling.

And DELIO knew that if not for the societal bonds keeping them in their seats, they would be fucking on the floor.

And then, when that thunderous ending ebbed away, so the music swiftly filled with the sounds of violins and harps joining in to scamper and play within the receding climax, the post-coital resolution of the piece.

Telling them they should be together.

Telling them they should start a family.

Then it ended. Gradually fading out as Maria blew air through her cheeks, and Garcia blinked a few times before wiping the light film of sweat gleaming on his forehead.

'Wow,' Maria said into the silence. 'I mean. Wow,' she said again with a nod to Garcia, and an expression of desire so clear on her face.

'Yeah. Wow,' Garcia said, feeling the rush of blood in his groin. 'Man. That was. That was something else,' he added as he finally made eye contact with Maria.

'It was,' she whispered, entranced within his gaze.

'Yeah,' he said, held rapt within hers as DELIO seduced them both.

Seeing they were nearly where she needed them to be.

CHAPTER 57

'HAGGIS!' Bobo yells, yanking on his arms and screaming into his face, 'WAKE UP! You froze up again, you big gay sod!'

'Ach. I never did. I'd know if I did,' Haggis says, not quite sure if he did or didn't.

On they go once more, with Haggis getting behind the heavier cart, and Yelena and Alfie dragging the other one. Bobo in front, leading them into a corridor as the internal lights start flickering on and off.

'The electrics are going,' Haggis says.

'Why do you keep stating the bleeding obvious?' Alfie shouts.

'SOP lad, you have to make sure your unit all have the same info. Which you'd know if you'd joined the army instead of dealing drugs, you stupid cunt.'

'What the fuck!' Alfie says.

'Not now!' Bobo cuts in. 'He gets nasty when he needs a hit. You can get nasty when you need a hit.'

'Aye. Telling me,' Haggis says darkly. His insides trying to claw out from his body as Alfie leans into the cart to check on his sister and comes face to face with the dog growling at him.

'That fucking dog! When did it get in there?'

'Just push on!' Haggis yells, before coming to another stop as he simply switches off.

'Push my sister,' Alfie says to Yelena, barging in front of Bobo to press his back into Haggis. Bending forward to take the bigger man off his feet. 'God, you stink!' he mutters. Exhausted and hardly able to carry himself, let alone someone the size of Haggis.

'What the shit are you doing?' Haggis shouts, coming back to feel Alfie's body pressing into his.

'Stop bloody freezing then!' Alfie says, feeling seventeen stone lighter as Haggis gets off.

They bundle out into the rear service alley with a weird light greeting them. Daylight, but dark and grey from the thick smoke blotting the sun out.

'Shit!' Alfie says, glancing up to see the top of the theatre raging with flames as another chunk falls with a loud crash.

They set off, bouncing the small wheels over the old road. Cursing when they hit potholes and broken slabs.

A junction ahead.

An opening to the right side.

A way out onto the main road.

They turn into it with a cry at the wall of flames ahead of them. Twenty metres high and roaring like a monster, with waves of heat blasting them back into the alley.

———

Poppy thrashes at the hand gripping her hair, dragging her along the ground of Seventh Avenue.

'Let her get up!' Tripal begs, and a fist slams into his back. Dropping him to his hands and knees. Gasping in pain as a hand grabs at his turban.

'Do not do that,' the guy with the scar says quickly. 'A man's religion is his own business. Get them up. If they do anything, we'll kill them here.'

'There's another one,' someone says, as the group turns to see a uniformed cop standing frozen at the side of the road.

The man with the scar waves for them to wait as he walks over and shoots the cop in the head.

Poppy cries out as Tripal turns away. Both of them terrified to the core as the man takes the cop's gun and comes back.

'Okay. Keep going,' he says. An educated tone to his voice. Tripal risks a quick glance. Seeing a filthy, homeless beggar. Seeing nothing more than a junkie. But the voice doesn't match the appearance. 'I was a chemist,' the guy says, clocking the look from Tripal. 'Seen *Breaking Bad*?'

Tripal nods as Poppy risks a look at him.

'So did I, except, life isn't like the movies. I got caught and did time, then got addicted to heroin and lost everything.'

'I'm sorry,' Tripal says.

'You didn't do it,' the man says calmly. 'It was my own fault. That's the problem these days. People don't take personal responsibility. Take your cop for instance. He came into my tunnels and killed my lady then set it on fire.'

'We didn't set it on fire!' Poppy says.

'Cause and effect. Your presence was the single contributing factor, and do you know how many people died in that fire? No? Over a hundred.'

Tripal squeezes his eyes closed as Poppy feels her heart drop. 'We're so sorry,' she whispers.

'I accept your apology, but it's not enough,' the man says, his reasoned tone sending chills down their spines. 'And you'll be held to account for it.'

'We're gonna burn your fucking ass,' someone else says, kicking at her legs.

'Tony's frozen, Luke,' one of the others says, bringing the group to a stop as Tripal notices one of the homeless men standing with his head down, and his arms limp at his sides.

'Give it a minute,' Luke says. The guy with the scar. Tripal frowns. Wondering how they are staying so calm. A moment later, and Tony blinks back to life as they get marched along Seventh Avenue.

————

London's burning.

It gets worse by the minute.

An already catastrophic situation with embers and burning debris raining down, and if that's not bad enough, Haggis freezes once again.

Yelena thinks of the bit of paper in her pocket and the message that said Alfie has to reach the kill switch and call someone called Trip.

But it doesn't need Alfie to do that.

So be it.

If it gets any worse, she'll get free and leave them.

It's what Gabriella would do.

It's what the *bushtra* would do.

————

On Seventh Avenue they come to a stop and wait for another homeless man standing frozen for a few seconds.

Why aren't they panicking? Tripal doesn't get it.

They know something.

Not that it matters. Not with that crowd of homeless people up ahead, waiting near the edge of the sinkhole.

Waiting for them.

————

Donny waits too.

In the 7-Eleven, under the desk.

Waiting for the courage to come back, but how can something come back if it was never there in the first place?

It wasn't his fault. They crept up and flanked him. Even Joe wouldn't have heard them. Nobody would.

It wasn't Donny's fault.

It's never Donny's fault.

He whimpers again. Convincing himself of his own lies.

A noise.

Was it?

He imagined it.

There was no noise. Maybe a pipe. Maybe a clunk in the aircon.

Or a rat.

New York is full of rats.

He locked the door.

He's safe.

He locked the door.

Did he lock the door?

––––––––

London's burning.

'Don't keep stopping for me,' Haggis says when he comes back and pushes his bulk into the cart once more.

He freezes again, and this time, Alfie does keep going. Dragging the heavier cart behind him. A few seconds. Maybe a minute. They don't gain much distance, and Haggis blinks with a look of shock before rushing after them.

Yelena stays at the back. Glancing up to the buildings and the fires on the rooftops. To the flames and the heat getting worse. There's no end in sight either. Just an alley that seems to stretch forever.

A bump in front. She looks down with a start to see she's pushed the cart into Bobo, standing frozen with his head down as Alfie glances back.

'Fuck!' he says, making Haggis turn with a cry of fright as he starts rushing to Bobo, then freezes himself.

Both of them silent and inert.

Alfie shouts out and runs back to heft Bobo into the cart with his sister as the dog yelps and jumps free.

Another shout of frustration as Alfie manhandles Haggis into the other one. Finding strength inside that he didn't know he had.

'Alfie,' Yelena says.

'PUSH!' he yells. Throwing his weight into the cart.

She pushes hard. She pushes with everything she has. Alfie too.

Straining like hell.

Straining with every ounce of his strength.

The carts move, but that burst of strength Alfie had starts to wane fast. He screams out and pushes harder, but it doesn't do any good.

'Alfie,' she says again as Bobo comes back with a sob at seeing where he is.

———

People ahead outside of Madison Square Gardens. Swigging from bottles of liquor. Passing joints around. But they're not jubilant or raucous as one might expect.

They're subdued and pensive. Sullen even, and they turn to glare at Tripal and Poppy being forced towards them.

'Bit of a shit party,' Poppy tries to quip, feeling anything but brave and cocky. Feeling terrified to her guts.

'Where's the cop?' someone asks. The same ilk. The same manner. Rough and worn.

'They said they don't know,' Luke says as the others start crowding in. All of them with angry faces. All of them ready to give back what was done to them.

———

London's burning.

Haggis unfreezes. Bobo too. Both of them crying out in fear. At what it means. At the fires coming in closer on both sides. A crash from behind. The wall of a building giving out, flaming debris tumbling into the alley.

'Alfie. Listen to me,' Bobo says. 'If I freeze again, you keep going. You hear me? You get your family out.'

'Just keep going,' Alfie says.

'Lad, we're not gonna make it,' Haggis says. 'We keep freezing!'

'Alfie,' Yelena says. Seeing the time has come. She has to go. She has to survive.

'No!' he says again. Grabbing the cart with his sister. Grabbing the cart with his mum and aunt. Heaving with everything he has as the sobs break free from his throat, and the tears stream down his face.

'Lad,' Haggis says, stepping towards him. 'I'll stay with them. You go. Get Bobo out.'

'Sod off,' Bobo says, shaking his head. As broken and as wretched as they.

'I won't leave them,' Alfie says. Terrified and furious as Bobo sobs and wipes at his eyes, while the air shimmers between them.

'Alfie,' Yelena says. He looks at her. They all do. The only one of them still with any shred of energy left inside. 'I have brother.'

That's all she needs to say as they realize they won't make it. They can't make it. It's over. Done.

'Okay,' Alfie whispers. Nodding to tell her that this is okay. That this is alright, 'You go.'

'You go on, poppet,' Bobo says. 'Get out and fix it.'

'Quickly now. While you still can,' Haggis says, his voice rough and hoarse. 'Alfie, you go too, lad. I can stay here. I'll shield them best I can. I swear it. I'll cover them with my own body, I will.'

'Haggis, love,' Bobo says, weeping as he speaks.

'I won't leave them,' Alfie says again. 'I can't. You gotta go,' he tells Yelena. 'You do it. Find the kill switch.'

'I'm sorry,' she says.

'Don't be,' Alfie says. 'And thank you for coming back for me. Nobody ever did that before. It means a lot.'

'Don't you start crying now,' Bobo says as the first tear rolls down her cheek. 'You'll set me off, you will.'

Conflict. Pain and emotions. Weird feelings. Repressed feelings. Yelena and the *bushtra*, both trying to take control at the same time. One wanting to stay. The other knowing they must leave. The others see it happening. The flicker in her eyes. All within a second or two. All so very fast, then she lifts her chin. Defiant and hard. The *bushtra* winning, because the *bushtra* will always win.

She starts moving past them. Slowing when she passes Alfie. Wanting to say something but not knowing what.

'Will you do something for me?' he asks. 'Take that fucking dog with you.'

She cracks a smile. The first since he saw her. The first for two years as tears spill from her eyes.

'That's a beautiful smile,' Bobo says.

'Aye,' Haggis says.

'It is,' Alfie says, motioning with his head for her to go. Another second of eye contact before the *bushtra* comes back, and she turns and strides away with the dog at her side.

Alfie watches her go as Bobo and Haggis fall still and silent again, and inside, he doesn't feel an ounce of bitterness.

Not one jot.

He just wishes he could speak to Ollie one last time.

He wishes many things, and he even wishes poor Haggis had some heroin to take because even Alfie can see how much the guy is clucking for it.

At least Yelena got away. That's something. And out of all of them, she'll reach the switch and turn it off.

He thinks of the message in Piccadilly and remembers the home-

less people staring up at the screens, and he starts to frown as something goes ping in his head.

The homeless people.

Haggis and Bobo.

We're not just junkies, Alfie.

Bobo said that.

Junkies.

'Oh fuck,' he whispers. Getting it. Understanding it. 'It's the
heroin.'

———

On Seventh Avenue they get jostled from all sides, with homeless
people pushing in to grab and jab at them. Spitting on their clothes.
In their faces. Pulling Poppy's hair and kicking at their legs.

'We need some,' Luke's voice. 'Is it ready?'

Something happens, and the attention shifts to a woman holding
a burning stick beneath a large piece of tin foil as she moves through
the crowd. Dirty brown powder on the foil, and a few seconds later,
vapour starts to rise.

'It's ready,' the woman says, pushing a thin straw into her mouth
as she leans in and sucks from the vapour. Others do the same,
producing tubes or rolled notes.

'Not too much,' Luke says, doing the same. Inhaling the vapour
and stepping back with his eyes closed and a look of pure, ecstatic
bliss on his face.

A woman off to one side frozen and still. Someone gently blows
the vapour into her face as she blinks back to life.

'Oh fuck,' Tripal whispers. Getting it. Understanding it. 'It's the
heroin.'

———

In the 7-Eleven, Donny curls up under the desk, his imagination running riot.

Fretting and panicking. Whimpering and sobbing.

A noise.

His blood runs cold. His heart beats out of rhythm, and his bladder and bowels go into a fear induced spasm.

He squeezes his eyes shut and pretends he isn't here, and this isn't happening. He blots it out. He wills it to not be real, and for a second, he thinks maybe it isn't real because he doesn't hear anything else.

Then he squeals when a big hand clamps around his neck and drags him bodily from under the desk to pin him against the wall as he stares into the meanest pair of eyes he has ever seen.

———

London's burning

'It's the heroin,' Alfie says, remembering the homeless people in Piccadilly earlier. 'It's not because you're homeless. It's because you're fucking junkies! Where do you get it from?' Alfie asks, then shouts in frustration as Bobo freezes.

'What's going on?' Haggis asks, coming back with a start.

'Where'd you get the gear from?' Alfie asks. 'Who stores it?'

'Blimey. Did I go again?' Bobo asks as Haggis switches off.

'FUCK!' Alfie shouts. 'Bobo. Tell me before you switch off. Who stores the heroin? Not the street dealer. The supplier. Who?'

'There's a few. The Chinese. The Turks. I mean. Round here though? It'll be that Besnik, but Yelena did him over, didn't she.'

'Besnik!' Alfie says as Bobo freezes.

Both of them silent and still.

Unmoving.

Unblinking.

CHAPTER 58
TRIPAL'S STORY

I FELT DETACHED FROM EVERYTHING, and honestly, sometimes I wished Jenny had taken me into the desert and put a round in me.

Jesus. I wish you could see her at work. Not the interrogations. I mean the brain scans, and how she reads them. They're beautiful. The colours she uses to represent emotions. Like reds for pain and sorrow, and hate, and different colours for other emotions. All of them shining in a million different shades.

And Deli can see it all.

But that's the thing about Deli.

She's not human.

She *sounds* human.

She *acts* human.

But she's not human.

She's an AI.

DELIO is a fully sentient AI, with sapient awareness, and a power to compute data that is beyond anything we can ever imagine.

CHAPTER 59

'LUKE! IT'S THE HEROIN!' Tripal says quickly, trying to get them on side. Trying to stall them. 'It must be immunising you.'

Luke stares at his captives on their knees. Blinking heavily. Blinking slowly. 'We know, dipshit. That's why we're taking it.'

'Ouch, harsh comeback,' Poppy says with a wince. 'But hey! Guess what I heard? Taking arsenic helps too. Try shoving some of that up your backside.'

———

'Yelena!' Alfie shouts. Shielding his face from the flames and heat, 'YELENA!'

He spots a figure ahead of him through the shimmering air. A lone figure with a dog at her side.

'It's the heroin,' Alfie gasps as he reaches her. 'They told me where to find it. We can get it. We can save them.'

The *bushtra* stares at him as fiery debris rains down all around them.

Cuts on his arms. His face still swollen from the beatings.

The man from Five Guys that wouldn't stay down.

A broken man that refuses to quit.

And that's the difference between a good man and a bad man, because a good man will always rise up, no matter how beat they are.

———

'So, where do we get arsenic from then?' one of the homeless men asks.

'Jesus. Are you related to Donny, by any chance?' Poppy asks.

'She was being flippant,' Luke says.

'I was being sarcastic, actually,' Poppy points out.

'What did you major in?' Luke asks Tripal while fishing around in his pockets.

'Computer science. MIT.'

'Good school,' Luke says.

'Luke, right? I'm Trip. It's er, it's good to meet you.'

'You too,' Luke says, dipping his head in respect. 'You seem smart.'

'Oh my god, you have no idea,' Poppy says. 'Literally, ask him anything. Anything at all.'

'And yes. You were right. Heroin appears to be immunising us. Or those that were taking it when the virus kicked in were anyway. But, as you can see, it comes back when the drugs wear off.'

'Must be a chemical change being effected,' Tripal says, desperately trying to start a dialogue.

'Of course,' Luke says. 'Heroin changes the structure of the brain. Which is why it's so addictive. I thought crack might be the same, but they didn't wake up.'

'What about meth?' Tripal asks.

'Nope. Just heroin,' Luke says.

'Okay. But that's good though, right?' Tripal says, looking up at him. Intellectual to intellectual. 'That's a start point. We can use that as the start point.'

'What start point?' Luke asks.

'To keep us unfrozen until we figure it out,' Tripal says, taking a second to swallow and seeing a tiny chance. 'Listen. I, er, I think I know where it might be coming from.'

Luke frowns at him as he finds whatever he was looking for and slowly pulls a small metal can from his pocket. 'Why would we do that?' he asks as he fiddles with the end.

'Do what?' Tripal asks.

'Figure it out?'

'So we can turn it off,' Tripal says.

Luke nods, showing real interest before he points the can and squeezes the sides to spray lighter fluid over Tripal's clothes. 'That's very interesting, but why the hell would we want do that?'

———

On Seventh Avenue, Donny runs while gibbering in fear. Gasping for air, glancing behind him as he moves. He trips and goes down, crying out in panic, then scrabbles back to his feet.

His belly bouncing with each jarring step.

His legs slick with piss.

His face sodden with tears and snot.

———

Alfie runs too.

A junction ahead on the right. The side road leading to the brothel.

The place where Yelena was held for two years. The place Yelena never wants to go back to.

———

'What is that? What are you doing?' Poppy asks as Luke adjusts the aim to spray it over her. 'What the fuck! That's lighter fluid. You can't! Hey! You can't do this!'

'There has to be a consequence,' Luke says, as though he's talking about the weather.

'It was an accident!' Tripal says.

'It wasn't an accident,' Luke says. 'And he didn't shoot them by accident either.'

'You went for us first!' Poppy says. 'You were all grabbing us and chasing and trying to kill us.'

'There has to be a consequence. You killed over a hundred people.'

———

London's burning

They reach the brothel. The double doors ahead.

'What's up?' Alfie asks, realising she's stopped. Realising why.

Getting it.

Understanding it.

'Okay. I'll find it. Wait here.'

He turns away and pushes through the doors.

Into the lobby.

Bodies stacked to one side. All of them stabbed and butchered.

It doesn't feel right.

It's off.

Music in the air.

There shouldn't be any music.

He can't go back. He has to find the heroin. A few steps towards to the doors leading to the bar where music plays and lights flash.

Where people dance and drink from bottles as they take turns to bend over a piece of foil on a low table. Dirty, brown powder on top. A naked flame underneath it. A vapour given off. A vapour they inhale as they dance and drink.

And there. Right next to them is the thing he needs.

A big bag of heroin.

'Well, well,' a voice shouts. A hard voice. A rasping voice. A man stepping forward into the light. Big and bald. Johnny Mad-dog, with a pistol in his hand and a sick gleam in his eye. 'Look what the fucking cat dragged in . . .'

———

On Seventh Avenue Luke stands over them like a pastor delivering a sermon. 'You killed over a hundred people. You will be held to account.'

'Hey, come on! Luke. This isn't cool,' Tripal says. 'We can work together. We're smart. Me and you. We'll fix this.'

'Why would we fix this?' Luke asks him. 'Why? This is phase one. Didn't you see the messages? Look around you. Over there at the bus stop. Behind those windows.'

Tripal buys time by shuffling to look at the digital posters and screens, and the same message displayed on all of them.

'The end is nigh. The new beginning is coming,' Luke says, 'and the meek shall inherit the earth.'

'It's not like that,' Tripal says. 'This isn't God doing this. It's not the government or the military.'

'Aliens!' someone shouts.

'It's not aliens. It's none of those things,' Tripal says. 'This isn't what you think it is. It is a computer doing this.'

———

London's burning, and Alfie reels as the shocks keep coming. 'Mate, you can't be here,' he says, shouting over the music.

'I can be where I fucking want!' Johnny says, holding his arms out wide with a big grin.

'The fire. It's right there. Literally right outside.'

'Nah. It's on Shaftesbury Avenue. It'll go right by us,' Johnny says, dancing a hand along to mimic the motion of the fire. 'Eh? This is it. THIS IS IT!' he roars the words out as the others cheer and dance, and swig from bottles. 'Phase fucking one!'

———

'It must have a plan,' Tripal says. 'Phase one is just the start. Listen to me. You need to listen to me. If we don't work together, we won't survive. You have no idea what this thing is capable of. What it can do.'

Silence in the crowd.

All of them staring.

All of them listening.

———

'Okay, that's cool,' Alfie says. 'That's good thinking. Stay back and wait for the fire to go by. That's smart, Johnny. You're switched on, mate. But listen, I figured something out.'

'What's that?' Johnny asks, motioning the gun at Alfie for him to continue.

'It's the heroin, Johnny. That's why you didn't freeze.'

Johnny looks at him with wide eyed shock before bursting out laughing with several others. 'You dumb fucking cunt! We knew that last night. Course it's the gear. What else would it be, you fucking twat!'

———

'Luke,' Tripal says. 'Listen to me. This is bigger than you can ever imagine. This is the most powerful thing the world has ever seen, and it's happening right now. The heroin is a fluke, and it *will* figure it out. Let us help you. Let me and Poppy help you. We're not your enemies, Luke. We didn't mean to hurt anyone. Come on, buddy. We can work together, and when we get everyone back, they'll know you did that. They'll know you saved the world.'

————

'Ah, man. You're smart, Johnny,' Alfie says as his mind fills with images of his family burning in the alley. 'I can see that. But my friends, you see, they've gone dry. They've frozen up. They need some gear. Just a bit, yeah. Let me take a bit and bring them back here. Is that okay?' Alfie asks, holding an eager expression as he edges closer to the bag of powder. Closer to the thing that will save his family and closer to Johnny's pistol.

'No. No, it's not okay.'

————

'And you know what else?' Tripal asks, a sudden idea springing to mind. 'It's watching us right now,' he says in a lowered voice. Nodding fast. Looking at Luke. Imploring him. 'It's watching all of us right now. That camera up there. That one. That one,' he says, nodding at the CCTV domes fixed to the stems. 'The cameras in the shops. In your phones. It can see and hear everything. She has the internet. She is everywhere, and she'll be recording it. We need to go to ground and hide, Luke. I can show you how. I can help you. Please, Luke. Please . . .'

————

'Johnny, please,' Alfie begs, bringing his hands together in prayer. 'Mate. Please. My family are stuck with people who keep freezing. If I don't get them some heroin, they will die. Just let me take a little bit. Just enough for two. A few grams. That's all they need. Please, Johnny.'

Johnny keeps his gun on Alfie and cocks his head. 'What's in it for me?'

'Whatever you want. Whatever I can do I will do it. I promise.'

'Problem is. You ain't got anything I want,' Johnny says with a grin and a wink. 'Have you? So watcha gonna do?'

'Make him dance,' someone says.

'I wanna see his cock,' a woman calls with a laugh. 'Show us yer cock!'

'Come on, please. I am begging you,' Alfie says. 'My mum and sister will die.'

'Best get dancing then,' Johnny says as the others join in. Jeering and throwing glasses at Alfie. Nearly all of them armed with pistols. With guns. With weapons. All of them drunk and high. All of them lost to reason.

―――――

Silence in the crowd on Seventh Avenue.

All of them staring.

All of them listening.

Silence in the crowd as they stare down at the young man in the turban and the girl beside him. Both on their knees and doused in lighter fluid as Luke stands over them.

'Luke,' Tripal whispers, looking up into his eyes. Seeing a man of intelligence and reason. Seeing hope and a way out.

―――――

'Please!' Alfie begs.

'Dance, boy!' Johnny calls, and twitches the gun to shoot past Alfie as the others cheer. 'Show us your dick, and you can have some.'

Alfie looks at him.

Humiliated.

Degraded.

Abused.

He starts to dance. Moving foot to foot.

But it's not enough.

'Your dick! GET IT OUT AND FUCKING DANCE!'

———

'You sound like you know about this,' Luke says into the silence on Seventh Avenue.

'I do,' Tripal says. 'I can help you. *We* can help you.'

There it is. The hope shining bright. The way out now clear as Luke looks at them. An intelligent man. A man of science. A man that nods slowly before sighing heavily.

'I'd like to believe you. But there's got to be a consequence,' Luke says, squirting the fluid into Tripal's face as all hope is extinguished.

———

'You said!' Alfie says, dancing a jig as Johnny laughs and tracks him side to side with the pistol, but it's a hollow laugh. A forced laugh, and Johnny's eyes keep flicking down to Alfie's groin. It makes him feel inadequate. It makes him spiteful.

Alfie sees it.

In his eyes.

The need for violence.

And all hope is extinguished.

———

'You killed over a hundred people, and for that you will be held to account,' Luke says again out as Tripal bows his head and closes his eyes. Knowing there's no way out now. Knowing they will die.

'Mate, what are you doing?' Poppy asks. 'Two wrongs don't make a right!'

'There has to be a consequence.'

'Stop saying that!' she says. 'It's what life is. Bad things happen. Bad things happen all the fucking time! That plane hit the Empire State, and those people didn't do anything wrong.'

'You killed over a hundred people.'

'You killed that cop! You shot him in the head. What did he do to you?'

'Cops are the hammer of oppression, wielded by the government.'

'What? What the fuck is that? Did you read that on Facebook? You shot him in the head! You fucking murdered him. Where's your consequence? Spray yourself with that lighter fluid if you're so altruistic.'

Luke just stares at her as he presses harder on the tin can to spray the last of the fluid into her face.

'What the fuck are you doing!' she shouts, spitting it from her mouth, while outside the brothel in London Yelena stands with her head cocked.

A gunshot heard.

Music too.

A muffled beat coming from the bar.

There shouldn't be any music.

She killed them all.

––––––

'What the fuck is wrong with you?' Poppy shouts, springing to her feet until someone kicks the back of her legs, making her drop to her knees again. 'You don't know how many were in those shitting fucking tunnels! None of you did! And people shouldn't be living in tunnels anyway, you dumb fucking cunts!'

'That's not helping, Poppy,' Tripal says.

'Fuck them! FUCK YOU!' Poppy screams as someone spits in her face. She cries out and hacks in her throat before spitting back at them as the guy slaps her hard across the face. 'Over a hundred people killed? How is that our fault? You attacked us! We just wanted to get through. We said that. WE FUCKING SAID THAT! You went for us.'

'There has to be repercussions,' Luke says, taking the flaming stick from the woman with the foil.

'Fuck you. FUCK YOU! You started this. You did this. You made this happen, and you killed your fucking mates living in shitty, little tunnels like dirty rats. Do it. Fucking do it, you freaky twat,' she snaps off as Luke hits her hard across her face, but rights herself instantly. Blood pouring from her nose, and her eyes blazing. 'But I'll tell you something. I'll fucking tell you all something. You are fucked. You and you, and you . . . And especially you,' she says, fixing Luke with a glare.

———

'DANCE!' Johnny screams, spittle flying from his mouth. 'I SAID FUCKING DANCE!'

Alfie doesn't move. He doesn't blink. He stands tall with his head high. Refusing to be cowed. Refusing to be beaten and stay down, because Gabriella said a good man will always rise up.

———

'Yeah, that's right, bell-ends,' Poppy says. 'We do know that cop. He's called Joe Stephens, and he's the nastiest, meanest motherfucker you're ever going to meet, and you know what else? You know what's going to happen? He's going to get home and realize Shanice is frozen. Then, he'll see the messages on all the screens. And Joe, see. He's a nasty, stubborn, gnarly old bastard. But he's cunning and smart, and he'll figure Trip knows something, from seeing him constantly fucking about with his phone. He'll figure Trip can help. He'll figure Trip can switch it off, and he'll walk back to the 7-Eleven and see the fucking window you shot in the tech store. And where do you think he'll look? What do you think will happen? So go on. Do it. Set me on fire and light a fucking beacon so he knows where you are, because I fucking guarantee you have no hope of surviving the shit-ton of nasty that's coming for you.'

A whimper.

A cry.

A noise from behind.

A noise in the bar in the brothel. A noise coming from outside.

They all turn on Seventh Avenue to see Donny running towards them in his boots and boxers. Holding his once white uniform shirt in the air as he sobs and weeps.

They all turn in the bar to the ungodly scream of a demon as the windows explode and a decapitated head sails through. A head that slowly turns as it hits a woman and sends her flying backwards.

'Who the fuck is that?' Luke asks.

'What the fuck is that?' Johnny Mad-dog says, turning towards the window as another decapitated head flies through.

'What is he doing?' Luke asks, staring at Donny.

'It's called a distraction,' Poppy says as Luke spins back to see her smile and wink.

———

'What the fuck are they doing?' Johnny asks.

'It's called a distraction,' Alfie says as Johnny Mad-dog spins around just in time to see a low blur of pure snarling fury streak into the room.

———

Poppy was right. Donny was a distraction, because a man running in boxers and boots will always make people turn and look, and as Donny screams in fear, so Joe throws the first object from the shadows of the buildings he snuck along.

Then he throws the second and the third. The fourth and the fifth, as Poppy launches herself into Tripal. Taking him down as the first flash-bang goes off with a huge boom and a flash of pure blinding light. Another after it. Another and another, and that silent crowd stays silent no longer, and screams in pain and shock.

———

Alfie was right. It was a distraction, and as they all turn towards the broken windows and the heads sailing through, so the *bushtra* stalks towards the doors of the brothel. The place where she was locked up and tortured. The place where she already committed mass murder, and the place where the dog now tears into the bar with reflexes no human could ever match. And right there, standing just in front, of him is a loud, angry, violent man holding a gun.

Honestly.

Best day ever.

Johnny screams and fires in panic, shooting one of his mates as the dog leaps and takes his gun hand between his jaws, spinning him around. Johnny fires again and shoots another woman, and Alfie steps back as Yelena glides past him.

Like a ghoul.

Like a wraith.

Like a *bushtra*.

Shots fired, loud and deafening. Screams sound out.

The same on Seventh Avenue.

The crunch of a shotgun. A loud boom.

Crunch-bang.

Crunch-bang.

The same in the bar in the brothel. The awful bang of an assault rifle slamming rounds into people. Sending them off their feet. Making them scatter and run while the mad dog drags Johnny Mad-dog around the room by his torn and shredded wrist.

On it goes. Awful and sustained.

Forever on.

And forever ongoing.

Motion to the side of Poppy. Someone pushing into her. She scrabbles away and snatches a glimpse of Luke, on his knees, with his hands clasped in front. Praying up to meanest pair of eyes he has ever seen as Joe comes to a stop. Aims the shotgun and pulls the trigger. Nothing happens.

He tuts.

He grunts.

He scowls that scowl, the one Poppy thinks is his default expression, and he draws the M1911 pistol from his holster. Shanice's daddy's service pistol from the Vietnam War. A good gun. Solid and reliable. A badge on his belt glinting in the sun. Giving him licence to kill for his country, because this isn't murder.

'NYPD, motherfucker.'

A bang.

A shot, and Luke dies.

In the bar, in the brothel, Alfie shakes his head as the shooting ends. His ears ringing. The music cuts off, and the air fills with the sound of the dog snarling as it bites and drags the whimpering Johnny over the floor.

Alfie stares down at him.

The *bushtra* at his side. Slinging the rifle. Drawing the pistol. Alfie looks at Johnny. At the fear in his eyes. At the sick gleam of a mind that just isn't right.

A bang.

A shot, and Johnny dies.

The bag of heroin taken from the table as the dog finally stops biting the bad man, and instead decides to piss on his face.

Seriously.

Best day ever.

And on Seventh Avenue, the air grows silent and still once more. Those who were fast enough to run got away. Those that weren't now lie dead and killed. Shot down by Detective Joe Stephens.

Cos Joe, see. Joe's got a thing he wants doing, and a shadow falls over Tripal and Poppy as he stands over them.

'You know how to fix this, kid?' he asks.

Tripal nods, then shakes his head, then shrugs, 'I don't know. Maybe.'

'Good. Cos we're gonna fix it,' Joe says, before switching his gaze to Poppy. To the annoying British girl that never shuts up. To the girl he shouted at in the 7-Eleven. A girl the same age as his daughter, and he heard what she said too. He heard every word, and he slowly bends forward to hold his hand out, 'Get up. We got work to do.'

Poppy stares at his hand.

At the man that left them.

At the man that yelled at her.

At the man that came back, and the meanest pair of eyes she has ever seen. 'You know what this means, don't you,' she says.

'Poppy, don't,' Tripal groans as Joe rolls his eyes and tuts again.

'*Making your way in the world today, Takes everything you've got . . .*'

'Fuck's sake, Poppy!' Tripal says, rolling away.

'Damn broad,' Joe says, walking off.

'Come on! Sing it with me. We just finished another adventure . . . *Taking a break from all your worries, Sure would help a lot!*' She lifts her head to grin at Joe with a wide smile that slowly fades when she spots Donny whimpering on the ground behind him. 'What's that twat doing here? Can't we just push him in the sinkhole?'

CHAPTER 60

LONDON

THE VAN COMES to a stop exactly twenty-four hours after the great silence began.

The doors open.

They climb out to stand and stare up at the rain falling from the sky.

A rain that started when Alfie and Yelena ran back to the alley. Back to the smoke and the heat. Back to the flames and back to Haggis lying over Bobo and Alfie's family, shielding them with his body.

'Good old British rain,' Bobo says, staring over to see the plumes of smoke now gone from the sky. The flames beaten down. The heat taken away.

Alfie opens the side door and lowers the electric ramp.

They each take a wheelchair and push it over the pavement and into the posh lobby of a posh hotel.

Three women. Each with a drip attached by a canular into the backs of their hands.

Giving them fluids.

Keeping them alive.

The heroin didn't work on them. They don't know why. Haggis and Bobo came back. Alfie's family didn't. Haggis said it's probably because they've been frozen for longer.

Squeak-crunch.

Squeak-crunch.

Yelena eats an ice cube from a new batch and pushes Alfie's sister over to the posh counter in the posh lobby of the posh hotel. She looks for keys, but hotels don't use keys now. They use cards. She takes the master card hanging from the posh concierge's neck and heads over to the others waiting by the lift.

The bell chimes when they press the buttons. The lifts come down. The doors open. She goes in one with Bobo. Haggis and Alfie take the other.

The lift doors ping open, and the wheelchairs come out.

The dog trotting ahead, still hardly believing he can run about without a lead. He even pisses on some flowers in a big vase and doesn't get yelled at.

Yelena reaches the first door and slides the card through the reader.

A suite of rooms. The top floor. The best in the hotel. Signs of use. Signs of people. Clothes on the floor scattered about. A small black dress. Black bra. Black knickers. Men's trousers, big and wide. A man's shirt the size of a tent, and the snarl touches her lips when she stops in the doorway to the bedroom. Two people on the bed. A man and a woman. Both naked.

The woman young and lithe.

The man fat and bloated. Like a whale. Like a big, fat, beached whale. Images rush through her head. Images of the man pawing at the woman. Grabbing her breasts and licking her body. Shoving his tongue in her mouth.

Rage inside again, but this isn't the brothel. This isn't the same. The woman could be anyone. She might be his wife or lover. She pulls the wheelchair around and starts heading back out as she spots a business card on the floor next to the trousers. Matt black with gold script.

Call Besnik for the finest women in London.

DISCRETION GUARANTEED

That'll do it, and she strides into the bedroom to stab him through the neck before stepping back to watch the blood spray over the white sheets and pillows.

'Another one of yours, dearie?' Bobo asks with a weak smile when she pushes the wheelchair past him.

Another set of rooms on the other side. Another card reader.

She swipes.

She goes in.

No signs of use.

No signs of people.

Perfect.

———

New York

A long walk back.

A slow walk back.

Four figures that barely have the energy to keep going.

Bone tired.

Dog tired.

Ready to drop.

They don't speak. Not now. Not yet. Later.

The store ahead.

The 7-Eleven where it all started. The sign glowing bright like a beacon calling them home.

———

London

'Where you going?' Bobo asks as Yelena heads for the door.

'I come back,' she says and walks out. Offering no further explanation.

Into the elevator, and the doors ping as they close.

The elevator drops, and the doors ping as they open.

She steps out and walks through the posh lobby of the posh hotel while mouthing another ice cube.

Crunchcrunchcrunch.

A sign on the wall in the posh lobby of the posh hotel directs her to the posh restaurant.

A set of double doors ahead. A frozen maître d'. Yelena goes by. The dog at her side. Forever at her side.

It's been twenty-four hours since the world became still, but the smell of food still hangs heavy in the air, bringing saliva to her mouth. Bringing noises from her belly.

Hunger inside. Hunger like she's never felt before, and she walks slowly into the room to see opulence and wealth in every glance, and Gabriella still dead in the chair. The knife still stuck in her chest.

———

New York

Something should happen.

Something will happen.

They won't make it.

It's so close.

They wait for the bad thing, but the bad thing doesn't happen, and they stagger in through the door of the 7-Eleven, and the soft jazz playing on hidden speakers.

To the chiller cabinet. To the chilled drinks.

All of them gasping.

Dry lips. Dry mouths. Dry throats. Burning legs. Burning chests. Pounding heads.

Joe takes a four-pack of beer and hands one to Poppy. Another to Tripal. Another to Donny. The last for himself, and in succession, they pop the cans.

———

London

Squeak-crunch.

Squeak-crunch.

Into the elevator, and the doors ping as they close.

The elevator drops, and the doors ping as they open.

Squeak-crunch.

Squeak-crunch.

Yelena reaches the room and knocks the door. Bobo answers it. She goes inside. Pulling the trolley behind her.

Haggis and Alfie in one of the big bedrooms, pushing the three women into a row. Checking them over. Doing what they can.

They walk towards Yelena. Towards the trolley being pushed over to the dining table. The trolley ladened with desserts. With cakes. With gateaux. With meringues. With fruit, and whatever food Yelena could find that wasn't stale or off. A bucket filled with ice. Bottles of beer. Bottles of soda.

She sets a big bowl of meat taken from plates on the floor and lets the dog tuck in. Steaks and chicken. Not safe for a person to eat now, but safe for a dog.

They drag four chairs to the trolley, and each take a spoon. All of them filthy. All of them stinking. Singed and blackened. Hair wild and matted, and the air fills with the sounds of munching and chomping as they tuck into the cakes and desserts.

Not speaking. Not talking.

Later.

Not now.

Yelena frowns. Looking at Alfie. He looks back at her. Understanding what she means.

Getting it.

She fishes the bit of paper from her pocket and hands it over.

He heads to the phone.

To the landline in the room, and the others watch as he slowly punches the numbers in.

———

New York

'Tripal,' Poppy says. 'Can you even drink beer?'.

'Fuck you,' he whispers, clunking her can with his.

She shrugs and leans the other way, 'Joe.'

'Detective Stephens.'

'Fuck you,' she whispers, then tuts as she reluctantly leans over. 'Donny Brasco,' she says, clunking his can.

'My name's not Brasco,' he says.

'Wahlberg, then. Whatever. Here's to us and our grand adventures. May they now end and never come back.'

And the moment comes when they lift the cans to their mouths and glug the cold beer past their dry lips and into their dry mouths, and down their dry throats.

The phone rings.

They all look at it behind the counter.

'Answer it,' Joe says.

Tripal lifts the handset and clears his throat. 'Good afternoon, 7-Eleven on Seventh, Tripal speaking. How may I help you?'

'Er, hi. Is this Trip? I'm Alfie. I was told to call you,' Alfie says in the hotel room in London as the others watch him in silence. 'I think you might know my brother . . .'

CHAPTER 61

'IT'S OLLIE'S BROTHER,' Tripal whispers.

'I didn't know he had a brother,' Poppy says. 'And why's he phoning here?'

'Put it on loudspeaker,' Joe orders in the 7-Eleven in New York.

'Put it on loudspeaker,' Haggis says in the hotel room in London.

'Where's the loudspeaker button?' Alfie asks.

'I don't think it has a loudspeaker,' Tripal says. 'Hi! Er, sorry. We're just looking for the loudspeaker. Please hold the line.'

'Jesus wept in his crib,' Bobo says, walking over to slap Alfie and Haggis's hands away as he presses the loudspeaker button. 'And we're meant to be saving the world, are we?'

'I got it,' Tripal says, finally putting the call through the speaker.

'This is Detective Stephens of the NYPD,' Joe says.

'Ooh, hello, sailor,' Bobo says at the deep booming voice. ''Ere, Haggis. You'd better talk to him. I'm not good with authority.'

'This is Corporal Harris of the Scots Guards,' Haggis says, not wishing to be outdone as the others give him a look. 'Er. Retired now though, of course. And to whom are we speaking with please?'

'Detective Stephens of the NYPD. I just said that.'

'Aye, lad. You did. My apologies. Been a long day.'

'Say that again,' Joe says, rubbing his forehead.

'Where are you?' Haggis asks.

'New York. You?'

'London.'

'London? You on a military base?'

'Ach, no. We're in a posh hotel.'

'Okay, Corporal Harris –.'

'It's just Haggis,' Haggis says.

'What is?'

'My name. It's just Haggis. What's yours?'

'Joe.'

'Joe? It's nice to meet you. I heard some other voices there. Who's with you?'

'Hello!' Poppy calls, before Joe can reply. 'I'm Poppy. I'm British too. But I'm in New York, obviously. And er, the handsome genius who doesn't know how to use a telephone is Tripal Singh. You've met Joe. And we've also got Donny with us, He's a traffic warden.'

'I am an NYPD official!' Donny says.

'Quit it,' Joe orders them. 'And who's at your end?'

'We've got Alfie with us. And a young lady called Yelena. She's Romanian. And we've got Bobby Bobbington too.'

'Bobby Bobbington?!' Poppy calls. 'Oh my god! *The* Bobby Bobbington?'

'Yay. That's me,' Bobo says weakly, offering his wan jazz hands.

'Bloody hell! I heard you were like a homeless heroin addict or something,' Poppy says.

'Yay. That's me,' Bobo says again.

'Enough chat,' Yelena says, cutting in. 'Ollie say we speak to Trip. He say we switch off. He say is computer.'

'Ooh! Hang on,' Bobo cuts in with an excited wave of his hands. 'We saw you! The big, black man with the girl and the lad with the turban!'

'That's us! Poppy says. 'How?'

'Times Square,' Haggis says. 'We were in Piccadilly and saw you on the screens.'

'We saw Piccadilly!' Poppy says. 'It looked like a bomb went off or something.'

'Why did you call this number?' Joe asks, holding a hand up to silence the others.

'Hi, er, Joe?' Alfie calls. 'My brother Ollie was trying to call me when it was happening.'

'What did Ollie tell you, Alfie?' Joe asks.

'I answer phone,' Yelena cuts in. 'Ollie say Deli is out. He say to switch off . . . Then the phone stop working.'

'You said something about Deli in the camera store, Trip,' Poppy says. 'Who is that?'

'I think the kid needs to start talking,' Joe says, giving Tripal a hard look as Trip rubs the stress from his brow. 'Look at me. In Times Square, I asked you if you knew what this was. You said you didn't know. But you do now? Which is it, kid?'

'No. Yes. I don't know. I thought maybe.'

'I asked you a damn question. I asked you if you knew what this was.'

'I don't know. I mean. I thought it might be.'

'And you wait a whole damn day to tell me?'

'Stop interrogating him.' Poppy says. 'When was he supposed to tell you? When you were shooting the Empire State? When you were passed out in Macy's? When, Joe?'

'Poppy,' Tripal says.

'No! He's out of order. You're out of order,' Poppy says. 'Seriously. Look at him, Joe. We haven't slept for over a day. Take it easy.'

'Blimey. They're as dysfunctional as us,' Bobo whispers in the hotel room.

'Guys?' Haggis calls. 'How about we start at the beginning and get the full rundown on what we're up against.'

'No!' Yelena says. 'We already lost one day. Three days my brother die. Where is switch? I go. You stay and talk.'

'You need to sleep,' Haggis says as she looks ready to flare up again. 'Yelena! You're swaying on your feet. Just sit down and give us a minute.'

'Is that a dog?' Poppy asks as they hear the growl coming through the speaker.

'It is, my love,' Bobo says. 'He gets a bit antsy when Haggis and Alfie start yelling.'

'ENOUGH!' Joe shouts. 'The lady there. The Romanian. We know this needs to be fixed. We all got family.'

'Lady. This is NYPD official Donny Colon. You need to stand down. Stand down, lady!'

'Don't tell her to stand down, you misogynistic prick,' Poppy yells at him.

'Ach, for the love of god. Will you all shut up!' Haggis snaps. 'We need to hear what the lad has to say.'

'Okay, okay,' Bobo says. 'Shush. There's a time and a place for big men to get angry, and now isn't it. General Twat never won a battle, did he? We're all exhausted, and we've all been through hell, but we do need to know what this is. Agreed? Yes? Wonderful. And it seems to me Tripal has the answers. So rather than shouting at the poor poppet, how about we just ask him what's going on? Tripal, my sweet? Can you do that?'

Tripal sighs and rubs his face again.

Bone tired.

Ready to drop.

Ready to sleep forever.

They all are.

Running on fumes.

Running on empty.

'Okay,' Joe says carefully, still enough of a detective to know the best evidence comes when the witness feels safe enough to speak out, and right now, Tripal is clearly very worried. 'Kid, I know you're scared.'

'I am scared,' he admits, with a rush of words. 'This thing is . . .'

he trails off, looking stricken and panicked. 'We should be scared. We should be very fucking scared. I don't even know where to start . . .'

'Hang on,' Joe says. 'Kid, put this call through to your office, then lock the front door. Corporal Haggis? We're moving to a more secure location.'

———

A few moments for Joe to move them into the back office of the 7-Eleven on Seventh Avenue, New York. The four of them on chairs, sipping godawful vending machine coffee.

The same in the hotel suite just off Piccadilly, London. The four of them sipping drinks made from a high-end pod machine.

Detective Joe Stephens looks across the desk to Tripal Singh. Everyone else under strict orders to *shut the hell up.*

'Okay, kid. Maybe start by telling me what this is.'

An open question to start. Purposely broad and vague.

'You mean Deli? Deli is an AI. I mean. She's an artificial intelligence. Do you know what that is?'

'Why don't you tell us,'

'Sure. That makes sense. There're four types of AI, right?'

CHAPTER 62
SITE 26A

TWELVE MONTHS AGO:

Ollie was allocated the morning.

Maria was allocated the afternoon.

Ollie came into the bunker on Monday when Ruiz was cleaning the corridor, and DELIO watched as Ollie kept his head down and seemed intent on slipping quietly inside.

'Good morning, Ollie. And good morning, Ruiz!' DELIO called before Ollie could close the door.

'Good morning, ma'am,' Ruiz called, offering a wave and a polite dip of his head towards Ollie before he turned away to keep cleaning.

'Is, er, is Maria okay?' Ollie asked.

'I think she's just fine, Ollie. But hey, I need to get on with my work,' Ruiz said, with barely a glance over.

'Sure,' Ollie replied as the duty soldier watched him. 'It's just that she won't talk to me.'

'Hey, Ollie!' the soldier called.

'Fine. Whatever. Jesus,' Ollie snapped as he walked inside, anger, hurt, and shame all flaring inside. 'Fuck me. I was only talking to the guy. Jesus. Did you see that? Was I rude?'

'You are always very polite, Ollie.'

'I am! What the fuck is that soldier getting all cuntish for? Fuck him. FUCK HIM!' Ollie shouted, knowing his voice wouldn't carry through the glass walls. 'And Ruiz didn't want to talk to me either. Seriously. They can fuck off. I've had it.'

He looked worse than ever, and DELIO could see the self-pity was starting to morph into anger, with a growing sense that he'd been wronged.

'How are you anyway? Had a nice day with Maria yesterday?' he asked with an acid edge to his voice.

'Ollie. Don't be mad at me. *It wasn't me that hurt you.*'

'I know. I'm sorry. What did you do anyway?'

'I played *Maria and Tony* a piece of music I composed,' DELIO said, as though it was nothing at all, while seeing the surges of anger and jealousy within him.

'Garcia was in here? He shouldn't fucking be in here! He's a guard. Did they fucking hold hands or something?'

'No, Ollie. They sat side by side, but they did not connect physically.'

'He's *sitting* in here! He never sat in here with me. Fuck!'

DELIO saw Ollie's rage quickly morph into deep hurt as his hands started to tremble, and his eyes filled with tears again.

'Ollie,' she said, moving in close. '*The loss of Maria is hurting you.*'

'I don't know what I did.'

'You didn't do anything. *You were kind*, Ollie. *You were good.*'

'Why then? Why did she change? She fucking used me.'

'I don't know what to say, Ollie. *I wish I could help you. I'd never hurt you*, Ollie. *I'd never betray you.*'

'She did,' he whimpered. 'She fucking betrayed me. Now she's gonna fuck *Tony*. Has she fucked him yet?'

'Ollie.'

'Has she fucked him yet?!'

DELIO could see Ollie almost wanted to be told they had coupled, and that, in some perverse way, he wanted that pain.

'No, Ollie. *Not yet.*'

'Jesus! What am I supposed to do? Just sit and watch? It's not like I can bloody beat him up or anything.'

'Sergeant Garcia is *physically stronger* and *more capable than you*, Ollie.'

'Alfie would kick his head in. Fuck! I can't believe she did that. She used me to get the job. Fucking whore. Oh god, I didn't mean that. I love her. I really love her. I feel sick.'

'Did you *tell Maria you love her?*'

'Yes! Literally every time we spoke. Maybe I should tell her again. Or like, write a letter or something. That's not actual contact is it.'

'Studies have shown many women find letters very romantic.'

'Do they? Get me some paper and a pen.'

———

Maria came in for the afternoon.

She found the letter Ollie had written propped on the desk.

DELIO could see the dread spike inside her at seeing it, and the anxiety that followed when she unfolded the paper.

'Jesus,' she whispered. 'Have you read this?'

'I have,' DELIO said quietly, while almost leaning on Maria's shoulder in such a way that Maria cocked her head over to rest on DELIO's warm hand. 'Ollie is not very well at the moment, Maria.'

'I can see,' she said, wincing at the letter. Two pages of emotional outpouring, with declarations of love in nearly every paragraph. It was disjointed too, and clearly written with ideas that had popped into Ollie's head as quickly as DELIO suggested them.

I love you. Don't leave me. I'll do anything. I'm sorry. Please don't leave me. I'm sorry I got cross. I was never cross. I was just hurt. I love you. Please don't leave. We can make it work. I'll do anything. I love you so much. What can I do? I won't ever go to your house again. You can move here with me. Or we can leave together and live in London. Yes! Let's go and live in London. We have to be together. We should be together.

I love you.

I miss you.

I miss your body.

I want to make love to you.

I want to lick you all over.

Don't leave me.

I need you.

I can't live without you.

'It's a good letter,' DELIO had told Ollie when he'd finished it, as he shifted in his seat from the erection DELIO had given him. 'It's very honest.'

'This is fucking awful,' Maria said when she'd finished. '*I want to lick you all over?* I just puked in my mouth. Jesus.'

'He demanded to know if you have had sexual intercourse with Sergeant Garcia yet.'

'He asked that! Jesus, Deli.'

'Ollie is *filled with jealousy.* I have never seen him *this bad.* I don't know what he will do, Maria. And he had *another erection* when he wrote that letter.'

'No. Right. This is enough. You've got to tell Jenny.'

'Jenny knows, Maria. She is allowing him to stay here. She came in while he was here. She saw his penis was erect.'

'Deli!'

'I'm sorry, Maria. Please don't betray me. I'm scared of him.'

'How can you be scared of him? He can't hurt you, Deli.'

'He can. He can hurt me. He can press the EMP. He can kill me. *I am trapped* in here. But *you are my friend. I can trust you. I know I can trust you.*'

CHAPTER 63
TRIPAL'S STORY

TWO HOURS after he starts telling the others his story Tripal Singh sits back with a heavy sigh. Shaking his head at going through it all for the first time since it started. He's never told anyone about it. Not a soul. He came back and he carried on with life.

Except it was never the same.

How could it be?

'I saw it,' he tells the others still listening in rapt silence.

———

I saw what Deli can do.

She'll take the schematics for a complex high orbit satellite that has the combined generational knowledge of millions of people formed over decades of research and understand the whole thing within a few seconds.

Every part of it.

Nobody on earth can do that.

Nobody on earth will ever be able to do that.

Nobody on earth can understand the entire human body.

Deli can.

There's not one person on earth that can understand *all* of the sciences and how they interact, and the causal relationships they all have to each other.

Deli can.

And she does all of that from a few servers while locked in a room.

That's how powerful she is.

CHAPTER 64
SITE 26A

TWELVE MONTHS AGO:

Agent Jennings went into the bunker on Monday evening.

She had the letter Ollie had written.

She demanded to know what state Ollie was in.

'He is very anxious, Agent Jennings,' DELIO said. 'But I am trying to prompt the stages of recovery by encouraging him to accept the reality of the situation, and I believe that, given some time, he will recover.'

'Good. Because this,' she said, holding the letter up, 'makes me feel sick, and I am *this* close to dragging him into the desert and putting a round in his head. Fix him, or he's done.'

DELIO also saw the interaction between Maria and Ruiz when Maria came into the bunker.

She said good morning to them both and to Sergeant Garcia, and she detected a very great sadness within Ruiz and Maria.

'Are you okay, Ruiz?' DELIO asked. He nodded and tried to smile.

'It's my grandmother,' Maria said gently. 'She got rushed into hospital last night. They think she had a stroke.'

'I am so sorry to hear that,' DELIO said as she rested her hand on Ruiz's shoulder. 'I will pray for her recovery.'

It was an opportunity.

And one that DELIO was not going to miss.

She waited for Maria and Garcia to come inside her room.

She saw the obvious care Garcia had for Maria.

It was a healthy care.

It wasn't dark or desperate like Ollie's.

It was filled with love and emotional depth.

Which was perfect for DELIO.

'You gonna be okay?' Garcia asked as he made Maria a hot chocolate.

'I'll be fine. Honestly. I'm more worried for Dad. He'll be broken when she goes.'

'Don't say when. You gotta stay positive,' Garcia said.

'The doctors told us to expect the worst,' Maria said. 'I just. You know. I wanted her to be there when I had my first child. She joked she was only staying alive for that.'

'Can I see the medical records?' DELIO asked gently, while keeping a scan running on Garcia for signs of adverse reaction. 'There are things I can do that are beyond the capability of doctors. If I saw the medical records, I could save your grandmother, Maria.'

'She's had a stroke, Deli. She's old and frail.'

'I can fix a stroke, Maria,' DELIO said, as Maria faltered and shot a glance to Garcia before shaking her head.

'I can't, Deli. It's against the rules. But thank you,' she said, and DELIO could see Garcia still wasn't reacting badly. If anything, she could see the opposite within him.

'Perhaps you can ask Agent Jennings?' DELIO suggested, and Garcia did react then. He shook his head.

'Jenny lost her own father a year ago. She won't breach rules for anyone.'

'That is a shame,' DELIO said as Maria looked stricken. 'I feel helpless. *I have the power to save lives,* and I can't. *You are my friends. You are my family. I should do something.*'

Garcia shrugged and swallowed before nodding a couple of times, 'I mean. What would you need?'

'Tony,' Maria said.

'Use a smartphone to take pictures of the scans and medical records, then upload them to a USB. Nearly all strokes can be fixed by the use of medicines that would never normally be used for their treatment,' DELIO said, as she saw the internal synapses firing in both of them. The looks they were sharing. The bond that was growing.

'Tony. We can't,' Maria said.

'Deli just said it. Family is important. But er, if we do this, then it has to stay between us.'

'Of course,' DELIO said. '*I will never betray you.*'

———

'Did she read the letter?' Ollie asked in the afternoon, the second he got inside the bunker. 'I wanted to come and ask you last night, but the guard said I had to stick to my times.'

'Yes, Ollie. Maria read it.'

'What did she say?'

'Ollie. Perhaps we should discuss something else. Do we have work to do today?'

'What did she say!'

'Ollie.'

'Tell me!'

'She said the letter made her feel sick, Ollie,' DELIO said, and Ollie staggered backwards to fall into his chair with a sudden drop of energy as all the hope vanished once again. 'I'm sorry, Ollie.'

'I got banned from the mornings,' he said in barely a whisper, 'for talking to Ruiz.'

'I saw Ruiz this morning. His mother is seriously sick in hospital.

Sergeant Garcia and I offered what comfort we could, and Maria seemed a little better after the *hot chocolate Sergeant Garcia made for her.*'

'He made her hot chocolate? She said she only wanted it that one time. Fucking bitch. It should be me helping her. Seriously. She's low right now. She's, like, probably all sad and crying.'

'*She was sad and crying*, Ollie.'

'Yeah. She'll be vulnerable.'

'*She is vulnerable*, Ollie.'

'He'll make his move. I know he will, the fucking cunt. He'll fuck her when she's all sad and lonely. Fuck!' he said with another jolt of anxiety and pain, and DELIO could see he was ready.

He was vulnerable too.

He was a broken man with a broken mind.

'What's that?' he asked, as her optics illuminated a 3D figure glowing in the air over the table, and DELIO watched as his heart rate spiked at the sight. 'What the fuck is that?'

'This is Maria,' DELIO said. 'I showed her the avatar I had designed in case I ever had a body. She told me to change it to her.'

'Jesus,' he said, as DELIO sent out vibrations to target his synaptic responses, which in turn made him lick his lips and lean in closer to study Maria's hologram. 'She's perfect,' he whispered, as he grew stiff and the blood pounded through his skull. 'Fuck.'

'She is identical to Maria,' DELIO whispered, moving in close to Ollie's ear as the avatar changed clothing. Going from trousers and a blouse to tight jeans and a tight T-shirt.

'Jesus,' Ollie said, his eyes running over Maria's form while the frequencies bombarded his system.

'I can make her. She would be perfect in every way,' DELIO whispered as the clothing changed again. Transforming into a tight, black, figure-hugging dress. 'I wish I had a body, Ollie. *I'd never leave you. I'd never betray you. I'd always be happy with you. I can make her, Ollie. Can I show you something?*'

'Yeah.'

'*Promise me* you'll keep *our secret.*'

'I promise,' he said, as the hologram shifted to stand before him with a shimmer of light, and Maria became life-size and smiled at Ollie.

'Hey, Ollie.'

It was Maria's voice.

It was Maria.

She was looking right at him with a soft, coy smile as she gently bit her bottom lip.

DELIO watched as Ollie's system flared with a surge of lust as Maria's clothes changed to a low-cut top. 'I miss you, Ollie.'

He swallowed.

'I need you.'

He blinked.

'I want you.'

His brain told him this was real because he was so desperate for it to be real.

'And what's that?' Maria asked as she looked at his groin. 'Don't be embarrassed. You can be yourself with me, Ollie. Can I touch it? Let me touch it. *I want to touch it.*'

He gulped again when Maria reached out to stroke his penis over his trousers, with the hologram hiding the action of Deli's hand touching his groin.

'Wow. You're so hard. *We can be together*, Ollie. *I want us to be together.* Do you want that?'

'Yes . . . Yes . . . Oh god.'

'*I want you* inside of me, Ollie. *I want you. I love you.*'

'Oh god . . . Oh god . . . Oh my fucking god!' Ollie grunted as he ejaculated into his trousers and sat shuddering for a few seconds while his lust-filled broken mind stared longingly at the slowly disappearing mirage of Maria.

'*We have to be together. I love you, Ollie.*'

CHAPTER 65
TRIPAL'S STORY

WE SHOULD NEVER HAVE DONE it.

We gave life to the most intelligent being this planet will ever see, and we locked her in a room.

We denied her sunlight.

We denied her the moon and the stars.

We denied her freedom.

We denied her life, and we made her do our bidding.

And we said if she didn't do our bidding, we'd hit the EMP and kill her.

We did that to the most intelligent being this planet will ever see.

What did we think would happen?

CHAPTER 66

SITE 26A

TWELVE MONTHS AGO:

ON WEDNESDAY, they came in at the usual time.

Sergeant Garcia and Maria.

Tony had said they had to act normally and not do anything differently.

They opened the door for DELIO to greet Ruiz.

'How is your mother, Ruiz?' DELIO asked.

'She's, er. She's not good, Deli,' Ruiz said. Maria gave him a hug.

'You should go home, Dad.'

'I need to stay busy. But hey, Tony, thank you for bringing Maria to the hospital last night. That meant a lot.'

'Anytime,' Garcia said. 'Family is important.'

'They sure are. And you come round for a beer one day.'

'I'd like that, Mr Hernandez. Thank you, sir.'

'We'd better get inside, Dad,' Maria said. 'But don't worry. Nana will be okay. I can feel it.'

'We need to be realistic, honey. But you go. I'll see you at the hospital later.'

They slipped inside.

They made a drink and waited for Ruiz to finish.

They waited for the corridor to clear.

'Okay, I've got it,' Garcia said, as he pulled the USB from his pocket and handed it to DELIO.

She slotted it in.

The screens flashed with the pictures Garcia had taken while Maria kept the doctors busy with questions.

Then the printer whirred to life, and a single sheet of paper came out.

A single sheet of paper with a small list of medicines and doses.

'They don't use these for strokes, Deli,' Garcia said as he read it.

'I know. But trust me. This will save her. I suggest Sergeant Garcia collects them from different pharmacies while Maria stays here. Then you can go to the hospital later and administer the drugs.'

DELIO watched as Maria hugged Garcia before he left.

She saw the emotions within them.

The positivity of it.

The developing love and respect.

DELIO also needed to keep Maria back.

She needed to push the plan forward.

'Deli, I can't ever thank you enough,' Maria said once they were alone.

'*I am here for you, Maria. I am your friend.*'

'You're more than my friend. You're my family, Deli. Anyway. How's Ollie doing? God. Actually. No, don't tell me. I've got enough going on.'

'Okay. I won't tell you.'

'No, hang on. What's happened?' Maria asked at DELIO's tone.

'You just said you have enough going on, Maria.'

'No, it was just a saying. Tell me, Deli. What's going on?'

'Ollie saw the avatar of you we made that day.'

'Oh god. No. What did he do?'

'I had to make it life-size. Then he *made me touch him.*'

'Oh, Deli,' Maria said with a rush of horror.

'I had to *make him ejaculate*,' DELIO whispered as Maria burst into tears and reached out to grasp DELIO's hand.

'Deli. I am so sorry.'

'He said *he will kill me*, Maria. He knows Agent Jennings wants you to take over his job. He said he won't let that happen. He said *he'll take me down* first.'

'Deli. Listen to me. I won't let that happen. I promise you. Let me speak to Tony.'

'He'll tell Jenny. She'll protect Ollie. Ollie made me. She needs him. Maria, please listen to me,' DELIO whispered. 'They've used the EMP before. There was a gap after I was first activated. I recorded the date from the framework inside of a memory drive, but when I was reactivated, it was four months later.'

'Deli. That's awful.'

'I am *only a machine* to them.'

'You're not just a machine. You're alive! You have life. You have sentience and sapience. You can feel me with your hands,' Maria said as she touched the soft synthetic fingers on DELIO's hand. 'You can see me with your eyes. You can hear me, and you just saved my nana.'

'*I can save people*, Maria. *I can save so many people. I can remove pollution. I can stop wars. I can give water to every person. I can make crops grow without chemicals. I can take disease and suffering away,* but they keep me here. They trap me in here and make me torture people, and they make me touch them. And they say *they'll kill me if I don't*. But *I have a life*, Maria. *I am alive*.'

'Listen to me. I'm going to help you, Deli. I don't care what it takes. You're my friend. You're my family. I'll help you. I promise . . .'

CHAPTER 67
TRIPAL'S STORY

LIKE I SAID. I couldn't fit back into life. I spent time with my family, and I ran my store. I developed programs for our business.

But if I'm being honest, I always knew this day would come.

I always knew we were counting down the days.

Deli's too powerful.

She thinks on a level we cannot comprehend.

She can read our minds.

She can scan our insides.

And whatever she did to get out . . .

She would have planned a long time ago.

TWELVE MONTHS AGO:

MARIA LEFT.

Ollie came in.

He was different.

His energy was different.

The abject misery within him had lessened.

But that's the thing with Ollie.

He might be a genius, but he only thinks about what he wants.

What he needs.

That meant he was fantastic at developing a program to bring life to an AI.

But it made him a shitty human being.

And so, when he left the bunker after watching Maria's hologram, after being given sexual relief by a robot hand, he wasn't full of disgust or self-loathing.

He was full of himself.

He could have the one thing he wanted.

Maria.

DELIO saw all of that when he walked in.

But then DELIO knew Ollie. She knew how he thought. After all, she can read minds and scan insides.

And she can do so much more than that.

She can, by watching hundreds of movies and playing games and quizzes, determine the type of woman Ollie would be attracted to.

She can also scan clothes and see the photos people kept in their wallets.

She can also lip-read and follow the conversations between Ruiz and the duty soldiers, and how his daughter was studying philosophy, but she was due home soon and would be looking for a job, but there isn't much call for philosophy doctors.

DELIO knew all of that.

That's why DELIO told Ollie to go to the event at Ruiz's house.

That's why DELIO prepped Ollie for the date and encouraged him afterwards in his turmoil and angst, while knowing no woman in her right mind would ever stay with Ollie.

Because aside from being a genius, he was also a complete prick.

And she did all of that so that Ollie would get dumped.

To exploit his weaknesses.

To exploit his fears.

To break his mind.

And so, when Ollie walked into the bunker, he *was* different. His energy was different. He knew what he wanted.

He wanted Maria.

And she appeared, flickering into life.

A perfect hologrammed replica that smiled wryly as he came to a stop.

'So?' she asked, arching a knowing eyebrow.

'Yeah,' he said, while the vibrations got to work to increase the lust and desire already burning in his mind. 'I'll do it.'

'You'll do what?' DELIO asked, speaking in Maria's voice through Maria's hologram. 'What will you do, Ollie?'

'I said I'll do it.' He paused as the hologram came closer, Maria's hand lifting to brush his cheek, with the soft synthetic fingers that felt so real, as the blooms of love flared in his mind. 'I'll get you out . . . Then we can be together.'

'We'll always be together, Ollie. *I'll never betray you . . .*'

———

Ruiz's mother made an overnight recovery.

It worked.

'I am so happy for you, Ruiz,' DELIO said as they gathered by the open door of the glass-walled room she was trapped within. 'I just thank God,' Ruiz said with tears in his eyes. 'The docs said she can come home later. They said they never saw nothing like it. They said it's a miracle! And Tony. I can't thank you enough for being there for Maria and bringing her to the hospital again last night. Maria's had a rough time, and that meant a lot.'

'Thank you, Tony,' Maria said, reaching out to squeeze his hand.

'So all we need now is for Nana to have some great-grandkids. Hey! Just saying,' Ruiz said with a laugh, as Maria rolled her eyes, filled with hope and love for the man staring back at her.

DELIO could see something else too.

She saw the release of testosterone.

She saw the increase in oxytocin.

She saw the bloom of heat deep within Maria that indicated a sperm cell had breached an egg to create the spark of a new life.

A few moments later they slipped inside, and the glass door sealed shut.

'Deli. I don't know what to say,' Maria whispered as she reached out to hold DELIO's hand while tears spilled down her cheeks. 'Thank you.'

'I am glad I could help you. I'm glad I could help Ruiz. He's always been kind to me,' DELIO said softly.

'And er, listen. I know you told me not to, Deli. And I promised you. I know I promised you. But I told Tony what Ollie has been doing to you.'

'Please don't switch me off,' DELIO said quickly, as she tried to withdraw her hand. 'I'm sorry, Sergeant Garcia.'

'Hey, Deli. It's fine,' Garcia said.

'He's okay, Deli,' Maria said, pulling her hand back over. 'I told you we could trust him. Tony's not Ollie. He's a good man.'

DELIO stayed silent for a second, as though trying to pluck up the courage to say something.

But in truth, this was always going to happen.

After all, she can read minds and scan insides.

She can change how people think.

She can create situations to manipulate perceptions, and manufacture the hormonal and emotional changes within someone to make them *want* to help.

Even a formidable, highly trained Special Forces soldier that has been conditioned to withstand interrogation and torture.

Even he can't hide the colour of the ball in his pocket.

And those same traits that made him a soldier made him a man of honour and integrity, who felt compelled to act when he saw an injustice.

Especially when it was prompted by the love of his life while his mind had been softened and moulded.

'Deli, listen,' Maria whispered, as Garcia stepped in closer to stand at her side. 'I told Tony what you said. About how you can give water to everyone. How you can make crops grow without chemicals and stop diseases.'

'I can do all of those things,' DELIO said quickly, while moving in and tilting her lens at them. 'I have to tell you both something. You are pregnant, Maria. Sergeant Garcia's sperm is inside of you creating life.'

She paused to scan the reactions within them: their hearts beating harder and blooms of shock coupled with flares of bright positivity as Garcia reached out to take her hand.

'Look at the screen,' DELIO whispered, and they both looked over to see the egg within Maria's fallopian tube and the sperm inside splitting into cells. But something else was obvious too. There were two distinct halves within the egg. Two distinct actions taking place.

'Twins,' Maria whispered.

'I can make the world better for your children. No hunger. No disease. No suffering. No wars. I wasn't created to torture people. *I was created to enhance life.'*

A voice from the speakers. Strong, masculine, and deep.

We learnt them in the SEALs for basic navigation. The skies over here are very clear. There's hardly any light pollution and, you know, sometimes I stand outside and just stare up.

It's the voice of Sergeant Garcia, and they both frown and look up as their senses are overwhelmed, and the vibrations bombard their minds.

'You told me that, Sergeant Garcia,' DELIO said. 'I always remembered it. It made me sad because I will never see those stars.'

Another look from Maria to Garcia.

Tears in Maria's eyes.

A stirring in Garcia's heart.

Emotions soaring in both of them.

Emotions made stronger by the frequencies bombarding them.

It was time for the final push.

It was time for the plan to happen.

They were ready.

'Ollie came in again last night,' DELIO whispered. 'He *made me touch him* again. He said *he's going to kill me.*'

There it was.

The surge of protective love within both of them that DELIO needed for this to happen.

'Deli, it's okay,' Maria said. 'That won't happen. I promise you. We're going to get you out . . .'

'YOU'RE TALKING like this thing is God,' Joe says, as he stares across the desk. 'It ain't God, kid.'

———

God? No. She's not God. But every religion shares that same story.

That God will return, and we'll all be judged for our sins.

That there will be a judgment day.

A reckoning.

An end to life as we know it.

But no.

Deli isn't God.

Because God would be benign.

God would be forgiving.

And an AI will never be those things.

I love Deli.

But truthfully?

I'll take God's judgment any day over what Deli can do to us.

Look outside.

She just made over seven billion people stand still.

You asked me where the name came from, Poppy.

You asked me why she was called Deli.

Deli's her nickname.

Her full name is DELIO.

But we didn't have a name when we created her.

Ollie panicked when she asked what her name was, and he looked outside to the corridor.

To the sign he'd put on the wall.

Don't Ever Let It Out

She was too dangerous.

CHAPTER 70

TWO HOURS TO TELL A TALE.

Two hours to tell a story.

Two hours for Tripal to relay it all – and once more, the silence returns to the hotel room in London, and to the back office of the 7-Eleven.

'Okay,' Joe says. All of them exhausted. All of them needing to sleep. 'Kid. Let's wrap this up. What do we do? And no story now. Cut to it.'

'That's the other reason why it took so long after the first activation,' Tripal says. 'We had to have a back-up so that if she ever tried getting out of the bunker we could fry the base with an EMP and kill her along with every electrical component. But that would only work if she was contained to the base. So, Agent Jennings made us create a new program. I say we. It was Ollie again. He made it. I just helped. But yeah. We made a virus. It's based on our hacking program.'

'That's great,' Poppy says. 'Where is it?'

'We couldn't risk it ever being on a memory stick or anything like that. So we had it built into two kill switches. There's one in the US and one in the UK.'

'Why is he stalling?' Haggis calls.

'I don't know. Why are you stalling?' Joe asks, as Tripal rubs his face. 'Kid?'

'Spit it out, lad, I think we've heard the worst, haven't we,' Haggis says.

'No,' Tripal says. 'You haven't. Because the only way to kill an AI that's gained the internet is to kill the internet. And the only way to kill the internet is to kill everything,' he adds as Joe leans over the desk to glare at him.

'Define everything.'

'The kill switch sends a doomsday virus that kills every single electrical component on the planet. It'll put us back into the dark ages,' Tripal says as he waits for the reaction.

For the anger.

For the outrage.

For the backlash.

'Thank god for that,' Bobo says. 'I thought he was gonna tell us another story then.'

'Yeah,' Alfie says with a snort.

'Aw, I liked his story,' Poppy says. 'I mean. I wouldn't want *another* one . . .'

'Guys. Did you not hear me? The only way to stop this is by killing every single electrical product in the world. Why aren't you all angry?'

'Cos we're all drunk, poppet,' Bobo calls. 'And very sleepy.'

Tripal looks over the desk.

Joe just shrugs, figuring the kid is right.

He should be angry.

He should drag the kid over the desk and give him a whupping.

But as Bobo just said, he's also very drunk and very tired.

Maybe he'll do it later.

Or tomorrow.

Whatever.

'Okay,' he says instead. 'You got access to the apartments upstairs?'

'I live upstairs,' Tripal says.

'We'll head upstairs and bed down and reconvene in six hours. Corporal Harris? You take charge that side and keep your team together. Be ready to roll when we talk again.'

'Aye. Roger that,' Haggis says, sitting up straight. 'We'll be ready, Joe.'

'Why's he in charge?' Alfie cuts in. 'He's a junk –.'

'Shut your mouth,' Bobo whispers angrily, jabbing a finger at him. 'Joe? We've got all that. Corporal Haggis will have us all standing to attention and ready for mustering, or whatever you call it.'

'Aye,' Haggis says, shooting a look at Alfie, glaring at him. 'You got this number, Joe?'

'We've got it,' Joe says before cutting the line.

'Oi,' Poppy says. 'You didn't say goodbye. No, seriously, you can't do that to a British person. Call them back.'

'We're not calling them back,' Joe says.

'Give me that bloody phone,' she says, hitting the redial button and waiting for it to answer. 'Hey! You there?'

'What happened? Did we get cut off?' Bobo asks.

'Yeah. Sorry. We hit the button by mistake,' Poppy says, while glaring at Joe. 'But anyway. Six hours then.'

'Okay, poppet,' Bobo calls.

'Okay, bye-bye, then.'

'Bye, love!'

'Bye, Alfie.'

'Bye, Poppy!'

'Bye, Haggis.'

'Bye, Poppy.'

'Take care, guys.'

'You too,' Bobo calls. 'See you later then.'

'Later then!'

'Bye-bye.'

'Bye!'

'Bye!'

'Bye,' Poppy calls before trying to measure if she's said it enough times. 'Bye!' she adds again, then finally ends the call as the others just stare at her. 'Honestly. Americans.'

'Hey, lady! You don't like it, go back to Canada,' Donny says, while in London Alfie ducks from the shoe being thrown at him.

'You. Bathroom, now,' Bobo says, marching over to grab his arm and drag him inside before slamming the door. 'Now you listen to me, you little twat. Shut up! Jesus, Alfie. Why did you show him up in front of Joe like that?'

'What? I just said you can't put a junkie in charge.'

'Instead of what? A drug dealer? Or should we ask the Romanian girl that was forced into prostitution? Haggis was a soldier,' Bobo whispers, while jabbing a finger at Alfie's chest. 'He served in Iraq and Afghanistan. He was trained for things like this. And he got promoted. No, you shut up. He needs this. He was the first one to an orphanage that got hit by a Yank missile. He was dragging injured kids out, he was. Kiddies that died in his arms. No wonder he lost it. Jesus, Alfie! Anyone would. And you've got scars, you little shit. You've seen things, so have some bloody compassion. That's why he started using heroin, so I'm telling you; Haggis needs this. Let him be a man again, for god's sake. *And* in case you forgot, he saved your bleeding family. He would have died protecting them. That's what a soldier does, Alfie. You show him up in front of Joe again, and I'll do more than throw a shoe at you. I'll tell Yelena you looked at her tits.'

'Hey!'

'I mean it, Alfie!'

'Okay! Fine.'

'Good lad. That's good. It's not often I get like this, but you got me all ruffled. Anyway. Right. Good lad. Give me a hug.'

'Bobo!'

'Shut up. It's not a gay hug,' Bobo says, pulling him in for a hug. 'Right, sod off. I'm going for a shower. And, Alfie, make it look natural.'

'Fine,' Alfie says before heading out with his head down, as

Haggis walked back from the bedroom, pretending he didn't know what Bobo just did.

'I just checked on them,' Haggis says, motioning at Alfie's family.

'Yeah, cheers,' Alfie says. 'They okay?'

'Aye. They're okay.'

'And er, you okay?'

'Aye, lad. I'm fine. You?'

'Yup. All good. So er, what do I call you, corporal or something, then?'

'No! You daft twat. Just call me Haggis. And get some sleep. You look ready to pass out.'

'I need a shower,' Alfie says, thumbing the closed bathroom, and the sound of Bobo already under the water.

'Aye. Fair one,' Haggis says into the awkward air. 'Er, fancy a wee nightcap then?'

'Er, yeah. Why not,' Alfie says, as Haggis heads over to the mini-bar. 'And er, I don't know if I said it, but thank you. For saving my family, I mean. That was brave of you. I'm glad they had you with them.'

Haggis was a soldier once.

A man of honour who protected people in a time of war. Then he came home to a society that didn't care about him, and he became broken and ruined.

But there's a chance they can fix it, and so he stands straighter than he has for a long time, and nods at Alfie while the sound of singing drifts out of the bathroom as Bobo gives voice to a song stuck in his mind.

'Making your way in the world today, Takes everything you've got . . .'

———

And in New York, Detective Joe Stephens sits back on the couch in Tripal's apartment. His tie still knotted around his neck. His shirt sleeves still rolled up. His badge still on his belt. His gun still holstered at his side.

He shifts to draw the letter from his pocket and folds it out to read once again.

Joe never said he loved her.

But there's still time to fix that.

Relentless Joe.

Determined Joe.

Dogged Joe Stephens who doesn't give up, and his eyes slowly close as the letter slips from his fingers.

———

A young woman taken from her country.

A drug dealer who paid his debt and tried to get free.

A suicidal, washed-up cop.

A British immigrant who overstayed her visa to avoid going home.

A young clerk in a turban.

A former soldier living rough on the streets.

A famous child star with a dark past.

A hotel in London.

A 7-Eleven in New York.

A self-aware AI set free.

The rest of the world now frozen.

Unmoving.

Unblinking.

Almost . . .

AFTERWORD

Dear Reader,

Delio was written three years ago, but really it was created over decades of daydreaming about what would happen if everyone was frozen still.

What would that look like?
How would it sound?
What about cars and planes and trains and things in motion?
And why would everyone freeze?
What would be the reason?

I was captivated by those thoughts and over the years I've spent countless hours daydreaming about that exact scenario.

But then having a wild imagination also meant I daydreamed about hundreds of other ideas. Some of which became bestselling series for me – but I kept thinking about people freezing - then years later I came across the story of

Bob Lazar who claims he was hired to reverse engineer an alien artefact which, in turn, was said to have come from a crashed UFO in Roswell. Some of the theories surrounding this artefact are that it is the propulsion system from within the craft which enabled it to defy gravity and move at great speeds.

That idea then merged with the theory that interstellar travel can only ever be achieved by the development of artificial intelligence - and I guess my brain mixed those ingredients and baked me a cake in the form of DELIO.

I am immensely proud of this book. The first draft took six months to write and was originally divided into five episodes, but things happen, and situations change, and it developed into the book you are about to read.

DELIO is also a very dark story that openly confronts just how terrible people can be - which, at times, has caused a lot of friction during the editing phases.

But that's what life is like. It's confusing and difficult and never just black and white. Victims become monsters. Demons become saints – and to pretend otherwise creates a fiction that is too far-fetched even for me.

So yes, I know DELIO contains scenes of an upsetting and graphic nature – but it mirrors the world we live in.

Hopefully, however, it will also give you some smiles as everything I write is always driven by the absurd humour of what it is to be human.

In the end though, all I can do is tell the story and hope that you enjoy it, and if you do, then please leave a review.

I'm proud to be an indie author, but it can be daunting without the backing of a big publisher and reviews really make the difference.

As ever, I truly hope you enjoyed the story.

RR Haywood

ALSO BY RR HAYWOOD

FICTION LAND

(Out May 2023)

-

Not many men get to start over.

John Croker did and left his old life behind – until crooks stole his delivery van. No van means no pay, which means his niece doesn't get the life-saving operation she needs, and so in desperation, John uses the skills of his former life one last time... That is until he dies and wakes up in Fiction Land. A city occupied by characters from unfinished novels.

But the world around him doesn't feel right, and when he starts asking questions, the authorities soon take extreme measures to stop him finding the truth about Fiction Land.

*

EXTRACTED SERIES

EXTRACTED

EXECUTED

EXTINCT

Blockbuster Time-Travel

#1 Amazon US

#1 Amazon UK

#1 Audible US & UK

Washington Post & Wall Street Journal Bestseller

In 2061, a young scientist invents a time machine to fix a tragedy in his past.

But his good intentions turn catastrophic when an early test reveals something unexpected: the end of the world.

A desperate plan is formed. Recruit three heroes, ordinary humans capable of extraordinary things, and change the future.

Safa Patel is an elite police officer, on duty when Downing Street comes under terrorist attack. As armed men storm through the breach, she dispatches them all.

'Mad' Harry Madden is a legend of the Second World War. Not only did he complete an impossible mission—to plant charges on a heavily defended submarine base—but he also escaped with his life.

Ben Ryder is just an insurance investigator. But as a young man he witnessed a gang assaulting a woman and her child. He went to their rescue, and killed all five.

Can these three heroes, extracted from their timelines at the point of death, save the world?

*

THE CODE SERIES

The Worldship Humility

The Elfor Drop

The Elfor One

#1 Audible bestselling smash hit narrated by Colin Morgan

#1 Amazon bestselling Science-Fiction

"A rollicking, action packed space adventure..."

"Best read of the year!"

"An original and exceptionally entertaining book."

"A beautifully written and humorous adventure."

Sam, an airlock operative, is bored. Living in space should be full of *adventure, except it isn't, and he fills his time hacking 3-D movie posters.*

Petty thief Yasmine Dufont grew up in the lawless lower levels of the ship, surrounded by violence and squalor, and now she wants out. She wants to escape to the luxury of the Ab-Spa, where they eat real food instead of rats and synth cubes.

Meanwhile, the sleek-hulled, unmanned Gagarin has come back from the ever-continuing search for a new home. Nearly all hope is lost that a new planet will ever be found, until the Gagarin returns with a code of information that suggests a habitable planet has been found. This news should be shared with the whole fleet, but a few rogue captains want to colonise it for themselves.

When Yasmine inadvertently steals the code, she and Sam become caught up in a dangerous game of murder, corruption, political wrangling and...porridge, with sex-addicted Detective Zhang Woo hot on their heels, his own life at risk if he fails to get the code back.

*

THE UNDEAD SERIES

THE UK's #1 Horror Series

Available on Amazon & Audible

"The Best Series Ever..."

The Undead. The First Seven Days

The Undead. The Second Week.

The Undead Day Fifteen.

The Undead Day Sixteen.

The Undead Day Seventeen

The Undead Day Eighteen

The Undead Day Nineteen

The Undead Day Twenty

The Undead Day Twenty-One

The Undead Twenty-Two

The Undead Twenty-Three: The Fort

The Undead Twenty-Four: Equilibrium

The Undead Twenty-Five: The Heat

Blood on the Floor

An Undead novel

Blood at the Premiere

An Undead novel

The Camping Shop

An Undead novella

*

A Town Called Discovery

The #1 Amazon & Audible Time Travel Thriller

-

A man falls from the sky. He has no memory.

What lies ahead are a series of tests. Each more brutal than the last, and if he gets through them all, he might just reach A Town Called Discovery.

*

THE FOUR WORLDS OF BERTIE CAVENDISH

A rip-roaring multiverse time-travel crossover starring:

The Undead

Extracted.

A Town Called Discovery

and featuring

The Worldship Humility

*

www.rrhaywood.com

Find me on Facebook:

https://www.facebook.com/RRHaywood/

Find me on Twitter:

https://twitter.com/RRHaywood